I0651026

THE QUEENS OF
VICTORIAN HORROR

RARE TALES OF TERROR
FROM THE
PENS OF FEMALE AUTHORS
OF THE VICTORIAN PERIOD

BY

VARIOUS AUTHORS

Copyright © 2013 Read Books Ltd.
This book is copyright and may not be
reproduced or copied in any way without
the express permission of the publisher in writing

British Library Cataloguing-in-Publication Data
A catalogue record for this book is available from the
British Library

CONTENTS

TRANSFORMATION

Mary Shelley

I have heard it said, that, when any strange, supernatural, and necromantic adventure has occured to a human being, that being, however desirous he may be to conceal the same, feels at certain periods torn up as it were by intellectual eathquake, and is forced to bare the inner depths of his spirit to another. I am a witness of the truth of this. I have dearly sworn to myself never to reveal to human ears the horrors to which I once, in excess of friendly pride, delivered myself over. The holy man who heard my confession, and reconciled me to the Church, is dead. None knows that once—

Why should it not be thus? Why tell a tale of impious tempting of Providence, and soul-subduing humiliation? Why? answer me, ye who are wise in the secrets of human nature! I only know that so it is; and in spite of strong resolve—of a pride that too much masters me—of shame, and even of fear, so to render myself odious to my species—I must speak.

Genoa! my birthplace—proud city! looking upon the blue Mediterranean—dost thou remember me in my boyhood, when thy cliffs and promontories, thy bright sky and gay vineyards, were my world? Happy time! when to the young heart the narrow-bounded universe, which leaves, by its very limitation, free scope to the imagination, enchains our physical energies, and, sole period in our lives, innocence and enjoyment are united. Yet, who can look back to childhood, and not remember its sorrows and its harrowing fears? I was born with the most imperious, haughty, tameless spirit. I quailed before my father only; and he, generous and noble, but capricious and tyrannical, at once fostered and checked the wild impetuosity of my character, making obedience necessary, but inspiring no respect for the motives which guided his commands. To be a man, free, independent; or, in better words, insolent and domineering, was the hope and prayer of my rebel heart.

My father had one friend, a wealthy Genoese noble, who in a political tumult was suddenly sentenced to banishment, and his property confiscated. The Marchese Torella went into exile alone. Like my father, he was a widower: he had one child, the almost infant Juliet, who was left under my father's guardianship. I should certainly have been unkind to the lovely girl, but that I was forced by my position to become her protector. A variety of childish incidents all tended to one point—to make Juliet see in me a rock of defence; I in her, one who must perish through the soft sensibility of her nature too rudely visited, but for my guardian care. We grew up together. The opening rose in May was not more sweet than this dear girl. An irradiation of beauty was spread over her face. Her form, her step, her voice—my heart weeps even now, to think of all of relying, gentle, loving, and pure, that she enshrined. When I was eleven and Juliet eight years of age, a cousin of mine, much older than either—he seemed to us a man—took great notice of my playmate; he called her his bride, and asked her to marry him. She refused, and he insisted, drawing her unwillingly towards him. With the countenance and emotions of a maniac I threw myself on him—I strove to draw his sword—I clung to his neck with the ferocious resolve to strangle him: he was obliged to call for assistance to disengage himself from me. On that night I led Juliet to the chapel of our house: I made her touch the sacred relics—I harrowed her child's heart, and profaned her child's lips with an oath, that she would be mine, and mine only.

Well, those days passed away. Torella returned in a few years, and became wealthier and more prosperous than ever. When I was seventeen, my father died; he had been magnificent to prodigality; Torella rejoiced that my minority would afford an opportunity of repairing my fortunes. Juliet

and I had been affianced beside my father's deathbed—
Torella was to be a second parent to me.

I desired to see the world, and I was indulged. I went to
Florence, to Rome, to Naples; thence I passed to Toulon, and
at length reached what had long been a bourne of my wishes,
Paris. There was wild work in Paris then. The poor king,
Charles the Sixth, now sane, now mad, now a monarch, now
an abject slave, was the very mockery of humanity. The queen,
the dauphin, the Duke of Burgundy, alternately friends and
foes—now meeting in prodigal feasts, now shedding blood
in rivalry—were blind to the miserable state of their country,
and the dangers that impended over it, and gave themselves
wholly up to dissolute enjoyment or savage strife. My
character still followed me. I was arrogant and self-willed; I
loved display, and above all, I threw off all control. My young
friends were eager to foster passions which furnished them
with pleasures. I was deemed handsome—I was master of
every knightly accomplishment. I was disconnected with any
political party. I grew a favourite with all: My presumption
and arrogance was pardoned in one so young: I became a
spoiled child. Who could control me? not the letters and
advice of Torella—only strong necessity visiting me in the
abhorred shape of an empty purse. But there were means
to refill this void. Acre after acre, estate after estate, I sold.
My dress, my jewels, my horses and their caparisons, were

almost unrivalled in gorgeous Paris, while the lands of my inheritance passed into possession of others.

The Duke of Orleans was waylaid and murdered by the Duke of Burgundy. Fear and terror possessed all Paris. The dauphin and the queen shut themselves up; every pleasure was suspended. I grew weary of this state of things, and my heart yearned for my boyhood's haunts. I was nearly a beggar, yet still I would go there, claim my bride, and rebuild my fortunes. A few happy ventures as a merchant would make me rich again. Nevertheless, I would not return in humble guise. My last act was to dispose of my remaining estate near Albaro for half its worth, for ready money. Then I despatched all kinds of artificers, arras, furniture to regal splendour, to fit up the last relic of my inheritance, my palace in Genoa. I lingered a little longer yet, ashamed at the part of the prodigal returned, which I feared I should play. I sent my horses. One matchless Spanish jannet I despatched to my promised bride: its caparisons flamed with jewels and cloth of gold. In every part I caused to be entwined the initials of Juliet and her Guido. My present found favour in hers and in her father's eyes.

Still to return a proclaimed spendthrift, the mark of impertinent wonder, perhaps of scorn, and to encounter singly the reproaches or taunts of my fellow-citizens, was no alluring prospect. As a shield between me and censure,

I invited some few of the most reckless of my comrades to accompany me: thus I went armed against the world, hiding a rankling feeling, half and half penitence, by bravado.

I arrived in Genoa. I trod the pavement of my ancestral palace. My proud step was no interpreter of my heart, for I deeply felt that, though surrounded by every luxury, I was a beggar. The first step I took in claiming Juliet must widely declare me such. I read contempt or pity in the looks of all. I fancied that rich and poor, young and old, all regarded me with derision. Torella came not near me. No wonder that my second father should expect a son's deference from me in waiting first on him. But, galled and stung by a sense of my follies and demerit, I strove to throw the blame on others. We kept nightly orgies in Palazzo Carega. To sleepless, riotous nights followed listless, supine mornings. At the Ave Maria we showed our dainty persons in the streets, scoffing at the sober citizens, casting insolent glances on the shrinking women. Juliet was not among them—no, no; if she had been there, shame would have driven me away, if love had not brought me to her feet.

I grew tired of this. Suddenly I paid the Marchese a visit. He was at his Villa, one among the many which deck the suburb of San Pietro d'Arena. It was the month of May, the blossoms of the fruit-trees were fading among thick, green foliage; the vines were shooting forth; the ground strewed with the fallen olive blooms; the firefly was in the myrtle hedge; heaven and earth wore a mantle of surpassing beauty. Torella welcomed me kindly, though seriously; and even his shade of displeasure soon wore away. Some resemblance to my father—some look and tone of youthful ingenuousness, softened the good old man's heart. He sent for his daughter— he presented me to her as her betrothed. The chamber became hallowed by a holy light as she entered. Hers was that cherub look, those large, soft eyes, full dimpled cheeks, and mouth of infantine sweetness, that expresses the rare union of happiness and love. Admiration first possessed me; she is mine! was the second proud emotion, and my lips curled with haughty triumph. I had not been the *enfant gate* of the beauties of France not to have learnt the art of pleasing the soft heart of woman. If towards men I was over-bearing, the deference I paid to them was more in contrast. I commenced my courtship by the display of a thousand gallantries to Juliet, who, vowed to me from infancy, had never admitted the devotion of others; and who, though accustomed to expressions of admiration, was uninitiated in the language of lovers.

For a few days all went well. Torella never alluded to my extravagance; he treated me as a favourite son. But the time came, as we discussed the preliminaries to my union with his daughter, when this fair face of things should be overcast. A contract had been drawn up in my father's lifetime. I had rendered this, in fact, void by having squandered the whole of the wealth which was to have been shared by Juliet and myself. Torella, in consequence, chose to consider this bond as cancelled, and proposed another, in which, though the wealth he bestowed was immeasurably increased, there were so many restrictions as to the mode of spending it, that I, who saw independence only in free career being given to my own imperious will, taunted him as taking advantage of my situation, and refused utterly to subscribe to his conditions. The old man mildly strove to recall me to reason. Roused pride became the tyrant of my thought: I listened with indignation—I repelled him with disdain.

"Juliet, thou art mine! Did we not interchange vows in our innocent childhood? Are we not one in the sight of God? and shall thy cold-hearted, cold-blooded father divide us? Be generous, my love, be just; take not away a gift, last treasure of thy Guido—retract not thy vows—let us defy the world, and, setting at nought the calculations of age, find in our mutual affection a refuge from every ill."

Fiend I must have been with such sophistry to endeavour to poison that sanctuary of holy thought and tender love. Juliet shrank from me affrighted. Her father was the best and kindest of men, and she strove to show me how, in obeying him, every good would follow. He would receive my tardy submission with warm affection, and generous pardon would follow my repentance—profitless words for a young and gentle daughter to use to a man accustomed to make his will law, and to feel in his own heart a despot so terrible and stern that he could yield obedience to nought save his own imperious desires! My resentment grew with resistance; my wild companions were ready to add fuel to the flame. We laid a plan to carry off Juliet. At first it appeared to be crowned with success. Midway, on our return, we were overtaken by the agonised father and his attendants. A conflict ensued. Before the city guard came to decide the victory in favour of our antagonists, two of Torella's servitors were dangerously wounded.

This portion of my history weighs most heavily with me. Changed man as I am, I abhor myself in the recollection. May none who hear this tale ever have felt as I. A horse driven to fury by a rider armed with barbed spurs was not more a slave than I to the violent tyranny of my temper. A fiend possessed my soul, irritating it to madness. I felt the voice of conscience within me; but if I yielded to it for a brief interval, it was only to be a moment after torn, as by a whirlwind, away—borne along on the stream of desperate rage—the plaything of the storms engendered by pride. I was imprisoned, and, at the instance of Torella, set free. Again, I returned to carry off both him and his child to France, which hapless country, then preyed on by freebooters and gangs of lawless soldiery, offered a grateful refuge to a criminal like me. Our plots were discovered. I was sentenced to banishment; and, as my debts were already enormous, my remaining property was put in the hands of commissioners for their payment. Torella again offered his mediation, requiring only my promise not to renew my abortive attempts on himself and his daughter. I spurned his offers, and fancied that I triumphed when I was thrust out from Genoa, a solitary and penniless exile. My companions were gone: they had been dismissed the city some weeks before, and were already in France. I was alone—friendless, with neither sword at my side, nor ducat in my purse.

I wandered along the sea-shore, a whirlwind of passion possessing and tearing my soul. It was as if a live coal had been set burning in my breast. At first I meditated on what *I should do*. I would join a band of freebooters. Revenge!— the word seemed balm to me; I hugged it, caressed it, till, like a serpent, it stung me. Then again I would abjure and despise Genoa, that little corner of the world. I would return to Paris, where so many of my friends swarmed; where my services would be eagerly accepted; where I would carve out a fortune with my sword, and make my paltry birthplace and the false Torella rue the day when they drove me, a new Coriolanus, from her walls. I would return to Paris—thus on foot—a beggar—and present myself in my poverty to those I had formerly entertained sumptuously? There was gall in the mere thought of it.

The reality of things began to dawn upon my mind, bringing despair in its train. For several months I had been a prisoner: the evils of my dungeon had whipped my soul to madness, but they subdued my corporeal frame. I was weak and wan. Torella had used a thousand artifices to administer to my comfort; I had detected and scorned them all, and I reaped the harvest of my obduracy. What was to be done? Should I crouch before my foe, and sue for forgiveness?—Die rather ten thousand deaths!—Never should they obtain that victory! Hate—I swore eternal hate! Hate from whom?—to whom!—From a wandering outcast—to a mighty noble! I and my feelings were nothing to them: already had they forgotten one so unworthy. And Juliet!—her angel face and sylph-like form gleamed among the clouds of my despair with vain beauty; for I had lost her—the glory and flower of the world! Another will call her his!—that smile of paradise will bless another!

Even now my heart fails within me when I recur to this rout of grimvisaged ideas. Now subdued almost to tears, now raving in my agony, still I wandered along the rocky shore, which grew at each step wilder and more desolate. Hanging rocks and hoar precipices overlooked the tideless ocean;

black caverns yawned; and for ever, among the seaworn recesses, murmured and dashed the unfruitful waters. Now my way was almost barred by an abrupt promontory, now rendered nearly impracticable by fragments fallen from the cliff. Evening was at hand, when, seaward, arose, as if on the waving of a wizard's wand, a murky web of clouds, blotting the late azure sky, and darkening and disturbing the till now placid deep. The clouds had strange, fantastic shapes, and they changed and mingled and seemed to be driven about by a mighty spell. The waves raised their white crests; the thunder first muttered, then roared from across the waste of waters, which took a deep purple dye, flecked with foam. The spot where I stood looked, on one side, to the widespread ocean; on the other, it was barred by a rugged promontory. Round this cape suddenly came, driven by the wind, a vessel. In vain the mariners tried to force a path for her to the open sea—the gale drove her on the rocks. It will perish!—all on board will perish! Would I were among them! And to my young heart the idea of death came for the first time blended with that of joy. It was an awful sight to behold that vessel struggling with her fate. Hardly could I discern the sailors, but I heard them. It was soon all over! A rock, just covered by the tossing waves, and so unperceived, lay in wait for its prey. A crash of thunder broke over my head at the moment that, with a frightful shock, the vessel dashed upon her unseen enemy. In a brief space of time she went to pieces. There I stood in safety; and there were my fellow-creatures battling, how hopelessly, with annihilation. Methought I saw them struggling—too truly did I hear their shrieks, conquering the barking surges in their shrill agony. The dark breakers threw hither and thither the fragments of the wreck: soon it disappeared. I had been fascinated to gaze till the end: at last I sank on my knees—I covered my face with my hands. I again looked up; something was floating on the billows towards the shore. It neared and neared. Was that a human form? It grew more and more distinct; and at last a mighty wave, lifting the whole freight, lodged it upon a rock. A human being bestriding a sea chest!—a human being! Yet was it one? Surely never such had existed before—a misshapen dwarf, with squinting eyes, distorted features, and body deformed, till it became a horror to behold. My blood, lately warming towards a fellow-being so snatched from a watery tomb, froze in my heart. The dwarf got off his chest; he tossed his straight, struggling hair from his odious visage.

"By St. Beelzebub!" he exclaimed, "I have been well bested." He looked round and saw me. "Oh, by the fiend! here is another ally of the mighty One. To what saint did you offer prayers, friend—if not to mine? Yet I remember you not on board."

I shrank from the monster and his blasphemy. Again he questioned me, and I muttered some inaudible reply. He continued:

"Your voice is drowned by this dissonant roar. What a noise the big ocean makes! Schoolboys bursting from the prison are not louder than these waves set free to play. They disturb me. I will no more of their ill-timed brawling. Silence, hoary One!—Winds, avaunt!—to your homes!—Clouds, fly to the antipodes, and leave our heaven clear!"

As he spoke, he stretched out his two long, lank arms, that looked like spider's claws and seemed to embrace with them the expanse before him. Was it a miracle? The clouds became broken and fled; the azure sky first peeped out, and then was spread a calm field of blue above us; the stormy gale was exchanged to the softly breathing west; the sea grew calm; the waves dwindled to riplets.

"I like obedience even in these stupid elements," said the dwarf. "How much more in the tameless mind of man! It was a well-got-up storm, you must allow—and all of my own making."

It was tempting Providence to interchange talk with this magician. But *Power*, in all its shapes, is respected by man. Awe, curiosity, a clinging facination, drew me towards him.

"Come, don't be frightened, friend," said the wretch: "I am good humoured when pleased; and something does please me in your well-proportioned body and handsome face, though you look a little woebegone. You have suffered a land—I, a sea wreck. Perhaps I can allay the tempest of your fortunes as I did my own. Shall we be friends?"—And he held out his hand; I could not touch it. "Well, then, companions—that will do as well. And now, while I rest after the buffeting I underwent just now, tell me why, young and gallant as you seem, you wander thus alone and downcast on this wild sea-shore."

The voice of the wretch was screeching and horrid, and his contortions as he spoke were frightful to behold. Yet he did gain a kind of influence over me, which I could not master, and I told him my tale. When it was ended, he laughed long and loud: the rocks echoed back the sound: hell seemed yelling around me.

"Oh, thou cousin of Lucifer!" said he; "so thou too hast fallen through thy pride; and, though bright as the son of Morning, thou art ready to give up thy good looks, thy bride, and thy well-being, rather than submit thee to the tyranny of good. I honour thy choice, by my soul!—So thou hast fled, and yield the day; and mean to starve on these rocks, and to let the birds peck out thy dead eyes, while thy enemy and thy bethrothed rejoice in thy ruin. Thy pride is strangely akin to humility, methinks."

As he spoke, a thousand fanged thoughts stung me to

the heart.

"What would you that I should do?" I cried.

"I!—Oh, nothing, but lie down and say your prayers before you die. But, were I you, I know the deed that should be done."

I drew near him. His supernatural powers made him an oracle in my eyes; yet a strange unearthly thrill quivered through my frame as I said, "Speak!—teach me—what act do you advise?"

"Revenge thyself, man!—humble thy enemies!—set thy foot on the old man's neck, and possess thyself of his daughter!"

"To the east and west I turn," cried I, "and see no means! Had I gold, much could I achieve; but, poor and single, I am powerless."

The dwarf had been seated on his chest as he listened to my story. Now he got off; he touched a spring; it flew open! What a mine of wealth—of blazing jewels, beaming gold, and pale silver—was displayed therein. A mad desire to possess this treasure was born within me.

"Doubtless," I said, "one so powerful as you could do all things."

"Nay," said the monster humbly, "I am less omnipotent than I seem. Some things I possess which you may covet; but I would give them all for a small share, or even for a loan of what is yours."

"My possessions are at your service," I replied bitterly—"my poverty, my exile, my disgrace—I make a free gift of them all."

"Good! I thank you. Add one other thing to your gift, and my treasure is yours."

"As nothing is my sole inheritence, what besides nothing would you have?"

"Your comely face and well-made limbs."

I shivered. Would this all-powerful monster murder me? I had no dagger. I forgot to pray—but I grew pale.

"I ask for a loan, not a gift," said the frightful thing: "lend me your body for three days—you shall have mine to cage your soul the while, and in payment, my chest. What say you to the bargain?—Three short days."

We are told that it is dangerous to hold unlawful talk; and well do I prove the same. Tamely written down, it may seem incredible that I should lend any ear to this proposition; but, in spite of his unnatural ugliness, there was something fascinating in a being whose voice could govern earth, air, and sea. I felt a keen desire to comply; for with that chest I could command the world. My only hesitation resulted from a fear that he would not be true to this bargain. Then I thought, I shall soon die here on these lonely sands, and the limbs he covets will be mine no more—it is worth the chance. And, besides, I knew that, by all the rules of art-magic, there were formula and oaths which none of its practisers dared break. I hesitated to reply; and he went on, now displaying his wealth, now speaking of the petty price he demanded, till it seemed madness to refuse. Thus is it—place our bark in the current of the stream, and down, over fall and cataract it is hurried; give up our conduct to the wild torrent of passion, and we are away, we know not whither.

He swore many an oath, and I adjured him by many a sacred name; till I saw this wonder of power, this ruler of the elements, shiver like an autumn leaf before my words; and as if the spirit spake unwillingly and perforce within him, at last, he, with broken Voice, revealed the spell whereby he might be obliged, did he wish to play me false, to render up the unlawful spoil. Our warm lifeblood must mingle to make and to mar the charm.

Enough of this unholy theme. I was persuaded—the thing was done. The morrow dawned upon me as I lay upon the shingles, and I knew not my own shadow as it fell from me. I felt myself changed to a shape of horror, and cursed my easy faith and blind credulity. The chest was there—there the gold and precious stones for which I had sold the frame of flesh which nature had given me. The sight a little stilled my emotions: three days would soon be gone.

They did pass. The dwarf had supplied me with a plenteous

store of food. At first I could hardly walk, so strange and out of joint were all my limbs; and my voice—it was that of the fiend. But I kept silent, and turned my face to the sun, that I might not see my shadow, and counted the hours, and ruminated on my future conduct. To bring Torella to my feet—to possess my Juliet in spite of him—all this my wealth could easily achieve. During dark night I slept, and dreamt of the accomplishment of my desires. Two suns had set—the third dawned. I was agitated, fearful. Oh expectation, what a frightful thing art thou, when kindled more by fear than hope! How dost thou twist thyself round the heart, torturing its pulsations! How dost thou dart unknown pangs all through our feeble mechanism, now seeming to shiver us like broken glass, to nothingness—now giving us afresh strength, which can *do* nothing, and so torments us by a sensation, such as the strong man must feel who cannot break his fetters, though they bend in his grasp. Slowly paced the bright, bright orb up the eastern sky; long it lingered in the zenith, and still more slowly wandered down the west: it touched the horizon's verge—it was lost! Its glories were on the summits of the cliff—they grew dun and grey. The evening star shone bright. He will soon be here.

He came not!—By the living heavens, he came not!—and night dragged out its weary length, and, in its decaying age, "day began to grizzle its dark hair"; and the sun rose again on the most miserable wretch that ever upbraided its light. Three days thus I passed. The jewels and the gold—oh, how I abhorred them!

Well, well—I will not blacken these pages with demoniac ravings. All too terrible were the thoughts, the raging tumult of ideas that filled my soul. At the end of that time I slept; I had not before since the third sunset; and I dreamt that I was at Juliet's feet, and she smiled, and then she shrieked—for she saw my transformation—and again she smiled, for still her beautiful lover knelt before her. But it was not I—it was he, the fiend, arrayed in my limbs, speaking with my voice, winning her with my looks of love. I strove to warn her, but my tongue refused its office; I strove to tear him from her, but I was rooted to the ground—I awoke with the agony. There were the solitary hoar precipices—there the splashing sea, the quiet strand, and the blue sky over all. What did it mean? was my dream but a mirror of the truth? was he wooing and winning my betrothed? I would on the instant back to Genoa—but I was banished. I laughed—the dwarf's yell burst from my lips—I banished! Oh no! they had not exiled the foul limbs I wore; I might with these enter, without fear of incurring the threatened penalty of death, my own, my native city.

I began to walk towards Genoa. I was somewhat accustomed to my distorted limbs; none were ever so ill-adapted for a straight-forward movement; it was with infinite difficulty that I proceeded. Then, too, I desired to avoid all the hamlets strewed here and there on the sea-beach, for I was unwilling to make a display of my hideousness. I was not quite sure that, if seen, the mere boys would not stone me to death as I passed, for a monster; some ungentle salutations I did receive from the few peasants or fishermen I chanced to meet. But it was dark night before I approached Genoa. The weather was so balmy and sweet that it struck me that the Marchese and his daughter would very probably have quitted the city for their country retreat. It was from Villa Torella that I had attempted to carry off Juliet; I had spent many an hour reconnoitring the spot, and knew each inch of ground in its vicinity. It was beautifully situated, embosomed in trees, on the margin of a stream. As I drew near, it became evident that my conjecture was right; nay, moreover, that the hours were being then devoted to feasting and merriment. For the house was lighted up; strains of soft and gay music were wafted towards me by the breeze. My heart sank within me. Such was the generous kindness of Torella's heart that I felt sure that he would not have indulged in public manifestations of rejoicing just after my unfortunate banishment, but for a cause I dared not dwell upon.

The country people were all alive and flocking about; it became necessary that I should conceal myself; and yet I longed to address some one, or to hear others discourse, or in any way to gain intelligence of what was really going on. At length, entering the walks that were in immediate vicinity to the mansion, I found one dark enough to veil my excessive frightfulness; and yet others as well as I were loitering in its shade. I soon gathered all I wanted to know—all that first made my very heart die with horror, and then boil with indignation. Tomorrow Juliet was to be given to the penitent, reformed, beloved Guido—tomorrow my bride was to pledge her vows to a fiend from hell! And I did this!— my accursed pride—my demoniac violence and wicked self-idolatry had caused this act. For if I had acted as the wretch who had stolen my form had acted—if, with a mien at once yielding and dignified, I had presented myself to Torella, saying, I have done wrong, forgive me; I am unworthy of your angel-child, but permit me to claim her hereafter, when my altered conduct shall manifest that I abjure my vices, and endeavour to become in some sort worthy of her. I go to serve against the infidels; and when my zeal for religion and my true penitence for the past shall appear to you to cancel my crimes, permit me again to call myself your son. Thus had he spoken; and the penitent was welcomed even as the prodigal son of Scripture: the fatted calf was killed for him; and he, still pursuing the same path, displayed such open-hearted regret for his follies, so humble a concession of all his rights, and so ardent a resolve to reacquire them by a life of contrition and virtue, that he quickly conquered the kind old man; and full pardon, and the gift of his lovely child, followed in swift succession.

Oh, had an angel from Paradise whispered to me to act thus! But now, what would be the innocent Juliet's fate? Would God permit the foul union—or, some prodigy destroying it, link the dishonoured name of Carega with the worst of crimes? Tomorrow at dawn they were to be married: there was but one way to prevent this—to meet mine enemy, and to enforce the ratification of our agreement. I felt that this could only be done by a mortal struggle. I had no sword—if indeed my distorted arms could wield a soldier's weapon—but I had a dagger, and in that lay my hope. There was no time for pondering or balancing nicely the question: I might die in the attempt; but besides the burning jealousy and despair of my own heart, honour, mere humanity, demanded that I should fall rather than not destroy the machinations of the fiend.

The guests departed—the lights began to disappear; it was evident that the inhabitants of the villa were seeking repose. I hid myself among the trees—the garden grew deserted—the gates were closed—I wandered round and came upon a window—ah! well did I know the same!—a soft twilight glimmered in the room—the curtains were half withdrawn. It was the temple of innocence and beauty. Its magnificence was tempered, as it were, by the slight disarrangements occasioned by its being dwelt in, and all the objects scattered around displayed the taste of her who hallowed it by her presence. I saw her enter with a quick light step—I saw her approach the window—she drew back the curtain yet further, and looked out into the night. Its breezy freshness played among her ringlets, and wafted them from the transparent marble of her brow. She clasped her hands, she raised her eyes to heaven. I heard her voice. Guido! she softly murmured—mine own Guido! and then, as if overcome by the fullness of her own heart, she sank on her knees;—her upraised eyes—her graceful attitude—the beaming thankfulness that lighted up her face—oh, these are tame words! Heart of mine, thou imagest ever, though thou canst not portray, the celestial beauty of that child of light and love.

I heard a step—a quick firm step along the shady avenue. Soon I saw a cavalier, richly dressed, young and, methought, graceful to look on, advance. I hid myself yet closer. The youth approached; he paused beneath the window. She arose, and again looking out she saw him, and said—I cannot, no, at this distant time I cannot record her terms of soft silver tenderness; to me they were spoken, but they were replied to by him.

"I will not go," he cried: "here where you have been, where your memory glides like some heaven-visiting ghost, I will pass the long hours till we meet, never, my Juliet, again, day or night, to part. But do thou, my love, retire; the cold morn and fitful breeze will make thy cheek pale, and fill with languor thy love-lighted eyes. Ah, sweetness! could I press one kiss upon them, I could, methinks, repose."

And then he approached still nearer, and methought he was about to clamber into her chamber. I had hesitated, not to terrify her; now I was no longer master of myself. I rushed forward—I threw myself on him—I tore him away—I cried, "O loathsome and foul-shaped wretch!"

I need not repeat epithets, all tending, as it appeared, to rail at a person I at present feel some partiality for. A shriek rose from Juliet's lips. I neither heard nor saw—I *felt* only mine enemy, whose throat I grasped, and my dagger's hilt; he struggled, but could not escape. At length hoarsely he breathed these words: "Do!—strike home! destroy this body—you will still live: may your life be long and merry!"

The descending dagger was arrested at the word, and he, feeling my hold relax, extricated himself and drew his sword, while the uproar in the house, and flying of torches from one room to the other, showed that soon we should be separated. In the midst of my frenzy there was much calculation:—fall I might, and so that he did not survive, I cared not for the death-blow I might deal against myself. While still, therefore, he thought I paused, and while I saw the villainous resolve to take advantage of my hesitation, in the sudden thrust he made at me, I threw myself on his sword, and at the same moment plunged my dagger, with a true, desperate aim, in his side. We fell together, rolling over each other, and the tide of blood that flowed from the gaping wound of each mingles on the grass. More I know not—I fainted.

Again I return to life: weak almost to death, I found myself stretched upon a bed—Juliet was kneeling beside it. Strange! my first broken request was for a mirror. I was so wan and ghastly, that my poor girl hesitated, as she told me afterwards; but, by the mass! I thought myself a right proper youth when I saw the dear reflection of my own well-known features. I confess it is a weakness, but I avow it, I do entertain a considerable affection for the countenance and limbs I behold, whenever I look at a glass; and have more mirrors in my house, and consult them oftener, than any beauty in Genoa. Before you too much condemn me, permit me to say that no one better knows than I the value of his own body; no one, probably, except myself, ever having had it stolen from him.

Incoherently I at first talked of the dwarf and his crimes, and reproached Juliet for her admission of his love. She thought me raving, as well she might; and yet it was some time before I could prevail on myself to admit that the Guido whose penitence had won her back for me was myself; and while I cursed bitterly the monstous dwarf, and blest the well-directed blow that had deprived him of life, I suddenly checked myself when I heard her say, Amen! knowing that him whom she reviled was my very self. A little reflection taught me silence—a little practice enabled me to speak of that frightful night without any very excessive blunder. The wound I had given myself was no mockery of one—it was long before I recovered—and as the benevolent and generous Torella sat beside me, talking such wisdom as might win friends to repentance, and mine own dear Juliet hovered near me, administered to my wants, and cheering me by her smiles, the work of my bodily cure and mental reform went on together. I have never, indeed, wholly recovered my strength—my cheek is paler since—my person a little bent. Juliet sometimes ventures to allude bitterly to the malice that caused this change, but I kiss her on the moment, and tell her all is for the best. I am a fonder and more faithful husband, and true is this—but for that wound, never had I called her mine.

I did not revisit the sea-shore, nor seek for the fiend's treasure; yet, while I ponder on the past, I often think, and my confessor was not backward in favouring the idea, that it might be a good rather than an evil spirit, sent by my guardian angel, to show me the folly and misery of pride. So well at least did I learn this lesson, roughly taught as I was, that I am known by all my friends and fellow-citizens by the name of Guido il Cortese.

THE OPEN DOOR

Mrs. Oliphant

I took the house of Brentwood on my return from India in 1800, for the temporary accommodation of my family, until I could find a permanent home for them. It had many advantages which made it peculiarly appropriate. It was within reach of Edinburgh, and my boy Roland, whose education had been considerably neglected, could go in and out to school, which was thought to be better for him than either leaving home altogether or staying there always with a tutor. The first of these expedients would have seemed preferable to me, the second commended itself to his mother. The doctor, like a judicious man, took the midway between. "Put him on his pony, and let him ride into the High School every morning; it will do him all the good in the world," Dr. Simson said; "and when it is bad weather there is the train." His mother accepted the solution of the difficulty more easily than I could have hoped; and our pale-faced boy, who had never known anything more invigorating than Simla, began to encounter the brisk breezes of the North in the subdued severity of the month of May. Before the time of the vacation in July we had the satisfaction of seeing him begin to acquire something of the brown and ruddy complexion of his schoolfellows. The English system did not commend itself to Scotland in these days. There was no little Eton at Fettes; nor do I think, if there had been, that a genteel exotic of that class would have tempted either my wife or me. The lad was doubly precious to us, being the only one left us of many; and he was fragile in body we believed, and deeply sensitive in mind. To keep him at home, and yet to send him to school—to combine the advantages of the two systems—seemed to be everything that could be desired. The two girls also found at Brentwood everything they wanted. They were near enough to Edinburgh to have masters and lessons as many as they required for completing that ending education which the young people seem to require nowadays. Their mother married me when she was younger than Agatha, and I should like to see them improve upon their mother! I myself was then no more than twenty-five—an age at which I see the young fellows now groping about them, with no notion what they are going to do with their lives. However, I suppose every generation has a conceit of itself which elevates it, in its own opinion, above that which comes after it.

Brentwood stands on that fine and wealthy slope of

country, one of the richest in Scotland, which lies between the Pentland Hills and the Firth. In clear weather you could see the blue gleam—like a bent bow, embracing the wealthy fields and scattered houses—of the great estuary on one side of you; and on the other the blue heights, not gigantic like those we had been used to, but just high enough for all the glories of the atmosphere, the play of clouds, and sweet reflections, which give to a hilly country an interest and a charm which nothing else can emulate. Edinburgh, with its two lesser heights—the Castle and the Calton Hill—its spires and towers piercing through the smoke, and Arthur's Seat lying crouched behind, like a guardian no longer very needful, taking his repose beside the well-beloved charge, which is now, so to speak, able to take care of itself without him—lay at our right hand. From the lawn and drawing-room windows we could see all these varieties of landscape. The colour was sometimes a little chilly, but sometimes, also, as animated and full of vicissitude as a drama. I was never tired of it. Its colour and freshness revived the eyes which had grown weary of arid plains and blazing skies. It was always cheery, and fresh, and full of repose.

The village of Brentwood lay almost under the house, on the other side of the deep little ravine, down which a stream—which ought to have been a lovely, wild, and frolicsome little river—flowed between its rocks and trees.

The river, like so many in that district had, however, in its earlier life been sacrificed to trade, and was grimy with paper-making. But this did not affect our pleasure in it so much as I have known it to affect other streams. Perhaps our water was more rapid—perhaps less clogged with dirt and refuse. Our side of the dell was charmingly *accidenté*, and clothed with fine trees, through which various paths wound down to the riverside and to the village bridge which crossed the stream. The village lay in the hollow, and climbed, with very prosaic houses, the other side. Village architecture does not flourish in Scotland. The blue slates and the grey stone are sworn foes to the picturesque; and though I do not, for my own part, dislike the interior of an old-fashioned pewed and galleried church, with its little family settlements on all sides, the square box outside, with its bit of a spire like a handle to lift it by, is not an improvement to the landscape. Still, a cluster of houses on differing elevations—with scraps of garden coming in between, a hedgerow with clothes laid out to dry, the opening of a street with its rural sociability, the women at their doors, the slow waggon lumbering along— gives a centre to the landscape. It was cheerful to look at, and convenient in a hundred ways. Within ourselves we had walks in plenty, the glen being always beautiful in all its phases, whether the woods were green in the spring or ruddy in the autumn. In the park which surrounded our house were the ruins of the former mansion of Brentwood, a much smaller and less important house than the solid Georgian edifice which we inhabited. The ruins were picturesque, however, and gave importance to the place. Even we, who were but temporary tenants, felt a vague pride in them, as if they somehow reflected a certain consequence upon ourselves. The old building had the remains of a tower, an indistinguishable mass of mason-work, overgrown with ivy, and the shells of walls attached to this were half filled up with soil. I had never examined it closely, I am ashamed to say. There was a large room, or what had been a large room, with the lower part of the windows still existing, on the principal floor, and underneath other windows, which were perfect, though half filled up with fallen soil, and waving with a wild growth of brambles and chance growths of all kinds. This was the oldest part of all. At a little distance were some very commonplace and disjointed fragments of the building, one of them suggesting a certain pathos by its very commonness and the complete wreck which it showed. This was the end of a low gable, a bit of grey wall, all encrusted with lichens, in which was a common doorway, Probably it had been a servants' entrance, a backdoor, or opening into what are called "the offices" in Scotland. No offices remained to be entered—pantry and kitchen had all been swept out of being; but there stood the doorway open and vacant, free to all the winds, to the rabbits, and every wild creature. It struck my eye, the first time I went to Brentwood, like a meloncholy comment upon a life that was over. A door that led to nothing—closed once perhaps with anxious care, bolted and guarded, now void of any meaning, It impressed me, I remember, from the first; so perhaps it may be said that my mind was prepared to attach to it an importance, which nothing justified.

The summer was a very happy period of repose for us all. The warmth of Indian suns was still in our veins. It seemed to us that we could never have enough of the greenness, the dewiness, the freshness of the northern landscape. Even its mists were pleasant to us, taking all the fever out of us, and pouring in vigour and refreshment. In autumn we followed the fashion of the time, and went away for a change which we did not in the least require. It was when the family had settled down for the winter, when the days were short and dark, and the rigorous reign of frost upon us, that the incidents occured which alone could justify me in intruding upon the world my private affairs. These incidents were, however, of so curious a character, that I hope my inevitable references to my own family and pressing personal interests will meet with a general pardon.

I was absent in London when these events began. In London an old Indian plunges back into the interests with which all his previous life has been associated, and meets old friends at every step. I had been circulating among some half-dozen of these—enjoying the return to my former life in shadow, though I had been so thankful in substance to throw it aside—and had missed some of my home letters, what with going down from Friday to Monday to old Benbow's place in the country, and stopping on the way back to dine and sleep at Sellar's and to take a look into Cross's stables, which occupied another day. It is never safe to miss one's letters. In this transitory life, as the Prayer-book says, how can one ever be certain what is going to happen? All was well at home. I knew exactly (I thought) what they would have to say to me: "The weather has been so fine that Roland has not once gone by train and he enjoys the ride beyond anything." "Dear papa, be sure that you don't forget anything, but bring us so-and-so and so-and-so"—a list as long as my arm. Dear girls and dearer mother! I would not for the world have forgotten their commissions or lost their little letters, for all the Benbows and Crosses in the world.

But I was confident in my home-comfort and peacefulness. When I got back to my club, however, three or four letters were lying for me, upon some of which I noticed the 'immediate' 'urgent', which old-fashioned people and anxious people still believe will influence the post-office and quicken the speed of the mails. I was about to open one of these, when the club porter brought me two telegrams, one of which, he said, had arrived the night before. I opened, as was to be expected, the last first, and this is what I read: "Why don't you come or answer? For God's sake come. He is much worse." This was a thunderbolt to fall upon a man's head who had only one son, and he the light of his eyes! The other telegram, which I opened with hands trembling so much that I lost time by my haste, was to much the same purport: "No better; doctor afraid of brain-fever. Calls for you day and night. Let nothing detain you." The first thing I did was to look up the time-tables to see if there was any way of getting off sooner than by the night train, though I knew well enough there was not! and then I read the letters, which furnished, alas! too clearly, all the details. They told me that the boy had been pale for some time, with a scared look. His mother had noticed it before I left home, but would not say anything to alarm me. This look had increased day by day; and soon it was observed that Roland came home at a wild gallop through the park, his pony panting and in foam, himself "as white as a sheet," but with the perspiration streaming from his forehead. For a long time he had resisted all questioning, but at length had developed such strange changes of mood, showing a reluctance to go to school, a desire to be fetched in the carriage at night—which was a ridiculous piece of luxury—an unwillingness to go out into the grounds, and nervous start at every sound, that his mother had insisted upon an explanation. When the boy—our boy Roland, who had never known what fear was—began to talk to her of voices he had heard in the park, and shadows that had appeared to him among the ruins, my wife promptly put him to bed and sent for Dr. Simson—which, of course, was the only thing to do.

I hurried off that evening, as may be supposed, with an anxious heart. How I got through the hours before the starting of the train, I cannot tell. We must all be thankful for the quickness of the railway when in anxiety; but to have thrown myself into a post-chaise as soon as horses could be put to, would have been a relief. I got to Edinburgh very early in the blackness of the winter morning, and scarcely dared look the man in the face at whom I gasped "What news?" My wife had sent the brougham for me, which I concluded, before the man spoke, was a bad sign. His answer was that stereotyped answer which leaves the imagination so wildly free—"Just the same." Just the same! What might that mean? The horses seemed to me to creep along the dark country road. As we dashed through the park I thought I heard someone moaning among the trees, and clenched my fist at him (whoever he might be) with fury. Why had the fool of a woman at the gate allowed anyone to come in and disturb the quiet of the place? If I had not been in such hot haste to get home, I think I should have stopped the carriage and got out to see what tramp it was that had made an entrance and chosen my grounds, of all places in the world—when my boy was ill!—to grumble and groan in. But I had no reason to complain of our slow pace here. The horses flew like lightning along the intervening path, and drew up at the door all panting, as if they had run a race. My wife stood waiting to receive me with a pale face, and a candle in her hand, which made her look paler still as the wind blew the flame about. "He is sleeping," she said in a whisper, as if her voice might wake him. And I replied, when I could find my voice, also in a whisper, as though the jingling of the horses' furniture and the sound of their hoofs must not have been more dangerous. I stood on the steps with her a moment, almost afraid to go in, now that I was here; and it seemed to me that I saw without observing, if I may say so, that the horses were unwilling to turn round, though their stables lay that way, or that the men were unwilling. These things occurred to me afterwards, though at the moment I was not capable of anything but to ask questions and to hear of the condition of the boy.

I looked at him from the door of his room, for we were afraid to go near, lest we should disturb that blessed sleep. It looked like actual sleep—not the lethargy into which my wife told me he would sometimes fall. She told me everything in the next room, which communicated with his, rising now and then and going to the door of communication; and in this there was much that was very startling and confusing to the mind. It appeared that ever since the winter began, since it was early dark and night had fallen before his return from school, he had been hearing voices among the ruins—at first only a groaning, he said, at which his pony was as much alarmed as he was, but by degrees a voice. The tears ran down my wife's cheeks as she described to me how he would start up in the night and cry out, "Oh, mother, let me in! oh, mother, let me in!" with a pathos which rent her heart. And she sitting there all the time, only longing to do everything his heart could desire! But though she would try to soothe him, crying: "You are at home, my darling. I am here. Don't you know me? Your mother is here," he would only stare at her, and after a while spring up again with the same cry. At other times he would be quite reasonable, she said, asking eagerly when I was coming, but declaring that he must go with me as soon as I did so, "to let them in". "The doctor thinks his nervous system must have received a shock," my wife said. "Oh, Henry, can it be that we have pushed him on too much with his work—a delicate boy like Roland?—and what is his work in comparison with his health? Even you would think little of honours or prizes if it hurt the boy's health." Even I! as if I were an inhuman father sacrificing my child to his ambition. But I would not increase her trouble by taking any notice. After a while they persuaded me to lie down, to rest, and to eat—none of which things had been possible since I received their letters. The mere fact of being on the spot, of course, in itself was a great thing and when I knew that I would be called in a moment, as soon as he was awake and wanted me, I felt capable, even in the dark, chill morning twilight, to snatch an hour or two's sleep. As it happened, I was so worn out with the strain of anxiety, and he so quieted and consoled by knowing I had come, that I was not disturbed till the afternoon, when the twilight had again settled down. There was just daylight enough to see his face when I went to him; and what a change in a fortnight! He was paler and more worn, I thought, than even in those dreadful days in the plains before we left India. His hair seemed to have grown long and lank; his eyes were like blazing lights projecting out of his white face. He got hold of my hand in a cold and tremulous clutch, and waved to everybody to go away. "Go away—even mother," he said, "go away." This went to her heart, for she did not like that even I should have more of the boy's confidence than herself; but my wife has never been a woman to think of herself, and she left us alone. "Are they all gone?" he said, eagerly. "They would not let me speak. The doctor treated me as if I were a fool. You know I am not a fool, papa."

"Yes, yes, my boy, I know; but you are ill, and quiet is so necessary. You are not only not a fool, Roland, but you are reasonable and understand. When you are ill you must deny yourself; you must not do everything that you might do being well."

He waved his thin hand with a sort of indignation.

"Then, father, I am not ill," he cried. "Oh, I thought when you came you would not stop me—you would see the sense of it! What do you think is the matter with me, all of you? Simson is well enough, but he is only a doctor. What do you think is the matter with me? I am no more ill than you are. A doctor, of course, he thinks you are ill the moment he looks at you—that's what he's there for—and claps you into bed."

"Which is the best place for you at present, my dear boy."

"I made up my mind," cried the little fellow, "that I would stand it till you came home. I said to myself, I won't frighten mother and the girls. But now, father," he cried, half jumping out of bed, "it's not illness—it's a secret."

His eyes shone so wildly, his face was so swept with strong feeling, that my heart sank within me. It could be nothing but fever that did it, and fever had been so fatal. I got him into my arms to put him back into bed. "Roland," I said, humouring the poor child, which I knew was the only way, "if you are going to tell me this secret to do any good, you know you must be quite quiet, and not excite yourself. If you excite yourself, I must not let you speak."

"Yes, father," said the boy. He was quiet directly, like a man, as if he quite understood. When I had laid him back on his pillow, he looked up at me with that grateful, sweet look with which children when they are ill, break one's heart, the water coming into his eyes in his weakness. "I was sure as soon as you were here you would know what to do," he said.

"To be sure, my boy. Now keep quiet, and tell it all out like a man." To think I was telling lies to my own child! for I did it only to humour him, thinking, poor little fellow, his brain was wrong.

"Yes, father. Father, there is some one in the park—some one that has been badly used."

"Hush, my dear; you remember, there is to be no excitement. Well, who is this somebody, and who has been ill-using him? We will soon put a stop to that."

"Ah," cried Roland, "but it is not so easy as you think. I don't know who it is. It is just a cry. Oh, if you could hear it! It gets into my head in my sleep. I heard it as clear as clear; and they think that I am dreaming—or raving perhaps" the boy said, with a sort of disdainful smile.

This look of his perplexed me; it was less like fever than I thought. "Are you quite sure you have not dreamt it,

Roland?" I said.

"Dreamt?—that!" He was springing up again when he suddenly bethought himself, and lay down flat with the same sort of smile on his face. "The pony heard it too," he said. "She jumped as if she had been shot. If I had not grasped at the reins—for I was frightened, father—"

"No shame to you, my boy," said I, though I scarcely knew why.

"If I hadn't held to her like a leech, she'd have pitched me over her head, and she never drew breath till we were at the door. Did the pony dream it?" he said, with a soft disdain, yet indulgence for my foolishness. Then he added slowly: "It was only a cry the first time, and all the time before you went away. I wouldn't tell you, for it was so wretched to be frightened. I thought it might be a hare or a rabbit snared, and I went in the morning and looked, but there was nothing. It was after you went I heard it really first, and this is what he says." He raised himself on his elbow close to me, and looked me in the face. " 'Oh, mother, let me in! oh, mother, let me in!'" As he said the words a mist came over his face, the mouth quivered, the soft features all melted and changed, and when he had ended these pitiful words, dissolved in a shower of heavy tears.

Was it a hallucination? Was it the fever of the brain? Was it the disordered fancy caused by great bodily weakness?

How could I tell? I thought it wisest to accept it as if it were all true.

"This is very touching, Roland," I said.

"Oh, if you had just heard it, father! I said to myself, 'if father heard it he would do something'; but mamma, you know, she's given over to Simson, and that fellow's a doctor, and never thinks of anything but clapping you into bed."

"We must not blame Simson for being a doctor, Roland."

"No, no," said my boy, with delightful toleration and indulgence; "oh, no; that's the good of him—that's what he's for; I know that. But you—you are different; you are just father: and you'll do something—directly, papa, directly—this very night."

"Surely," I said. "No doubt, it is some little lost child."

He gave me a sudden, swift look, investigating my face as though to see whether, after all, this was everything my eminence as "father" came to—no more than that? Then he got hold of my shoulder, clutching it with his thin hands: "Look here," he said, with a quiver in his voice; "suppose it wasn't—living at all!"

"My dear boy, how then could you have heard it?" I said.

He turned away from me, with a pettish exclamation—"As if you didn't know better than that!"

"Do you want to tell me it is a ghost?" I said.

Roland withdrew his hand; his countenance assumed an

aspect of great dignity and gravity; a slight quiver remained about his lips. "Whatever it was—you always said we were not to call names. It was something—in trouble. Oh, father, in terrible trouble!"

"But, my boy," I said—I was at my wits' end—"if it was a child that was lost, or any poor human creature—But Roland, what do you want me to do?"

"I should know if I was you," said the child eagerly. "That is what I always said to myself—'Father will know.' Oh, papa, papa, to have to face it night after night, in such terrible, terrible trouble! and never be able to do it any good. I don't want to cry; it's like a baby, I know; but what can I do else?—out there all by itself in the ruin, and nobody to help it. I can't bear it, I can't bear it!" cried my generous boy. And in his weakness he burst out, after many attempts to restrain it, into a great childish fit of sobbing and tears.

I do not know that I ever was in a greater perplexity in my life; and afterwards, when I thought of it, there was something comic in it too. It is bad enough to find your child's mind possessed with the conviction that he has seen—or heard—a ghost. But that he should require you to go instantly and help that ghost, was the most bewildering experience that had ever come my way. I am a sober man myself, and not superstitious—at least any more than everybody is superstitious. Of course I do not believe in ghosts; but I don't deny, any more than other people, that there are stories which I cannot pretend to understand. My blood got a sort of chill in my veins at the idea that Roland should be a ghost-seer; for that generally means a hysterical temperament and weak health, and all that men most hate and fear for their children. But that I should take up his ghost and right its wrongs, and save it from its trouble, was such a mission as was enough to confuse any man. I did my best to console my boy without giving any promise of this astonishing kind; but he was too sharp for me. He would have none of my caresses. With sobs breaking in at intervals upon his voice, and the raindrops hanging on his eye-lids, he yet returned to the charge.

"It will be there now—it will be there all the night. Oh think, papa, think, if it was me! I can't rest for thinking of it. Don't!" he cried, putting away my hand—"don't! You go and help it, and mother can take care of me."

"But, Roland, what can I do?"

My boy opened his eyes, which were large with weakness and fever and gave me a smile such, I think, as sick children only know the secret of. "I was sure you would know as soon as you came. I always said—'Father will know': and mother," he cried, with a softening of repose upon his face, his limbs relaxing, his form sinking with a luxurious ease in his bed—"mother can come and take care of me."

I called her, and saw him turn to her with the complete dependence of a child, and then I went away and left them, as perplexed a man as any in Scotland. I must say, however, I had this consolation, that my mind was greatly eased about Roland. He might be under a hallucination, but his head was clear enough, and I did not think him so ill as everybody else did. The girls were astonished even at the ease with which I took it. "How do you think he is?" they said in a breath, coming round me, laying hold of me. "Not half so ill as I expected," I said; "not very bad at all," "Oh, papa, you are a darling," cried Agatha, kissing me, and crying upon my shoulder; while little Jeanie, who was as pale as Roland, clasped both her arms round mine, and could not speak at all. I knew nothing about it, not half so much as Simson; but they believed in me; they had a feeling that all would go right now. God is very good to you when your children look to you like that. It makes one humble, not proud. I was not worthy of it; and then I recollected that I had to act the part of a father to Roland's ghost, which made me almost laugh, though I might just as well have cried. It was the strangest mission that ever was entrusted to mortal man.

It was then I remembered suddenly the looks of the men when they turned to take the brougham to the stables in the dark that morning: they had not liked it, and the horses had not liked it. I remembered that even in my anxiety about

Roland I had heard them tearing along the avenue back to the stables, and had made a memorandum mentally that I must speak of it. It seemed to me that the best thing I could do was to go to the stables now and make a few inquiries. It is impossible to fathom the minds of rustics; there might be some devilry of practical joking, for anything I knew; or they might have some interest in getting up a bad reputation for the Brentwood avenue. It was getting dark by the time I went out, and nobody who knows the country will need to be told how black is the darkness of a November night under high laurel bushes and yew-trees. I walked into the heart of the shrubberies two or three times, not seeing a step before me, till I came out upon the broader carriage-road, where the trees opened a little, and there was a faint grey glimmer of sky visible, under which the great limes and elms stood darkling like ghosts; but it grew black again as I approached the corner where the ruins lay. Both eyes and ears were on the alert, as may be supposed; but I could see nothing in the absolute gloom, and, so far as I can recollect, I heard nothing. Nevertheless, there came a strong impression upon me that somebody was there. It is a sensation which most people have felt. I have seen when it has been strong enough to awake me out of sleep, the sense of some one looking at me. I suppose my imagination had been affected by Roland's story; and the mystery of the darkness is always full of suggestions. I stamped my feet violently on the gravel to rouse myself, and called out sharply, "Who's there?" Nobody answered, nor did I expect any one to answer, but the impression had been made. I was so foolish that I did not like to look back, but went sideways, keeping an eye on the gloom behind. It was with great relief that I spied the light in the stables, making a sort of oasis in the darkness. I walked very quickly into the midst of that lighted and cheerful place, and thought the clank of the groom's pail one of the pleasantest sounds I had ever heard. The coachman was the head of this little colony, and it was to his house I went to pursue my investigations. He was a native of the district, and had taken care of the place in the absence of the family for years; it was impossible but that he must know everything that was going on, and all the traditions of the place. The men, I could see, eyed me anxiously when I thus appeared at such an hour among them, and followed me with their eyes to Jarvis's house, where he lived alone with his old wife, their children being all married and out in the world. Mrs. Jarvis met me with anxious questions. How was the poor young gentleman? but the others knew, I could see by their faces, that not even this was the foremost thing in my mind.

"Noises?—ou ay, there'll be noises—the wind in the trees, and the water soughing down the glen. As for tramps, Cornel, no, there's little o' that kind of cattle about here; and

Merran at the gate's a careful body." Jarvis moved about with some embarrassment from one leg to another as he spoke. He kept in the shade, and did not look at me more than he could help. Evidently his mind was perturbed, and he had reasons for keeping his own counsel. His wife sat by, giving him a quick look now and then, but saying nothing. The kitchen was very snug, and warm, and bright—as different as could be from the chill and mystery of the night outside.

"I think you are trifling with me, Jarvis," I said.

"Triflin', Cornel? no me. What would I trifle for? If the deevil himsel' was in the auld hoose, I have no interest in't one way or another—"

"Sandy, hold your peace!" cried his wife imperatively.

"And what am I to hold my peace for, wi' the Cornel standing there asking a' thae questions? I'm saying, if the deevil himsel'—"

"And I'm telling ye hold your peace!" cried the woman, in great excitement. "Dark November weather and lang nichts, and us that ken a' we ken. How daur ye name—a name that shouldna be spoken?" She threw down her stocking and got up, also in great agitation. "I tell't ye you never could keep it. It's no a thing that will hide; and the haill toun kens as weel as you or me. Tell the Cornel straight out—or see, I'll do it. I dinna hold wi' your secrets; and a secret that the haill toun kens!" She snapped her fingers with an air of large disdain.

As for Jarvis, ruddy and big as he was, he shrank to nothing before this decided woman. He repeated to her two or three times her own adjuration, "Hold your peace!" then, suddenly changing his tone, cried out, "Tell him then, confound ye! I'll wash my hands o't. If a' the ghosts in Scotland were in the auld hoose, is that ony concern o' mine?"

After this I elicited without much difficulty the whole story. In the opinion of the Jarvises, and of everybody about, the certainty that the place was haunted was beyond all doubt. As Sandy and his wife warmed to the tale, one tripping up another in their eagerness to tell everything, it gradually developed as distinct a superstition as I ever heard, and not without poetry and pathos. How long it was since the voice had been heard first, nobody could tell with certainty. Jarvis's opinion was that his father, who had been coachman at Brentwood before him, had never heard anything about it, and that the whole thing had arisen within the last ten years, since the complete dismantling of the old house: which was a wonderfully modern date for a tale so well authenticated. According to these witnesses, and to several whom I questioned afterwards, and who were all in perfect agreement, it was only in the months of November and December that "the visitation" occured. During these months, the darkest of the year, scarcely a night passed without the recurrence of these inexplicable cries. Nothing, it was said, had ever been seen—at least nothing that could be identified. Some people, bolder or more imaginative than the others, had seen the darkness moving, Mrs Jarvis said, with unconscious poetry. It began when night fell and continued, at intervals, till day broke. Very often it was only an inarticulate cry and moaning, but sometimes the words which had taken possession of my poor boy's fancy had been distinctly audible—"Oh, mother, let me in!" The Jarvises were not aware that there had ever been any investigation into it. The estate of Brentwood had lapsed into the hands of a distant branch of the family, who had lived but little there; and of the many people who had taken it, as I had done, few had remained through two Decembers. And nobody had taken the trouble to make a very close examination into the facts. "No, no," Jarvis said, shaking his head. "No, no, Cornel. Wha wad set themsels up for a laughin'-stock to a' the country-side, making a wark about a ghost? Naebody believes in ghosts. It bid to be the wind in the trees, the last gentleman said, or some effec' o' the water wrastlin' among the rocks. He said it was a' quite easy explained: but he gave up the hoose. And when you cam, Cornel, we were awfu' anxious you should never hear. What for should I have spoiled the bargain and hairmed the property for nothing?"

"Do you call my child's life nothing?" I said in the trouble of the moment, unable to restrain myself. "And instead of telling this all to me, you have told it to him—to a delicate boy, a child unable to sift evidence, or judge for himself, a tender-hearted young creature—"

I was walking about the room with an anger all the hotter that I felt it to be most likely quite unjust. My heart was full of bitterness against the stolid retainers of a family who were content to risk other people's children and comfort rather than let the house lie empty. If I had been warned I might have taken precautions, or left the place, or sent Roland away, a hundred things which now I could not do; and here I was with my boy in a brain-fever, and his life, the most precious life on earth, hanging in the balance, dependent on whether or not I could get to the reason of a commonplace ghost-story! I paced about in high wrath, and seeing what I was to do; for, to take Roland away, even if he were able to travel, would not settle his agitated mind; and I feared even that a scientific explanation of refracted sound, or reverberation, or any other of the easy certainties with which we elder men are silenced, would have very little effect upon the boy.

"Cornel," said Jarvis, solemnly, "ond *she'll* bear me witness—the young gentleman never heard a word from me—no, nor from either groom or gardener; I'll gie ye my word for that. In the first place, he's no a lad that invites ye to talk. There are some that are, and some that arena. Some will draw ye on, till ye've tellt them a' the clatter of the toun, and a' ye ken, and whiles mair. But Maister Roland, his mind's fu' of his books. He's aye civil and kind, and a fine lad; but no that sort. And ye see it's for a' our interest, Cornel, that you should stay at Brentwood. I took it upon me mysel' to pass the word—'No a syllable to Maister Roland, nor to the young leddies—no a syllable'. The women-servants, that have little reason to be out at night, ken little or nothing about it. And some think it grand to have a ghost so long as they're no in the way of coming across it. If you had been tellt the story to begin with, maybe ye would have thought so yourself."

This was true enough, though it did not throw any light upon my perplexity. If we had heard of it to start with, it is possible that all the family would have considered the possession of a ghost a distinct advantage. It is the fashion of the times. We never think what a risk it is to play with young imaginations, but cry out, in the fashionable jargon, "A ghost!—nothing else was wanted to make it perfect." I should not have been above this myself. I should have smiled, of course, at the idea of the ghost at all, but then to feel that it was mine would have pleased my vanity. Oh, yes, I claim no exemption. The girls would have been delighted. I could fancy their eagerness, their interest, and excitement. No; if we had been told, it would have done no good—we should have made the bargain all the more eagerly, the fools that we are. "And there has been no attempt to investigate it," I said, "to see what it really is?"

"Eh, Cornel," said the coachman's wife, "wha would investigate, as ye call it, a thing that nobody believes in? Ye would be the laughing-stock of a' the country-side, as my man says."

"But you believe in it," I said, turning upon her hastily. The woman was taken by surprise. She made a step backward out of my way.

"Lord, Cornel, how ye frichten a body! Me!—there's awful strange things in this world. An unlearned person doesna ken what to think. But the minister and the gentry they just laugh in your face. Inquire into the thing that is not! Na, na, we just let it be."

"Come with me, Jarvis," I said, hastily, "and we'll make an attempt at least. Say nothing to the men or to anybody. I'll come back after dinner, and we'll make a serious attempt to see what it is, if it is anything. If I hear it—which I doubt— you may be sure I shall never rest till I make it out. Be ready for me about ten o'clock."

"Me, Cornel!" Jarvis said, in a faint voice. I had not been looking at him in my own preoccupation, but when I did so, I found that the greatest change had come over the fat and ruddy coachman. "Me Cornel!" he repeated, wiping the perspiration from his brow. His ruddy face hung in flabby folds, his knees knocked together, his voice seemed half extinguished in his throat. Then he began to rub his hands and smile upon me in a deprecating, imbecile way. "There's nothing I wouldna do to pleasure ye, Cornel," taking a step further back. "I'm sure *she* kens I've aye said I never had to do with a mair fair, weelspoken gentleman—" Here Jarvis came to a pause, again looking at me, rubbing his hands.

"Well?" I said.

"But eh, sir!" he went on, with the same imbecile yet insinuating smile, "if ye'll reflect that I am no used to my feet. With a horse atween my legs, or the reins in my hand, I'm maybe nae worse than other men; but on fit, Cornel— It's no the—bogles;—but I've been cavalry, ye see," with a little hoarse laugh, "a' my life. To face a thing ye didna understan'—on you feet, Cornel—"

"Well, sir, if I do it," said I tartly, "why shouldn't you?"

"Eh, Cornel, there's an awfu' difference. In the first place, ye tramp about the haill country-side, and think naething of it; but a walk tires me mair than a hunard miles' drive; and then ye'e a gentleman, and do your ain pleasure; and your'e no so auld as me; and it's for your ain bairn, ye see, Cornel; and then—"

"He believes in it, Cornel, and you dinna believe in it," the woman said.

"Will you come with me?" I said, turning to her.

60

She jumped back, upsetting her chair in her bewilderment. "Me!" with a scream, and then fell into a sort of hysterical laugh. "I wouldna say but what I would go; but what would the folk say to hear of Cornel Mortimer with an auld silly woman at his heels?"

The suggestion made me laugh too, though I had little inclination for it. "I'm sorry you have so little spirit, Jarvis," I said. "I must find some one else, I suppose."

The beautiful Mary Shelley—who looked the most unlikely person to have created a monster such as that of Baron Frankenstein.

In supernatural stories by Victorian women it was not uncommon for the phantom to appear when the heroine was in bed. Here are two almost identical scenes from two completely different stories: (above) A Horrible Honeymoon by Mrs. Edith Cuthell and (below) The Figure in White, Anonymous.

Jarvis, touched by this, began to remonstrate, but I cut him short. My butler was a soldier who had been with me in India, and was not supposed to fear anything—man or devil—certainly not the former; and I felt that I was losing time. The Jarvises were too thankful to get rid of me. They attended me to the door with the most anxious courtesies. Outside, the two grooms stood close by, a little confused by my sudden exit. I don't know if perhaps they had been listening—at least standing as near as possible, to catch any scrap of the conversation. I waved my hand to them as I went past, in answer to their salutations, and it was very apparent to me that they were also glad to see me go.

And it will be thought very strange, but it would be weak not to add, that I myself, though bent on the investigation I have spoken of, pledged to Roland to carry it out, and feeling that my boy's health, perhaps his life, depended on the result of my inquiry—I felt the most unaccountable reluctance to pass these ruins on my way home. My curiosity was intense; and yet it was all my mind could do to pull my body along. I daresay the scientific people would describe it the other way, and attribute my cowardice to the state of my stomach. I went on; but if I had followed my impulse, I should have turned and bolted. Everything in me seemed to cry out against it; my heart thumped, my pulses all began, like sledge-hammers, beating against my ears and every sensitive part. It was very dark, as I have said; the old house, with its shapeless tower, loomed a heavy mass through the darkness, which was only not entirely so solid as itself. On the other hand, the great dark cedars of which we were so proud seemed to fill up the night. My foot strayed out of the path in my confusion and the gloom together, and I brought myself up with a cry as I felt myself knock against something solid. What was it? The contact with hard stone and lime, and prickly bramble-bushes, restored me a little to myself. "Oh, it's only the old gable," I said aloud, with a little laugh to reassure myself. The rough feeling of the stones reconciled me. As I groped about thus, I shook off my visonary folly. What so easily explained as that I should have strayed from the path in the darkness? This brought me back to common existence, as if I had been shaken by a wise hand out of all the silliness of superstition. How silly it was, after all! What did it matter which path I took? I laughed again, this time with better heart—when suddenly, in a moment, the blood was chilled in my veins, a shiver stole along my spine, my faculties seemed to forsake me. Close by me at my side, at my feet, there was a sigh. No, not a groan, not a moaning, not anything so tangible—a perfectly soft, faint, inarticulate sigh. I sprang back, and my heart stopped beating. Mistaken! no, mistake was impossible. I heard it as clearly as I hear myself speak; a long, soft, weary sigh, as if drawn to the utmost, and emptying out a load of sadness that filled the breast. To hear this in the solitude, in the dark, in the night (though it was still early), had an effect which I cannot describe. I feel it now—something cold creeping over me, up into my hair, and down to my feet, which refused to move. I cried out with a trembling voice, "Who is there?" as I had done before—but there was no reply.

I got home—I don't quite know how; but in my mind there was no longer any indifference as to the thing, whatever it was, that haunted these ruins. My scepticism disappeared like a mist. I was as firmly determined that there was something as Roland was. I did not for a moment pretend to myself that it was possible I could be deceived; there were movements and noises which I understand all about, crackling of small branches in the frost, and little rolls of gravel on the path, such as have a very eerie sound sometimes, and perplex you with wonder as to who has done it, *when there is no real mystery*; but I assure you all these little movements of nature don't affect you one bit *when there is something*. I understood *them*. I did not understand the sigh. That was not simple nature; there was meaning in it—feeling, the soul of a creature invisible. This is the thing that human nature trembles at—a creature invisible, yet with sensations, feelings, a power somehow of expressing itself. I had not the same sense of unwillingness to turn my back upon the scene of the mystery which I had experienced in going to the stables; but I almost ran home, impelled by eagerness to get everything done that had to be done in order to apply myself to finding it out. Bagley was in the hall as usual when I went in. He was always there in the afternoon, always with the appearance of perfect occupation, yet, so far as I know, never doing anything. The door was open, so that I hurried in without any pause, breathless; but the sight of his calm regard, as he came to help me off with my overcoat, subdued me in a moment. Anything out of the way, anything incomprehensible faded to nothing in the presence of Bagley. You saw and wondered how *he* was made: the parting of his hair, the tie of his white neck-cloth, the fit of his trousers, all perfect as works of art; but you could see how they were done, which makes all the difference. I flung myself upon him, so to speak, without waiting to note the extreme unlikeness of the man to anything of the kind I meant. "Bagley," I said, "I want you to come out with me tonight to watch for—"

"Poachers, Colonel," he said, a gleam of pleasure running all over him.

"No, Bagley; a great deal worse," I cried.

"Yes, Colonel; at what hour, sir?" the man said; but then I had not told him what it was.

It was ten o'clock when we set out. All was perfectly quiet

indoors. My wife was with Roland, who had been quite calm, she said, and who (though, no doubt, the fever must run its course) had been better since I came. I told Bagley to put on a thick greatcoat over his evening coat, and did the same myself—with strong boots; for the soil was like a sponge, or worse. Talking to him, I almost forgot what we were going to do. It was darker even than it had been before, and Bagley kept very close to me as we went along. I had a small lantern in my hand, which gave us a partial guidance. We had come to the corner where the path turns. On one side was the bowling-green, which the girls had taken possession of for their croquet-ground—a wonderful enclosure surrounded by high hedges of holly, three hundred years old and more; on the other, the ruins. Both were black as night; but before we got so far, there was a little opening in which we could just discern the trees and the lighter line of the road. I thought it best to pause there and take breath. "Bagley, I said, "there is something about these ruins I don't understand. It is there I am going. Keep your eyes open and your wits about you. Be ready to pounce upon any stranger you see—anything, man or woman. Don't hurt, but seize—anything you see." "Colonel," said Bagley, with a little tremor in his breath, "they do say there's things there—as is neither man nor woman." There was no time for words. "Are you game to follow me, my man? that's the question," I said. Bagley fell in without a word, and saluted. I knew then I had nothing to fear.

We went, so far as I could guess, exactly as I had come, when I heard that sigh. The darkness, however, was so complete that all marks, as of trees or paths, disappeared. One moment we felt our feet on the gravel, another sinking noiselessly into the slippery grass, that was all. I had shut up my lantern, not wishing to scare any one, whoever it might be. Bagley followed, it seemed to me, exactly in my footsteps as I made my way, as I supposed, towards the mass of the ruined house. We seemed to take a long time groping along seeking this; the squash of the wet soil under our feet was the only thing that marked our progress. After a while I stood still to see, or rather feel, where we were. The darkness was very still, but no stiller than is usual in a winter's night. The sounds I have mentioned—the crackling of twigs, the roll of a pebble, the sound of some rustle in the dead leaves, or creeping creature on the grass were audible when you listened, all mysterious enough when your mind is disengaged, but to me cheering now as signs of the livingness of nature, even in the death of the frost. As we stood still there came up from the trees in the glen the prolonged hoot of an owl. Bagley started with alarm, being in a state of general nervousness, and not knowing what he was afraid of. But to me the sound was encouraging and pleasant, being so comprehensible. "An owl," I said, under my breath. "Y—es, Colonel," said Bagley, his teeth chattering. We stood still about five minutes, while it broke into the still brooding of the air, the sound widening out in circles, dying upon the darkness. This sound, which is not a cheerful one, made me almost gay. It was natural, and relieved the tension of the mind. I moved on with new courage, my nervous excitement calming down.

When all at once, quite suddenly, close to us, at our feet, there broke out a cry. I made a spring backwards in the first moment of surprise and horror, and in doing so came sharply against the same rough masonry and brambles that had struck me before. This new sound came upwards from the ground—a low, moaning, wailing voice, full of suffering and pain. The contrast between it and the hoot of the owl was indescribable; the one with a wholesome wildness and naturalness that hurt nobody—the other a sound that made one's blood curdle, full of human misery. With a great deal of fumbling—for in spite of everything I could do to keep up my courage my hands shook—I managed to remove the slide of my lantern. The light leaped out like something living, and made the place visible in a moment. We were what would have been inside the ruined building had anything remained but the gable-wall which I have descibed. It was close to us, the vacant doorway in it going out straight into the blackness outside. The light showed the bit of wall, the ivy glistening upon it in clouds of dark green, the bramble-branches waving, and below, the open door—a door that led to nothing. It was from this the voice came which died out just as the light flashed upon this strange scene. There was a moment's silence, and then it broke forth again. The sound was so near, so penetrating, so pitiful, that, on the nervous start I gave, the light fell out of my hand. As I groped for it in the dark my hand was clutched by Bagley, who I think must have dropped upon his knees; but I was too much perturbed myself to think much of this. He clutched at me in the confusion of his terror, forgetting all his usual decorum. "For God's sake, what is it, sir?" he gasped. If I yielded, there was evidently an end of both of us. "I can't tell," I said, "any more than you; that's what we've got to find out: up, man, up!" I pulled him to his feet. "Will you go round and examine the other side, or will you stay here with the lantern?" Bagley gasped at me with a face of horror. "Can't we stay together, Colonel?" he said—his knees were trembling under him. I pushed him against the corner of the wall, and put the light into his hands. "Stand fast till I come back; shake yourself together, man; let nothing pass you," I said. The voice was within two or three feet of us, of that there could be no doubt.

I went myself to the other side of the wall, keeping close to it. The light shook in Bagley's hand, but tremulous though it was, shone out through the vacant door, one oblong block of light marking all the crumbling corners and hanging masses of foliage. Was that something dark huddled in a heap by the side of it? I pushed forward across the light in the doorway, and fell upon it with my hands; but it was only a juniper-bush growing close against the wall. Meanwhile, the sight of my figure crossing the doorway had brought Bagley's nervous excitement to a height: he flew at me, gripping my shoulder. "I've got him, Colonel! I've got him!" he cried, with a voice of sudden exultation. He thought it was a man, and was at once relieved. But at that moment the voice burst forth again be-between us, at our feet—more close to us than any separate being could be. He dropped off from me, and fell against the wall, his jaw dropping as if he were dying. I suppose, at the same moment, he saw that it was me whom he had clutched. I, for my part, had scarcely more command of myself. I snatched the light out of his hand, and flashed it all about me wildly. Nothing—the juniper-bush which I thought I had never seen before, the heavy growth of the glistening ivy, the brambles waving. It was close to my ears now, crying, crying, pleading as if for life. Either I heard the same words Roland had heard, or else, in my excitement, his imagination got possession of mine. The voice went on, growing into distinct articulation, but wavering about, now from one point, now from another, as if the owner of it were moving slowly back and forward—"Mother! mother!" and then an outburst of wailing. As my mind steadied, getting accustomed (as one's mind gets accustomed to anything), it seemed to me as if some uneasy, miserable creature was pacing up and down before a closed door. Sometimes—but that must have been excitement—I thought I heard a sound like knocking, and then another burst, "Oh, mother! mother!" All this close, close to the space where I was standing with my lantern—now before me, now behind me: a creature restless, unhappy, moaning, crying, before the vacant doorway, which no one could either shut or open more.

"Do you hear it, Bagley? do you hear what it is saying?" I cried, stepping in through the doorway. He was lying against the wall—his eyes glazed, half dead with terror. He made a motion of his lips as if to answer me, but no sounds came; then lifted his hand with a curious imperative movement as if ordering me to be silent and listen. And how long I did so I cannot tell. It began to have an interest, an exciting hold on me, which I could not describe. It seemed to call up visibly a scene any one could understand—a something shut out, restlessly wandering to and fro; sometimes the voice dropped, as if throwing itself down—sometimes wandered off a few paces, growing sharp and clear. "Oh, mother, let me in! oh, mother, mother, let me in! oh, let me in!" every word was clear to me. No wonder the boy had gone wild with pity. I tried to steady my mind upon Roland, upon his conviction that I could do something, but my head swam with the excitement, even when I partially overcame the terror. At last the words died away, and there was a sound of sobs and moaning. I cried out, "In the name of God who are you?" with a kind of feeling in my mind that to use the name of God was profane, seeing that I did not believe in ghosts or anything supernatural; but I did it all the same, and waited, my heart giving a leap of terror lest there should be a reply. Why this should have been I cannot tell, but I had a feeling that if there was an answer, it would be more than I could bear. But there was no answer; the moaning went on, and then, as if it had been real, the voice rose, a little higher again, the words recommenced, "Oh, mother, let me in! oh, mother, let me in!" with an expresion that was heart-breaking to hear.

As if it had been real! What do I mean by that? I suppose I got less alarmed as the thing went on. I began to recover the use of my senses—I seemed to explain it all to myself by saying that this had once happened, that it was a recollection of a real scene. Why there should have seemed something quite satisfactory and composing in this explanation I cannot tell, but so it was. I began to listen almost as if it had been a play, forgetting Bagley, who, I almost think, had fainted, leaning against the wall. I was startled out of this strange spectatorship that had fallen upon me by the sudden rush of something which made my heart jump once more, a large black figure in the doorway waving its arms. "Come in! come in! come in!" it shouted out hoarsely at the top of a deep bass voice, and then poor Bagley fell down senseless across the threshold. He was less sophisticated than I—he had not been able to bear it any longer. I took him for something supernatural, as he took me, and it was some time before I awoke to the necessities of the moment. I remembered only after, that from the time I began to give my attention to the man, I heard the other voice no more. It was some time before I brought him to. It must have been a strange scene; the lantern making a luminous spot in the darkness, the man's white face lying on the black earth, I over him, doing what I could for him. Probably I should have been thought to be murdering him had any one seen us. When at last I succeeded in pouring a little brandy down his throat he sat up and looked about him wildly. "What's up?" he said; then recognizing me, tried to struggle to his feet with a faint "Beg your pardon, Colonel." I got him home as best I could, making him lean upon my arm. The great fellow was as weak as a child. Fortunately he did not for some time remember what had happened. From the time Bagley fell the voice had stopped, and all was still.

"You've got an epidemic in your house, Colonel," Simson

said to me next morning. "What's the meaning of it all? Here's your butler raving about a voice. This will never do, you know; and so far as I can make out, you are in it too."

"Yes, I am in it, doctor. I thought I had better speak to you. Of course you are treating Roland all right—but the boy is not raving, he is as sane as you or me. It's all true."

"As sane as—I—or you. I never thought the boy insane. He's got cerebral excitement, fever. I don't know what you've got. There's something very queer about the look of your eyes."

"Come," said I, "you can't put us all to bed, you know. You had better listen and hear the symptons in full."

The doctor shrugged his shoulders, but he listened to me patiently. He did not believe a word of the story, that was clear; but he heard it all from beginning to end. "My dear fellow," he said, "the boy told me just the same. It's an epidemic. When one person falls a victim to this sort of thing, it's as safe as can be—there's always two or three."

"Then how do you account for it!—that's a different matter; there's no accounting for the freaks our brains are subject to. If it's delusion; if it's some trick of the echoes or the winds—some phonetic disturbance or other—"

"Come with me tonight, and judge for yourself," I said.

Upon this he laughed aloud, then said, "That's not such a bad idea; but it would ruin me for ever if it were known that

John Simson was ghost-hunting."

"There it is," said I; "you dart down on us who are un-learned with your phonetic disturbances, but you daren't examine what the thing really is for fear of being laughed at. That's science!"

"It's not science—it's common sense," said the doctor. "The thing has delusion on the front of it. It is encouraging an unwholesome tendency even to examine. What good could come of it? Even if I am convinced, I shouldn't believe."

"I should have said so yesterday; and I don't want you to be convinced or to believe," said I. "If you prove it to be a delusion, I shall be very much obliged to you for one. Come; somebody must go with me."

"You are cool," said the doctor. "You've disabled this poor fellow of yours, and made him—on that point—a lunatic for life; and now you want to disable me. But for once, I'll do it. To save appearance, if you'll give me a bed, I'll come over after my last rounds."

It was agreed that I should meet him at the gate, and that we should visit the scene of last night's occurrences before we came to the house, so that nobody might be the wiser. It was scarcely possible to hope that the cause of Bagley's sudden illness should not somehow steal into the knowledge of the servants at least, and it was better that all should be done as quietly as possible. The day seemed to me a very long one.

I had to spend a certain part of it with Roland, which was a terrible ordeal for me—for what could I say to the boy? The improvement continued, but he was still in a very precarious state, and the trembling vehemence with which he turned to me when his mother left the room filled me with alarm. "Father!" he said, quietly. "Yes, my boy; I am giving my best attention to it—all is being done that I can do. I have not come to any conclusion—yet. I am neglecting nothing you said," I cried. What I could not do was to give his active mind any encouragement to dwell upon the mystery. It was a hard predicament, for some satisfaction had to be given him. He looked at me very wistfully, with the great blue eyes which shone so large and brilliant out of his white and worn face. "You must trust me," I said. "Yes, father. Father understands," he said to himself, as if to soothe some inward doubt. I left him as soon as I could. He was the most precious thing I had on earth, and his health my first thought; but yet somehow, in the excitement of this other subject, I put that aside, and preferred not to dwell upon Roland, which was the most curious part of it all.

That night at eleven I met Simson at the gate. He had come by train, and I let him in gently myself. I had been so much absorbed in the coming experiment that I passed the ruins in going to meet him, almost without thought, it you can understand that. I had my lantern; and he showed me a coil of taper which he had ready for use. "There is nothing like light," he said, in his scoffing tone. It was a very still night, scarcely a sound, but not so dark. We could keep the path without difficulty as we went along. As we approached the spot we could hear a low moaning, broken occasionally by a bitter cry. "Perhaps that is your voice," said the doctor; "I thought it must be something of the kind. That's a poor brute caught in some of these infernal traps of yours; you'll find it among the bushes somewhere." I said nothing. I felt no particular fear, but a triumphant satisfaction in what was to follow. I led him to the spot where Bagley and I had stood on the previous night. All was silent as a winter night could be—so silent that we heard far off the sound of the horses in the stables, the shutting of a window at the house. Simson lighted his taper and went peering about, poking into all the corners. We looked like two conspirators lying in wait for some unfortunate traveller; but not a sound broke the quiet. The moaning had stopped before we came up; a star or two shone over us in the sky, looking down as if surprised at our proceedings. Dr. Simson did nothing but utter subdued laughs under his breath. "I thought as much," he said. "It is just the same with tables and all other kinds of ghostly apparatus; a sceptic's presence stops everything. When I am present nothing ever comes off. How long do you think it will be necessary to stay here? Oh, I don't complain; only, when *you* are satisfied, I am—quite."

I will not deny that I was disappointed beyond measure by this result. It made me look like a credulous fool. It gave the doctor such a pull over me as nothing else could. I should point all his morals for years to come, and his materialism, his scepticism, would be increased beyond endurance. "It seems, indeed," I said, "that there is to be no—" "Manifestation," he said, laughing; "that is what all the mediums say. No manifestations, in consequence of the presence of an unbeliever." His laugh sounded very uncomfortable to me in the silence; and it was now near midnight. But that laugh seemed the signal; before it died away the moaning we had heard before was resumed. It started from some distance off, and came towards us, nearer and nearer, like some one walking along and moaning to himself. There could be no idea now that it was a hare caught in a trap. The approach was slow, like that of a weak person, with little halts and pauses. We heard it coming along the grass straight towards the vacant doorway. Simson had been a little startled by the first sound. He said hastily, "That child has no business to be out so late." But he felt as well as I, that this was no child's voice. As it came nearer, he grew silent, and going to the doorway with his taper, stood looking out towards the sound. The taper being unprotected blew about in the night air, though there was scarcely any wind. I threw the light of my lantern steady and white across the same space. It was a blaze of light in the midst of the blackness. A little icy thrill had gone over me at the first sound, but as it came close, I confess that my only feeling was satisfaction. The scoffer could scoff no more. The light touched his own face, and showed a very perplexed countenance. If he was afraid, he concealed it with great success, but he was perplexed. And then all that had happened on the previous night was enacted once more. It fell strangely upon me with a sense of repetition. Every cry, every sob seemed the same as before. I listened almost without any emotion at all in my own person, thinking of its effect upon Simson. He maintained a very bold front on the whole. All that coming and going of the voice was, if our ears could be trusted, exactly in front of the vacant blank doorway, blazing full of light, which caught and shone in the glistening leaves of the great hollies at a little distance. Not a rabbit could have crossed the turf without being seen; but there was nothing. After a time, Simson, with a certain caution and bodily reluctance, as it seemed to me, went out with his roll of taper into this space. His figure showed against the holly in full outline. Just at this moment the voice sank, as was its custom, and seemed to fling itself down at the door. Simson recoiled violently, as if some one had come up against him, then turned, and held his taper low as if examining something. "Do you see anybody?" I cried in a whisper, feeling the chill of nervous panic steal over me at this action. "It's nothing but a—confounded juniper-bush," he said. This I knew very well to be nonsense, for the juniper-bush was on the other side. He went about after this round and round, poking his taper everywhere, then returned to me on the inner side of the wall. He scoffed no longer; his face was contracted and pale. "How long does this go on?" he whispered to me, like a man who does not wish to interrupt some one who is speaking. I had become too much perturbed myself to remark whether the successions and changes of the voice were the same as last night. It suddenly went out in the air almost as he was speaking, with a soft, reiterated sob dying away. If there had been anything to be seen, I should have said that the person was at that moment crouching on the ground close to the door.

We walked home very silent afterwards. It was only when we were in sight of the house that I said, "What do you think of it?" "I can't tell what to think of it," he said, quickly. He took—though he was a very temperate man—not the claret I was going to offer him, but some brandy from the tray, and swallowed it almost undiluted. "Mind you, I don't believe a word of it," he said, when he had lighted his candle; "but I can't tell what to think," he turned round to add, when he was half-way upstairs.

All of this, however, did me no good with the solution of my problem. I was to help this weeping, sobbing thing, which was already to me as distinct a personality as anything I knew—or what should I say to Roland? It was on my heart that my boy would die if I could not find some way of helping this creature. You may be surprised that I should speak of it in this way. I did not know if it was man or woman; but I no more doubted that it was a soul in pain than I doubted my own being; and it was my business to soothe this pain—to deliver it, if that was possible. Was ever such a task given to an anxious father trembling for his only boy? I felt in my heart, fantastic as it may appear, that I must fulfil this somehow, or part with my child; and you may conceive that rather than do that I was ready to die. But even my dying would not have advanced me—unless by bringing me into the same world with that seeker at the door.

Next morning Simson was out before breakfast, and came in with evident signs of the damp grass on his boots, and a look of worry and weariness, which did not say much for the night he had passed. He improved a little after breakfast, and visited his two patients, for Bagley was still an invalid. I went out with him on his way to the train, to hear what he had to say about the boy. "He is going on very well," he said; "there are no complications as yet. But mind you, that's not a boy to be trifled with, Mortimer. Not a word to him about last night." I had to tell him then of my last interview with Roland, and of the impossible demand he had made upon me—by which, though he tried to laugh, he was much discomposed, as I could see. "We must just perjure ourselves all round," he said, "and swear you exorcised it"; but the man was too kind-hearted to be satisfied with that. "It's frightfully serious for you, Mortimer. I can't laugh as I should like to. I wish I saw a way out of it, for your sake. By the way," he added shortly, "didn't you notice that juniper-bush on the left-hand side?" "There was one on the right hand of the door. I noticed you made that mistake last night." "Mistake!" he cried with a curious low laugh, pulling up the collar of his coat as though he felt the cold—"there's no juniper there this morning, left or right. Just go and see." As he stepped into the train a few minutes after, he looked back upon me and beckoned me for a parting word. "I'm coming back tonight," he said.

I don't think I had any feeling about this as I turned away from that common bustle of the railway, which made my private preoccupations feel so strangely out of date. There had been a distinct satisfaction in my mind before that his scepticism had been so entirely defeated. But the more serious part of the matter pressed upon me now. I went straight from the railway to the manse, which stood on a little plateau on the side of the river opposite to the woods of Brentwood.

The minister was one of a class which is not so common in Scotland as it used to be. He was a man of good family, well educated in the Scotch way, strong in philosophy, not so strong in Greek, strongest of all in experience—a man who had "come across", in the course of his life, most people of note that had ever been in Scotland—and who was said to be very sound in doctrine, without infringing the toleration with which old men, who are good men, are generally endowed. He was old-fashioned; perhaps he did not think so much about the troublous problems of theology as many of the young men, nor ask himself any hard questions about the Confession of Faith—but he understood human nature, which is perhaps better. He received me with a cordial welcome. "Come away, Colonel Mortimer," he said; "I'm all the more glad to see you, that I feel it's a good sign for the boy. He's doing well?—God be praised—and the Lord bless him and keep him. He has many a poor body's prayers—and that can do nobody harm."

"He will need them all, Dr. Moncrieff," I said, "and your counsel too." And I told him the story—more than I had told Simson. The old clergyman listened to me with many suppressed exclamations, and at the end the water stood in his eyes.

"That's just beautiful," he said. "I do not mind to have heard anything like it; it's as fine as Burns when he wished deliverance to one—that is prayed for in no kirk. Ay, ay! so he would have you console the poor lost spirit? God bless the boy! There's something more than common in that, Colonel Mortimer. And also the faith of him in his father!—I would like to put that into a sermon." Then the old gentleman gave me an alarmed look, and said, "No, no; I was not meaning a sermon; but I must write it down for the *Children's Record*." I saw the thought that passed through his mind. Either he thought, or he feared I would think, of a funeral sermon. You may believe this did not make me more cheerful.

I can scarcely say that Dr. Moncrieff gave me any advice. How could any one advise on such a subject? But he said, "I think I'll come too. I'm an old man; I'm less liable to be frighted than those that are further off the world unseen. It behoves me to think of my own journey there. I've no cut-and-dry beliefs on the subject. I'll come too; and maybe at the moment the Lord will put into our heads what to do."

This gave me a little comfort—more than Simson had given me. To be clear about the cause of it was not my grand desire. It was another thing that was in my mind—my boy. As for the poor soul at the open door, I had no more doubt, as I have said, of its existence than I had of my own. It was no ghost to me. I knew the creature, and it was in trouble. That was my feeling about it, as it was Roland's. To hear it first was a great shock to my nerves, but not now; a man will get accustomed to anything. But to do something for it was the great problem; how was I to be serviceable to a being that was invisible, that was mortal no longer? "Maybe at the moment the Lord will put it into our heads." This is very old-fashioned phraseology, and a week before, most likely, I should have smiled (though always with kindness) at Dr. Moncrieff's credulity; but there was a great comfort, whether rational or otherwise I cannot say, in the mere sound of the words.

The road to the station and the village lay through the glen—not by the ruins; but though the sunshine and the fresh air, and the beauty of the trees, and the sound of the water were all very soothing to the spirits, my mind was so full of my own subject that I could not refrain from turning to the right hand as I got to the top of the glen, and going straight to the place which I may call the scene of all my thoughts. It was lying full in the sunshine, like all the rest of the world. The ruined gable looked due east, and in the present aspect of the sun the light streamed down through the doorway as our lantern had done, throwing a flood of light upon the damp grass beyond. There was a strange suggestion in the open door—so futile, a kind of emblem of vanity—all free around, so that you could go where you pleased, and yet that semblance of an enclosure—that way of entrance, unnecessary, leading to nothing. And why any creature should pray and weep to get in—to nothing: or be kept out—by nothing! You could not dwell upon it, or it made your brain go round. I remembered however, what Simson said about the juniper, with a little smile on my own mind as to the inaccuracy of recollection, which even a scientific man will be guilty of. I could see now the light of my lantern gleaming upon the wet glistening surface of the spiky leaves at the right hand—and he ready to go to the stake for it that it was the left! I went round to make sure. And then I saw what he had said. Right or left there was no juniper at all. I was confounded by this, though it was entirely a matter of detail: nothing at all: a bush of brambles waving, the grass growing up to the very walls. But after all, though it gave me a shock for a moment, what did that matter? There were marks as if a number of footsteps had been up and down in front of the door; but these might have been our steps; and all was bright, and peaceful, and still. I poked about the other ruin—the larger ruins of the old house—for some time, as I had done before. There were marks upon the grass here and there, I could not call them footsteps, all about; but that told for nothing one way or another. I had examined the ruined rooms closely the first day. They were half filled up with soil and *debris*, withered brackens and bramble—no refuge for any one there. It vexed me that Jarvis should see me coming from that spot when he came up to me for his orders. I don't know whether my nocturnal expeditions had got wind among the servants. But there was a significant look in his face. Something in it I felt was like my own sensation when Simson in the midst of his scepticism was struck dumb. Jarvis felt satisfied that his veracity had been put beyond question. I never spoke to a servant of mine in such a peremptory tone before. I sent him away "with a flea in his lug," as the man described it afterwards. Interference of any kind was intolerable to me at such a moment.

But what was strangest of all was, that I could not face Roland. I did not go to his room as I would have naturally done at once. This the girls could not understand. They saw there was some mystery in it. "Mother has gone to lie down," Agatha said; "he had such a good night." "But he wants you so, papa!" cried little Jeanie, always with her two arms embracing mine in a pretty way she had. I was obliged to go at last—but what could I say? I could only kiss him, and tell him to keep still—that I was doing all I could. There is something mystical about the patience of a child. "It will come all right won't it, father?" he said. "God grant it may! I hope so, Roland." "Oh yes, it will come all right." Perhaps he understood that in the midst of my anxiety I could not stay with him as I should have done otherwise. But the girls were more surprised than it is possible to describe. They looked at me with wondering eyes. "If I were ill, papa, and you only stayed with me a moment, I should break my heart," said Agatha. But the boy had a sympathetic feeling. He knew that of my own will I would not have done it. I shut myself up in the library, where I could not rest, but kept pacing up and down like a caged beast. What could I do? and if I could do nothing, what would become of my boy? These were the questions that, without ceasing, pursued each other through my mind.

Simson came out to dinner, and when the house was all still, and most of the servants in bed, we went out and met Dr. Moncrieff, as we had appointed, at the head of the glen. Simson, for his part, was disposed to scoff at the doctor. "If there are to be any spells, you know, I'll cut the whole concern," he said. I did not make him any reply. I had not invited him; he could go or come as he pleased. He was very talkative, far more than suited my humour, as we went on. "One thing is certain, you know, there must be some human agency," he said. "It is all bosh about apparitions. I never have investigated the laws of sound to any great extent, and there's a great deal in ventriloquism that we don't know much about." "If it's the same to you," I said, "I wish you'd keep all that to yourself, Simson. It doesn't suit my state of mind." "Oh, I hope I know how to respect idiosyncrasy," he said. The very tone of his voice irritated me beyond measure.

These scientific fellows, I wonder people put up with them as they do, when you have no mind for their cold-blooded confidence. Dr. Moncrieff met us about eleven o'clock, the same time as on the previous night. He was a large man, with a venerable countenance and white hair—old, but in full vigour, and thinking less of a cold night walk than many a younger man. He had his lantern as I had. We were fully provided with means of lighting the place, and we were all of us resolute men. We had a rapid consultation as we went up, and the result was that we divided to different posts. Dr. Moncrieff remained inside the wall—if you can call that inside where there was no wall but one. Simson placed himself on the side next the ruins, so as to intercept any communication with the old house, which was what his mind was fixed upon. I was posted on the other side. To say that nothing could come near without being seen was self-evident. It had been so also on the previous night. Now, with our three lights in the midst of the darkness, the whole place seemed illuminated. Dr. Moncrieff's lantern, which was a large one, without any means of shutting up—an old-fashioned lantern with a pierced and ornamental top—shone steadily, the rays shooting out of it upward into the gloom. He placed it on the grass, where the middle of the room, if this had been a room, would have been. The usual effect of the light streaming out of the doorway was prevented by the illumination which Simson and I on either side supplied. With these differences, everything seemed as on the previous night.

Quite a number of the occult stories written by women during Victoria's reign contained a strong moral lesson—as in this case where the phantom is rebuking the terrified mother for ill-treating her child.

The Victorians had very fixed ideas on what ghosts looked like and how they behaved—this clever mock-up by a photographer of the period illustrates their convictions exactly.

And what occured was exactly the same, with the same air of repetition, point for point, as I had formerly remarked. I declare that it seemed to me as if I were pushed against, put aside, by the owner of the voice as he paced up and down in his trouble—though these are perfectly futile words, seeing that the stream of light from my lantern, and that from Simson's taper, lay broad and clear, without a shadow, without the smallest break, across the entire breadth of the grass. I had ceased even to be alarmed, for my part. My heart was rent with pity and trouble—pity for the poor suffering human creature that moaned and pleaded so, and trouble for myself and my boy. God! if I could not find any help—and what help could I find?—Roland would die.

We were all perfectly still till the first outburst was exhausted, as I knew (by experience) it would be. Dr. Moncrieff, to whom it was new, was quite motionless on the other side of the wall, as we were in our place. My heart had remained almost at its usual beating during the voice. I was used to it; it did not rouse all my pulses as it did at first. But just as it threw itself sobbing at the door (I cannot use other words), there suddenly came something which sent the blood coursing through my veins and my heart into my mouth. It was a voice inside the wall—the minister's well-known voice. I would have been prepared for it in any kind of adjuration, but I was not prepared for what I heard. It came out with a sort of stammering, as if too much moved for utterance. "Willie, Willie! Oh, God preserve us! is it you?"

These simple words had an effect upon me that the voice

of the invisible creature had ceased to have. I thought the old man, whom I had brought into this danger, had gone mad with terror. I made a dash round to the other side of the wall, half crazed with the thought. He was standing where I had left him, his shadow thrown vague and large upon the grass by the lantern which stood at his feet. I lifted my own light to see his face as I rushed forward. He was very pale, his eyes wet and glistening, his mouth quivering with parted lips. He neither saw nor heard me. We that had gone through this experience before, had crouched towards each other to get a little strength to bear it. But he was not even aware that I was there. His whole being seemed absorbed in anxiety and tenderness. He held out his hands, which trembled, but it seemed to me with eagerness, not fear. He went on speaking all the time. "Willie, if it is you—and it's you, if it is not a delusion of Satan—Willie, lad! why come ye here frighting them that know you not? Why came ye not to me?"

He seemed to wait for an answer. When his voice ceased, his countenance, every line moving, continued to speak. Simson gave me another terrible shock, stealing into the open doorway with his light, as much awe-stricken, as wildly curious as I. But the minister resumed, without seeing Simson, speaking to some one else. His voice took a tone of expostulation—

"Is this right to come here? Your mother's gone with your name on her lips. Do you think she would ever close her door on her own lad? Do ye think the Lord will close the door, ye faint-hearted creature? No!—I forbid ye! I forbid ye!" cried the old man. The sobbing voice had begun to resume its cries. He made a step forward, calling out the last words in a voice of command. "I forbid ye! Cry out no more to man. Go home, ye wandering spirit! go home! Do you hear me?—me that christened ye, that have struggled with ye, that have wrestled for ye with the Lord!" Here the loud tones of his voice sank into tenderness. "And her too, poor woman! poor woman; her you are calling upon. She's no here. You'll find her with the Lord. Go there and seek her, not here. Do you hear me, lad? go after her there. He'll let you in, though it's late. Man, take heart! if you will lie and sob and greet, let it be at heaven's gate, and no your poor mother's ruined door."

He stopped to get his breath: and the voice had stopped, not as it had done before, when its time was exhausted and all its repetitions said, but with a sobbing catch in the breath as if overruled. Then the minister spoke again, "Are you hearing me, Will? Oh, laddie, you've liked the beggarly elements all your days. Be done with them now. Go home to the Father—the Father! Are you hearing me?" Here the old man sank down upon his knees, his face raised upwards, his hands held up with a tremble in them, all white in the light in the midst of the darkness. I resisted as long as I could, though I cannot tell why—then I, too, dropped upon my knees. Simson all the time stood in the doorway, with an expression, his eyes wild, staring. It seemed to be to him, that image of blank ignorance and wonder, that we were praying. All the time the voice, with a low arrested sobbing, lay just where he was standing as I thought.

"Lord," the minister said—"Lord, take him into Thy everlasting habitations. The mother he cries to is with Thee. Who can open to him but Thee? Lord, when is it too late for Thee, or what is too hard for Thee? Lord, let that woman there draw him inower! Let her draw him inower!"

I sprang forward to catch something in my arms that flung itself wildly within the door. The illusion was so strong, that I never paused till I felt my forehead graze against the wall and my hands clutch the ground—for there was nobody there to save from falling, as in my foolishness I thought. Simson held out his hand to me to help me up. He was trembling and cold, his lower lip hanging, his speech almost inarticulate. "It's gone," he said, stammering—"it's gone!" We leant upon each other for a moment, trembling so much both of us that the whole scene trembled as if it were going to dissolve and disappear; and yet as long as I live I will never forget it—the shining of the strange lights, the blackness all round, the kneeling figure with all the whiteness of the light concentrated on its white venerable head and uplifted hands. A strange solemn stillness seemed to close all round us. By intervals a single syllable, "Lord! Lord!" came from the old minister's lips. He saw none of us, nor thought of us. I never knew how long we stood, like sentinels guarding him at his prayers, holding our lights in a confused dazed way, not knowing what we did. But at last he rose from his knees, and standing up at his full height, raised his arms, as the Scotch manner is at the end of a religious service, and solemnly gave the apostolical benediction—to what? to the silent earth, the dark woods, the wide breathing atmosphere—for we were but spectators gasping an Amen!

It seemed to me that it must be the middle of the night, as we all walked back. It was in reality very late. Dr. Moncrieff put his arm into mine. He walked slowly, with an air of exhaustion. It was as if we were coming from a death-bed. Something hushed and solemnised the very air. There was that sense of relief in it which there always is at the end of a death-struggle. And nature persistent, never daunted, came back in all of us, as we returned into the ways of life. We said nothing to each other, indeed, for a long time; but when we got clear of the trees and reached the opening near the house, where we could see the sky, Dr. Moncrieff himself was the first to speak. "I must be going," he said, "it's very late, I'm afraid. I will go down the glen, as I came."

"But not alone. I am going with you, doctor."

"Well, I will not oppose it. I am an old man, and agitation wearies more than work. Yes; I'll be thankful of your arm. Tonight, Colonel, you've done me more good turns than one."

I pressed his hand on my arm, not feeling able to speak. But Simson, who turned with us, and who had gone along all this time with his taper flaring, in entire unconsciousness, came to himself, apparently at the sound of our voices, and put out that wild little torch with a quick movement, as if of shame. "Let me carry your lantern," he said; "it is heavy." He recovered with a spring, and in a moment, from the awe-stricken spectator he had been, became himself sceptical and cynical "I should like to ask you a question," he said. "Do you believe in purgatory Doctor? It's not in the tenets of the Church, so far as I know."

"Sir," said Dr. Moncrieff, "an old man like me is sometimes not very sure what he believes. There is just one thing I am certain of—and that is the loving-kindness of God."

"But I thought that was in this life. I am no theologian—"

"Sir," said the old man, again with a tremor in him which I could feel going over all his frame, "if I saw a friend of mine within the gates of hell, I would not despair but his Father would take him by the hand still—if he cried like *yon*."

"I allow it is very strange—very strange. I cannot see through it. That there must be human agency, I feel sure. Doctor, what made you decide upon the person and the name?"

The minister put out his hand with the impatience which a man might show if he were asked how he recognised his brother. "Tuts!" he said, in familiar speech—then more solemnly, "how should I not recognise a person that I know better—far better—than I know you?"

"Then you saw the man?"

Dr. Moncrieff made no reply. He moved his hand again with a little impatient movement, and walked on, leaning heavily on my arm. And we went on for a long time without another word, threading the dark paths, which were steep and slippery with the damp of the winter. The air was very still—not more than enough to make a faint sighing in the branches, which mingled with the sound of the water to which we were descending. When we spoke again, it was about indifferent matters—about the height of the river, and the recent rains. We parted with the minister at his own door, where his old housekeeper appeared in great perturbation, waiting for him. "Eh, me, minister! the young gentleman will be worse?" she cried.

"Far from that—better. God bless him!" Dr.

Moncrieff said.

I think if Simson had begun again to me with his questions, I should have pitched him over the rocks as we returned up the glen; but he was silent, by a good inspiration. And the sky was clearer than it had been for many nights, shining high over the trees, with here and there a star faintly gleaming through the wilderness of dark and bare branches. The air, as I have said, was very soft in them, with a subdued and peaceful cadence. It was real, like every natural sound, and came to us like a hush of peace and relief. I thought there was a sound in it as of the breath of a sleeper, and it seemed clear to me that Roland must be sleeping, satisfied and calm. We went up to his room when we went in. There we found the complete hush of rest. My wife looked up out of a doze, and gave me a smile; "I think he is a great deal better: but you are very late," she said in a whisper, shading the light with her hand that the doctor might see his patient. The boy had got back something like his own colour. He woke as we stood all round his bed. His eyes had the happy half-awakened look of childhood, glad to shut again, yet pleased with the interruption and glimmer of the light. I stooped over him and kissed his forehead, which was moist and cool. "All is well, Roland," I said. He looked up at me with a glance of pleasure, and took my hand and laid his cheek upon it, and so went to sleep.

For some nights after, I watched among the ruins, spending all the dark hours up to midnight patrolling about the bit of wall which was associated with so many emotions; but I heard nothing, and saw nothing beyond the quiet course of nature: nor, so far as I am aware, has anything been heard again. Dr. Moncrieff gave me the history of the youth, whom he never hesitated to name. I did not ask, as Simson did, how he recognised him. He had been a prodigal—weak, foolish, easily imposed upon, and "led away," as people say. All that we had heard had passed actually in life, the Doctor said. The young man had come home thus a day or two after his mother died—who was no more than the housekeeper in the old house—and distracted with the news, had thrown himself down at the door and called upon her to let him in. The old man could scarcely speak of it for tears. To me it seemed as if—heaven help us, how little do we know about anything!—a scene like that might impress itself somehow upon the hidden heart of nature. I do not pretend to know how, but the repetition had struck me at the time as, in its terrible strangeness and incomprehensibility, almost mechanical—as if the unseen actor could not exceed or vary, but was bound to reenact the whole. One thing that struck me, however, greatly, was the likeness between the old minister and my boy in the manner of regarding these strange phenomena. Dr. Moncrieff was not terrified, as I had been myself, and all the rest of us. It was no "ghost", as I fear we all vulgarly considered it, to him—but a poor creature whom he knew under these conditions, just as he had known him in the flesh, having no doubt of his identity. And to Roland it was the same. This spirit in pain—if it was a spirit—this voice out of the unseen—was a poor fellow-creature in misery, to be succoured and helped out of his trouble, to my boy. He spoke to me quite frankly about it when he got better. "I knew father would find out some way," he said. And this was when he was strong and well, and all idea that he would turn hysterical or become a seer of visions had happily passed away.

I must add one curious fact which does not seem to me to have any relation to the above, but which Simson made great use of, as the human agency which he was determined to find somehow. We had examined the ruins very closely at the time of these occurrences; but afterwards, when all was over, as we went casually about them one Sunday afternoon in the idleness of that unemployed day, Simson with his stick penetrated an old window which had been entirely blocked up with fallen soil. He jumped down into it in great excitement, and called me to follow. There we found a little hole—for it was more a hole than a room—entirely hidden under the ivy ruins, in which there was a quantity of straw laid in a corner, as if some one had made a bed there, and some remains of crusts about the floor. Some one had lodged there, and not very long before, he made out; and that this unknown being was the author of all the mysterious sounds we heard he is convinced. "I told you it was human agency," he said, triumphantly. He forgets, I suppose, how he and I stood with our lights seeing nothing, while the space between us was audibly traversed by something that could speak, and sob, and suffer. There is no argument with men of this kind. He is ready to get up a laugh against me on this slender ground. "I was puzzled myself—I could not make it out—but I always felt convinced human agency was at the bottom of it. And here it is—and a clever fellow he must have been," the Doctor says.

Bagley left my service as soon as he got well. He assured me it was no want of respect; but he could not stand "them kind of things," and the man was so shaken and ghastly that I was glad to give him a present and let him go. For my own part, I made a point of staying out the time, two years, for which I had taken Brentwood; but I did not renew my tenancy.

THE ITALIAN'S STORY

Miss Catherine Crowe

"How well your friend speaks English!" I remarked one day to an acquaintance when I was abroad, alluding to a gentleman who had just quitted the room. "What is his name?"

"Count Francesco Ferraldi."

"I suppose he has been in England?"

"Oh, yes; he was exiled and taught Italian there. His history is very curious and would interest you, who like wonderful things."

"Can you tell it me?"

"Not correctly, as I never heard it from himself. But I believe he has no objection to tell it—with the exception of the political transactions in which he was concerned, and which caused his being sent out of the Austrian dominions; that part of it, I believe, he thinks it not prudent to allude to. We'll ask him to dinner, if you'll meet him, and perhaps we may persuade him to tell the story." Accordingly, the meeting took place; we dined *en petit comité*—and the Count very good-naturedly yielded to our request; "but you must excuse me," he said "beginning a long way back, for my story commences three hundred years ago.

"Our family claims to be of great antiquity, but we were not very wealthy till about the latter half of the tenth century when Count Jacopo Ferraldi made very considerable additions to the property; not only by getting, but also by saving—he was, in fact, a miser. Before that period the Ferraldis had been warriors, and we could boast of many distinguished deeds of arms recorded in our annals; but Jacopo, although by the death of his brother he ultimately inherited the title and estates, had begun life as a younger son, and being dissatisfied with his portion, had resolved to increase it by commerce.

"Florence then was a very different city to what it is now; trade flourished, and its merchants had correspondence and large dealings with all the chief cities of Europe. My ancestor invested his little fortune so judiciously, or so fortunately, that he trebled it in his first venture; and as people grow rapidly rich who gain and don't spend, he soon had wealth to his heart's content. But I am wrong in using that term as applied to him—he was never content with his gains but still worked to add to them, for he grew to love the money for itself and not for what it might purchase.

"At length, his two elder brothers died, and as they left no issue, he succeeded to their inheritance and dwelt in the palace of his ancestors; but instead of circulating his riches he hoarded them; and being too miserly to entertain his friends and neighbours, he lived like an anchorite in his splendid halls, exulting in his possessions but never enjoying them. His great pleasure and chief occupation seems to have been counting his money, which he kept hidden in strange out-of-the-way places, or in strong iron chests clamped to the floors and walls. But, notwithstanding these precautions, and that he guarded it like a watch-dog, to his great dismay he one day missed a sum of two thousand pounds which he had concealed in an ingeniously contrived receptacle under the floor of his dining-room, the existence of which was only known to the man who made it; at least, so he believed. Small as was this sum in proportion to what he possessed, the shock was tremendous; he rushed out of his house like a madman with the intention of dragging the criminal to justice but when he arrived at the man's shop he found him in bed and at the point of death. His friends and the doctor swore that he had not quitted it for a fortnight; in short, according to their showing, he was taken ill on his return from working at the Count's, the very day he finished the job.

"If this were true, he could not be the thief, as the money

was not deposited there until some days afterwards, and although the Count had his doubts, it was not easy to disprove what everybody swore, more especially as the man died on the following day, and was buried. Baffled and furious, he next fell foul of his two servants—he kept but two, for he only inhabited a small part of the palace. There was not the slightest reason to suspect them, nor to suppose they knew anything of the hiding-place, for every precaution had been used to conceal it; moreover, he had found it locked as he himself had locked it after depositing the money, and he was quite sure the key had never been absent from his own person. Nevertheless, he discharged them and took no others. The thief, whoever he was, had evinced so much ingenuity, that he trembled to think what such skill might compass with opportunity. So he resolved to afford none; and henceforth to have his meals sent in from a neighbouring eating-house, and to have a person once a week to sweep and clean his rooms, whom he could keep an eye on while it was doing. As he had no clue to the perpetrators of the robbery, and the man whom he had most reason to suspect was dead, he took no futher steps in the business, but kept it quiet lest he should draw too much attention towards his secret hoards; nevertheless, though externally calm, the loss preyed on his mind and caused him great anguish.

"Shortly after this occurrence he received a letter from

a sister of his who had several years before married an Englishman, saying that her husband was dead, and it being advisable that her dear and only son should enter into commerce, that she was going to send him to Florence, feeling assured that her brother would advise him for the best, and enable him to employ the funds he brought with him advantageously.

"This was not pleasing intelligence; he did not want to promote anybody's interest but his own, and he felt that the young man would be a spy on his actions, an intruder in his house, and no doubt an expectant and greedy heir, counting the hours until he died; for this sister and her family were his nearest of kin, and would inherit if he left no will to the contrary. However, his arrival could not be prevented; letters travelled slowly in those days, and ere his could reach England his nephew would have quitted it, so he resolved to give him a cold reception and send him back as soon as he could.

"In the meantime, the young man had started on his journey full of hope and confidence, and immediately on his arrival hastened to present himself to this rich uncle who was to show him the path he had himself followed to fortune. It was not for his own sake alone he coveted riches, but his mother and sister were but poorly provided for, and they had collected the whole of their little and risked it upon this venture, hoping, with the aid of their relative, to be amply repaid for the present sacrifice.

"A fine open-countenance lad was Arthur Allen, just twenty years of age; such a face and figure had not beamed on those halls for many a day. Well brought up and well instructed too; he spoke Italian as well as English, his mother having accustomed him to it from infancy.

"Though he had heard his uncle was a miser, he had no conception of the extent to which the mania had arisen; and his joyous anticipations were somewhat damped when he found himself so coldly received, and when he looked into those hard grey eyes and contracted features that had never expanded with a genial smile; so fearing the old man might be apprehensive that he had come as an applicant or for assistance to set him up in trade, he hastened to inform him of the true state of the case, saying that they had got together two thousand pounds.

" 'Of course, my mother,' he said, 'would not have entrusted my inexperience with such a sum; but she desired me to place it in your hands, and to act entirely under your direction.'

"To use the miser's own expression—for we have learnt all these particulars from a memoir left by himself—'When I heard these words the devil entered into me, and I bade the youth bring me the money and dine with me on the following day.'

"I dare say you will think the devil had entered into him long before; however, now he had recognised his presence, but that did not deter him from following his counsel.

"Pleased that he had so far thawed his uncle's frigidity, Arthur arrived the next day with his money-bags at the appointed hour, and was received in an inner chamber; their contents were inspected and counted, and then placed in one of the old man's iron chests. Soon afterwards, the tinkle of the bell announced that the waiter from the neighbouring *traiteur's* had brought the dinner, and the host left the room to see that all was ready. Presently he re-entered, and led his guest to the table. The repast was not sumptuous, but there was a bottle of old Lachryma Christi which he much recommended, and which the youth tasted with great satisfaction. But strange! He had no sooner swallowed the first glass, than his eyes began to stare—there was a gurgle in his throat—a convulsion passed over his face—and his body stiffened.

" 'I did not look up,' says the old man in his memoir, 'for I did not like to see the face of the boy that had sat down so hearty to his dinner, so I kept on eating mine—but I heard the gurgle, and I knew what had happened; and presently, lest the servant should come to fetch the dinner things, I pushed the table aside and opened the receptacle from which my two thousand pounds had been stolen—curses on the thief!—and I laid the body in it, and the wine therewith. I locked it and drove in two strong nails. Then I put back the table, moved away the lad's chair and plate, unlocked the door which was fast, and sat down to finish my dinner. I could not help chuckling as I ate, to think how his had been spoilt.

" 'I closed up that apartment, as I thought there might be a smell that would raise observation, and I selected one on the opposite side of the gallery for my dining-room. All went well until the following day. I counted my two thousand pounds again and again, and I kept gloating over the recovery of it—for I felt as if it was my own money, and I had a right to seize it where I could. I wrote also to my sister, saying that her son had not arrived; but that when he did I would do my best to forward his views. My heart was light that day—they say that's a bad sign.

" 'Yes, all was so far well; but the next day we were two of us at dinner! And yet I had invited no guests; and the next—and the next—and so on—always! As I was about to sit down, he entered and took a chair opposite me, an unbidden guest. I ceased dining at home, but it made no difference; he came, dine where I would. This preyed on me; I tried not to mind, but I could not help it. Argument was vain. I lost my appetite, and was reduced nearly to death's door. At last, driven to desperation, I consulted Fra Giuseppe. He had been a fast fellow in his time, and it was said he had been too impatient for his father's succession, howbeit, the old man died suddenly; Giuseppe spent the money and then took to religion. I thought he was a proper person to consult, so I told him my case. He recommended repentance and restitution. I tried but I could not repent, for I had got the money; but I thought, perhaps, if I parted with it to another, I might be released; so I looked about for an advantageous purchase, and hearing that Bartolomeo Malfi was in difficulties, I offered him two thousand pounds, money down for his land—I knew it was worth three times the sum. We signed the agreement, and then I went home and opened the door of the room where it was; but lo! he sat there upon the chest where the money was fast locked, and I could not get it. I peeped in two or three times, but he was always there; so I was obliged to expend other moneys in this purchase, which vexed me, albeit the bargain was a good one. Then I consulted Giuseppe again, and he said nothing would do but restitution—but that was bad, so I waited; and I said to myself, "I'll eat and care not whether he sit there or not." But woe be to him! He chilled the marrow of my bones, and I could not away with him; so I said one day, "What if I go to England with the money?" And he bowed his head.'

"The old man accordingly took the money-bags from the chest and started for England. His sister and her daughter were still living in the house they had inhabited during the husband's lifetime; in short it was their own; and being attached to the place they hoped, if the young man succeeded in his undertakings, to be able to keep it. It was a small house with a garden full of flowers, which the ladies cultivated themselves. The village church was close at hand, and the churchyard joined the garden. The poor ladies had become very uneasy at not hearing of Arthur's arrival; and when the old man presented himself and declared he had never seen anything of him, great was their affliction and dismay; for it was clear that some misfortune had happened to the boy, or he had appropriated the money and gone off in some other direction. They scarcely admitted the possibility of the last contingency, although it was the one their little world universally adopted, in spite of his being a very well conducted and affectionate youth; but people said it was too great a temptation for his years, and blamed his mother for entrusting him with so much money. Whichever it was, the blow fell very heavy on them all ways, for Arthur was their sole stay and support, and they loved him dearly.

"Since he had set out on this journey, the old man had been relieved from the company of his terrible guest, and was beginning to recover himself a little, but it occasioned him a severe pang when he remembered that this immunity was to be purchased with the sacrifice of two thousand pounds, he set himself to think how he could jockey the ghost. But while he was deliberating on this subject, an event happened that alarmed him for the immediate safety of the money.

He had found, on the road, that the great weight of a certain chest he brought with him had excited observation whenever his luggage had to be moved; on his arrival two labouring men had been called in to carry it into the house, and he had overheard some remarks that induced him to think they had drawn a right conclusion with regard to its contents. Subsequently, he saw these two men hovering round the house in a suspicious manner, and he was afraid to leave it or go to sleep at night, lest he should be robbed.

"So far we learn from Jacopo Ferraldi himself; but here the memoir stops and tradition says that he was found one morning murdered in his bed and his chest rifled. All the family, that is the mother and daughter and their one servant, were accused of the murder; and notwithstanding their protestation of innocence were declared guilty and executed.

"The memoir I have quoted was found on his dressing-table, and he appears to have been writing it when he was surprised by the assassins; for the last words were—"I think I've baulked them, and nobody will understand the . . .' then comes a large blot and a mark, as if the pen had fallen out of his hand. It seems wonderful that this man, so suspicious and secretive, should thus have entrusted to paper what it was needful he should conceal; but the case is not singular; it has been remarked in similar instances when some mystery is pressing on a human soul, that there exists an irresistible desire to communicate it, notwithstanding the peril of betrayal; and when no other confidant can be found, the miserable wretch has often had recourse to paper.

"The family of Arthur Allen being now extinct, a cousin of Jacopo's, who was a penniless soldier, succeeded to the title and estate, and the memoir, with a full account of what had happened, being forwarded to Italy, inquiries were made about the missing two thousand pounds; but it was not forthcoming; and it was at first supposed that the ladies had some accomplice who had carried it off. Subsequently, however, one of the two men who had borne the money-chest into the house, at the period of the old man's arrival, was detected in endeavouring to dispose of some Italian gold and a diamond ring, which Jacopo was in the habit of wearing. This led to investigation, and he ultimately confessed to the murder committed by himself and his companion, thus exonerating the unfortunate women. He nevertheless declared that they had not rifled the strong box as they could not open it, and were disturbed by the barking of a dog before they could search for the keys. The box itself they were afraid to carry away, it being a remarkable one and liable to attract notice; and that therefore their only booty was some loose coin and some jewels that were found on the old man's person. But this was not believed, especially as his accomplice could not be found and appeared, on inquiry, to have left that part of the country immediately after the catastrophe.

"There the matter rested for nearly two centuries and a half. Nobody sorrowed for Jacopo Ferraldi, and the fate of the Allens was a matter of indifference to the public, who were glad to see the estate fall into the hands of his successor, who appears to have made a much better use of his riches. The family, in the long period that elapsed, had many vicissitudes; but at the period of my birth my father inhabited the same old palace, and we were in tolerably affluent circumstances. I was born there, and I remember as a child the curiosity I used to feel about the room with the secret receptacle under the floor where Jacopo had buried the body of his guest. It had been found there and received Christian burial; but the receptacle still remained and the room was shut up, being said to be haunted. I never *saw* anything extraordinary, but I can bear witness to the frightful groans and moans that issued from it sometimes at night, when, if I could persuade anybody to accompany me, I used to stand in the gallery and listen with wonder and awe. But I never passed the door alone, nor would any of the servants do so after dark. There had been an attempt made to exclude the sounds by walling up the door; but so far from this succeeding they became twenty times worse, and as the wall was a disfigurement as well as a failure, the unquiet spirit was placated by taking it down again.

"The old man's memoir is always preserved among the family papers, and his picture still hangs in the gallery. Many strangers who have heard something of this extraordinary story, have asked to see it. The palace is now inhabited by an Austrian nobleman. Whether the ghost continues to annoy the inmates by his lamentations, I do not know.

"I now," said Count Francesco, "come to my personal history. Political reasons a few years since obliged me to quit Italy with my family. I had no resources except a little ready money that I had brought with me, and I had resolved to utilise some musical talent which I had cultivated for my amusement. I had not voice enough to sing in public, but I was capable of giving lessons and was considered, when in Italy, a successful amateur. I will not weary you with the sad details of my early residence in England; you can imagine the difficulties that an unfortunate foreigner must encounter before he can establish a connexion. Suffice it to say that my small means were wholly exhausted, and very often I, and what was worse, my wife and child, were in want of bread, and indebted to one of my more prosperous countrymen for the very necessaries of life. I was almost in despair, and I do not know what rash thing I might have done if I was a single man; but I had my family depending on me, and it was my duty not to sink under my difficulties however great they were.

"One night I had been singing at the house of a nobleman, in St. James's Square, and had received some flattering compliments from a young man who appeared to be very fond of Italian music, and to understand it. My getting to this party was a stroke of good luck in the first instance, for I was quite unknown to the host, but Signor A., an acquaintance of mine, who had been engaged for the occasion, was taken ill at the last moment, and had sent me with a note of introduction to apply for his place.

"I knew, of course, that I should be well paid for my services, but I would gladly have accepted half the sum I expected if I could have had it that night, for our little treasury was wholly exhausted, and we had not sixpence to purchase a breakfast for the following day. When the great hall door shut upon me, and I found myself on the pavement, with all the luxury and splendour on one side, and I and my desolation on the other, the contrast struck me cruelly, for I too, had been rich, and dwelt in illuminated palaces, and had a train of liveried servants at my command, and sweet music had echoed through my halls. I felt desperate, and drawing my hat over my eyes I began pacing the square, forming wild plans for the relief or escape from my misery. No doubt I looked frantic, for you know we Italians have such a habit of gesticulating, that I believe my thoughts were accompanied by movements that must have excited notice. But I was too much absorbed to observe anything, till I was roused by a voice saying, 'Signor Ferraldi, still here this damp chilly night! Are you not afraid for your voice—it is worth taking care of.'

" 'To what purpose,' I said savagely, 'It will not give me bread!'

"If the interruption had not been so sudden, I should not have made such an answer, but I was surprised into it before I knew who had addressed me. When I looked up I saw it was the young man I had met at Lord L.'s, who had complimented me on my singing. I took off my hat and begged his pardon, and was about to move away when he took my arm.

" 'Excuse me,' he said, 'let us walk together,' and then after a little pause, he added, with an apology,' 'I think you are an exile.'

" 'I am,' I said.

" 'And I think,' he continued, 'I have surprised you out of

a secret that you would not voluntarily have told me. I know well the hardships that beset many of your countrymen—as good gentlemen as we are ourselves—when you are obliged to leave your country; and I beg therefore you will not think me impertinent or intrusive, if I beg you to be frank with me and tell me how you are situated!'

"This offer of symphathy was evidently so sincere, and it was so welcome, at such a moment, that I did not hesitate to comply with my new friend's request—I told him everything—adding that in time I hoped to get known, and that then I did not fear being able to make my way; but that meanwhile we were in danger of starving.

"During this conversation we were walking round and round the square, where in fact he lived. Before we parted at his door, he had persuaded me to accept a gift, I call it, for he had then no reason to suppose I should ever be able to repay him, but he called it an advance of ten guineas upon some lessons I was to give him—the first instalment of which was to be paid the following day.

"I went home with a comparatively light heart, and the next morning waited upon my friendly pupil, whom I found, as I expected, a very promising scholar. He told me with a charming frankness that he had not much influence in fashionable society, for his family, though rich, was *parvenue*, but he said he had two sisters, as fond of music as himself, who would be shortly in London, and would be delighted to take lessons, as I had just the voice they liked to sing with them.

"This was the first auspicious incident that had occurred to me, nor did the omen fail in its fulfilment. I received great kindness from the family when they came to London. I gave them lessons, sung at their parties, and they took every opportunity of recommending me to their friends.

"When the end of the season approached, however, I felt somewhat about the future—there would be no parties to sing at, and my pupils would all be leaving town. But my new friends, whose name, by the way, was Greathead, had a plan for me in their heads, which they strongly recommended me to follow. They said they had a house in the country with a large neighbourhood—in fact near a large watering-place; and if I went there during the summer months, they did not doubt my getting plenty of teaching; adding, 'We are much greater people there than we are here, you see; and our recommendation will go a great way.'

"I followed my friends' advice, and soon after they left London I joined them at Salton, which was the name of their place. As I had left my wife and children in London with very little money, I was anxious that they should join me as soon as possible; and therefore the morning after my arrival I proceeded to look for a lodging at Salton and to take measures to make my object known to the residents and visitors there. My business done, I sent my family directions for their journey, and then returned to Salton to spend a few days, as I had promised my kind patrons.

"The house was modern; in fact, it had been built by Mr. Greathead's grandfather, who was the architect of their fortunes; the grounds were extensive, and the windows looked on a fine lawn, a picturesque ruin, a sparkling rivulet, and a charming flower garden. There could not be a prettier view than we enjoyed while sitting at breakfast. It was my first experience of the lovely and graceful English homes, and it fully realised all my expectations, both within doors and without. After breakfast Mr. Greathead and his son asked me to accompany them round the grounds, as they were contemplating some alterations.

" 'Among other things,' said Mr. Greathead, 'we want to turn this rivulet; but my wife has a peculiar fancy for that old hedge, which is exactly in the way, and she won't let me root it up.'

"The hedge alluded to enclosed two sides of the flower garden, but seemed out of place, I thought.

" 'Why!' said I, 'What is Mrs. Greathead's attachment to the hedge?'

" 'Why? it's very old; it formerly bordered the church yard, for that old ruin you see there is all that remains of the parish church; and this flower garden, I fancy, is all the more brilliant for the rich soil of the burial-ground. But what is remarkable is that the hedge and that side of the garden are full of Italian flowers, and always have been so long as anybody can remember. Nobody seems to know how it happened, but they must spring up from some old seeds that have been long in the ground. Look at this cyclamen growing wild in the hedge.'

"The subject of the alterations was renewed at dinner, and Mrs. Greathead, still objecting to the removal of the hedge, her younger son, whose name was Harry, said, 'It is all very well for mother to pretend it is for the sake of the flowers, but I am quite sure that the real reason is that she is afraid of offending the ghost.'

" 'What nonsense, Harry,' she said. 'You must not believe him, Mr. Ferraldi.'

" 'Well, mother,' said the boy, 'you know you will never be convinced that that was not a ghost you saw.'

" 'Never mind what it was,' she said; 'I won't have the hedge removed.' Presently, she added, 'I suppose you would laugh at any one believing in a ghost, Mr. Ferraldi.'

" 'Quite the contrary,' I answered; 'I believe in them myself, and upon very good grounds—for we have a celebrated ghost in our family.'

" 'Well,' she said, 'Mr. Greathead and the boys laugh at

me; but when I came to live here, upon the death of Mr. Greathead's grandfather—for his father never inhabited the place, having died by accident before the old gentlemen—I never heard a word of the place being haunted; and, perhaps, I should not have believed it if I had. But one evening, when the younger children were gone to bed, and Mr. Greathead and George were sitting with some friends in the dining-room, I and my sister, who was staying with me, strolled into the garden. It was the month of August, and a bright starlight night. We were talking on a very interesting matter, for my sister had that day received an offer from the gentleman she afterwards married. I mention this to show you that we were not thinking of anything supernatural, but, on the contrary, that our minds were quite absorbed with the subject we were discussing. I was looking on the ground, as one does, when listening intently to what another person in saying. My sister was speaking when she suddenly stopped, and laid her hand upon my arm, saying "who's that?"

" 'I raised my eyes and saw, not many yards from us, an old man, withered and thin, dressed in a curious antique fashion, with a high-peaked hat on his head. I could not conceive who he could be, or what he was doing there, for it was close to the flower garden. So we stood still and observed him. I don't know whether you saw the remains of an old tombstone in a corner of the garden? It is said to be that of a former rector of the parish; the date, 1550, is still legible upon it. The old man walked from one side of the hedge to the stone, and seemed to be counting his steps. He walked like a person pacing the ground, to measure it; then he stopped and appeared to be noting the result of his measurement with a pencil and paper he held in his hand. Then he did the same thing the other side of the hedge, pacing up to the old tombstone and back.

" 'There was a talk, at that time, of removing the hedge and digging up the old tombstone; and it occurred to me that my husband might have been speaking to somebody about it, and that this man might be concerned in the business, though, still, his dress and appearance puzzled me. It seemed odd, too, that he took no notice of us; and I might have remarked that we heard no footsteps, though we were quite close enough to do so—but these circumstances did not strike me then. However, I was just going to advance, and ask him what he was doing, when I felt my sister's hand release the hold she had of my arm, and she sank to the ground. At that same instant I lost sight of the mysterious old man, who suddenly disappeared.

" 'My sister had not fainted; but she said her knees bent under her, and she had slipped down, collapsed by terror. I did not feel very comfortable myself, I assure you; but I lifted her up, and we hastened back to the house and told what we had seen. The gentlemen went out, and, of course, saw nothing, and laughed at us. Shortly afterwards, when Harry was born, I had a nurse from the village and she asked me one day if I had ever happened to see "the old gentleman that walks!" I had ceased to think of the circumstance, and inquired what old gentleman she meant. And then she told me that, long ago, a foreign gentleman had been murdered here. That is in the old house that Mr. Greathead's grandfather pulled down when he built this—and that, ever since, the place has been haunted, and nobody will pass by the hedge and the old tombstone after dark: for that is the spot where the ghost confines himself.'

" 'But I should think,' said I, 'that so far from desiring to preserve these objects, you would wish them removed since the ghost would, probably, cease to visit the spot at all.'

" 'Quite the contrary,' answered Mr. Greathead. 'The people of the neighbourhood say that the former possessor of the place entertained the same idea, and had resolved to move them; but that then the old man became very troublesome and was even seen in the house. The nurse positively assured me that her mother had told her old Mr. Greathead had also intended to remove them; but that he quite suddenly counter-ordered the directions he had given and, though he did not confess to anything of the sort, the people all believed that he had seen the ghost. Certain it is, that this hedge has always been maintained by the proprietors of the place.'

"The young men laughed and quizzed their mother for indulging in such superstitions; but the lady was quite firm in her opposition; alleging that, independently of all considerations connected with the ghost, she liked the hedge on account of the Italian flowers, and she liked the old tombstone on account of its antiquity.

"Consequently some other plan was devised for Mr. Greathead's alterations, which led the course of the rivulet quite clear of the hedge and the tombstone.

"In a few days my family arrived, and I established myself at the place for the summer. The speculation answered well, and through the recommendation of Mr. and Mrs. Greathead, and their personal kindness to myself and my wife, we passed the time very pleasantly. When the period for our returning to London approached, they invited us to spend a fortnight with them before our departure, and, accordingly, the day we gave up our lodgings, we removed to their house.

"Preparations for turning the rivulet had then commenced; and soon after my arrival, I walked out with Mr. Greathead to see the works. There was a boy, about fourteen, amongst the labourers; and while we were standing close to him, he picked up something and handed it to Mr. Greathead saying,

'Is this yours, sir?' which, on examination, proved to be a gold coin of the sixteenth century—the date on it was 1545. Presently the boy, who was digging, picked up another, and then several more.

" 'This becomes interesting,' said Mr. Greathead, 'I think we are coming upon some buried treasure,' and he whispered to me that he had better not leave the spot.

"Accordingly, he stayed there till it was time to dress for dinner; and, feeling interested, I remained also. In the interval, many more coins were found—and when he went in, he dismissed the workmen and sent a servant to watch the place, for he saw by the men's faces that if he had not happened to be present, he would probably never have heard of the discovery. A few more turned up the following day, and then the store seemed exhausted. When the villagers heard of this money being discovered, they all looked upon it as the explanation of the old gentleman haunting that particular spot. No doubt he had buried the money, and it remained to be seen whether, now that it was found, his spirit would be at rest.

"My two children were with me at Salton on this occasion. They slept in a room on the third floor, and one morning my wife, having told me that the younger of the two seemed unwell, I went upstairs to look at her. It was a cheerful room, with two little white beds in it, and several old prints and samplers, and bits of work such as you see in nurseries. After I had spoken to the child, and while my wife was speaking to the maid, I stood with my hands in my pockets idly looking at these things. Among them was one that arrested my attention because at first I could not understand it, nor see why this discoloured parchment, with a few lines and dots on it, should have been framed and glazed. There were some words here and there which I could not decipher; so I lifted the frame off the nail and carried it to the window. Then I saw that the words were in Italian, written in a crabbed, old-fashioned hand, and the whole seemed to be a plan, or sketch, rudely drawn of what I thought at first was a camp—but, on closer examination, I saw was part of a churchyard, with tombstones, from one of which various lines were drawn to various dots, and among these lines were numbers, and here and there a word such as *right, left,* etc. There were also two lines forming a right angle, which intersected the whole, and after contemplating the thing for some time, it struck me that it was a rude sort of map of the old churchyard and the hedge, which had formed the subject of conversation some days before.

"At breakfast I mentioned what I had observed to Mr. and Mrs. Greathead, and they said they believed it was; it had been found when the old house was pulled down, and was kept on account of antiquity.

" 'Of what period is it?' I asked, 'and how happens it to have been made by an Italian?'

" 'The last question I can't answer,' said Mr. Greathead, 'but the date is on it, I believe.'

" 'No,' said I, 'I examined it particularly—there is no date.'

" 'Oh, there is a date and name, I think—but I never examined it myself.' And to settle the question he desired his son Harry to run and fetch it, adding, 'You know, Italian architects and designers of various kinds were not rare in this country a few centuries ago.'

"Harry brought the frame, and we were confirmed in our conjectures of what it represented, but we could find no date or name.

" 'And yet I think I've heard there was one,' said Mr. Greathead. 'Let us take it out of the frame.'

"This was easily done, and we found the date and the name inside."

The Count paused in his story and then added:

"I dare say you can guess it?"

"Jacopo Ferraldi?" I said.

"It was," he answered, "and it immediately occurred to me that he had buried the money supposed to have been stolen on the night he was murdered, and that this was the plan to guide him to finding it again. So I told Mr. Greathead the story I have now told you, and mentioned my reasons for supposing that if I was correct in my surmise, more gold would be found.

"With the old man's map as our guide, we immediately set to work—the whole family vigorously joining in the search; and, as I expected, we found that the tombstone in the garden was the point from which all the lines were drawn, and that the dots indicated where the money lay. It was in different heaps, and appeared to have been enclosed in bags, which had rotted away with time. We found the whole sum mentioned in the memoir, and Mr. Greathead, being Lord of the Manor, was generous enough to make it all over to me, as being the lawful heir, which, however, I was certainly not—for it was the spoil of a murderer and a thief and it properly belonged to the Allens. But that family had become extinct; at least, so we believed, when the two unfortunate ladies were executed, and I accepted the gift with much gratitude and a quiet conscience. It relieved us from our pressing difficulties and enabled me to wait for better times."

"And," said I, "now of the ghost? was he pleased or otherwise by the *dénouement?*"

"I cannot say," replied the Count. "I have not heard of his being seen since. I believe, however, that the villagers, who understand these things better than we do, say that they should not be surprised if he allowed the hedge and tombstone to be removed now without opposition—but Mr. Greathead, on the contrary, wished to retain them as mementoes of these curious circumstances."

THE GHOST

Mrs. Henry Wood

The moon was high in the heavens, lighting up the tower of the cathedral, illuminating its pinnacles, glittering through the elm trees, bringing forth into view even the dark old ivy on the preberdal houses. A fair night—all too fair for the game that was going to be played in it.

When the Helstoneleigh college boys resolved upon what they were pleased to term a "lark"—and, to do them justice, they regarded this, their prospective night's work, in no graver light—they carried it out artistically, with a completeness, a skill, worthy of a better cause. Several days had they been hatching this—laying their plans, arranging the details; it would be their own bungling fault if it miscarried. But the college boys were no bunglers.

Stripped of its details, the bare plot was to exhibit a "ghost" in the cloisters, and to get Charley Channing, a harmless but timid fellow scholar, to pass through them. The boys had been too wise to let it come to the knowledge of their seniors; and the most difficult part of the business had been old Ketch, the caretaker—but that was managed.

The moonlight shone peacefully on the college, and the conspirators were stealing up, by ones and twos, to their place of meeting round the dark trunks of the elm trees. Fine as it was overhead, it was less so underfoot. The previous day had been a wet one, the night had been wet, and also the forepart of the present day. Schoolboys are not particularly given to reticence, and a few more than the original conspirators had been taken into the plot. They were winding up now, in the weird moonlight, for the hour was approaching.

At this point we must pay a visit to Mr. Ketch in his lodge at his supper hour. Mr. Ketch had changed his hour for that important meal. Growing old with age or with lumbago, he found early rest congenial to his bones, as he informed his friends; so he supped at seven, and retired afterwards. Since the summer he had taken to having his pint of ale brought to him, deeming it more prudent not to leave his lodge and the keys to fetch it. This was known to the boys, and it rendered their plans a little more difficult.

Mr. Ketch, I say, sat in his lodge, having locked up the cloisters about an hour, sneezing and wheezing, for he was suffering from a cold, caught the day previously in the wet. He was spelling over a weekly twopenny newspaper, borrowed from the public-house, by the help of a flaring tallow candle and a pair of spectacles, of which one glass was out. Cynically severe was he over everything he read, for it was in the nature of Mr. Ketch to be. As the three-quarters past six chimed out from the cathedral clock, his door was suddenly opened, and a voice called out "Beer!" Mr. Ketch's supper ale had arrived.

But the arrival did not give the gentleman pleasure, and he started up in what we might call a fury. Dashing his one-eyed glasses on the table, he attacked the man—

"What d'ye mean with your 'beer' at this time o' the evening? It wants a quarter to seven! Haven't you got no clock at your place? D'ye think I shall take it in now?"

"Well, it just comes to this," said the man, who was the brewer at the public-house, and made himself useful at odd jobs in his spare time: "if you don't like to take it in now, you can't have it at all, of my bringing. I be a-going up to t'other end of the town, and shan't be back this side of ten."

Mr. Ketch with much groaning and grumbling, took the ale and poured it into a jug of his own—a handsome jug, that had been in the wars and lost its spout and handle—giving back the public house jug to the man. "You serve me such an impertinant trick again as to bring my ale a quarter of an hour aforehand, that's all!" snarled he.

The man received the jug and went off whistling; he had the pleasure of knowing Mr. Ketch and his temper well.

That gentleman shut his door with a bang, and proceeded to get out his customary bread and cheese. Not that he had any great love for a bread-and-cheese supper, as a matter of taste he would very much have preferred something more dainty; only dainties and Mr. Ketch's pocket didn't agree.

"They wants to be took down a notch, that public—sending out a man's supper beer a quarter afore seven, when it ain't ordered to come till seven strikes. Much they care it if stops a-waiting and a-flattening, and gets undrinkable! Be I a slave that I should be forced to swaller my supper afore my tea have well gone down, just to please them? they have got a sight too much custom, that's what it is."

He took a slight draught of the offending ale, and was critically surveying the loaf before applying to it that green-handled knife of his, when a second summons was heard at the door—a very timid one this time.

Mr. Ketch flung down the bread and the knife. "What's the reason I can't get a meal in quiet? Who is it?"

There was no response to this, save a second faint tapping.

"Come in!" roared out he. "Pull the string o' the latch."

But nobody came in, in spite of this lucid direction; and the timid tapping, which seemed to proceed from very small knuckles, was repeated again. Mr. Ketch was fain to go, grunting, and open it.

A young damsel of eight or so, in a tattered tippet and a large bonnet—probably her mother's—stood there curtsying. "Please, sir, Mr. Ketch is wanted."

Mr. Ketch was rather taken aback at this strange address, and surveyed its messenger in astonishment. "Who be you? and who wants him?" growled he.

"Please, sir, it's a gentleman as is a-waiting at the big green gates," was the reply. "Mr. Ketch is to go to him this minute—he told me to come and say so; and if you didn't make haste, he should be gone."

"Can't you speak consistent?" snarled Ketch. "Who is the gentleman?"

"Please, sir, I think it is the bishop."

This put Ketch in a fluster. The "big green gates" could only have reference to the private entrance to the bishop's garden, which entrance his lordship used when attending the cathedral. That the bishop was in Helstoneleigh Ketch knew. He had arrived that day, after a short absence. What on earth could he want with *him*? Never doubting, in his hurry, the genuineness of the message, Ketch pulled his door to, and stepped off, the young messenger having already decamped. The green gates were not one minute's walk from the lodge—though a projecting buttress of the cathedral prevented the one being in sight of the other—and old Ketch gained them and looked around.

Where was the bishop? The iron gates, the garden, the white stones at his feet, the towering cathedral aloft, all lay cold and calm in the moolight, but of human sound or sight there was none. The gates were locked when he came to try them and he could not see the bishop anywhere.

He was not likely to see him. Steven Bywater, the lad who took upon himself much of the plot's acting part—of which, to give him his due, he was boldly capable—had been on the watch in the street near the cathedral for a messenger that would suit his purpose. Seeing this young damsel hurrying along with a jug in her hand, possibly to buy beer for *her* home supper, he waylaid her.

"Little ninepins, would you like to get threepence?" asked he. "You shall have it if you'll carry a message for me close by."

"Little ninepins" had probably never had a whole threepenny piece to herself in her young life; she caught at the tempting suggestion, and Bywater drilled into her his instructions, finding her excessively stupid over the process. Perhaps that was all the better. "Now mind, you are *not* to say who wants Mr. Ketch unless he asks," repeated he for about the fifth time, as she was departing to do the errand. "If he asks, say you think it's the bishop."

So she went and delivered it. But had old Ketch's temper allowed him to go into minute questioning, he might have discovered the trick. Bywater stealthily followed the child near the lodge, screening himself from observation; and as soon as old Ketch hobbled out of it, he popped in, snatched the cloister keys from their nail, and deposited a piece of paper, folded as a note, on Ketch's table. Then he made off.

Back came Ketch after a while. He did not quite know what to make of it, but rather inclined to the opinion that the bishop had not waited for him. "He might have wanted me to take an errand round to the deanery," soliloquised he. And this thought had caused him to tarry about the gate, so that he was absent from his lodge quite ten minutes. The first thing he saw on entering was the bit of paper on the table. He seized and opened it, grumbling aloud that folks used his home just as they pleased, going in and out without reference to his presence or his absence. The note, written in pencil, purported to be from an acquaintance, one Joseph Jenkins. It ran as follows.—

"My old father is coming up to our place
tonight to eat a bit of supper, and he
says he should like you to join him, which
I and Mrs. J. shall be happy if you will,
at seven o'clock. It's tripe and onions.
Yours
J. Jenkins.

Now, if there was one delicacy known to this world more delicious to old Ketch's palate than another it was tripe, seasoned with plenty of onions. His mouth watered as he read. He was aware that it was—to use the phraseology of Helstoneleigh—"tripe night". On two nights in the week tripe was sold in the town ready dressed, onions and all. This was one; and Ketch anticipated a glorious treat. In too great a hurry to cast so much as a glance round his lodge (crafty Bywater had been deep), not stopping even to put up the loaf and the cheese and the green-handled knife, only drinking the beer, away hobbled Ketch as fast as his lumbago would allow him, locking safely his door, and not having observed the absence of the keys.

"He ain't a bad sort, Joe Jenkins," allowed he, conciliated beyond everything at the prospect the invitation held out, and talking to himself as he limped away towards the street. "He don't write a bad hand neither! It's a plain un—not one o' them new-fangled scrawls that you can't read. Him and his wife held up their heads a cut above me—oh, yes they have, though, for all Joe's humbleness. Old Jenkins has always said we'd have a supper together some night, him and me; I suppose this is it."

The first chimes of the cathedral clock gave notice of the hour seven! Old Ketch broke out all in a heat, and tried to hobble along Seven o'clock! What if, through being late, his share of the tripe and onions should be eaten!

Peeping out every now and then from the deep shade cast by one of the angles of the cathedral, and as swiftly and cautiously drawn back again, was a trencher, apparently watching Ketch. As soon as that functionary was fairly launched on his way, the trencher came out entirely, and went flying at a swift pace round the college to the Boundaries.

Bywater, by the help of the filched keys, was now safe in the cloisters, absorbed with his companions in the preparation for the grand event of the night. In point of fact, they were getting up Pierce senior. Their precise mode of doing that need not be given. They had requisites in abundance, having disputed among themselves which should be at the honour of the contribution, and the result was an over prodigality.

"That's seven!" exclaimed Bywater in an agony, as the clock struck. "Make haste, Pierce! The young one was to come out at a quarter-past. If you're not ready, it will ruin all."

"I shall be ready and waiting, if you don't bother," was the response of Pierce. "I wonder if old Ketch is safely off."

"What a stunning fright Ketch would be in if he came in here and met the ghost!" exclaimed Hurst. "He'd never think it was anything less than the Old Gentleman come for him."

A chorus of laughter, which Hurst himself hushed. It would not do for noise to be heard in the cloisters at that hour.

There was nothing to which poor Charley Channing was more sensitive than to ridicule on the subject of his unhappy failing—the propensity to fear; and there is no failing to which schoolboys are more intolerant. Of moral courage—that is, of courage in the cause of right—Charles had plenty; of physical courage, little. Apart from the misfortune of having had supernatural terror implanted in him in childhood, he would never have been physically brave. Schoolboys cannot understand that this shrinking from danger (I speak of palpable danger), which they call cowardice, nearly always emanates from a superior intellect. Where the mental powers are of a high order, the imagination unusually awakened, danger is sure to be keenly perceived, and sensitively shrunk from. In proportion will be the shrinking dread of ridicule. Charles Channing possessed this dread in a remarkable degree. You may therefore judge how he felt when he found it mockingly alluded to by Bywater.

On this very day that we are writing of, Bywater caught Charles, and imparted to him in profound confidence an important secret—that a choice few of the boys were about to play old Ketch a trick, obtain the keys, and have a game in the cloisters by moonlight. A place in the play, he said, had been assigned to Charles. Charles hesitated—not because it might be wrong so to cheat Ketch (Ketch was the common enemy of the boys, of Charley as of the rest), but because he had plenty of lessons to do. This was Bywater's opportunity; he chose to interpret the hesitation differently.

"So you are afraid, Miss Charley! Ho, ho! Do you think the cloisters will be dark? that the moon won't keep the ghosts away? I say, it *can't* be true, what I heard the other day, that you dare not be in the dark, lest ghosts should come and run away with you!"

"Nonsense, Bywater!" returned Charley, changing colour like a conscious girl.

"Well, if you are *not* afraid, you'll come and join us," sarcastically returned Bywater. "We shall have stunning good sport. There'll be about a dozen of us. Rubbish to your lessons! You need not be away from them more than an hour. It won't be *dark*, Miss Channing."

After this nothing would have kept Charley away, fearing their ridicule. He promised faithfully to be in the cloisters at a quarter-past seven.

Accordingly, the instant tea was over, he got to his lessons. Thus was he engaged when another student, Hamish, entered.

"What sort of night is it, Hamish?" asked Charles thinking of the projected night play.

"Fine," replied Hamish.

The silence was resumed. Hamish turned himself round to the fire and said no more. Charles's ears were listening for the quarter-past seven; and the moment it chimed out, he quitted his work, took his trencher coat from the hall, and departed saying nothing to anybody.

He went along whistling past the deanery; it, and the cathedral tower rising above it, looked gray in the moonlight. He picked up a stone and sent it right into one of the elm trees; some of the birds, disturbed from their roost, flew out, croaking, over his head. In the old days of superstition it might have been looked upon as an ill omen, coupled with what was to follow. Ah, Charley if you could but foresee what is before you! If Mrs. Channing, from her far-off sojourn, could but know what grievous ill is about to overtake her boy!

Poor Charley suspected nothing. He was whistling a merry tune, laughing, boy-like, at the discomfiture of the cawing rooks, and anticipating the stolen game he and his friends were about to take part in on forbidden ground.

At that minute he saw a boy come forth from the cloisters, and softly whistle to him, as if in token that he was being waited for. Charley answered the whistle, and set off at a run.

Which of the boys it was he could not tell; the outline of the form and the college cap were visible enough in the moonlight, but not the face. When he gained the cloister entrance he could no longer see him, but supposed the boy had preceded him into the cloisters. On went Charley, groping his way down the narrow passage. "Where are you?" called out he.

There was no answer. Once in the cloisters, a faint light came in from the open windows overlooking the burial-yard—a very faint light, indeed, for the buildings all round it were so high as almost to shut out a view of the sky; you must go close to the window-frame before you could see it.

"I—s-a-a-y!" roared Charley again, at the top of his voice, "where are you all? Is nobody here?"

There came neither response nor sign of it. One faint sound certainly did seem to strike upon his ear from behind; it was like the click of a lock being turned. Charley looked sharply round, but all seemed still again. The low, dark, narrow passage was behind him; the dim cloisters were before him; he was standing at the corner formed by the east and south quadrangles, and the pale burial-ground in their midst, with its damp grass and its gravestones, looked cold and lonesome in the moonlight.

The strange silence—it was not the silence of daylight—struck upon Charles with dismay. "You fellows there!" he called out again in desperation. "What's the good of playing up this nonsense?"

The tones of his voice died away in the echoes of the cloisters, but of other answer there was none. At that instant a rook, no doubt disturbed by the sound, came diving down and flopped its wings across the burial-ground. The sight of something moving there nearly startled Charles out of his senses, and the matter was not much mended when he discovered it was only a bird. He turned and flew down the passage to the entrance quicker than he had come up it; but, instead of passing out, he found the iron gate closed. What could have shut it? There was no wind. And if there had been a wind ever so boisterous, it could scarcely have moved that little low gate, for it opened inwards.

Charles seized it to pull it open. It resisted his efforts. He tried to shake it, but little came of that, for the gate was fastened firmly. Bit by bit stole the conviction over his mind that he was locked in.

Then a panic seized him. He was locked in the ghostly cloisters, close to the graves of the dead—on the very spot where, as idle tales went, the monks of bygone ages came out of those recording stones under his feet and showed themselves at midnight. Not a step could he take round the cloisters but his foot must press those stones. To be locked in the cloisters might be nothing for brave, grown, sensible men, but for many a boy it would have been a great deal, and for Charles Channing it was awful.

That he was alone he never doubted. He believed—as fully as belief, or any other feeling could flash into his horrified mind and find a place in it—that By water had decoyed him into the cloisters and left him there. All the dread terrors of childhood rose up before him. To say that he was mad in that moment might not be quite correct, but it is certain his mind was not perfectly sane. His whole body, his face, his hair, grew damp in an instant, as does one in mortal agony; and with a smothered cry, which was not like that of a human being, he turned and fled through the cloisters, in the vague hope to find the other gate open.

It may be difficult for some of you to understand this excessive terror, albeit the situation was not a particularly desirable one. A college boy, in these enlightened days, laughs at supernatural tales as the delusions of ignorance in ages past; but for those who have had the misfortune to be imbued in infancy with superstitions, as was Charles Channing, the terror exists still, college boys though they may be. He could not have told (had he been collected enough to tell anything) what his precise dread was as he flew through the cloisters. None can at these moments. A sort of bugbear rises up in the mind, and they shrink from it, though they see not what its exact nature may be; but it is a bugbear that can neither be faced nor borne.

Feeling like one about to die; feeling as if death, in that awful moment, might be a boon rather than the contrary, Charles sped down the east quadrangle and turned into the north. At the extremity of the north side, forming the angle between it and the west, commenced the narrow passage similar to the one he had just traversed, which led to the west gate of egress. A faint glimmering of the white-flagged stones beyond this gate gave a promise it was open. A half-uttered sound of thankfulness escaped him, and he sped on.

Ah, but what was that? What was it that he came upon in the middle of the north quadrangle, standing within the niches? A towering form, with a ghostly face, telling of the dead, a mysterious, supernatural-looking blue flame lighting it up round about. It came out of the niche and advanced slowly upon him.

An awful cry escaped from his heart, and went ringing up to the roof of the cloisters. Oh, that the dean, sitting in his deanery adjacent to the cloisters, could have heard that helpless cry of anguish! No, no; there could be no succour for a place that was supposed to be empty and closed.

Back to the locked gate with perhaps the apparition following him? or forward *past* IT to the open door of egress? Which was it to be? In these moments there can be no reason to guide the course; but there is instinct; and instinct took that ill-fated child to the open door.

How he got past the sight it is impossible to tell. Had it been right in front of his path he never would have got past it. But it had made a halt when just beyond the niche, not coming out very far. With his poor hands stretched out and his breath leaving him, Charles did get by, and made for the door, the ghost bringing up the rear with a yell; while those old cloister niches when he was fairly gone, grew alive with moving figures, which came out of their dark corners and shrieked aloud with laughter.

Away, he knew not whither—away, like one who is being pursued by an unearthly phantom, deep catchings of his breath, as will follow undue bodily exertion, telling of something not right within; wild, low, abrupt sounds breaking from him at intervals—thus he flew, turning to the left, which took him towards . . . the river. Anywhere from the dreaded cloisters; anywhere from the old grey ghostly edifice; anywhere in his dread and agony! He dashed past the boat-house, down the steps, turning on to the river pathway, and—

Whether the light hanging at the boat-house deceived his sight—whether the slippery mud caused him to lose his footing—whether he was running too quickly and could not stop himself in time—or whether, in his irrepressible fear, he threw himself unconsciously in, to escape what might be behind him, will never be known. Certain it is, the unhappy boy went plunging into the river, another and a last wild cry escaping him as the waters closed over his head . . .

THE OLD NURSE'S STORY

Mrs. Gaskell

You know, my dears, that your mother was an orphan, and an only child; and I dare say you have heard that your grandfather was a clergyman up in Westmorland, where I come from. I was just a girl in the village school, when, one day, your grandmother came in to ask the mistress if there was any scholar there who would do for a nurse maid; and mighty proud I was, I can tell ye, when the mistress called me up, and spoke to my being a good girl at my needle, and a steady, honest girl, and one whose parents were very respectable, though they might be poor. I thought I should like nothing better than to serve the pretty young lady, who was blushing as deep as I was as she spoke of the coming baby, and what I should have to do with it. However, I see you don't care so much for this part of my story as for what you think is to come, so I'll tell you at once. I was engaged and settled at the parsonage before Miss Rosamond (that was the baby, who is now your mother) was born. To be sure, I had little enough to do with her when she came, for she was never out of her mother's arms, and slept by her all night long; and proud enough was I sometimes when missis trusted her to me.

There never was such a baby before or since, though you've all of you been fine enough in your turns; but for sweet, winning ways, you've none of you come up to your mother. She took after her mother, who was a real lady born; a Miss Furnivall, a granddaughter of Lord Furnivall's, in Northumberland. I believe she had neither brother nor sister, and had been brought up in my lord's family till she had married your grandfather, who was just a curate, son to a shopkeeper in Carlisle—but a clever, fine gentleman as ever was—and one who was a right-down hard worker in his parish, which was very wide, and scattered all abroad over the Westmorland Fells. When your mother, little Miss Rosamond, was about four or five years old, both her parents died in a fortnight—one after the other. Ah! that was a sad time. My pretty young mistress and me was looking for another baby, when my master came home from one of his long rides, wet and tired, and took the fever he died of; and then she never held up her head again, but just lived to see her dead baby, and have it laid on her breast before she sighed away her life. My mistress had asked me, on her death-bed, never to leave Miss Rosamond; but if she had never spoken a word, I would have gone with the little child to the end of the world.

The next thing, and before we had well stilled our sobs, the executors and guardians came to settle the affairs. They were my poor young mistress's own cousin, Lord Furnivall, and Mr. Esthwaithe, my master's brother, a shopkeeper in Manchester; not so well-to-do then as he was afterwards, and with a large family rising about him. Well! I don't know if it were their settling, or because of a letter my mistress wrote on her death-bed to her cousin, my lord; but somehow it was settled that Miss Rosamond and me were to go to Furnivall Manor House, in Northumberland, and my lord spoke as if it had been her mother's wish that she should live with his family, and as if he had no objections, for that one or two more or less could make no difference in so grand a household. So though that was not the way in which I should have wished the coming of my bright and pretty pet to have been looked at—who was like a sunbeam to any family, be it ever so grand—I was well pleased that all the folks in the Dale should stare and admire when they heard I was going to be young lady's maid at my Lord Furnivall's at Furnivall Manor.

But I made a mistake in thinking we were to go and live

where my lord did. It turned out that the family had left Furnivall Manor House fifty years or more. I could not hear that my poor young mistress had ever been there, though she had been brought up in the family; and I was sorry for that, for I should have liked Miss Rosamond's youth to have passed where her mother's had been.

My lord's gentlemen, from whom I asked so many questions as I durst, said that the Manor House was at the foot of the Cumberland Fells, and a very grand place; that an old Miss Furnivall, a great-aunt of my lord's, lived there, with only a few servants; but that it was a very healthy place, and my lord had thought that it would suit Miss Rosamond very well for a few years, and that her being there might perhaps amuse his old aunt.

I was bidden by my lord to have Miss Rosamond's things ready by a certain day. He was a stern, proud man, as they say all the Lords Furnivall were; and he never spoke a word more than was necessary. Folk did say he had loved my young mistress; but that, because she knew that his father would object, she would never listen to him, and married Mr. Esthwaite, but I don't know. He never married, at any rate. But he never took much notice of Miss Rosamond; which I thought he might have done if he had cared for her dead mother. He sent his gentleman with us to Manor House, telling him to joint him at Newcastle that same evening; so there was no great length of time for him to make us known to all the strangers before he, too, shook us off; and we were left, two lonely young things (I was not eighteen), in the great, old Manor House.

It seems like yesterday that we drove there. We had left our own dear parsonage very early, and we had both cried as if our hearts would break, though we were travelling in my lord's carriage, which I thought so much of once. And now it was long past noon on a September day, and we stopped to change horses for the last time at a little town all full of colliers and miners. Miss Rosamond had fallen asleep, but Mr. Henry told me to waken her, that she might see the park and the Manor House as we drove up. I thought it rather a pity; but I did what he bade me, for fear he should complain of me to my lord. We had left all signs of a town, or even a village, and were then inside the gates of a large wild park—not like the parks here in the north, but with rocks, and the noise of running water, and gnarled thorn-trees, and old oaks all white and peeled with age.

The road went up about two miles, and then we saw a great and stately house, with many trees close around it, so close that in some places their branches dragged against the walls when the wind blew; and some huge broken down; for no one seemed to take much charge of the place; to lop the wood, or to keep the moss-covered carriageway in order.

Only in front of the house all was clear. The great oval drive was without a weed; and neither tree nor creeper was allowed to grow over the long, many-windowed front; at both sides of which a wing projected, which were each the ends of other side fronts, for the house, although it was so desolate, was even grander than I expected. Behind it rose the fells, which seemed unenclosed and bare enough; and on the left-hand of the house, as you stood facing it, was a little, old-fashioned flower garden, as I found out afterwards. A door opened out upon it from the west front; it had been scooped out of the thick dark wood for some old Lady Furnivall; but the branches of the great forest trees had grown and overshadowed it again, and there were very few flowers that would live there at that time.

When we drove up to the great front entrance, and went into the hall I thought we should be lost—it was so large, and vast, and grand. There was a chandelier, all of bronze, hung down from the middle of the ceiling; and I had never seen one before, and looked at it all in amaze. Then, at one end of the hall, was a great fire-place, as large as the sides of the houses in my country, with massy andirons and dogs to hold the wood; and by it were heavy, old-fashioned sofas. At the opposite end of the hall, to the left as you went in—on the western side—was an organ built into the wall, and so large that it filled up the best part of that end. Beyond it, on the same side, was a door; and opposite, on each side of the fire-place, were also doors leading to the east front; but those I never went through as long as I stayed in the house, so I can't tell you what lay beyond.

The afternoon was closing in, and the hall, which had no fire lighted in it, looked dark and gloomy, but we did not stay there a moment. The old servant, who had opened the door for us, bowed to Mr. Henry, and took us in through the door at the farther side of the great organ, and led us through several smaller halls and passages into the west drawing-room, where he said that Miss Furnivall was sitting. Poor little Miss Rosamond held very tight to me, as if she were scared and lost in that great place, and as for myself, I was not much better. The west drawing-room was very cheerful-looking, with a warm fire in it, and plenty of wood, comfortable furniture about. Miss Furnivall was an old lady not far from eighty, I should think, but I do not know. She was thin and tall, and had a face as full of fine wrinkles as if they had been drawn all over it with a needle's point. Her eyes were very watchful, to make up, I suppose, for her being so deaf as to be obliged to use a trumpet.

Sitting with her, working at the same great piece of tapestry, was Mrs. Stark, her maid and companion, and almost as old as she was. She had lived with Miss Furnivall ever since they were both young, and now she seemed more like a friend than a servant; she looked so cold and grey and stony—as if she had never loved or cared for anyone; and I don't suppose she did for anyone except her mistress; and, owing to the great deafness of the latter, Mrs. Stark treated her very much as if she were a child. Mr. Henry gave some message from my lord, and then he bowed good-bye to us all—taking no notice of my sweet little Miss Rosamond's outstretched hand—and left us standing there, being looked at by the two ladies through their spectacles.

I was right glad when they rung for the old footman who had shown us in at first, and told him to take us to our rooms. So we went out of that great drawing-room, and into another sitting-room, and out of that, and then up a great flight of stairs, and along a broad gallery—which was something like a library, having books all down one side and windows and writing-tables all down the other—till we came to our rooms, which I was not sorry to hear were just over the kitchens; for I began to think I should be lost in that wilderness of a house. There was an old nursery that had been used for all the little lords and ladies long ago, with a pleasant fire burning in the grate, and the kettle boiling on the hob, and tea-things spread out on the table; and out of that room was the night-nursery, with a little crib for Miss Rosamond close to my bed. And old James called up Dorothy, his wife, to bid us welcome; and both he and she were so hospitable and kind that by and by Miss Rosamond and me felt quite at home; and by the time tea was over, she was sitting on Dorothy's knee, and chattering away as fast as her little tongue could go.

I soon found out that Dorothy was from Westmorland, and that bound her and me together, as it were; and I would never wish to meet with kinder people than were old James and his wife. James had lived pretty nearly all his life in my lord's family, and thought there was no one so grand as they. He even looked down a little on his wife; because, till he had married her, she had never lived in any but a farmer's household. But he was very fond of her, as well he might be. They had one servant under them, to do all the rough work. Agnes, they called her; and she and me and James and Dorothy, with Miss Furnivall and Mrs. Stark, made up the family; always remembering my sweet Miss Rosamond. I used to wonder what they had done before she came, they thought so much of her now. Kitchen and drawing-room, it was all the same. The hard, sad Miss Furnivall, and the cold Mrs. Stark, looked pleased when she came fluttering in like a bird, playing and pranking hither and thither, with a continual murmur, and pretty prattle of gladness. I am sure, they were sorry many a time when she flitted away into the kitchen, though they were too proud to ask her to stay with them, and were a little surprised at her taste; though to be sure, as Mrs. Stark said, it was not to be wondered at, remembering what stock her father had come of.

The great, old rambling house was a famous place for little Miss Rosamond. She made expeditions all over it, with me at her heels; all except the east wing, which was never opened, and whither we never thought of going. But in the western and northern part was many a pleasant room; full of things that were curiosities to us, though they might not have been to people who had seen more. The windows were darkened by the sweeping boughs of the trees, and the ivy which had overgrown them: but, in the green gloom, we could manage to see old China jars and carved ivory boxes, and great heavy books, and, above all, the old pictures.

Once, I remember, my darling would have Dorothy go with us to tell us who they all were; for they were all portraits of some of my lord's family, though Dorothy could not tell us the names of every one. We had gone through most of the rooms, when we came to the old state drawing-room over the hall, and there was a picture of Miss Furnivall; or, as she was called in those days, Miss Grace, for she was the younger sister. Such a beauty she must have been! but with such a set, proud look, and such scorn looking out of her handsome eyes, with her eyebrows just a little raised, as if she were wondering how anyone could have the impertinence to look at her; and her lip curled at us, as we stood there gazing. She had a dress on, the like of which I had never seen before, but it was all the fashion when she was young: a hat of some soft white stuff like beaver, pulled a little over her brows, and a beautiful plume of feathers sweeping round it on one side; and her gown of blue satin was open in front to a quilted white stomacher.

"Well, to be sure!" said I, when I had gazed my fill. "Flesh is grass, they do say; but who would have thought that Miss Furnivall had been such an out-and-out beauty, to see her now?"

"Yes," said Dorothy. "Folks change sadly. But if what my master's father used to say was true, Miss Furnivall, the elder sister, was handsomer than Miss Grace. Her picture is here somewhere; but, if I show it you, you must never let on, even to James, that you have seen it. Can the little lady hold her tongue, think you?" asked she.

I was not so sure, for she was such a little sweet, bold, open-spoken child, so I set her to hide herself; and then I helped Dorothy to turn a great picture, that leaned with its face towards the wall, and was not hung up as the others were. To be sure, it beat Miss Grace for beauty; and, I think, for scornful pride too, though in that matter it might be hard to choose. I could have looked at it an hour, but Dorothy seemed half frightened at having shown it to me and hurried it back again, and bade me run and find Miss Rosamond, for that there were some ugly places about the house, where she should like ill for the child to go. I was a brave, high-spirited girl, and thought little of what the old woman said, for I liked hide-and-seek as well as any child in the parish; so off I ran to find my little one.

As winter drew on, and the days grew shorter, I was sometimes almost certain that I heard a noise as if someone was playing on the great organ in the hall. I did not hear it every evening; but, certainly, I did very often; usually when I was sitting with Miss Rosamond, after I had put her to bed, and keeping quite still and silent in the bedroom. Then I used to hear it booming and swelling away in the distance. The first night, when I went down to my supper, I asked Dorothy who had been playing music, and James said very shortly that I was a gowk to take the wind soughing among the trees for music; but I saw Dorothy look at him very fearfully, and Bessy, the kitchen-maid, said something beneath her breath, and went quite white. I saw they did not like my question, so I held my peace till I was with Dorothy alone, when I knew I could get a good deal out of her.

So, the next day, I watched my time, and I coaxed and asked her who it was that played the organ; for I knew that it was the organ and not the wind well enough, for all I had kept silence before James. But Dorothy had had her lesson, I'll warrant, and never a word could I get from her. So then

I tried Bessy, though I had always held my head rather above her, as I was evened to James and Dorothy, and she was little better than their servant. So she said I must never, never tell; and if I ever told, I was never to say *she* had told me; but it was a very strange noise, and she had heard it many a time, but most of all on winter nights, and before storms; and folks did say, it was the old lord playing on the great organ in the hall, just as he used to do when he was alive; but who the old lord was, or why he played, and why he played on stormy winter evenings in particular, she either could not or would not tell me. Well! I told you I had a brave heart; and I thought it was rather pleasant to have that grand music rolling about the house, let who would be the player; for now it rose above the great gusts of wind, and wailed and triumphed just like a living creature, and then it fell to a softness most complete; only it was always music and tunes, so it was nonsense to call it the wind.

I thought at first that it might be Miss Furnivall who played, unknown to Bessy; but one day when I was in the hall by myself, I opened the organ and peeped all above it and around it, as I had done to the organ in Crosthwaite Church once before, and I saw it was all broken and destroyed inside, though it looked so brave and fine; and then, though it was noonday, my flesh began to creep a little, and I shut it up, and ran away pretty quickly to my own bright nursery; and

I did not like hearing the music for some time after that, any more than James and Dorothy did.

All this time Miss Rosamond was making herself more and more beloved. The old ladies liked her to dine with them at their early dinner; James stood behind Miss Furnivall's chair, and I behind Miss Rosamond's all in state; and, after dinner, she would play about in a corner of the great drawing-room, as still as any mouse, while Miss Furnivall slept, and I had my dinner in the kitchen. But she was glad enough to come to me in the nursery afterwards; for, as she said, Miss Furnivall was so sad, and Mrs. Stark so dull; but she and I were merry enough; and, by and by, I got not to care for that weird, rolling music, which did one no harm, if we did not know where it came from.

That winter was very cold. In the middle of October the frosts began, and lasted many, many weeks. I remember, one day at dinner, Miss Furnivall lifted up her sad, heavy eyes said to Mrs. Stark, "I am afraid we shall have a terrible winter," in a strange kind of meaning way. But Mrs. Stark pretended not to hear, and talked very loud of something else. My little lady and I did not care for the frost; not we! As long as it was dry we climbed up the steep brows, behind the house, and went up on the Fells, which were bleak, and bare enough, and there we ran races in the fresh, sharp air; and once we came down by a new path that took us past the two old gnarled holly trees, which grew about half way down by the east side of the house.

But the days grew shorter and shorter; and the old lord—if it was he—played more and more stormily and sadly on the great organ. One Sunday afternoon—it must have been towards the end of November—I asked Dorothy to take charge of little Missy when she came out of the drawing-room, after Miss Furnivall had had her nap; for it was too cold to take her with me to church, and yet I wanted to go. And Dorothy was glad enough to promise, and was so fond of the child that all seemed well; and Bessy and I set off briskly, though the sky hung heavy and black over the white earth, as if the night had never fully gone away; and the air, though still, was very biting and keen.

"We shall have a fall of snow," said Bessy to me. And sure enough, even while we were in church, it came down thick, in great, large flakes, so thick it almost darkened the windows. It had stopped snowing before we came out, but it lay soft, thick and deep beneath our feet as we tramped home. Before we got to the hall the moon rose, and I think it was lighter then—what with the moon, and what with the white dazzling snow—than it had been when we went to church, between two and three o'clock. I have not told you that Miss Furnivall and Mrs. Stark never went to church; they used to read the prayers together, in their quiet, gloomy way; they seemed to feel the Sunday very long with their tapestry-work to be busy at.

So when I went to Dorothy in the kitchen, to fetch Miss Rosamond and take her upstairs with me, I did not much wonder when the old woman told me that the ladies had kept the child with them, and that she had never come to the kitchen, as I had bidden her when she was tired of behaving pretty in the drawing-room. So I took off my things and went to find her, and bring her to her supper in the nursery. But when I went into the best drawing-room there sat the two old ladies, very still and quiet, dropping out a word now and then but looking as if nothing so bright and merry as Miss Rosamond had ever been near them. Still I thought she might be hiding from me; it was one of her pretty ways; and that she had persuaded them to look as if they knew nothing about her; so I went softly peeping under this sofa, and behind that chair, making believe I was sadly frightened at not finding her.

"What's the matter, Hester?" said Mrs. Stark sharply. I don't know if Miss Furnivall had seen me, for, as I told you, she was very deaf, and she sat quite still, idly staring into the fire, with her hopeless face. "I'm only looking for my little Rosy-Posy," I replied, still thinking that the child was there, and near me, though I could not see her.

"Miss Rosamond is not here," said Mrs. Stark. "She went

away more than an hour ago to find Dorothy." And she too turned and went on looking into the fire.

My heart sank at this, and I began to wish I had never left my darling. I went back to Dorothy and told her. James was gone out for the day, but she and me and Bessy took lights and went up into the nursery first, and then we roamed over the great large house, calling and entreating Miss Rosamond to come out of her hiding-place, and not frighten us to death in that way. But there was no answer; no sound.

"Oh!" said I at last. "Can she have got into the east wing and hidden there?"

But Dorothy said it was not possible, for that she herself had never been there; that the doors were always locked, and my lord's steward had the keys, she believed; at any rate, neither she nor James had ever seen them. So I said I would go back and see if, after all, she was not hidden in the drawing-room, unknown to the old ladies; and if I found her there I said I would whip her well for the fright she had given me; but I never meant to do it. Well, I went back to the west drawing-room, and I told Mrs. Stark we could not find her anywhere, and asked for leave to look all about the furniture there, for I thought now, that she might have fallen asleep in some warm hidden corner; but no! we looked, Miss Furnivall got up and looked, trembling all over, and she was nowhere there; then we set off again, everyone in the house, and looked in all the places we had searched before, but we could not find her. Miss Furnivall shivered and shook so much that Mrs. Stark took her back into the warm drawing-room; but not before they had made me promise to bring her to them when she was found. Welladay! I began to think she never would be found, when I bethought me to look out into the great front court, all covered with snow.

I was upstairs when I looked out; but it was such clear moonlight I could see, quite plain, two little footprints, which might be traced from the hall door and round the corner of the east wing. I don't know how I got down, but I tugged open the great, stiff hall door; and, throwing the skirt of my own gown over my head for a cloak, I ran out. I turned the east corner, and there a black shadow fell on the snow; but when I came again into the moonlight, there were the little foot-marks going up—up to the Fells. It was bitter cold; so cold that the air almost took the skin off my face as I ran, but I ran on, crying to think how my poor little darling must be perished and frightened. I was within sight of the holly trees when I saw a shepherd coming down the hill, bearing something in his arms wrapped in his maud. He shouted to me, and asked me if I had lost a bairn; and, when I could not speak for crying, he bore towards me, and I saw my wee bairnie lying still, and white, and stiff, in his arms, as if she had been dead. He told me he had been up the Fells to gather in his sheep, before the deep cold of night came on, and that under the holly trees (black marks on the hill-side, where no other bush was for miles around) he had found my little lady—my lamb—my queen—my darling—stiff and cold, in the terrible sleep which is frost-begotten.

Oh! the joy, and the tears of having her in my arms once again! for I would not let him carry her; but took her, maud and all, into my own arms, and held her near my own warm neck and heart, and felt the life stealing slowly back again into her little gentle limbs. But she was still insensible when we reached the hall, and I had no breath for speech. We went in by the kitchen door.

"Bring the warming-pan," said I; and I carried her upstairs, and began undressing her by the nursery fire, which Bessy had kept up. I called my little lammie all the sweet and playful names I could think of—even while my eyes were blinded by my tears; and at last, oh! at length she opened her large, blue eyes. Then I put her into her warm bed, and sent Dorothy down to tell Miss Furnivall that all was well; and I made up my mind to sit by my darling's bedside the live-long night. She fell away into a soft sleep as soon as her pretty head had touched the pillow, and I watched by her until morning light; when she wakened up bright and clear—or so I thought at first—and, my dears, so I think now.

She said that she had fancied that she should like to go to Dorothy, for that both the old ladies were asleep, and it was very dull in the drawing-room; and that, as she was going through the west lobby, she saw the snow through the high window falling—falling—soft and steady. But she wanted to see it lying pretty and white on the ground; so she made her way into the great hall; and then, going to the window, she saw it bright and soft upon the drive; but while she stood there, she saw a little girl, not so old as she was, "but so pretty," said my darling, "and this little girl beckoned to me to come out; and oh, she was so pretty and so sweet, I could not choose but go." And then this other little girl had taken her by the hand, and side by side the two had gone round the east corner.

"Now you are a naughty little girl, and telling stories," said I. "What would your good mamma, that is in heaven, and never told a story in her life, say to her little Rosamond, if she heard her—and I dare say she does—telling stories!"

"Indeed, Hester," sobbed out my child, "I'm telling you true. Indeed I am."

"Don't tell me!" said I, very stern. "I tracked you by your footmarks through the snow; there were only yours to be seen; and if you had had a little girl to go hand in hand with you up the hill, don't you think the footprints would have gone along with yours?"

"I can't help it, dear, dear Hester," said she, crying, "if they did not. I never looked at her feet, but she held my hand fast and tight in her little one, and it was very, very cold. She took me up the Fell path, up to the holly trees; and there I saw a lady weeping and crying; but when she saw me, she hushed her weeping, and smiled very proud and grand, and took me on her knee, and began to lull me to sleep; and that's all, Hester—but that is true, and my dear mamma knows it is," said she, crying. So I thought the child was in a fever, and pretended to believe her, as she went over her story—over and over again, and always the same. At last Dorothy knocked at the door with Miss Rosamond's breakfast; and she told me the old ladies were down in the eating-parlour, and that they wanted to speak to me. They had both been into the night-nursery the evening before, but it was after Miss Rosamond was asleep; so they had only looked at her—not asked me any questions.

"I shall catch it," thought I to myself, as I went along the north gallery. "And yet," I thought, taking courage, "it was in their charge I left her; and it's they that's to blame for letting her steal away unknown and unwatched." So I went in boldly and told my story. I told it all to Miss Furnivall, shouting it close to her ear; but when I came to the mention of the other little girl out in the snow, coaxing and tempting her out, and willing her up to the grand and beautiful lady by the holly tree, she threw her arms up—her old and withered arms—and cried aloud, "Oh! Heaven, forgive! Have mercy!"

Mrs. Stark took hold of her; roughly enough, I thought; but she was past Mrs. Stark's management, and spoke to me, in a kind of wild warning and authority.

"Hester, keep her from that child! It will lure her to her death! That evil child! Tell her it is a wicked, naughty child." Then Mrs. Stark hurried me out of the room; where, indeed, I was glad enough to go; but Miss Furnivall kept shrieking out, "Oh! have mercy! Wilt Thou never forgive! It is many a long year ago—"

I was very uneasy in my mind after that. I durst never leave Miss Rosamond, night or day, for fear lest she might slip off again, after some fancy or other; and all the more because I thought I could make out that Miss Furnivall was crazy, from their odd ways about her; and I was afraid lest something of the same kind (which might be in the family, you know) hung over my darling. And the great frost never ceased all this time; and whenever it was a more stormy night than usual, between the gusts, and through the wind, we heard the old lord playing on the great organ. But, old lord or not, wherever Miss Rosamond went, there I followed; for my love for her, pretty, helpless orphan, was stronger than fear for the grand and terrible sound. Besides, it rested with me to keep her cheerful and merry, as beseemed her age. So we played together, and wandered together, here and there, and everywhere; for I never dared to lose sight of her again in that large and rambling house. And so it happened, that one afternoon, not long before Christmas Day, we were playing together on the billiard-table in the great hall (not that we knew the way of playing, but she liked to roll the smooth, ivory balls with her pretty hands, and I liked to do whatever she did); and, by and by, without our noticing it, it grew dusk indoors, though it was still light in the open air, and I was thinking of taking her back into the nursery, when, all of a sudden, she cried out:

"Look! Hester, look! there is my poor little girl out in the snow!"

I turned towards the long narrow windows, and there, sure enough, I saw a little girl, less than my Miss Rosamond—dressed all unfit to be out of doors such a bitter night—crying, and beating against the window-panes, as if she wanted to be let in. She seemed to sob and wail, till Miss Rosamond could bear it no longer, and was flying to the door to open it, when, all of a sudden, and close up upon us, the great organ pealed out so loud and thundering, it fairly made me tremble; and all the more, when I remembered me that, even in the stillness of that dead-cold weather, I had heard no sound of little battering hands upon the window glass, although the Phantom Child had seemed to put forth all its force; and, although I had seen it wail and cry, no faintest touch of sound had fallen upon my ears. Whether I remembered all this at the very moment, I do not know; the great organ sound had so stunned me into terror; but this I know: I caught up Miss Rosamond before she got the hall door opened, and clutched her, and carried her away, kicking and screaming, into the large bright kitchen, where Dorothy and Agnes were busy with their mince pies.

"What is the matter with my sweet one?" cried Dorothy, as I bore in Miss Rosamond, who was sobbing as if her heart would break.

"She won't let me open the door for my little girl to come in; and she'll die if she is out on the Fells all night. Cruel, naughty Hester," she said, slapping me; but she might have struck harder, for I had seen a look of ghastly terror on Dorothy's face, which made my very blood run cold.

"Shut the back-kitchen door fast, and bolt it well," said she to Agnes. She said no more; she gave me raisins amd almonds to quiet Miss Rosamond: but she sobbed about the little girl in the snow, and would not touch any of the good things. I was thankful when she cried herself to sleep in bed. Then I stole down to the kitchen and told Dorothy I had made up my mind. I would carry my darling back to my father's house in Applethwaite; where, if we lived humbly, we lived at peace. I said I had been frightened enough with the old lord's organ-playing; but now that I had seen for myself this little moaning child, all decked out as no child in the neighbourhood could be, beating and battering to get in, yet always without any sound or noise—with the dark wound on her right shoulder; and that Miss Rosamond had known it again for the phantom that had nearly lured her to her death (which Dorothy knew was true); I would stand it no longer.

I saw Dorothy change colour once or twice. When I had done she told me she did not think I could take Miss Rosamond with me, for that she was my lord's ward, and I had no right over her; and she asked me, would I leave the child that I was so fond of just for sounds and sights that could do me no harm; and that they had all had to get used to in their turns? I was all in a hot, trembling passion; and I said it was very well for her to talk, that knew what these sights and noises betokened, and that had, perhaps, had something to do with the Spectre-Child while it was alive. And I taunted her so, that she told me all she knew, at last, and then I wished I had never been told, for it only made me afraid more than ever.

She said she had heard the tale from old neighbours, that were alive when she was first married; when folks used to come to the hall sometimes, before it had got such a bad name on the country-side: it might not be true, or it might, what she had been told.

The old lord was Miss Furnivall's father—Miss Grace as Dorothy called her, for Miss Maude was the elder, and Miss Furnivall by rights. The old lord was eaten up with pride. Such a proud man was never seen or heard of; and his daughters were like him. No one was good enough to wed them, although they had choice enough; for they were the great beauties of their day, as I had seen by their portraits where they hung in the state drawing-room. But, as the old saying is, "Pride will have a fall"; and these two haughty beauties fell in love with the same man, and he no better than a foreign musician whom their father had down from London to play music with him at the Manor House. For above all things, next to his pride, the old lord loved music. He could play on nearly every instrument that ever was heard of: and it was a strange thing it did not soften him; but he was a fierce, dour old man, and had broken his poor wife's heart with his cruelty, they said. He was mad after music, and would pay any money for it. So he got this foreigner to come; who made such beautiful music, that they said the very birds on the trees stopped their singing to listen. And, by degrees, this foreign gentleman got such a hold over the old lord that nothing would serve him but that he must come every year; and it was he that had the great organ brought from Holland and built up in the hall, where it stood now.

He taught the old lord to play on it; but many and many a time, when Lord Furnivall was thinking of nothing but his fine organ, and his finer music, the dark foreigner was walking abroad in the woods with one of the young ladies; now Miss Maude, and then Miss Grace.

Miss Maude won the day and carried off the prize—such as it was; and he and she were married, all unknown to anyone; and before he made his next yearly visit, she had been confined of a little girl at a farm-house on the Moors, while her father and Miss Grace thought she was away at Doncaster Races. But though she was a wife and a mother she was not a bit softened, but as haughty and as passionate as ever; and perhaps more so, for she was jealous of Miss Grace, to whom her foreign husband paid a deal of court—by way of blinding her—as he told his wife. But Miss Grace triumphed over Miss Maude, and Miss Maude grew fiercer and fiercer, both with her husband and with her sister; and the former—who could easily shake off what was disagreeable, and hide himself in foreign countries—went away a month before his usual time that summer, and half threatened that he would never come back again.

Meanwhile, the little girl was left at the farm-house, and her mother used to have her horse saddled and gallop wildly over the hills to see her once every week at the very least—for where she loved, she loved; and where she hated, she hated. And the old lord went on playing—playing on his organ; and the servants thought the sweet music he made had soothed down his awful temper, of which (Dorothy said) some terrible tales could be told. He grew infirm too, and had to walk with a crutch; and his son—that was the present Lord Furnivall's father—was with the army in America, and the other son at sea; so Miss Maude had it pretty much her own way, and she and Miss Grace grew colder and bitterer to each other every day; till at last they hardly ever spoke, except when the old lord was by. The foreign musician came again the next summer, but it was for the last time; for they led him such a life with their jealousy and their passions that he grew weary, and went away, and never was heard of again. And Miss Maude, who had always meant to have her marriage acknowledged when her father should be dead, was left now a deserted wife—whom nobody knew to have been married—with a child that she dared not own, although she loved it to distraction; living with a father whom she feared, and a sister whom she hated.

When the next summer passed over and the dark foreigner never came, both Miss Maude and Miss Grace grew gloomy and sad; they had a haggard look about them, though they looked handsome as ever. But by and by Miss Maude brightened; for her father grew more and more infirm, and more than ever carried away by his music; and she and Miss

Grace lived almost entirely apart, having separate rooms, the one on the west side, Miss Maude on the east—those very rooms which were now shut up. So she thought she might have her little girl with her, and no one need ever know except those who dared not speak about it, and were bound to believe that it was, as she said, a cottager's child she had taken a fancy to. All this, Dorothy said, was pretty well known; but what came afterwards no one knew, except Miss Grace and Mrs. Stark, who was even then her maid, and much more of a friend to her than ever her sister had been. But the servants supposed, from words that were dropped, that Miss Maude had triumphed over Miss Grace, and told her that all the time the dark foreigner had been mocking her with pretended love he was her own husband; the colour left Miss Grace's cheek and lips that very day for ever, and she was heard to say many a time that sooner or later she would have her revenge; and Mrs. Stark was for every spying about the east rooms.

One fearful night, just after the New Year had come in, when the snow was lying thick and deep, and the flakes were still falling—fast enough to blind any one who might be out and abroad—there was a great and violent noise heard, and the old lord's voice above all, cursing and swearing awfully; and the cries of a little child; and the proud defiance of a fierce woman; and the sound of a blow; and a dead stillness;

and moans and waitings dying away on the hillside! Then
the old lord summoned all his servants, and told them, with
terrible oaths, and words more terrible, that his daughter had
disgraced herself, and that he had turned her out of doors—
her, and her child—and that if ever they gave her help,
or food, or shelter, he prayed that they might never enter
heaven. And, all the while, Miss Grace stood by him, white
and still as any stone; and when he had ended she heaved a
great sigh, as much as to say her work was done, and her end
was accomplished. But the old lord never touched his organ
again, and died within the year; and no wonder! for, on the
morrow of that wild and fearful night, the shepherds coming
down the Fell side, found Miss Maude sitting all crazy and
smiling, under the holly trees, nursing a dead child—with a
terrible mark on its right shoulder. "But that was not what
killed it," said Dorothy; "it was the frost and the cold. Every
wild creature was in its hole, and every beast in its fold—
while the child and its mother were turned out to wander
on the Fells! And now you know all, and I wonder if you are
less frightened now?"

I was more frightened than ever; but I said I was not. I
wished Miss Rosamond and myself well out of that dreadful
house for ever; but I would not leave her, and I dared not
take her away. But oh! how I watched her, and guarded her!
We bolted the doors and shut the window-shutters fast, and

an hour or more before dark rather than leave them open five minutes too late. But my little lady still heard the weird child crying and mourning; and not all we could do or say could keep her from wanting to go to her, and let her in from the cruel wind and the snow. All this time, I kept away from Miss Furnivall and Mrs. Stark as much as ever I could; for I feared them—I knew no good could be about them, with their grey, hard faces, and their dreamy eyes looking back into the ghastly years that were gone. But, even in my fear, I had a kind of pity—for Miss Furnivall, at least. Those gone down to the pit can hardly have a more hopeless look than that which was ever on her face. At last I even got so sorry for her—who never said a word but what was quite forced from her—that I prayed for her; and I taught Miss Rosamond to pray for one who had done a deadly sin; but often, when she came to those words, she would listen, and start up from her knees, and say, "I hear my little girl plaining and crying very sad—Oh! let her in, or she will die!"

One night—just after New Year's Day had come at last, and the long winter had taken a turn, as I hoped—I heard the west drawing-room bell ring three times, which was a signal for me. I would not leave Miss Rosamond alone, for all she was asleep—for the old lord had been playing wilder than ever—and I feared lest my darling should waken to hear the Spectre-Child; see her I knew she could not—I had fastened the windows too well for that. So I took her out of her bed and wrapped her up in such outer clothes as were most handy, and carried her down to the drawing-room, where the old ladies sat at their tapestry-work as usual. They looked up when I came in, and Mrs. Stark asked, quite astounded, "Why did I bring Miss Rosamond there, out of her warm bed?" I had begun to whisper, "Because I was afraid of her being tempted out while I was away, by the wild child in the snow," when she stopped me short (with a glance at Miss Furnivall), and said Miss Furnivall wanted me to undo some work she had done wrong, and which neither of them could see to unpick. So I laid my pretty dear on the sofa, and sat down on a stool by them, and hardened my heart against them, as I heard the wind rising and howling.

Miss Rosamond slept on sound, for all the wind blew so; and Miss Furnivall said never a word, nor looked round when the gusts shook the windows. All at once she started up to her full height, and put up one hand, as if to bid us listen.

"I hear voices!" said she, "I hear terrible screams—I hear my father's voice!"

Just at that moment my darling wakened with a sudden start: "My little girl is crying, oh, how she is crying!" and she tried to get up and go to her, but she got her feet entangled in the blanket, and I caught her up; for my flesh had begun to creep at these noises, which they heard while we could catch no sound. In a minute or two the noises came, gathered fast, and filled our ears; we, too, heard voices and screams, and no longer heard the winter's wind that raged abroad. Mrs. Stark looked at me, and I at her, but we dared not speak. Suddenly Miss Furnivall went towards the door, out into the ante-room, through the west lobby, and opened the door into the great hall. Mrs. Stark followed, and I durst not be left, though my heart almost stopped beating for fear. I wrapped my darling tight in my arms and went out with them. In the hall the screams were louder than ever; they sounded to come from the east wing—nearer and nearer—close on the other side of the locked-up doors—close behind them. Then I noticed that the great bronze chandelier seemed all alight, though the hall was dim, and that a fire was blazing in the vast hearth-place, though it gave no heat; and I shuddered up with terror, and folded my darling closer to me. But as I did so, the east door shook, and she, suddenly struggling to get free from me, cried, "Hester, I must go! My little girl is there; I hear her; she is coming! Hester, I must go!"

I held her tight with all my strength; with a set will, I held her. If I had died my hands would have grasped her still, I was so resolved in my mind. Miss Furnivall stood listening, and paid no regard to my darling, who had got down to the ground and whom I, upon my knees now, was holding with both my arms clasped round her neck; she still striving and crying to get free.

All at once the east door gave way with a thundering crash, as if torn open in a violent passion, and there came into that broad and mysterious light, the figure of a tall old man, with grey hair and gleaming eyes. He drove before him, with many a relentless gesture of abhorrence, a stern and beautiful woman, with a little child clinging to her dress.

"Oh, Hester! Hester!" cried Miss Rosamond. "It's the lady! the lady below the holly trees; and my little girl is with her. Hester! Hester! let me go to her; they are drawing me to them. I feel them, I feel them. I must go!"

Again she was almost convulsed by her efforts to get away; but I held her tighter and tighter, till I feared I should do her a hurt; but rather that than let her go towards those terrible phantoms. They passed along towards the great hall door, where the winds howled and ravened for their prey; but before they reached that, the lady turned; and I could see that she defied the old man with a fierce and proud defiance; but then she quailed—and then she threw up her arms wildly and piteously to save her child—her little child—from a blow from his uplifted crutch.

And Miss Rosamond was torn as by a power stronger than mine, and writhed in my arms, and sobbed (for by this time the poor darling was growing faint).

"They want me to go with them on to the Fells—they are drawing me to them. Oh, my little girl! I would come, but cruel, wicked Hester holds me very tight." But when she saw the uplifted crutch she swooned away, and I thanked God for it. Just at this moment—when the tall old man, his hair streaming as in the blast of a furnace, was going to strike the little shrinking child—Miss Furnivall, the old woman by my side cried out, "Oh, Father! Father! spare the little innocent child!" But just then I saw—we all saw—another phantom shape itself, and grow clear out of the blue and misty light that filled the hall; we had not seen her till now, for it was another lady who stood by the old man, with a look of relentless hate and triumphant scorn. That figure was very beautiful to look upon, with a soft white hat drawn down over the proud brows and a red and curling lip. It was dressed in an open robe of blue satin. I had seen that figure before. It was the likeness of Miss Furnivall in her youth; and the terrible phantoms moved on, regardless of old Miss Furnivall's wild entreaty—and the uplifted crutch fell on the right shoulder of the little child, and the younger sister looked on, stony and deadly serene. But at that moment the dim lights and the fire that gave no heat went out of themselves, and Miss Furnivall lay at our feet stricken down by the palsy—death stricken.

Yes, she was carried to her bed that night never to rise

again. She lay with her face to the wall muttering low but muttering always: "Alas! alas! what is done in youth can never be undone in age! What is done in youth can never be undone in age!"

THE PHANTOM COACH

Miss Amelia Edwards

The circumstances I am about to relate to you have truth to recommend them. They happened to myself, and my recollection of them is as vivid as if they had taken place only yesterday. Twenty years, however, have gone by since that night. During those twenty years I have told the story to but one other person. I tell it now with a reluctance which I find it difficult to overcome. All I entreat, meanwhile, is that you will abstain from forcing your own conclusions upon me. I want nothing explained away. I desire no arguments. My mind on this subject is quite made up, and, having the testimony of my own senses to rely upon, I prefer to abide by it.

Well! It was just twenty years ago, and within a day or two of the end of the grouse season. I had been out all day with my gun, and had had no sport to speak of. The wind was due east; the month, December; the place, a bleak wide moor in the far north of England. And I had lost my way. It was not a pleasant place in which to lose one's way, with the first feathery flakes of a coming snowstorm just fluttering down upon the heather, and the leaden evening closing in all round. I shaded my eyes with my hand, and stared anxiously into the gathering darkness, where the purple moorland melted into a range of low hills, some ten or twelve miles distant. Not the faintest smoke-wreath, not the tiniest cultivated patch, or fence, or sheep-track, met my eyes in any direction. There was nothing for it but to walk on, and take my chance of finding what shelter I could, by the way. So I shouldered my gun again, and pushed wearily forward; for I had been on foot since an hour after daybreak, and had eaten nothing since breakfast.

Meanwhile, the snow began to come down with ominous steadiness, and the wind fell. After this, the cold became more intense, and the night came rapidly up. As for me, my prospects darkened with the darkening sky, and my heart grew heavy as I thought how my young wife was already watching for me through the window of our little inn parlour, and thought of all the suffering in store for her throughout this weary night. We had been married four months, and, having spent our autumn in the Highlands, were now lodging in a remote little village situated just on the verge of the great English moorlands. We were very much in love, and, of course, very happy. This morning, when we parted, she had implored me to return before dusk, and I had promised her that I would. What would I not have given to have kept my word!

Even now, weary as I was, I felt that with a supper, an hour's rest, and a guide, I might still get back to her before midnight, if only guide and shelter could be found.

And all this time, the snow fell and the night thickened. I stopped and shouted every now and then, but my shouts seemed only to make the silence deeper. Then a vague sense of uneasiness came upon me, and I began to remember stories of travellers who had walked on and on in the falling snow until, wearied out, they were fain to lie down and sleep their lives away. Would it be possible, I asked myself, to keep on thus through all the long dark night? Would there not come a time when my limbs must fail and my resolution give way? When I, too, must sleep the sleep of death. Death! I shuddered. How hard to die just now, when life lay all so bright before me! How hard for my darling, whose whole loving heart—but that thought was not to be borne! To banish it, I shouted again, louder and longer, and then listened eagerly. Was my shout answered, or did I only fancy that I heard a far-off cry? I halloed again, and again the echo followed. Then a wavering speck of light came suddenly out of the dark, shifting, disappearing, growing momentarily nearer and brighter. Running towards it at full speed, I found myself to my great joy, face to face with an old man and a lantern.

"Thank God!" was the exclamation that burst involuntarily from my lips.

Blinking and frowning, he lifted his lantern and peered into my face.

"What for?" growled he, sulkily.

"Well—for you. I began to fear I should be lost in the snow."

"Eh, then, folks do get cast away hereabouts fra' time to time, an' what's to hinder you from bein' cast away likewise, if the Lord's so minded?"

"If the Lord is so minded that you and I shall be lost together, friend, we must submit," I replied; "but I don't mean to be lost without you. How far am I now from Dwolding?"

"A gude twenty mile, more or less."

"And the nearest village?"

"The nearest village is Wyke, an' that's twelve mile t'other side."

"Where do you live, then?"

"Out yonder," said he, with a vague jerk of the lantern.

"You're going home, I presume?"

"Maybe I am."

"Then I'm going with you."

The old man shook his head, and rubbed his nose reflectively with the handle of the lantern.

"It ain't o' no use," growled he. He 'ont let you in—not he."

"We'll see about that," I replied briskly. "Who is He?"

"The master."

"Who is the master?"

"That's nowt to you," was the unceremonious reply.

"Well, well; you lead the way, and I'll engage that the master shall give me shelter and a supper tonight."

"Eh, you can try him!" muttered my reluctant guide; and, still shaking his head, he hobbled, gnome-like, away through the falling snow. A large mass loomed up presently out of the darkness, and a huge dog rushed out, barking furiously.

"Is this the house?" I asked.

"Ay, it's the house. Down, Bey!" And he fumbled in his pocket for the key.

I drew up close behind him, prepared to lose no chance of entrance, and saw in the little circle of light shed by the lantern that the door was heavily studded with iron nails, like the door of a prison. In another minute he had turned the key and I had pushed past him into the house.

Once inside, I looked round with curiosity, and found myself in a great raftered hall, which served, apparently, a variety of uses. One end was piled to the roof with corn, like a barn. The other was stored with flour-sacks, agricultural implements, casks, and all kinds of miscellaneous lumber; while from the beams overhead hung rows of hams, flitches, and bunches of dried herbs for winter use. In the centre of the floor stood some huge object gauntly dressed in a dingy wrapping-cloth, and reaching half-way to the rafters. Lifting a corner of this cloth, I saw to my surprise, a telescope of very considerable size, mounted on a rude movable platform, with four small wheels. The tube was made of painted wood, bound round with bands of metal rudely fashioned; the speculum, so far as I could estimate its size in the dim light, measured at least fifteen inches in diameter. While I was yet examining the instrument, and asking myself whether it was not the work of some self-taught optician, a bell rang sharply.

"That's for you," said my guide, with a malicious grin, "Yonder's his room."

He pointed to a low black door at the opposite side of the hall, I crossed over, rapped somewhat loudly, and went in, without waiting for an invitation. A huge, white-haired old man rose from a table covered with books and papers, and confronted me sternly.

"Who are you?" said he. "How came you here? What do you want?"

"James Murray, barrister-at-law. On foot across the moor.

Meat, drink and sleep."

He bent his bushy brows into a portentous frown.

"Mine is not a house of entertainment," he said, haughtily. "Jacob, how dared you admit this stranger?"

"I didn't admit him," grumbled the old man. "He followed me over the muir, and shouldered his way in before me. I'm no match for six foot two."

"And pray, sir, by what right have you forced an entrance into my house?"

"The same by which I should have clung to your boat, if I were drowning. The right of self-preservation."

"Self-preservation?"

"There's an inch of snow on the ground already," I replied, briefly; "and it would be deep enough to cover my body before daybreak."

He strode to the window, pulled aside a heavy curtain, and looked out.

"It is true," he said. "You can stay, if you choose, till morning. Jacob, serve the supper."

With this he waved me to a seat, resumed his own, and became at once absorbed in the studies from which I had disturbed him.

I placed my gun in a corner, drew a chair to the hearth, and examined my quarters at leisure. Smaller and less incongruous in its arrangements than the hall this room contained, nevertheless, much to awaken my curiosity. The floor was carpetless. The whitewashed walls were in parts scrawled over with strange diagrams, and in others covered with shelves crowded with philosophical instruments, the uses of many of which were unknown to me. On one side of the fireplace, stood a bookcase filled with dingy folios; on the other, a small organ, fantastically decorated with painted carvings of medieval saints and devils. Through the half-opened door of a cupboard at the further end of the room, I saw a long array of geological specimens, surgical preparations, crucibles, retorts, and jars of chemicals; while on the mantleshelf beside me, amid a number of small objects, stood a model of the solar system, a small galvanic battery, and a microscope. Every chair had its burden. Every corner was heaped high with books. The very floor was littered over with maps, casts, papers, tracings, and learned lumber of all conceivable kinds.

I stared about me with an amazement increased by every fresh object upon which my eyes chanced to rest. So strange a room I had never seen; yet seemed it stranger still, to find such a room in a lone farmhouse amid those wild and solitary moors! Over and over again, I looked from my host to his surroundings, and from his surroundings back to my host, asking myself who and what he could be? His head was singularly fine; but it was more the head of a poet than of a philosopher. Broad in the temples, prominent over the eyes, and clothed with a rough profusion of perfectly white hair, it had all the ideality and much of the ruggedness that characterizes the head of Louis von Beethoven. There were the same deep lines about the mouth, and the same stern furrows in the brow. There was the same concentration of expression. While I was yet observing him, the door opened, and Jacob brought in the supper. His master then closed his book, rose, and with more courtesy of manner than he had yet shown, invited me to the table.

A dish of ham and eggs, a loaf of brown bread, and a bottle of admirable sherry, were placed before me.

"I have but the homeliest farmhouse fare to offer you, sir," said my entertainer. "Your appetite, I trust, will make up for the deficiencies of our larder."

I had already fallen upon the viands, and now protested, with the enthusiasm of a starving sportsman, that I had never eaten anything so delicious.

He bowed stiffly, and sat down to his own supper, which consisted, primitively, of a jug of milk and a basin of porridge. We ate in silence, and, when we had done, Jacob removed the tray. I then drew my chair back to the fireside. My host, somewhat to my surprise, did the same, and turning abruptly towards me, said:

"Sir, I have lived in strict retirement for three-and-twenty years. During that time, I have not seen as many strange faces, and I have not read a single newspaper. You are the first stranger who has crossed my threshold for more than four years. Will you favour me with a few words of information respecting that outer world from which I have parted company so long?"

"Pray interrogate me," I replied. "I am heartily at your service."

He bent his head in acknowledgement; leaned forward, with his elbows resting on his knees and his chin supported in the palms of his hands; stared fixedly into the fire; and proceeded to question me.

His inquiries related chiefly to scientific matters, with the later progress of which, as applied to the practical purposes of life, he was almost wholly unacquainted. No student of science myself, I replied as well as my slight information permitted; but the task was far from easy, and I was much relieved when, passing from interrogation to discussion, he began pouring forth his own conclusions upon the facts which I had been attempting to place before him. He talked, and I listened spellbound. He talked till I believe he almost forgot my presence, and only thought aloud. I had never heard anything like it then; I have never heard anything like it since. Familiar with all systems of all philosophies, subtle in analysis, bold in generalisation, he poured forth his thought in an uninterrupted stream, and, still leaning forward in the same moody attitude with his eyes fixed upon the fire, wandered from topic to topic, from speculation to speculation like an inspired dreamer. From practical science to mental philosophy; from electricity in the wire to electricity in the nerve; from Watts to Mesmer, from Mesmer to Reichenbach, from Reichenbach to Swedenborg, Spinoza, Condillac, Descartes, Berkeley, Aristotle, Plato, and the Magi and mystics of the East, were transitions which, however bewildering in their variety and scope, seemed easy and harmonious upon his lips as sequences in music. By-and-by—I forget now by what link of conjecture or illustration—he passed on to that field which lies beyond the boundary line of even conjectural philosophy, and reaches no man knows whither. He spoke of the soul and its aspirations; of the spirit and its powers; of second sight; of prophecy; of those phenomena which, under the names of ghosts, spectres, and supernatural appearances, have been denied by the sceptics and attested by the credulous of all ages.

"The world," he said, "grows hourly more and more sceptical of all that lies beyond its own narrow radius; and our men of science foster the fatal tendency. They condemn as fable all that resists experiment. They reject as false all that cannot be brought to the test of the laboratory or the dissecting-room. Against what superstition have they waged so long and obstinate a war, as against the belief in apparitions? And yet what superstition has maintained its hold upon the minds of men so long and so firmly? Show me any fact in physics, history, in archaeology, which is supported by testimony so wide and so various. Attested by all races of men, in all ages, and in all climates, by the soberest sages of antiquity, by the rudest savage of today, by the Christian, the Pagan, the Pantheist, the Materialist, this phenomenon is treated as a nursery tale by the philosophers of our century. Circumstantial evidence weighs with them as a feather in the balance. The comparison of causes with effects, however valuable in physical science, is put aside as worthless and unreliable. The evidence of competent witnesses, however conclusive in a court of justice, counts for nothing. He who pauses before he pronounces, is condemned as a trifler. He who believes, is a dreamer or a fool."

He spoke with bitterness, and, having said thus, relapsed for some minutes into silence. Presently he raised his head from his hands, and added, with an altered voice and manner:

"I, sir, paused, investigated, believed, and was not ashamed to state my convictions to the world. I, too, was branded as a visionary, held up to ridicule by my contemporaries, and hooted from that field of science in which I had laboured with honour during all the best years of my life. These things happened just three-and-twenty years ago. Since then, I have lived as you see me living now, and the world has forgotten me, as I have forgotten the world. You have my history."

"It is a very sad one," I murmured, scarcely knowing what to answer.

"It is a very common one," he replied. "I have only suffered for the truth, as many a better and wiser man has suffered before me.

He rose, as if desirous of ending the conversation, and went over to the window.

"It has ceased snowing," he observed, as he dropped the curtain, and came back to the fireside.

"Ceased!" I exclaimed, starting eagerly to my feet. "Oh, if it were only possible—but no! it is hopeless. Even if I could find my way across the moor, I could not walk twenty miles tonight."

"Walk twenty miles tonight!" repeated my host. "What are you thinking of?"

"Of my wife," I replied, impatiently. "Of my young wife, who does not know that I have lost my way, and who is at this moment breaking her heart with suspense and terror."

"Where is she?"

"At Dwolding, twenty miles away."

"At Dwolding," he echoed, thoughtfully. "Yes, the distance,

it is true, is twenty miles; but—are you so very anxious to save the next six or eight hours?"

"So very, very anxious, that I would give ten guineas at this moment for a guide and a horse."

"Your wish can be gratified at a less costly rate," said he, smiling. "The night mail from the north, which changes horses at Dwolding, passes within five miles of this spot, and will be due at a certain cross-road in about an hour and a quarter. If Jacob were to go with you across the moor, and put you into the old coach-road, you could find your way, I suppose, to where it joins the new one?"

"Easily—gladly."

He smiled again, rang the bell, gave the old servant his directions, and, taking a bottle of whiskey and a wineglass from the cupboard in which he kept his chemicals, said:

"The snow lies deep, and it will be difficult walking tonight on the moor. A glass of usquebaugh before you start?"

I would have declined the spirit, but he pressed it on me, and I drank it. It went down my throat like liquid flame, and almost took my breath away.

"It is strong," he said; "but it will keep out the cold. And now you have no moments to spare. Good night!"

I thanked him for his hospitality, and would have shaken hands, but that he had turned away before I could finish my sentence. In another minute I had traversed the hall, Jacob had locked the outer door behind me, and we were out on the wide white moor.

Although the wind had fallen, it was still bitterly cold. Not a star glimmered in the vault overhead. Not a sound, save the rapid crunching of the snow beneath our feet, disturbed the heavy stillness of the night. Jacob, not too well pleased with his mission, shambled on before in sullen silence, his lantern in his hand, and his shadow at his feet. I followed, with my gun over my shoulder, as little inclined for conversation as himself. My thoughts were full of my late host. His voice yet rang in my ears. His eloquence yet held my imagination captive. I remember to this day, with surprise, how my overexcited brain retained whole sentences and parts of sentences, troops of brilliant images, and fragments of splendid reasoning, in the very words in which he had uttered them. Musing thus over what I had heard, and striving to recall a lost link here and there, I strode on at the heels of my guide, absorbed and unobservant. Presently—at the end, as it seemed to me, of only a few minutes—he came to a sudden halt, and said:

"Yon's your road. Keep the stone fence to your right hand, and you can't fail of the way."

"This, then, is the old coach-road?"

"Ay, 'tis the old coach-road."

"And how far do I go, before I reach the cross-roads?"

"Nigh upon three mile."

I pulled out my purse, and he became more communicative.

"The road's a fair road enough," said he, "for foot passengers; but 'twas over steep and narrow for the northern traffic. You'll mind where the parapet's broken away, close again the sign-post. It's never been mended since the accident."

"What accident?"

"Eh, the night mail pitched right over into the valley below—a gude fifty feet an' more—just at the worst bit o' road in the whole country."

"Horrible! Were many lives lost?"

"All. Four were found dead, and t'other two died next morning."

"How long is it since this happened?"

"Just nine year."

"Near the sign-post, you say? I will bear it in mind. Good night."

"Gude night, sir, and thankee." Jacob pocketed his half-crown, made a faint pretence of touching his hat, and trudged back by the way he had come.

I watched the light of his lantern till it quite disappeared, and then turned to pursue my way alone. This was no longer matter of the slightest difficulty, for, despite the dead darkness overhead, the line of stone fence showed distinctly enough against the pale gleam of the snow. How silent it seemed now, with only my footsteps to listen to; how silent and how solitary! A strange disagreeable sense of loneliness stole over me. I walked faster. I hummed a fragment of a tune. I cast up enormous sums in my head, and accumulated them at compound interest. I did my best, in short, to forget the startling speculations to which I had but just been listening, and, to some extent, I succeeded.

Meanwhile, the night air seemed to become colder and colder, and though I walked fast I found it impossible to keep myself warm. My feet were like ice. I lost sensation in my hands, and grasped my gun mechanically. I even breathed with difficulty, as though, instead of traversing a quiet north-country highway, I were scaling the uppermost heights of some gigantic Alp. This last symptom became presently so distressing, that I was forced to stop for a few minutes, and lean against the stone fence. As I did so, I chanced to look back up the road, and there, to my infinite relief, I saw a distant point of light, like the gleam of an approaching lantern. I at first concluded that Jacob had retraced his steps and followed me; but even as the conjecture presented itself, a second light flashed into sight—a light evidently parallel with the first, and approaching at the same rate of motion. It needed no second thought to show me that these must be the carriage-lamps of some private vehicle, though it seemed strange that any private vehicle should take a rqgd professedly disused and dangerous.

There could be no doubt, however, of the fact, for the lamps grew larger and brighter every moment, and I even fancied I could already see the dark outline of the carriage between them. It was coming up very fast, and quite noiselessly, the snow being nearly a foot deep under the wheels.

And now the body of the vehicle became distinctly visible behind the lamps. It looked strangely lofty. A sudden suspicion flashed upon me. Was it possible that I had passed the cross-roads in the dark without observing the sign-post, and could this be the very coach which I had come to meet?

No need to ask myself that question a second time, for here it came round the bend of the road, guard and driver, one outside passenger, and four steaming greys, all wrapped in a soft haze of light, through which the lamps blazed out, like a pair of fiery meteors.

I jumped forward, waved my hat, and shouted. The mail came down at full speed, and passed me. For a moment I feared that I had not been seen or heard, but it was only for a moment. The coachman pulled up; the guard, muffled to the eyes in capes and comforters, and apparently sound asleep in the rumble, neither answered my hail nor made the slightest effort to dismount; the outside passenger did not even turn his head. I opened the door for myself, and looked in, There were but three travellers inside, so I stepped in, shut the door, slipped into the vacant corner, and congratulated myself on my good fortune.

The atmosphere of the coach seemed, if possible, colder than that of the outside air, and was pervaded by a singularly damp and disagreeable smell. I looked round at my fellow-passengers. They were all three men, and all silent. They did not seem to be asleep, but each leaned back in his corner of the vehicle, as if absorbed in his own reflections. I attempted to open a conversation.

"How intensely cold it is tonight," I said, addressing my opposite neighbour.

He lifted his head, looked at me, but made no reply.

"The winter," I added, "seems to have begun in earnest."

Although the corner in which he sat was so dim that I could distinguish none of his features very clearly, I saw that his eyes were still turned full upon me. And yet he answered never a word.

At any other time I should have felt, and perhaps expressed, some annoyance, but at the moment I felt too ill to do either. The icy coldness of the night air had struck a chill to my very marrow, and the strange smell inside the coach was affecting me with an intolerable nausea. I shivered from head to foot, and, turning to my left-hand neighbour, asked if he had any objection to an open window?

He neither spoke nor stirred.

I repeated the question more loudly, but with the same result. Then I lost patience, and let the sash down. As I did so the leather strap broke in my hand, and I observed that the glass was covered with a thick coat of mildew, the accumulation, apparently, of years. My attention being thus drawn to the condition of the coach, I examined it more narrowly, and saw by the uncertain light of the outer lamps that it was in the last stage of dilapidation. Every part of it was not only out of repair, but in a condition of decay. The sashes splintered at a touch. The leather fittings were crusted over with mould, and literally rotting from the woodwork. The floor was almost breaking away beneath my feet. The whole machine, in short, was foul with damp, and had evidently been dragged from some outhouse in which it had been mouldering away for years, to do another day or two of duty on the road.

I turned to the third passenger, whom I had not yet addressed, and hazarded one more remark.

"This coach," I said, "is in a deplorable condition. The regular mail, I suppose, is under repair?"

He moved his head slowly, and looked me in the face, without speaking a word. I shall never forget that look while I live. I turned cold at heart under it. I turn cold at heart even now when I recall it. His eyes glowed with a fiery unnatural lustre. His face was livid as the face of a corpse. His bloodless lips were drawn back as if in the agony of death, and showed the gleaming teeth between.

The words that I was about to utter died upon my lips, a strange horror—a dreadful horror—came upon me. My sight had by this time become used to the gloom of die coach, and I could see with tolerable distinctness. I turned to my opposite neighbour. He, too, was looking at me, with the same startling pallor in his face, and the same stony glitter in his eyes. I passed my hand across my brow. I turned to the passenger on the seat beside my own, and saw—oh heaven! how shall I describe what I saw? I saw that he was no living man—that none of them were living men, like myself! A pale phosphorescent light—the light of putrefaction—played upon their awful faces; upon their hair, dank with the dews of the grave; upon their clothes, earth-stained and dropping to pieces; upon their hands, which were as the hands of corpses long buried. Only their eyes, their terrible eyes, were living; and those eyes were all turned menacingly upon me!

A shriek of terror, a wild unintelligible cry for help and mercy, burst from my lips as I flung myself against the door, and strove in vain to open it.

In that single instant, brief and vivid as a landscape beheld in the flash of summer lightning, I saw the moon shining down through a rift of stormy cloud—the ghastly sign-post rearing its warning finger by the wayside—the broken parapet—the plunging horses—the black gulf below. Then, the coach reeled like a ship at sea. Then, came a mighty crash—a sense of crushing pain—and then, darkness.

It seemed as if years had gone by when I awoke one morning from a deep sleep, and found my wife watching by my bedside. I will pass over the scene that ensued, and give you, in half a dozen words, the tale she told me with tears of thanksgiving. I had fallen over a precipice, close against the junction of the old coach-road and the new, and had only been saved from certain death by lighting upon a deep snowdrift that had accumulated at the foot of the rock beneath. In this snowdrift I was discovered at daybreak, by a couple of shepherds, who carried me to the nearest shelter, and brought a surgeon to my aid. The surgeon found me in a state of raving delirium with a broken arm and a compound fracture of the skull. The letters in my pocket-book showed my name and address; my wife was summoned to nurse me; and, thanks to youth and a fine constitution, I came out of danger at last. The place of my fall, I need scarcely say, was precisely that at which a frightful accident had happened to the north mail nine years before.

I never told my wife the fearful events which I have just related to you. I told the surgeon who attended me; but he treated the whole adventure as a mere dream born of the fever in my brain. We discussed the question over and over again, until we found that we could discuss it with temper no longer, and then we dropped it. Others may form what conclusions they please—I *know* that twenty years ago I was the fourth inside passenger in that Phantom Coach.

THE LIFTED VEIL

Mary Ann Evans

I

The time of my end approaches. I have lately been subject to attacks of *angina pectoris*; and in the ordinary course of things, my physician tells me, I may fairly hope that my life will not be protracted many months. Unless, then, I am cursed with an exceptional physical constitution, as I am cursed with an exceptional mental character, I shall not much longer groan under the wearisome burden of this earthly existence. If it were to be otherwise—if I were to live on to the age most men desire and provide for—I should for once have known whether the miseries of delusive expectation can out-weigh the miseries of true prevision. For I foresee when I shall die, and everything that will happen in my last moments.

Just a month from this day, on September 20, 1850, I shall be sitting in this chair, in this study, at ten o'clock at night, longing to die, weary of incessant insight and foresight, without delusions and without hope. Just as I am watching a tongue of blue flame rising in the fire, and my lamp is burning low, the horrible contraction will begin in my chest. I shall only have time to reach the bell, and pull it violently, before the sense of suffocation will come. No one will answer my bell. I know why. My two servants are lovers, and will have quarrelled. My housekeeper will have rushed out of the house in a fury, two hours before, hoping that Perry will believe she has gone to drown herself. Perry is alarmed at last, and is gone out after her. The little scullery-maid is asleep on a bench: she never answers the bell; it does not wake her. The sense of suffocation increases: my lamp goes out with a horrible stench: I make a great effort, and snatch at the bell again. I long for life, and there is no help. I thirsted for the unknown: the thirst is gone. O God, let me stay with the known, and be weary of it. I am content. Agony of pain and suffocation—and all the while the earth, the fields, the pebbly brook at the bottom of the rookery, the fresh scent after the rain, the light of the morning through my chamber window, the warmth of the hearth after the frosty air—will darkness close over them for ever?

Darkness—darkness—no pain—nothing but darkness: but I am passing on and on through the darkness: my thought stays in the darkness, but always with a sense of moving onward . . .

Before that time comes, I wish to use my last hours of ease and strength in telling the strange story of my experience. I have never fully unbosomed myself to any human being; I have never been encouraged to trust much in the sympathy of my fellow men. But we have all a chance of meeting with some pity, some tenderness, some charity, when we are dead: it is the living only who cannot be forgiven—the living only from whom men's indulgence and reverence are held off, like the rain by the hard east wind. While the heart beats, bruise it—it is your only opportunity; while the eye can still turn towards you with moist, timid entreaty, freeze it with an icy unanswering gaze; while the ear, that delicate messenger to the inmost sanctuary of the soul, can still take in the tones of kindness, put it off with hard civility, or sneering compliment, or envious affectation of indifference; while the creative brain can still throb with the sense of injustice, with the yearning for brotherly recognition—make haste— oppress it with your ill-considered judgements, your trivial comparisons, your careless misrepresentations. The heart will by and by be still—*ubi saeva indignatio ulterius cor lacerare nequit*; the eye will cease to entreat; the ear will be deaf; the brain will have ceased from all wants as well as from all work. Then your charitable speeches may find vent; then you may remember and pity the toil and the struggle and the failure; then you may give due honour to the work achieved;

then you may find extenuation for errors, and may consent to bury them.

That is a trivial schoolboy text; why do I dwell on it? It has little reference to me, for I shall leave no works behind me for men to honour. I have no near relatives who will make up, by weeping over my grave, for the wounds they inflicted on me when I was among them. It is only the story of my life that will perhaps win a little more sympathy from strangers when I am dead, than I ever believed it would obtain from my friends while I was living.

My childhood perhaps seems happier to me than it really was, by contrast with all the after-years. For then the curtain of the future was as impenetrable to me as to other children: I had all their delight in the present hour, their sweet indefinite hopes for the morrow; and I had a tender mother: even now, after the dreary lapse of long years, a slight trace of sensation accompanies the remembrance of her caress as she held me on her knee—her arms round my little body, her cheek pressed on mine. I had a complaint of the eyes that made me blind for a little while, and she kept me on her knee from morning till night. That unequalled love soon vanished out of my life, and even to my childish consciousness it was as if that life had become more chill. I rode my little white pony with the groom by my side as before, but there were no loving eyes looking at me as I mounted, no glad arms opened to me when I came back. Perhaps I missed my mother's love more than most children of seven or eight would have done, to whom the other pleasures of life remained as before; for I was certainly a very sensitive child. I remember still the mingled trepidation and delicious excitement with which I was affected by the tramping of the horses on the pavement in the echoing stables, by the loud resonance of the grooms' voices, by the booming bark of the dogs as my father's carriage thundered under the archway of the courtyard, by the din of the gong as it gave notice of luncheon and dinner. The measured tramp of soldiery which I sometimes heard—for my father's house lay near a county town where there were large barracks—made me sob and tremble; and yet when they were gone past, I longed for them to come back again.

I fancy my father thought me an odd child, and had little fondness for me; though he was very careful in fulfilling what he regarded as a parent's duties. But he was already past the middle of life, and I was not his only son. My mother had been his second wife, and he was five-and-forty when he married her. He was a firm, unbending, intensely orderly man, in root and stem a banker, but with a flourishing graft of the active landholder, aspiring to county influence: one of those people who are always like themselves from day to day, who are uninfluenced by the weather, and neither know melancholy nor high spirits. I held him in great awe, and appeared more timid and sensitive in his presence than at other times; a circumstance which, perhaps, helped to confirm him in the intention to educate me on a different plan from the prescriptive one with which he had complied in the case of my elder brother, already a tall youth at Eton. My brother was to be his representative and successor; he must go to Eton and Oxford, for the sake of making connexions, of course: my father was not a man to underrate the bearing of Latin satirists or Greek dramatists on the attainment of an aristocratic position. But intrinsically, he had slight esteem for "those dead but sceptred spirits"; having qualified himself for forming an independent opinion by reading Potter's *Aeschylus*, and dipping into Francis's *Horace*. To this negative view he added a positive one, derived from a recent connexion with mining speculations; namely, that a scientific education was the really useful training for a younger son. Moreover, it was clear that a shy, sensitive boy like me was not fit to encounter the rough experience of a public school. Mr. Letherall had said so very decidedly. Mr. Letherall was a large man in spectacles, who one day took my small head between his large hands, and pressed it here and there in an exploratory, suspicious manner—then placed each of his great thumbs on my temples, and pushed me a little way from him, and stared at me with glittering spectacles. The contemplation appeared to displease him, for he frowned sternly, and said to my father, drawing his thumbs across my eyebrows—

"The deficiency is there, sir—there; and here," he added, touching the upper sides of my head, "here is the excess. That must be brought out, sir, and this must be laid to sleep."

I was in a state of tremor, partly at the vague idea that I was the object of reprobation, partly in the agitation of my first hatred—hatred of this big, spectacled man, who pulled my head about as if he wanted to buy and cheapen it.

I am not aware how much Mr. Letherall had to do with the system afterwards adopted towards me, but it was presently clear that private tutors, natural history, science, and the modern languages, were the appliances by which the defects of my organisation were to be remedied. I was very stupid about machines, so I was to be greatly occupied with them: I had no memory for classification, so it was particularly necessary that I should study systematic zoology and botany; I was hungry for human deeds and humane motions, so I was to be plentifully crammed with the mechanical powers, the elementary bodies, and the phonomena of electricity and magnetism. A better-constituted boy would certainly have profited under my intelligent tutors, with their scientific apparatus; and would, doubtless, have found the phenomena of elecricity and magnetism as fascinating as I was, every

Thursday, assured they were. As it was, I could have paired off, for ignorance of whatever was taught me, with the worst Latin scholar that was ever turned out of a classical academy. I read Plutarch, and Shakespeare, and Don Quixote by the sly, and supplied myself in that way with wandering thoughts, while my tutor was assuring me that "an improved man, as distinguished from an ignorant one, was a man who knew the reason why water ran downhill." I had no desire to be this improved man; I was glad of the running water; I could watch it and listen to it gurgling among the pebbles and bathing the bright green water-plants, by the hour together. I did not want to know *why* it ran; I had perfect confidence that there were good reasons for what was so very beautiful.

There is no need to dwell on this part of my life. I have said enough to indicate that my nature was of the sensitive, unpractical order, and that it grew up in an uncongenial medium, which could never foster it into happy, healthy development. When I was sixteen I was sent to Geneva to complete my course of education; and the change was a very happy one to me, for the first sight of the Alps, with the setting sun on them, as we descended the Jura, seemed to me like an entrance into heaven; and the three years of my life there were spent in a perpetual sense of exaltation, as if from a draught of delicious wine, at the presence of Nature in all her awful loveliness. You will think, perhaps, that I must have been a poet, from this early sensibility to Nature. But my lot was not so happy as that. A poet pours forth his song and *believes* in the listening ear and answering soul, to which his song will be floated sooner or later. But the poet's sensibility without his voice—the poet's sensibility that finds no vent but in silent tears on the sunny bank, when the noonday light sparkles on the water, or in an inward shudder at the sound of harsh human tones, the sight of a cold human eye—this dumb passion brings with it a fatal solitude of soul in the society of one's fellowmen. My least solitary moments were those in which I pushed off in my boat, at evening, towards the centre of the lake; it seemed to me that the sky, and the glowing mountain-tops, and the wide blue water, surrounded me with a cherishing love such as no human face had shed on me since my mother's love had vanished out of my life. I used to do as Jean Jacques did—lie down in my boat and let it glide where it would, while I looked up at the departing glow leaving one mountain-top after the other, as if the prophet's chariot of fire were passing over them on its way to the home of light. Then, when the white summits were all sad and corpse-like, I had to push homeward, for I was under careful surveillance, and was allowed no late wanderings. This disposition of mine was not favourable to the formation of intimate friendships among the numerous youths of my own age who are always to be found studying at Geneva. Yet I made *one* such friendship; and, singularly enough, it was with a youth whose intellectual tendencies were the very reverse of my own. I shall call him Charles Meunier; his real surname—an English one, for he was of English extraction—having since become celebrated. He was an orphan, who lived on a miserable pittance while he pursued the medical studies for which he had a special genius. Strange! that with my vague mind, susceptible and unobservant, hating inquiry and given up to contemplation, I should have been drawn towards a youth whose strongest passion was science. But the bond was not an intellectual one; it came from a source that can happily blend the stupid with the brilliant, the dreamy with the practical: it came from community of feeling. Charles was poor and ugly, derided by Genevese *gamins*, and not acceptable in drawing-rooms. I saw that he was isolated, as I was, though from a different cause, and stimulated by a sympathetic resentment, I made timid advances towards him. It is enough to say that there sprang up as much comradeship between us as our different habits would allow; and in Charles's rare holidays we went up to the Saleve together, or took the boat to Vevay, while I listened dreamily to the monologues in which he unfolded his bold conceptions of future experiment and discovery. I mingled them confusedly in my thought with glimpses of blue water and delicate floating cloud, with the notes of birds and the distant glitter of the glacier. He knew quite well that my mind was half absent, yet he liked to talk to me in this way; for don't we talk of our hopes and our projects even to dogs and birds when they love us? I have mentioned this one friendship because of its connexion with a strange and terrible scene which I shall have to narrate in my subsequent life.

This happier life at Geneva was put an end to by a severe illness, which is partly a blank to me, partly a time of dimly-remembered suffering, with the presence of my father by my bed from time to time. Then came the languid monotony of convalescence, the days gradually breaking into variety and distinctness as my strength enabled me to take long and longer drives. On one of these more vividly remembered days, my father said to me, as he sat beside my sofa—

"When you are quite well enough to travel, Latimer, I shall take you home with me. The journey will amuse you and do you good, for I shall go through the Tyrol and Austria, and you will see many new places. Our neighbours, the Filmores, are come; Alfred will join us at Basle, and we shall all go together to Vienna, and back by Prague . . ."

My father was called away before he had finished his sentence, and he left my mind resting on the word *Prague*, with a strange sense that a new and wondrous scene was breaking upon me: a city under the broad sunshine, that seemed to me as if it were summer sunshine of a long-past century arrested in its course—unrefreshed for ages by dews of night, or the rushing rain-cloud; scorching the dusty, weary, time-eaten grandeur of a people doomed to live on in the stale repetition of memories, like deposed and superannuated kings in their regal gold inwoven tatters. The city looked so thirsty that the broad river seemed to me a sheet of metal; and the blackened statues, as I passed under their blank gaze, along the unending bridge, with their ancient garments and their saintly crowns, seemed to me the real inhabitants and owners of this place, while the busy, trivial men and women, hurrying to and fro, were a swarm of ephemeral visitants infesting it for a day. It is such grim, stony beings as these, I thought, who are the fathers of ancient faded children, in those tanned time-fretted dwellings that crowd the steep before me; who pay their court in the worn and crumbling pomp of the palace which stretches its monotonous length on the height; who worship wearily in the stifling air of the churches, urged by no fear or hope, but compelled by their doom to be ever old and undying, to live on in the rigidity of habit, as they live on in perpetual midday, without the repose of night or the new birth of morning.

A stunning clang of metal suddenly thrilled through me, and I became conscious of the objects in my room again: one of the fire-irons had fallen as Pierre opened the door to bring me my draught. My heart was palpitating violently, and I begged Pierre to leave my draught beside me; I would take it presently.

As soon as I was alone again, I began to ask myself whether I had been sleeping. Was this a dream—this wonderfully distinct vision—minute in its distinctness down to a patch of rainbow light on the pavement, transmitted through a coloured lamp in the shape of a star—of a strange city, quite unfamiliar to my imagination! I had seen no picture of Prague: it lay in my mind as a mere name, with vaguely-remembered historical associations—ill-defined memories of imperial grandeur and religious wars.

Nothing of this sort had ever occurred in my dreaming experience before, for I had often been humiliated because my dreams were only saved from being utterly disjointed and commonplace by the frequent terrors of nightmare. But I could not believe that I had been asleep, for I remembered distinctly the gradual breaking-in of the vision upon me, like the new images in a dissolving view, or the growing distinctness of the landscape as the sun lifts up the veil of the morning mist. And while I was conscious of this incipient vision, I was also conscious that Pierre came to tell my father Mr. Filmore was waiting for him, and that my father hurried out of the room. No, it was not a dream; was it—the thought was full of tremulous exultation—was it the poet's nature in me, hitherto only a troubled yearning sensibility, now manifesting itself suddenly as spontaneous creation? Surely it was in this way that Homer saw the plain of Troy, that Dante saw the abodes of the departed, that Milton saw the earthward flight of the Tempter. Was it that my illness had wrought some happy change in my organisation—given a firmer tension to my nerves—carried off some dull obstruction? I had often read of such effects—in works of fiction at least. Nay; in genuine biographies I had read of the subtilising or exalting influence of some diseases on the mental powers. Did not Novalis feel his inspiration intensified under the progress of consumption?

When my mind had dwelt for some time on this blissful idea, it seemed to me that I might perhaps test it by an exertion of my will. The vision had begun when my father was speaking of our going to Prague. I did not for a moment believe it was really a representation of that city; I believed—I hoped it was a picture that my newly liberated genius had painted in fiery haste, with the colours snatched from lazy memory. Suppose I were to fix my mind on some other place—Venice, for example, which was far more familiar to my imagination than Prague: perhaps the same sort of result would follow. I concentrated my thoughts on Venice; I stimulated my imagination with poetic memories, and strove to feel myself present in Venice, as I had felt myself in Prague. But in vain. I was only colouring the Canaletto engravings that hung in my old bedroom at home; the picture was a shifting one, my mind wandering uncertainly in search of more vivid images; I could see no accident of form or shadow without conscious labour after the necessary conditions. It was all prosaic effort, not rapt passivity, such as I had experienced half an hour before. I was discouraged; but I remembered that inspiration was fitful.

For several days I was in a state of excited expectation, watching for a recurrence of my new gift. I sent my thoughts ranging over my world of knowledge, in the hope that they would find some object which would send a re-awakening vibration through my slumbering genius. But no; my world remained as dim as ever, and that flash of strange light refused to come again, though I watched for it with palpitating eagerness.

Mrs. Margaret Oliphant, gentle and quietly-spoken, wrote the most hair-raising stories.

Mrs. Elizabeth Gaskell, prim and pretty wife of a noted Victorian humanitarian.

Mrs. Charlotte Eliza Riddell was and outstanding writer of macabre stories.

Mary Ann Evans, who wrote under the name of George Eliot, a well- known novelist.

Illustrated heading for a vampire story by Miss Mary Braddon, published in 1896.

The brilliant Victorian artist, George Cruikshank, illustrated several macabre tales by women—here is a typical example of his extraordinary and evocative skill entitled *The Death of Lady Rookwood*.

My father accompanied me every day in a drive and a gradually lengthening walk as my powers of walking increased; and one evening he had agreed to come and fetch me at twelve the next day, that we might go together to select a musical box, and other purchases rigorously demanded of a rich Englishman visiting Geneva. He was one of the most punctual of men and bankers, and I was always nervously anxious to be quite ready for him at the appointed time. But, to my surprise, at a quarter past twelve he had not appeared. I felt all the impatience of a convalescent who has nothing particular to do, and who has just taken a tonic in the prospect of immediate exercise that would carry off the stimulus.

Unable to sit still and reserve my strength, I walked up and down the room, looking out on the current of the Rhone, just where it leaves the dark-blue lake; but thinking all the while of the possible causes that could detain my father.

Suddenly I was conscious that my father was in the room, but not alone: there were two persons with him. Strange! I had heard no footsteps, I had not seen the door open; but I saw my father, and at his right hand our neighbour Mrs. Filmore, whom I remembered very well, though I had not seen her for five years. She was a commonplace middle aged woman, in silk and cashmere; but the lady on the left of my father was not more than twenty, a tall, slim, willowy figure with luxuriant blond hair, arranged in cunning braids and folds that looked almost too massive for the slight figure and the small-featured, thin-lipped face they crowned. But the face had not a girlish expression: the features were sharp, the pale grey eyes at once acute, restless, and sarcastic. They were fixed on me in half-smiling curiosity, and I felt a painful sensation as if a sharp wind were cutting me. The pale-green dress, and the green leaves that seemed to form a border about her pale blond hair, made me think of a Water-Nixie—for my mind was full of German lyrics, and this pale, fatal-eyed woman, with the green weeds, looked like a birth from some cold sedgy stream, the daughter of an aged river.

"Well, Latimer, you thought me long," my father said . . .

But while the last word was in my ears, the whole group vanished, and there was nothing between me and the Chinese painted folding-screen that stood before the door. I was cold and trembling; I could only totter forward and throw myself on the sofa. This strange new power had manifested itself again . . . But *was* it a power? Might it not rather be a disease—a sort of intermittent delirium, concentrating my energy of brain into moments of unhealthy activity, and leaving my saner hours all the more barren? I felt a dizzy sense of unreality in what my eye rested on; I grasped the bell convulsively, like one trying to free himself from nightmare, and rang it twice. Pierre came with a look of alarm in his face.

"Monsieur ne se trouve pas bien?" he said anxiously.

"I'm tired of waiting, Pierre," I said, as distinctly and emphatically as I could, like a man determined to be sober in spite of wine; "I'm afraid something has happened to my father—he's usually so punctual. Run to the Hotel des Bergues and see if he is there."

Pierre left the room at once, with a soothing " *Bien, Monsieur"*; and I felt the better for this scene of simple, walking prose. Seeking to calm myself still further, I went into my bedroom, adjoining the *salon*, and opened a case of *eau-de-Cologne*; took out a bottle; went through the process of taking out the cork very neatly, and then rubbed the reviving spirit over my hands and forehead, and under my nostrils, drawing a new delight from the scent because I had procured it by slow details of labour, and by no strange sudden madness. Already I had begun to taste someting of the horror that belongs to the lot of a human being whose nature is not adjusted to simple human conditions.

Still enjoying the scent, I returned to the *salon*, but it was not unoccupied, as it had been before I left it. In front of the Chinese folding-screen there was my father, with Mrs. Filmore on his right hand, and on his left—the slim, blond-haired girl, with the keen face and the keen eyes fixed on me in half-smiling curiosity.

"Well, Latimer, you thought me long," my father said . . .

I heard no more, felt no more, till I became conscious that I was lying with my head low on the sofa, Pierre and my father by my side. As soon as I was thoroughly revived, my father left the room, and presently returned, saying—

"I've been to tell the ladies how you are, Latimer. They were waiting in the next room. We shall put off our shopping expedition today."

Presently he said, "That young lady is Bertha Grant, Mrs Filmore's orphan niece. Filmore has adopted her, and she lives with them, so you will have her for a neighbour, when we go home—perhaps for a near relation; for there is a tenderness between her and Alfred, I suspect, and I should be gratified by the match, since Filmore means to provide for her in every way as if she were his daughter. It had not occurred to me that you knew about her living with the Filmores."

He made no further allusion to the fact of my having fainted at the moment of seeing her, and I would not for the world have told him the reason: I shrank from the idea of disclosing to any one what might be regarded as a pitiable peculiarity, most of all from betraying it to my father, who would have suspected my sanity ever after.

I do not mean to dwell with particularity on the details

of my experience. I have described these two cases at length, because they had definite, clearly traceable results in my after-lot.

Shortly after this last occurrence—I think the very next day—I began to be aware of a phase in my abnormal sensibility, to which, from the languid and slight nature of my intercourse with others since my illness, I had not been alive before. This was the obtrusion on my mind of the mental process going forward in first one person, and then another, with whom I happened to be in contact: the vagrant, frivolous ideas and emotions of some uninteresting acquaintance— Mrs. Filmore, for example—would force themselves on my consciousness like an importunate, ill-played musical instrument, or the loud activity of an imprisoned insect. But this unpleasant sensibility was fitful, and left me moments of rest, when the souls of my companions were once more shut out from me, and I felt a relief such as silence brings to wearied nerves. I might have believed this importunate insight to be merely a diseased activity of the imagination, but that my prevision of incalculable words and actions proved it to have a fixed relation to the mental process in other minds. But this superadded consciousness, wearying and annoying enough when it urged on me the trivial experience of indifferent people, became an intense pain and grief when it seemed to be opening to me the souls of those who were in a close relation to me—when the rational talk, the graceful attentions, the wittily-turned phrases, and the kindly deeds, which used to make the web of their characters, were seen as if thrust asunder by a microscope vision, that showed all the intermediate frivolities, all the suppressed egoism, all the struggling chaos of puerilities, meanness, vague capricious memories, and indolent make-shift thoughts, from which human words and deeds emerge like leaflets covering a fermenting heap.

At Basle we were joined by my brother Alfred, now a handsome, self-confident man of six-and-twenty—a thorough contrast to my fragile, nervous, ineffectual self. I believe I was held to have a sort of half-womanish, half-ghostly beauty; for the portrait-painters, who are thick as weeds at Geneva, had often asked me to sit to them, and I had been the model of a dying minstrel in a fancy picture. But I thoroughly disliked my own physique and nothing but the belief that it was a condition of poetic genius would have reconciled me to it. That brief hope was quite fled, and I saw in my face now nothing but the stamp of a morbid organisation, framed for passive suffering—too feeble for the sublime resistance of poetic production. Alfred, from whom I had been almost constantly separated, and who, in his present stage of character and appearance, came before me as a perfect stranger, was bent on being extremely friendly and brother-like to me. He had the superficial kindness of a good-humoured, self-satisfied nature, that fears no rivalry, and has encountered no contrarieties. I am not sure that my disposition was good enough for me to have been quite free from envy towards him, even if our desires had not clashed, and if I had been in the healthy human condition which admits of generous confidence and charitable construction. There must always have been an antipathy between our natures. As it was, he became in a few weeks an object of intense hatred to me; and when he entered the room, still more when he spoke, it was as if a sensation of grating metal had set my teeth on edge. My diseased consciousness was more intensely and continually occupied with his thoughts and emotions, than with those of any other person who came in my way. I was perpetually exasperated with the petty promptings of his conceit, with his love of patronage, with his self-complacent belief in Bertha Grant's passion for him, with his half-pitying contempt for me—seen not in the ordinary indications of intonation and phrase and slight action, which an acute and suspicious mind is on the watch for, but in all their naked skinless complication.

For we were rivals, and our desires clashed, though he was not aware of it. I have said nothing yet of the effect Bertha Grant produced in me on a nearer acquaintance. That effect was chiefly determined by the fact that she made the only exemption, among all the human beings about me, to my unhappy gift of insight. About Bertha I was always in a state of uncertainty: I could watch the expression of her face, and speculate on its meaning; I could ask for her opinion with the real interest of ignorance; I could listen for her words and watch for her smile with hope and fear: she had for me the fascination of an unravelled destiny. I say it was this fact that chiefly determined the strong effect she produced on me: for, in the abstract, no womanly character could seem to have less affinity for that of a shrinking, romantic, passionate youth than Bertha's. She was keen, sarcastic, unimaginative, prematurely cynical, remaining critical and unmoved in the most impressive scenes, inclined to dissect all my favourite poems, and especially contemptuous towards the German lyrics which were my pet literature at that time. To this moment I am unable to define my feeling towards her: it was not ordinary boyish admiration, for she was the very opposite, even to the colour of her hair, of the ideal woman who still remained to me the type of loveliness; and she was without that enthusiasm for the great and good, which, even at the moment of her strongest dominion over me, I should have declared to be the highest element of character. But there is no tyranny more complete than that which a self-centered negative nature exercises over a morbidly sensitive nature perpetually craving sympathy and support. The most independent people feel the effect of a man's silence in heightening their value for his opinion—feel an additional triumph in conquering the reverence of a critic habitually captious and satirical: no wonder, then, that an enthusiastic self-distrusting youth should watch and wait before the closed secret of a sarcastic woman's face, as if it were the shrine of the doubtfully benignant deity who ruled his destiny. For a young enthusiast is unable to imagine the total negation in another mind of the emotions which are stirring his own; they may be feeble, latent, inactive, he thinks, but they are there—they may be called forth; sometimes, in moments of happy hallucination, he believes they may be there in all the greater strength because he sees no outward sign of them. And this effect, as I have intimated, was heightened to its utmost intensity in me, because Bertha was the only being who remained for me in the mysterious seclusion of soul that renders such youthful delusion possible. Doubtless there was another sort of fascination at work—that subtle physical attraction which delights in cheating our psychological predictions, and in compelling the men who paint sylphs, to fall in love with some *bonne et brave femme*, heavy-heeled and freckled.

Bertha's behaviour towards me was such as to encourage all my illusions, to heighten my boyish passion, and make me more and more dependant on her smiles. Looking back with my present wretched knowledge, I conclude that her vanity and love of power were intensely gratified by the belief that I had fainted on first seeing her purely from the strong impression her person had produced on me. The most prosaic woman likes to believe herself the object of a violent, a poetic passion; and without a grain of romance in her Bertha had that spirit of intrigue which gave piquancy to the idea that the brother of the man she meant to marry was dying with love and jealousy for her sake. That she meant to marry my brother, was what at that time I did not believe; for though he was assiduous in his attentions to her, and I knew well enough that both he and my father had made up their minds to this result, there was not yet an understood engagement—there had been no explicit declaration; and Bertha habitually, while she flirted with my brother, and accepted his homage in a way that implied to him a thorough recognition of its intention, made me believe, by the subtlest looks and phrases—feminine nothings which could never be quoted against her—that he was really the object of her secret ridicule; that she thought him, as I did, a coxcomb, whom she would have pleasure in disappointing. Me she openly petted in my brother's presence, as if I were too young and sickly ever to be thought of as a lover; and that was the view he took of me. But I believe she must inwardly have delighted in the tremors into which she threw me by the coaxing way in which she patted my curls, while she laughed at my quotations. Such caresses were always given in the presence of our friends; for when we were alone together, she affected a much greater distance towards me, and now and then took the opportunity, by words or slight actions, to stimulate my foolish timid hope that she really preferred me. And why should she not follow her inclination? I was not a year younger than she was, and she was an heiress, who would soon be of age to decide for herself.

The fluctuations of hope and fear, confined to this one channel, made each day in her presence a delicious torment. There was one deliberate act of hers which especially helped to intoxicate me. When we were at Vienna her twentieth birthday occurred, and as she was very fond of ornaments, we all took the opportunity of the splendid jewellers' shops in that Teutonic Paris to purchase her a birthday present of jewellery. Mine, naturally, was the least expensive; it was an opal ring—the opal was my favourite stone, because it seems to blush and turn pale as if it had a soul. I told Bertha so when I gave it her, and said that it was an emblem of the poetic nature, changing with the changing light of heaven and of woman's eyes. In the evening she appeared elegantly dressed and wearing conspicuously all the birthday presents except mine. I looked eagerly at her fingers, but saw no opal. I had no opportunity of noticing this to her during the evening;

but the next day, when I found her seated near the window alone, after breakfast, I said, "You scorn to wear my poor opal. I should have remembered that you despised poetic natures, and should have given you coral, or turquoise, or some other opaque unresponsive stone." "Do I despise it?" she answered, taking hold of a delicate gold chain which she always wore round her neck and drawing out the end from her bosom with my ring hanging to it; "it hurts me a little, I can tell you," she said, with her usual dubious smile, "to wear it in that secret place; and since your poetical nature is so stupid as to prefer a more public position, I shall not endure the pain any longer."

She took off the ring from the chain and put it on her finger, smiling still, while the blood rushed to my cheeks, and I could not trust myself to say a word of entreaty that she would keep the ring where it was before.

I was completely fooled by this, and for two days shut myself up in my room whenever Bertha was absent, that I might intoxicate myself afresh with the thought of this scene and all it implied.

I should mention that during these two months—which seemed a long life to me from the novelty and intensity of the pleasures and pains I underwent—my diseased participation in other peoples' consciousness continued to torment me; now it was my father, and now my brother, now Mrs. Filmore or her husband, and now our German courier, whose stream of thought rushed upon me like a ringing in the ears not to be got rid of, though it allowed my own impulses and ideas to continue their uninterrupted course. It was like a preternaturally heightened sense of hearing, making audible to one a roar of sound where others find perfect stillness. The weariness and disgust of this involuntary intrusion into other souls was counteracted only by my ignorance of Bertha, and my growing passion for her; a passion enormously stimulated, if not produced, by that ignorance. She was my oasis of mystery in the dreary desert of knowledge. I had never allowed my diseased condition to betray itself, or to drive me into any unusual speech or action, except once, when, in a moment of peculiar bitterness against my brother, I had forestalled some words which I knew he was going to utter—a clever observation, which he had prepared beforehand. He had occasionally a slightly-affected hesitation in his speech, and when he paused an instant after the second word, my impatience and jealousy impelled me to continue the speech for him, as if it were something we had both learned by rote. He coloured and looked astonished, as well as annoyed; and the words had no sooner escaped my lips than I felt a shock of alarm lest such an anticipation of words—very far from being words, of course, easy to divine—should have betrayed me as an exceptional being, a sort of quiet energumen, whom every one, Bertha above all, would shudder at and avoid. But I magnified, as usual, the impression any word or deed of mine could produce on others; for no one gave any sign of having noticed my interruption as more than a rudeness, to be forgiven me on the score of my feeble nervous condition.

While this superadded consciousness of the actual was almost constant with me, I had never had a recurrence of that distinct prevision which I have described in relation to my interview with Bertha; and I was waiting with eager curiosity to know whether or not my vision of Prague would prove to have been an instance of the same kind. A few days after the incident of the opal ring, we were paying one of our frequent visits to the Lichtenberg Palace. I could never look at many pictures in succession; for pictures, when they are at all powerful, affect me so strongly that one or two exhaust all my capability of contemplation. This morning I had been looking at Giorgione's picture of the cruel-eyed woman, said to be a likeness of Lucrezia Borgia. I had stood long alone before it, fascinated by the terrible reality of that cunning, relentless face, till I felt a strange poisoned sensation, as if I had long been inhaling a fatal odour, and was just beginning to be conscious of its effects. Perhaps even then I should not have moved away, if the rest of the party had not returned to this room, and announced that they were going to the

Belvedere Gallery to settle a bet which had arisen between my brother and Mr. Filmore about a portrait. I followed them dreamily, and was hardly alive to what occurred till they had all gone up to the gallery, leaving me below; for I refused to come within sight of another picture that day. I made my way to the Grand Terrace, since it was agreed that we should saunter in the gardens when the dispute had been decided. I had been sitting here a short space, vaguely conscious of trim gardens, with a city and green hills in the distance, when, wishing to avoid the proximity of the sentinel, I rose and walked down the broad stone steps, intending to seat myself farther on in the gardens. Just as I reached the gravel-walk, I felt an arm slipped within mine, and a light hand gently pressing my wrist. In the same instant a strange intoxicating numbness passed over me, like the continuance or climax of the sensation I was still feeling from the gaze of Lucrezia Borgia. The gardens, the summer sky, the consciousness of Bertha's arm being within mine, all vanished, and I seemed to be suddenly in darkness, out of which there gradually broke a dim firelight, and I felt myself sitting in my father's leather chair in the library at home. I knew the fireplace— the dogs for the wood-fire—the black marble chimney-piece with the white marble medallion of the dying Cleopatra in the centre, Intense and hopeless misery was pressing on my soul; the light became stronger, for Bertha was entering with a candle in her hand—Bertha, my wife—with cruel eyes, with green jewels and green leaves on her white ball-dress; every hateful thought within her present to me . . . "Madman, idiot! why don't you kill yourself, then?" It was a moment of hell. I saw into her pitiless soul—saw its barren worldliness, its scorching hate—and felt it clothe me round like an air I was obliged to breathe. She came with her candle and stood over me with a bitter smile of contempt; I saw the great emerald brooch on her bosom, a studded serpent with diamond eyes. I shuddered—I despised this woman with the barren soul and mean thoughts; but I felt helpless before her, as if she clutched my bleeding heart, and would clutch it till the last drop of life-blood ebbed away. She was my wife, and we hated each other. Gradually the hearth, the dim library, the candle-light disappeared—seemed to melt away into a background of light, the green serpent with the diamond eyes remaining a dark image on the retina. Then I had a sense of my eyelids quivering, and the living daylight broke in upon me; I saw gardens, and heard voices; I was seated on the steps of the Belvedere Terrace, and my friends were round me.

The tumult of mind into which I was thrown by this hideous vision made me ill for several days, and prolonged our stay in Vienna. I shuddered with horror as the scene recurred to me; and it recurred constantly, with all its minutiae, as if they had been burnt into my memory; and yet, such is the madness of the human heart under the influence of its immediate desires, I felt a wild hell-braving joy that Bertha was to be mine; for the fulfilment of my former prevision concerning her first appearance before me, left me little hope that this last hideous glimpse of the future was the mere diseased play of my own mind, and had no relation to external realities. One thing alone I looked towards as a possible means of casting doubt on my terrible conviction—the discovery that my vision of Prague had been false—and Prague was the next city on our route.

Meanwhile, I was no sooner in Bertha's society again, than I was as completely under her sway as before. What if I saw into the heart of Bertha, the matured woman—Bertha, my wife? Bertha, the *girl*, was a fascinating secret to me still: I trembled under her touch; I felt the witchery of her presence; I yearned to be assured of her love. The fear of poison is feeble against the sense of thirst. Nay, I was just as jealous of my brother as before—just as much irritated by his small patronising ways; for my pride, my diseased sensibility, were there as they had always been, and winced as inevitably under every offence as my eye winced from an intruding mote. The future, even when brought within the compass of feeling by a vision that made me shudder, had still no more than the force of an idea, compared with the force of present emotion—of my love for Bertha, of my dislike and jealousy towards my brother.

It is an old story, that men sell themselves to the tempter, and sign a bond with their blood, because it is only to take effect at a distant day; then rush on to snatch the cup their souls thirst after with an impulse not the less savage because there is a dark shadow beside them for evermore. There is no short cut, no patent tram-road, to wisdom: after all the centuries of invention, the soul's path lies through the thorny wilderness which must be still trodden in solitude, with bleeding feet, with sobs for help, as it was trodden by them of old time.

My mind speculated eagerly on the means by which I should become my brother's successful rival, for I was still too timid, in my ignorance of Bertha's actual feeling, to venture on any step that would urge from her an avowal of it. I thought I should gain confidence even for this, if my vision of Prague proved to have been veracious; and yet, the horror of that certitude! Behind the slim girl Bertha, whose words and looks I watched for, whose touch was bliss, there stood continually that Bertha with the fuller form, the harder eyes, the more rigid mouth—with the barren, selfish soul laid bare; no longer a fascinating secret, but a measured fact, urging itself perpetually on my unwilling sight. Are you unable to give me your sympathy—you who read this? Are you unable to imagine this double consciousness at work within me, flowing on like two parallel streams which never mingle their waters and blend into a common hue? Yet you must have known something of the presentiments that spring from an insight at war with passion; and my visions were only like presentiments intensified to horror. You have known the powerlessness of ideas before the might of impulse; and my visions, when once they had passed into memory, were mere ideas—pale shadows that beckoned in vain, while my hand was grasped by the living and the loved.

In after-days I thought with bitter regret that if I had foreseen something more or something different—if instead of that hideous vision which poisoned the passion it could not destroy, or if even along with it I could have had a foreshadowing of that moment when I looked on my brother's face for the last time, some softening influence would have been shed over my feeling towards him: pride and hatred would surely have been subdued into pity, and the record of those hidden sins would have been shortened. But this is one of the vain thoughts with which we men flatter ourselves. We try to believe that the egoism within us would have easily been melted, and that it was only the narrowness of our knowledge which hemmed in our generosity, our awe, our human piety, and hindered them from submerging our hard indifference to the sensations and emotions of our fellows.

Our tenderness and self-renunciation seem strong when our egoism has had its day—when, after our mean striving for a triumph that is to be another's loss, the triumph comes suddenly, and we shudder at it, because it is held out by the chill hand of death.

Our arrival in Prague happened at night, and I was glad of this, for it seemed like a deferring of a terrible decisive moment, to be in the city for hours without seeing it. As we were not to remain long in Prague, but to go on speedily to Dresden, it was proposed that we should drive out the next morning and take a general view of the place, as well as visit some of its specially interesting spots, before the heat became oppressive—for we were in August, and the season was hot and dry. But it happened that the ladies were rather late at their morning toilet, and to my father's politely-repressed but perceptible annoyance, we were not in the carriage till the morning was far advanced. I thought with a sense of relief, as we entered the Jew's quarter, where we were to visit the old synagogue, that we should be kept in this flat, shut-up part of the city, until we should all be too tired and too warm to go farther, and so we should return without seeing more than the streets through which we had already passed. That would give me another day's suspense—suspense, the only form in which a fearful spirit knows the solace of hope. But, as I stood under the blackened, groined arches of that old synagogue, made dimly visible by the seven thin candles in the sacred lamp, while our Jewish cicerone reached down the Book of the Law, and read to us in its ancient tongue—I felt a shuddering impression that this strange building, with its shrunken lights, this surviving withered remnant of medieval Judaism, was of a piece with my vision. Those darkened dusty Christian saints, with their loftier arches and their larger candles, needed the consolatory scorn with which they might point to a more shrivelled death-in-life than their own.

As I expected, when we left the Jews' quarter the elders of our party wished to return to the hotel. But now, instead of rejoicing in this, as I had done beforehand, I felt a sudden overpowering impulse to go on at once to the bridge, and put an end to the suspense I had been wishing to protract. I declared, with unusual decision, that I would get out of the carriage and walk on alone; they might return without me. My father, thinking this merely a sample of my usual "poetic nonsense," objected that I should only do myself harm by walking in the heat; but when I persisted, he said angrily that I might follow my own absurd devices, but that Schmidt (our courier) must go with me. I assented to this, and set off with Schmidt towards the bridge. I had no sooner passed from under the archway of the grand old gate leading on to the bridge, than a trembling seized me, and I turned cold under the midday sun; yet I went on; I was in search of something—a small detail which I remembered with special intensity as part of my vision. There it was—the patch of rainbow light on the pavement transmitted through a lamp in the shape of a star.

II

Before the autumn was at an end, and while the brown leaves still stood thick on the beeches in our park, my brother and Bertha were engaged to each other, and it was understood that their marriage was to take place early in the next spring. In spite of the certainty I had felt from that moment on the bridge at Prague, that Bertha would one day be my wife, my constitutional timidity and distrust had continued to be-numb me, and the words in which I had sometimes premeditated a confession of my love, had died away unuttered. The same conflict had gone on within me as before—the longing for an assurance of love from Bertha's lips, the dread lest a word of contempt and denial should fall upon me like a corrosive acid. What was the conviction of a distant necessity to me? I trembled under a present glance, I hungered after a present joy, I was clogged and chilled by a present fear. And so the days passed on: I witnessed Bertha's engagement and heard her marriage discussed as if I were under a conscious nightmare—knowing it was a dream that would vanish, but feeling stifled under the grasp of hard-clutching fingers.

When I was not in Bertha's presence—and I was with her very often, for she continued to treat me with a playful patronage that wakened no jealousy in my brother—I spent my time chiefly in wandering, in strolling, or taking long rides while the daylight lasted, and then shutting myself up with my unread books; for books had lost the power of chaining my attention. My self-consciousness was heightened to that pitch of intensity in which our own emotions take the form of a drama which urges itself imperatively on our contemplation, and we begin to weep, less under the sense of our suffering than at the thought of it. I felt a sort of pitying anguish over the pathos of my own lot: the lot of a being finely organized for pain, but with hardly any fibres that responded to pleasure—to whom the idea of future evil robbed the present of its joy, and for whom the idea of future good did not still the uneasiness of a present yearning or a present dread. I went dumbly through that stage of the poet's suffering, in which he feels the delicious pang of utterance, and makes an image of his sorrows.

I was left entirely without remonstance concerning this dreamy wayward life: I knew my father's thought about me: "That lad will ever be good for anything in life: he may waste his years in an insignificant way on the income that falls to him: I shall not trouble myself about a career for him."

One mild morning in the beginning of November, it happened that I was standing outside the portico patting lazy old Caesar, a Newfoundland almost blind with age, the only dog that ever took any notice of me—for the very dogs shunned me, and fawned on the happier people about me—

when the groom brought up my brother's horse which was to carry him to the hunt, and my brother himself appeared at the door, florid, broad-chested, and self-complacent, feeling what a good-natured fellow he was not to behave insolently to us all on the strength of his great advantages.

"Latimer, old boy," he said to me in a tone of compassionate cordiality, "what a pity it is you don't have a run with the hounds now and then! The finest thing in the world for low spirits!"

"Low spirits!" I thought bitterly, as he rode away; "that is the sort of phrase with which coarse, narrow natures like yours think to describe experience of which you can know no more than your horse knows. It is to such as you that the good of this world falls: ready dullness, healthy selfishness, good-tempered conceit—these are the keys to happiness."

The quick thought came, that my selfishness was even stronger than his—it was only a suffering selfishness instead of an enjoying one. But then, again, by exasperating insight into Alfred's self-complacent soul, his freedom from all the doubts and fears, the unsatisfied yearnings, the exquisite tortures of sensitiveness, that had made the web of my life, seemed to absolve me from all bonds towards him. This man needed no pity, no love; those fine influences would have been as little felt by him as the delicate white mist is felt by the rock it caresses. There was no evil in store for *him*: if he was not to marry Bertha, it would be because he had found a lot pleasanter to himself.

Mr. Filmore's house lay not more than half a mile beyond our own gates, and whenever I knew my brother was gone in another direction, I went there for the chance of finding Bertha at home. Later on in the day I walked thither. By a rare accident was she alone, and we walked out in the grounds together, for she seldom went on foot beyond the trimly-kept gravel walks. I remember what a beautiful sylph she looked to me as the low November sun shone on her blond hair, and she tripped along teasing me with her usual light banter, to which I listened half-fondly, half-moodily; it was all the sign Bertha's mysterious inner self ever made to me. Today perhaps the moodiness predominated, for I had not yet shaken off the access of jealous hate which my brother had raised in me by his parting patronage. Suddenly I interrupted and startled her by saying, almost fiercely, "Bertha, how can you love Alfred?"

She looked at me with surprise for a moment, but soon her light smile came again, and she answered sarcastically, "Why do you suppose I love him?"

"How can you ask that, Bertha?"

"What! your wisdom thinks I must love the man I'm going to marry? The most unpleasant thing in the world. I should quarrel with him; I should be jealous of him; our *ménage* would be conducted in a very ill-bred manner. A little quiet contempt contributes greatly to the elegance of life."

"Bertha, that is not your real feeling. Why do you delight in trying to deceive me by inventing such cynical speeches?"

"I need never take the trouble of invention in order to deceive you, my small Tasso"—(that was the mocking name she usually gave me). "The easiest way to deceive a poet is to tell him the truth."

She was testing the validity of her epigram in a daring way, and for a moment the shadow of my vision—the Bertha whose soul was no secret to me—passed between me and the radiant girl, the playful sylph whose feelings were a fascinating mystery. I suppose I must have shuddered, or betrayed in some other way my momentary chill of horror.

"Tasso!" she said, seizing my wrist, and peeping round into my face, "are you really beginning to discern what a heartless girl I am? Why, you are not half the poet I thought you were; you were actually capable of believing the truth about me."

The shadow passed from between us, and was no longer the object nearest to me. The girl whose light fingers grasped me, whose elfish charming face looked into mine—who, I thought, was betraying an interest in my feelings that she would not have directly avowed—this warm breathing presence again possessed my senses and imagination like a returning siren melody which had been overpowered for an instant by the roar of threathening waves. It was a moment as delicious to me as the waking up to a consciousness of youth after a dream of middle age. I forgot everything but my passion, and said with swimming eyes:

"Bertha, shall you love me when we are first married? I wouldn't mind if you really loved me only for a little while."

Her look of astonishment, as she loosed my hand and started away from me, recalled me to a sense of my strange, my criminal indiscretion.

"Forgive me," I said, hurriedly, as soon as I could speak again; "I did not know what I was saying."

"Ah, Tasso's mad fit has come on, I see," she answered quietly, for she had recovered herself sooner than I had. "Let him go home and keep his head cool. I must go in, for the sun is setting."

I left her—full of indignation against myself. I had let slip words which, if she reflected on them, might rouse in her a suspicion of my abnormal mental condition—a suspicion which of all things I dreaded. And besides that, I was ashamed of the apparent baseness I had committed in uttering them to my brother's betrothed wife. I wandered home slowly, entering our park through a private gate instead of by the lodges. As I approached the house, I saw a man dashing off at full speed from the stable-yard across the park. Had any accident happened at home? No; perhaps it was only one of my father's peremptory business errands that required this headlong haste.

Some of the illustrations which accompanied tales by the Gentlewomen of Evil reached a high standard of artistic merit. And—as in this case—were quite unnervingly ghoulish.

Another favourite subject with women novelists of the period were staring, disembodied eyes which came to terrorize in the night. These illustrations are (left) from The Horror of Studley Grange by Mrs. Benson, and (right) from The Eyes of Terror by Mrs. L. T. Meade, which is included in this anthology.

Nevertheless I quickened my pace without any distinct motive, and was soon at the house. I will not dwell on the scene I found there. My brother was dead—had been pitched from his horse, and killed on the spot by a concussion of the brain.

I went up to the room where he lay, and where my father was seated beside him with a look of rigid despair. I had shunned my father more than any one since our return home, for the radical antipathy between our natures made my insight into his inner self a constant affliction to me. But now, as I went up to him, and stood beside him in sad silence, I felt the presence of a new element that blended us as we had never been blent before. My father had been one of the most successful men in the money-getting world: he had had no sentimental sufferings, no illness. The heaviest trouble that had befallen him was the death of his first wife. But he married my mother soon after; and I remembered he seemed exactly the same, to my keen childish observation, the week after her death as before. But now, at last, a sorrow had come—the sorrow of old age, which suffers the more from the crushing of its pride and its hopes, in proportion as the pride and hope are narrow prosaic. His son was to have been married soon—would probably have stood for the borough at the next election. That son's existence was the best motive that could be alleged for making new purchases of land every year to round off the estate. It is a dreary thing to live on doing the same things year after year, without knowing why we do them. Perhaps the tragedy of disappointed youth and passion is less piteous than the tragedy of disappointed age and worldliness.

As I saw into the desolation of my father's heart, I felt a movement of deep pity towards him, which was the beginning of a new affection—an affection that grew and strengthened in spite of the strange bitterness with which he regarded me in the first month or two after my brother's death. If it had not been for the softening influence of my compassion for him—the first deep compassion I had ever felt—I should have been stung by the perception that my father transferred the inheritance of an eldest son to me with a mortified sense that fate had compelled him to the unwelcome course of caring for me as an important being. It was only in spite of himself that he began to think of me with anxious regard. There is hardly any neglected child for whom death has made vacant a more favoured place, who will not understand what I mean.

Gradually, however, my new deference to his wishes, the effect of that patience which was born of my pity for him, won upon his affection, and he began to please himself with the endeavour to make me fill my brother's place as fully as my feebler personality would admit. I saw that the prospect which by and by presented itself of my becoming Bertha's husband was welcome to him, and he even contemplated in my case what he had not intended in my brother's—that his son and daughter-in-law should make one household with him. My softened feeling towards my father made this the happiest time I had known since childhood—these last months in which I retained the delicious illusion of loving Bertha, of longing and doubting and hoping that she might love me. She behaved with a certain new consciousness and distance towards me after my brother's death; and I too was under a double constraint—that of delicacy towards my brother's memory, and of anxiety as to the impression my abrupt words had left on her mind. But the additional screen this mutual reserve erected between us only brought me more completely under her power: no matter how empty the adytum, so that the veil be thick enough. So absolute is our soul's need of something hidden and uncertain for the maintenance of that doubt and hope and effort which are the breath of its life, that if the whole future were laid bare to us beyond today, the interest of all mankind would be bent on the hours that lie between; we should pant after the uncertainties of our one morning and our one afternoon; we should rush fiercely to the Exchange of our last possibility of speculation, of success, of disappointment: we should have a glut of political prophets foretelling a crisis or a no-crisis within the only twenty-four hours left open to prophecy. Conceive the condition of the human mind if all propositions whatsoever were self-evident except one, which was to become self-evident at the close of a summer's day, but in the meantime might be the subject of question, of hypothesis, of debate. Art and philosophy, literature and science, would fasten like bees on that one proposition which had the honey of probability in it, and be the more eager because their enjoyment would end with sunset. Our impulses, our spiritual activities, no more adjust themselves to the idea of their future nullity, than the beating of our heart, or the irritability of our muscles.

Bertha, the slim, fair-haired girl, whose present thoughts and emotions were an enigma to me amidst the fatiguing obviousness of the other minds around me, was as absorbing to me as a single unknown today—as a single hypothetic proposition to remain problematic till sunset; and all the cramped, hemmed-in belief and disbelief, trust and distrust, of my nature, welled out in this one narrow channel.

And she made me believe that she loved me. Without ever quitting her tone of *badinage* and playful superiority, she intoxicated me with the sense that I was necessary to her, that she was never at ease unless I was near her, submitting to her playful tyranny. It costs a woman so little effort to besot us in this way! A half-repressed word, a moment's unexpected silence, even an easy fit of petulance on our account, will serve us as *hashish* for a long while. Out of the subtlest web of scarcely perceptible signs, she set me weaving the fancy that she had always unconsciously loved me better than Alfred, but that, with the ignorant fluttered sensibility of a young girl, she had been imposed on by the charm that lay for her in the distinction of being admired and chosen by a man who made so brilliant a figure in the world as my brother. She satirised herself in a very graceful way for her vanity and ambition. What was it to me that I had the light of my wretched prevision on the fact that now it was I who possessed at least all but the personal part of my brother's advantages? Our sweet illusions are half of them conscious illusions like effects of colour that we know to be made up of tinsel, broken glass, and rags.

We were married eighteen months after Alfred's death, one cold, clear morning in April, when there came hail and sunshine both together; and Bertha, in her white silk and pale-green leaves, and the pale hues of her hair and face, looked like the spirit of the morning. My father was happier than he had thought of being again: my marriage, he felt sure, would complete the desirable modification of my character, and make me practical and wordly enough to take my place in society among sane men. For he delighted in Bertha's tact and acuteness, and felt sure she would be mistress of me, and make me what she chose: I was only twenty-one, and madly in love with her. Poor father! He kept that hope a little while after our first year of marriage, and it was not quite extinct when paralysis came and saved him from utter disappointment.

I shall hurry through the rest of my story, not dwelling so much as I have hitherto done on my inward experience. When people are well known to each other, they talk rather of what befalls them externally, leaving their feelings and sentiments to be inferred.

We lived in a round of visits for some time after our return home, giving splendid dinner-parties, and making a sensation in our neighbourhood by the new lustre of our equipage, for my father had reserved this display of his increased wealth for the period of his son's marriage; and we gave our acquaintances liberal opportunity of remarking that it was a pity I made so poor a figure as an heir and a bridegroom. The nervous fatigue of this existence, the insincerities and platitudes which I had to live through twice over—through my inner and outward sense—would have been maddening to me, if I had not had that sort of intoxicated callousness which came from the delights of a first passion. A bride and bridegroom surrounded by all the appliances of wealth, hurried through the day by the whirl of society, filling their solitary moments with hastily-snatched caresses, are prepared for their future life together as the notice is prepared for the cloister—by experiencing its utmost contrast.

Through all these crowded, excited months, Bertha's inward self remained shrouded from me, and I still read her thoughts only through the language of her lips and demeanour: I had still the human interest of wondering whether what I did and said pleased her, of longing to hear a word of affection, of giving a delicious exaggeration of meaning to her smile. But I was conscious of a growing difference in her manner towards me; sometimes strong enough to be called haughty coldness, cutting and chilling me as the hail had done that came across the sunshine on our marriage morning; sometimes only perceptible in the dexterous avoidance of a *tête-à-tête* walk or dinner to which I had been looking forward. I had been deeply pained by this—had even felt a sort of crushing of the heart, from the sense that my brief day of happiness was near its setting; but still I remained dependent on Bertha, eager for the last rays of a bliss that would soon be gone for ever, hoping and watching for some after-glow more beautiful from the impending light.

I remember—how should I not remember?—the time when that dependance and hope utterly left me, when the sadness I had felt in Bertha's growing estrangement became a joy that I looked back upon with longing as a man might look back on the last pains in a paralysed limb. It was just after the close of my father's last illness, which had necessarily withdrawn us from society and thrown us more upon each other. It was the evening of my father's death. On that evening the veil which had shrouded Bertha's soul from me—had made me find in her alone among my fellow-beings the blessed possibility of mystery, and doubt, and expectations—was first withdrawn. Perhaps it was the first day since the beginning of my passion for her, in which that passion was completely neutralized by the presence of an absorbing feeling of another kind. I had been watching by my father's death-bed: I had been witnessing the last fitful yearning glance his soul had cast back on the spent inheritance of life—the last faint consciousness of love he had gathered from the pressure of my hand. What are all our personal loves when we have been sharing in that supreme agony? In the first moments when we come away from the presence of death, every other relation to the living is merged, to our feeling, in the great relation of a common nature and a common destiny.

In that state of mind I joined Bertha in her private sitting-room. She was seated in a leaning posture on a settee, with her back towards the door; the great rich coils of her pale blond hair surmounting her small neck, visible above the back of the settee. I remember, as I closed the door behind me, a cold tremulousness seizing me, and a vague sense of being hated and lonely—vague and strong, like a presentiment. I know how I looked at that moment, for I saw myself in Bertha's thought as she lifted her cutting grey eyes, and looked at me: a miserable ghost-seer, surrounded by phantoms in the noonday, trembling under a breeze when the leaves were still, without appetite for the common objects of human desires, but pining after the moonbeams. We were front to front with each other, and judged each other. The terrible moment of complete illumination had come to me, and I saw that the darkness had hidden no landscape from me, but only a blank prosaic wall: from that evening forth, through the sickening years which followed, I saw all round the narrow room of this woman's soul—saw petty artifice and mere negation where I had delighted to believe in coy sensibilities and in wit at war with latent feeling—saw the light floating vanities of the girl defining themselves into the systematic coquetry, the scheming selfishness, of the woman—saw repulsion and antipathy harden into cruel hatred, giving pain only for the sake of wreaking itself.

For Bertha too, after her kind, felt the bitterness of disillusion. She had believed that my wild poet's passion for her would make me her slave; and that, being her slave, I should execute her will in all things. With the essential shallowness of a negative, unimaginative nature, she was unable to conceive the fact that sensibilities were anything else than weaknesses. She had thought my weaknesses would put me in her power, and she found them unmanageable forces. Our positions were reversed. Before marriage she had completely mastered my imagination, for she was a secret to me; and I created the unknown thought before which I trembled as if it were hers. But now that her soul was laid open to me, now that I was compelled to share the privacy of her motives, to follow all the petty devices that preceded her words and acts, she found herself powerless with me, except to produce in me the chill shudder of repulsion—powerless, because I could be acted on by no lever within her reach. I was dead to worldly ambitions, to social vanities, to all the incentives within the compass of her narrow imagination, and I lived under influences utterly invisible to her.

She was really pitiable to have such a husband, and so all the world thought. A graceful, brilliant woman, like Bertha, who smiled on morning callers, made a figure in ballrooms, and was capable of that light repartee which, from such a woman, is accepted as wit, was secure of carrying off all sympathy from a husband who was sickly, abstracted and, as some suspected, crack-brained. Even the servants in our house gave her the balance of their regard and pity. For there were no audible quarrels between us; our alienation, our repulsion from each other, lay within the silence of our own hearts; and if the mistress went out a great deal, and seemed to dislike the master's society, was it not natural, poor thing? The master was odd. I was kind and just to my dependants, but I excited in them a shrinking, half-contemptuous pity; for this class of men and women are but slightly determined in their estimate of others by general considerations, or even experience, of character. They judge of persons as they judge of coins, and value those who pass current at a high rate.

After a time I interfered so little with Bertha's habits that it might seem wonderful how her hatred towards me could grow so intense and active as it did. But she had begun to suspect, by some involuntary betrayal of mind, that there was an abnormal power of penetration in me—that fitfully, at least, I was strangely cognizant of her thoughts and intentions, and she began to be haunted by a terror of me, which alternated every now and then with defiance. She meditated continually how the incubus could be shaken off her life—how she could be freed from this hateful bond to a being whom she at once despised as an imbecile, and dreaded as an inquisitor. For a long while she lived in the hope that my evident wretchedness would drive me to the commission of suicide; but suicide was not in my nature. I was too completely swayed by the sense that I was in the grasp of unknown forces, to believe in my power of self-release. Towards my own destiny I had become entirely passive; for my one ardent desire had spent itself, and impulse no longer predominated over knowledge. For this reason I never thought of taking any steps towards a complete separation, which would have made our alienation evident to the world. Why should I rush for help to a new course, when I was only suffering from the consequences of a deed which had been the act of my intensest will? That would have been the logic of one who had desires to gratify, and I had no desires. But Bertha and I lived more and more aloof from each other. The rich find it easy to live married and apart.

That course of our life which I have indicated in a few sentences filled the space of years. So much misery—so slow and hideous a growth of hatred and sin, may be compressed into a sentence! And men judge of each other's lives through this summary medium. They epitomize the experience of their fellow-mortal, and pronounce judgement on him in neat syntax, and feel themselves wise and virtuous—conquerors over the temptations they define in well-selected predicates. Seven years of wretchedness glide over the lips of the man who has never counted them out in moments of chill disapointment, of head and heart throbbings, of dread and vain wrestling, of remorse and despair. We learn *words* by rote, but not their meaning; *that* must be paid for with our life-blood, and printed in the subtle fibres of our nerves.

But I will hasten to finish my story. Brevity is justified at once to those who readily understand, and to those who will never understand.

Some years after my father's death, I was sitting by the dim firelight in my library one January evening—sitting in the leather chair that used to be my father's—when Bertha appeared at the door, with a candle in her hand, and advanced towards me. I knew the ball-dress she had on—the white ball-dress, with the green jewels, shone upon by the light of the wax candle which lit up the medallion of the dying Cleopatra on the mantelpiece. Why did she come to me before going out? I had not seen her in the library, which was my habitual place, for months. Why did she stand before me with the candle in her hand, with her cruel contemptuous eyes fixed on me, and the glittering serpent, like a familar demon, on her breast? For a moment I thought this fulfilment of my vision at Vienna marked some dreadful crisis in my fate, but I saw nothing in Bertha's mind, as she stood before me except scorn for the look of overwhelming misery with which I sat before her . . . "Fool, idiot, why don't you kill yourself, then?"—that was her thought. But at length her thoughts reverted to her errand, and she spoke aloud. The apparently indifferent nature of the errand seemed to make a ridiculous anticlimax to my prevision and agitation.

"I have had to hire a new maid. Fletcher is going to be married, and she wants me to ask you to let her husband have the public-house and farm at Molton. I wish him to have it. You must give the promise now, because Fletcher is going tomorrow morning—and quickly, because I'm in a hurry."

"Very well; you may promise her," I said, indifferently, and Bertha swept out of the library again.

I always shrank from the sight of a new person, and all the more when it was a person whose mental life was likely to weary my reluctant insight with wordly ignorant trivialities. But I shrank especially from the sight of this new maid, because her advent had been announced to me at a moment to which I could not cease to attach some fatality: I had a vague dread that I should find her mixed up with the dreary drama of my life—that some new sickening vision would reveal her to me as an evil genius. When at last I did unavoidably meet her, the vague dread was changed into definite disgust. She was a tall, wiry, dark-eyed woman, this Mrs. Archer, with a face handsome enough to give her coarse hard nature the odious finish of bold, self-confident coquetry. That was enough to make me avoid her, quite apart from the contemptuous feeling with which she contemplated me. I seldom saw her; but I perceived that she rapidly became a favourite with her mistress, and, after the lapse of eight or nine months, I began to be aware that there had arisen in Bertha's mind towards this woman a mingled feeling of fear and dependance, and that this feeling was associated with ill-defined images of candle-light scenes in her dressing-room, and the locking-up of something in Bertha's cabinet. My interviews with my wife had become as brief and so rarely solitary, that I had no opportunity of perceiving these images in her mind with more definiteness. The recollections of the past become contracted in the rapidity of thought till they sometimes bear hardly a more distinct resemblance to the external reality than the forms of an oriental alphabet to the objects that suggested them.

Besides, for the last year or more a modification had been going forward in my mental condition, and was growing more and more marked. My insight into the minds of those around me was becoming dimmer and more fitful, and the ideas that crowded my double consciousness became less and less dependent on any personal contact. All that was personal in me seemed to be suffering a gradual death, so that I was losing the organ through which the personal agitations and projects of others could affect me. But along with this relief from wearisome insight, there was a new development of what I concluded—as I have since found rightly—to be a prevision of external scenes. It was as if the relation between me and my fellow-men was more and more deadened, and my relation to what we call the inanimate was quickened into new life. The more I lived apart from society, and in proportion as my wretchedness subsided from the violent throb of agonised passion into the dullness of habitual pain, the more frequent and vivid became such visions as that I had had of Prague—of strange cities, of sandy plains, of gigantic ruins, of midnight skies with strange bright constellations, of mountain-passes, of grassy nooks flecked with the afternoon sunshine through the boughs: I was in the midst of such scenes, and in all of them one presence seemed to weigh on me in all these mighty shapes—the presence of something unknown and pitiless. For continual suffering had annihilated religious faith within me: to the utterly miserable—the unloving and the unloved—there is no religion possible, no worship but a worship of devils. And beyond all these, and continually recurring, was the vision of my death—the pangs, the suffocation, the last struggle, when life would be grasped at in vain.

Things were in this state near the end of the seventh year. I had become entirely free from insight, from my abnormal cognizance of any other consciousness than my own, and instead of intruding involuntarily into the world of other minds, was living continually in my own solitary future. Bertha was aware that I was greatly changed. To my surprise she had of late seemed to seek opportunities of remaining in my society, and had cultivated that kind of distant yet familiar talk which is customary between a husband and wife who live in polite and irrevocable alienation. I bore this with languid submission, and without feeling enough interest in her motives to be roused into keen observation; yet I could not help perceiving something triumphant and excited in her carriage and the expression of her face—something too subtle to express itself in words or tones, but giving one the idea that she lived in a state of expectation or hopeful suspense. My chief feeling was satisfaction that her inner self was once more shut from me; and I almost revelled for the moment in the absent melancholy that made me answer her at cross purposes, and betray utter ignorance of what she had been saying. I remember well the look and the smile with which she one day said, after a mistake of this kind on my part: "I used to think you were a clairvoyant and that was the reason why you were so bitter against other clairvoyants, wanting to keep your monopoly; But I see now you have become rather duller than the rest of the world."

I said nothing in reply. It occured to me that her recent obtrusion of herself upon me might have been prompted by the wish to test my power of detecting some of her secrets; but I let the thought drop again at once: her motives and her deeds had no interest for me, and whatever pleasures she might be seeking, I had no wish to baulk her. There was still pity in my soul for every living thing, and Bertha was living—was surrounded with possibilities of misery.

Just at this time there occurred an event which roused me somewhat from my inertia, and gave me an interest in the passing moment that I had thought impossible for me. It was a visit from Charles Meunier, who had written me word that he was coming to England for relaxation from too strenuous labour, and would like to see me. Meunier had now a European reputation; but his letter to me expressed that keen remembrance of an early regard, an early debt of sympathy, which is inseperable from nobility of character: and I too felt as if his presence would be to me like a transient resurrection into a happier pre-existence.

He came, and as far as possible, I renewed our old pleasure of making *tête-à-tête* excursions, though, instead of mountains and glaciers and the wide blue lake, we had to content ourselves with mere slopes and ponds and artificial plantations. The years had changed us both, but with what different result! Meunier was now a brilliant figure in society, to whom elegant women pretended to listen, and whose acquaintance was boasted of by noblemen ambitious of brains. He repressed with the utmost delicacy any betrayal of the shock which I am sure he must have received from our meeting, or of a desire to penetrate into my condition and circumstances, and sought by the utmost exertion of his charming social powers to make our reunion agreeable. Bertha was much struck by the unexpected fascinations of a visitor whom she had expected to find presentable only on the score of his celebrity, and put forth all her coquetries and accomplishments. Apparently she succeeded in attracting his admiration, for his manner towards her was attentive and flattering. The effect of his presence on me was so benignant, especially in those renewals of our old *tête-à-tête* wanderings, when he poured forth to me wonderful narratives of his professional experience, that more than once, when his talk turned on the psychological relations of disease, the thought crossed my mind that, if his stay with me were long enough,

I might possibly bring myself to tell this man the secrets of my lot. Might there not lie some comprehension and sympathy ready for me in his large susceptible mind? But the thought only flickered feebly now and then, and died out before it could become a wish. The horror I had of again breaking in on the privacy of another soul, made me, by an irrational instinct, draw the shroud of concealment more closely around my own, as we automatically perform the gesture we feel to be wanting in another.

When Meunier's visit was approaching its conclusion, there happened an event which caused some excitement in our household, owing to the surprisingly strong effect it appeared to produce on Bertha—on Bertha, the self-possessed, who usually seemed inaccessible to feminine agitations, and did even hate in a self-restrained hygienic manner. This event was the sudden severe illness of her maid, Mrs. Archer. I have reserved to this moment the mention of a circumstance which had forced itself on my notice shortly before Meunier's arrival, namely, that there had been some quarrel between Bertha and this maid, apparently during a visit to a distant family, in which she had accompanied her mistress. I had overheard Archer speaking in a tone of bitter insolence, which I should have thought an adequate reason for immediate dismissal. No dismissal followed; on the contrary, Bertha seemed to be silently putting up with personal inconveniences from the exhibitions of this woman's temper. I was the more astonished to observe that her illness seemed a cause of strong solicitude to Bertha; that she was at the bedside night and day, and would allow no one else to officiate as head-nurse. It happened that our family doctor was out on a holiday, an accident which made Meunier's presence in the house doubly welcome, and he apparently entered into the case with an interest which seemed so much stronger than the ordinary professional feeling, that one day when he had fallen into a long fit of silence, after visiting her, I said to him:

"Is this a very peculiar case of disease, Meunier?"

"No," he answered, "it is an attack of peritonitis, which will be fatal, but which does not differ physically from many other cases that have come under my observation. But I'll tell you what I have on my mind. I want to make an experiment on this woman, if you will give me permission. It can do her no harm—will give her no pain—for I shall not make it until life is extinct to all purposes of sensation. I want to try the effect of transfusing blood into her arteries after the heart has ceased to beat for some minutes. I have tried the experiment again and again with animals that have died of this disease, with astounding results, and I want to try it on a human subject. I have the small tubes necessary, in a case I have with me, and the rest of the apparatus could be prepared readily. I should use my own blood—take it from my own arm. This woman won't live through the night, I'm convinced, and I want you to promise me your assistance in making the experiment. I can't do without another hand, but it would perhaps not be well to call in a medical assistant from among your provincial doctors. A disagreeable foolish version of the thing might get abroad."

"Have you spoken to my wife on the subject?" I said, "because she appears to be peculiarly sensitive about this woman: she has been a favourite maid."

"To tell you the truth," said Meunier, "I don't want her to know about it. There are always insuperable difficulties with women in these matters, and the effect on the supposed dead body may be startling. You and I will sit up together, and be in readiness. When certain symptoms appear I shall take you in, and at the right moment we must arrange to get every one else out of the room."

I need not give our further conversation on the subject. He entered very fully into the details, and overcame my repulsion from them, by exciting in me a mingled awe and curiosity concerning the possible results of his experiment.

We prepared everything, and he instructed me in my part as assistant. He had not told Bertha of his absolute conviction that Archer would not survive through the night, and endeavoured to persuade her to leave the patient and take a night's rest. But she was obstinate, suspecting die fact that death was at hand, and supposing that he wished merely to save her nerves. She refused to leave the sick-room. Meunier and I sat up together in the library, he making frequent visits to the sick-room, and returning with the information that the case was taking precisely the course he expected. Once he said to me, "Can you imagine any cause of ill-feeling this woman has against her mistress, who is so devoted to her?"

"I think there was some misunderstanding between them before her illness. Why do you ask?"

"Because I have observed for the last five or six hours— since, I fancy, she has lost all hope of recovery—there seems a strange prompting in her to say something which pain and failing strength forbid her to utter; and there is a look of hideous meaning in her eyes, which she turns continually towards her mistress. In this disease the mind often remains singularly clear to the last."

"I am not surprised at an indication of malevolent feeling in her," I said. "She is a woman who has always inspired me with distrust and dislike, but she managed to insinuate herself into her mistress's favour." He was silent after this, looking at the fire with an air of absorption, till he went upstairs again. He stayed away longer than usual, and on returning, said to me quietly, "Come now."

I followed him to the chamber where death was hovering.

The dark hangings of the large bed made a background that gave a strong relief to Bertha's pale face as I entered. She started forward as she saw me enter, and then looked at Meunier with an expression of angry inquiry; but he lifted up his hand as if to impose silence, while he fixed his glance on the dying woman and felt her pulse. The face was pinched and ghastly, a cold perspiration was on the forehead, and the eyelids were lowered so as to conceal the large dark eyes. After a minute or two, Meunier walked round to the other side of the bed where Bertha stood, and with his usual air of gentle politeness towards her begged her to leave the patient under our care—everything should be done for her—she was no longer in a state to be conscious of an affectionate presence. Bertha was hesitating, apparently almost willing to believe his assurance and to comply. She looked round at the ghastly dying face, as if to read the confirmation of that assurance, when for a moment the lowered eyelids were raised again, and it seemed as if the eyes were looking towards Bertha, but blanky. A shudder passed through Bertha's frame, and she returned to her station near the pillow, tacitly implying that she would not leave the room.

The eyelids were lifted no more. Once I looked at Bertha as she watched the face of the dying one. She wore a rich *pegnoir*, and her blond hair was half covered by a lace cap: in her attire she was, as always, an elegant woman, fit to figure in a picture of modern aristocratic life: but I asked myself how that face of hers could ever have seemed to me the face of a woman born of woman, with memories of childhood, capable of pain, needing to be fondled? The features at that moment seemed to preternaturally sharp, the eyes were so hard and eager—she looked like a cruel immortal, finding her spiritual feast in the agonies of a dying race. For across those hard features there came something like a flash when the last hour had been breathed out, and we all felt that the dark veil had completely fallen. What secret was there between Bertha and this woman? I turned my eyes from her with a horrible dread lest my insight should return, and I should be obliged to see what had been breeding about two unloving women's hearts. I felt that Bertha had been watching for the moment of death as the sealing of her secret: I thanked Heaven it could remain sealed for me.

Meunier said quietly, "She is gone." He then gave his arm to Bertha, and she submitted to be led out of the room.

I suppose it was at her order that two female attendants came into the room, and dismissed the younger one who had been present before. When they entered, Meunier had already opened the artery in the long thin neck that lay rigid on the pillow, and I dismissed them, ordering them to remain at a distance till we rang: the doctor, I said, had an operation to perform—he was not sure about the death. For the next twenty minutes I forgot everything but Meunier and the experiment in which he was so absorbed that I think his senses would have been closed against all sounds or sights which had no relation to it. It was my task at first to keep up the artificial respiration in the body after the transfusion had been effected, but presently Meunier relieved me, and I could see the wondrous slow return of life; the breast began to heave, the inspirations became stronger, the eyelids quivered, and the soul seemed to have returned beneath them. The artificial respiration was withdrawn: still the breathing continued, and there was a movement of the lips.

Just then I heard the handle of the door moving: I suppose Bertha had heard from the women that they had been dismissed: probably a vague fear had arisen in her mind, for she entered with a look of alarm. She came to the foot of the bed and gave a stifled cry.

The dead woman's eyes were wide open, and met hers in full recognition of hate. With a sudden strong effort, the hand that Bertha had thought for ever still was pointed towards her, and the haggard face moved. The gasping eager voice said:

"You mean to poison your husband . . . the poison is in the black cabinet . . . I got it for you . . . you laughed at me, and told lies about me behind my back, to make me disgusting . . . because you were jealous . . . are you sorry .

. . now?"

The lips continued to murmur, but the sounds were no longer distinct. Soon there was no sound—only a slight movement: the flame had leaped out, and was being extinguished the faster. The wretched woman's heart-strings had been set to hatred and vengeance; the spirit of life had swept the chords for an instant, and was gone again for ever. Great God! Is this what it is to live again . . . to wake up with our unstilled thirst upon us, with our unuttered curses rising to our lips, with our muscles ready to act out their half-committed sins?

Bertha stood pale at the foot of the bed, quivering and helpless, despairing of devices, like a cunning animal whose hiding-places are surrounded by swift-advancing flame. Even Meunier looked paralysed; life for that moment ceased to be a scientific problem to him. As for me, this scene seemed of one texture with the rest of my existence: horror was my familiar, and this new revelation was only like an old pain recurring with new circumstances.

Since then Bertha and I have lived apart—she in her own neighbourhood, the mistress of half our wealth, I as a wanderer in foreign countries, until I came to this Devonshire nest to die. Bertha lives pitied and admired; for what had I against that charming woman, whom every one but myself could have been happy with? There had been no witness of the scene in the dying room except Meunier, and while Meunier lived his lips were sealed by a promise to me.

Once or twice, weary of wandering, I rested in a favourite spot, and my heart went out towards the men and women and children whose faces were becoming familiar to me; But I was driven away again in terror at the approach of my old insight—driven away to live continually with the one Unknown Presence revealed and yet hidden by the moving curtain of the earth and sky. Till at last disease took hold of me and forced me to rest here—forced me to live in dependence on my servants. And then the curse of insight— of my double consciousness, came again, and has never left me. I knew all their narrow thoughts, their feeble regard, their half-wearied pity.

It is the 20th September, 1850. I know these figures I have just written, as if they were a long familiar inscription. I have seen them on this page in my desk unnumbered times, when the scene of my dying struggle has opened upon me . . .

EVELINE'S VISITANT

Miss Braddon

It was at a masked ball at the Palais Royal that my fatal quarrel with my first cousin André de Brissac began. The quarrel was about a woman. The women who followed the footsteps of Philip of Orleans were the causes of many such disputes; and there was scarcely one fair head in all that glittering throng which, to a man versed in social histories and mysteries, might not have seemed bedabbled with blood.

I shall not record the name of her for love of whom André de Brissac and I crossed one of the bridges, in the dim August dawn on our way to the waste ground beyond the church of Saint-Germain des Prés.

There were many beautiful vipers in those days, and she was one of them. I can feel the chill breath of that August morning blowing in my face, as I sit in my dismal chamber at my château of Puy Verdun tonight, alone in the stillness, writing the strange story of my life. I can see the white mist rising from the river, the grim outline of the Châtelet, and the square towers of Notre Dame black against the pale-grey sky. Even more vividly can I recall André's fair young face, as he stood opposite me with his two friends—scoundrel's both, and like eager for that unnatural fray. We were a strange group to be seen in a summer sunrise, all of us fresh from the heat and clamour of the Regent's saloons—André in a quaint hunting-dress copied from a family portrait at Puy Verdun, I costumed as one of Law's Mississippi Indians; the other men in like garish frippery, adorned with broideries and jewels that looked wan in the pale light of dawn.

Our quarrel had been a fierce one—a quarrel which could have but one result, and that the direst. I had struck him; and the welt raised by my open hand was crimson upon his fair, womanish face as he stood opposite to me. The eastern sun shone on the face presently, and dyed the cruel mark with a deeper red; but the sting of my own wrongs was fresh, and I had not yet learned to despise myself for that brutal outrage.

To André de Brissac such an insult was most terrible. He was the favourite of Fortune, the favourite of woman; and I was nothing—a rough soldier who had done my country good service, but in the boudoir of a Parabère a mannerless boor.

We fought, and I wounded him mortally. Life had been

very sweet to him; and I think that a frenzy of despair took possession of him when he felt the life-blood ebbing away. He beckoned me to him as he lay on the ground. I went, and knelt at his side.

"Forgive me, André!" I murmured.

He took no more heed of my words than if that piteous entreaty had been the idle ripple of the river near at hand.

"Listen to me, Hector de Brissac," he said. "I am not one who believes that a man has done with earth because his eyes glaze and his jaw stiffens. They will bury me in the old vault at Puy Verdun; and you will be master of the château. Ah, I know how lightly they take things in these days, and how Dubois will laugh when he hears that Ca has been killed in a duel. They will bury me, and sing masses for my soul; but you and I have not finished our affair yet, my cousin. I will be with you when you least look to see me—I, with this ugly scar upon the face that women have praised and loved. I will come to you when your life seems brightest. I will come between you and all that you hold fairest and dearest. My ghostly hand shall drop a poison in your cup of joy. My shadowy form shall shut the sunlight from your life. Men with such iron will as mine can do what they please, Hector de Brissac. It is my will to haunt you when I am dead."

All this in short, broken sentences he whispered into my ear. I had need to bend my ear close to his dying lips; but the iron will of André de Brissac was strong enough to do battle with Death, and I believe he said all he wished to say before his head fell back upon the velvet cloak they had spread beneath him, never to be lifted again.

As he lay there, you would have fancied him a fragile stripling, too fair and frail for the struggle called life; but there are those who remember the brief manhood of André de Brissac, and who can bear witness to the terrible force of that proud nature.

I stood looking down at the young face with that foul mark upon it, and God knows I was sorry for what I had done.

Of these blasphemous threats which he had whispered in my ear I took no heed. I was a soldier, and a believer. There was nothing absolutely dreadful to me in the thought that I had killed this man. I had killed many men on the battlefield; and this one had done me a cruel wrong.

My friends would have had me cross the frontier to escape the consequences of my act; but I was ready to face those consequences, and I remained in France. I kept aloof from the court, and received a hint that I had best confine myself to my own province. Many masses were chanted in the little chapel of Puy Verdun for the soul of my dead cousin, and his coffin filled a niche in the vault of our ancestors.

His death had made me a rich man; and the thought that

it was so made my newly acquired wealth very hateful to me. I lived a lonely existence in the old château, where I rarely held converse with any but the servants of the household, all of whom had served my cousin, and none of whom liked me.

It was a hard and bitter life. It galled me, when I rode through the village, to see the peasant children shrink away from me. I have seen old women cross themselves stealthily as I passed by. Strange reports had gone forth about me; and there were those who whispered that I had given my soul to the Evil One as the price of my cousin's heritage. From my boyhood I had been dark of visage and stern of manner; and hence, perhaps no woman's love had ever been mine. I remembered my mother's face in all its changes of expression; but I can remember no look of affection that ever shone on me. The other woman, beneath whose feet I laid my heart, was pleased to accept my homage, but she never loved me; and the end was treachery.

I had grown hateful to myself, and had well-nigh begun to hate my fellow-creatures, when a feverish desire seized upon me, and I pined to be back in the press and throng of the busy world once again. I went back to Paris, where I kept myself aloof from the court, and where an angel took compassion on me.

She was the daughter of an old comrade, a man whose

merits had been neglected, whose achievements had been ignored, and who sulked in his shabby lodging like a rat in a hole, while all Paris went mad with the Scotch Financier, and gentlemen and lackeys were trampling one another to death in the Rue Quincampoix. The only child of this little cross-grained old captain of dragoons was an incarnate sunbeam, whose mortal name was Eveline Duchalet.

She loved me. The richest blessings of our lives are often those which cost us least. I wasted the best years of my youth in the worship of a wicked woman, who jilted and cheated me at last. I gave this meek angel but a few courteous words—a little fraternal tenderness—and lo, she loved me. The life which had been so dark and desolate grew bright beneath her influence; and I went back to Puy Verdun with a fair young bride for my companion.

Ah, how sweet a change there was in my life and in my home! The village children no longer shrank appalled as the dark horseman rode by, the village crones no longer crossed themselves; for a woman rode by his side—a woman whose charities had won the love of all those ignorant creatures, and whose companionship had transformed the gloomy lord of the château into a loving husband and gentle master. The old retainers forgot the untimely fate of my cousin, and served me with cordial willingness, for love of their young mistress.

There are no words which can tell the pure and perfect happiness of that time. I felt like a traveller who had traversed the frozen seas of an arctic region, remote from human love or human companionship, to find himself all of a sudden in the bosom of a verdant valley, in the sweet atmosphere of home. The change seemed too bright to be real; and I strove in vain to put away from my mind the vague suspicion that my new life was but some fantastic dream.

So brief were those halcyon hours, that, looking back on them now, it is scarcely strange if I am still half inclined to fancy the first days of my married life could have been no more than a dream.

Neither in my days of gloom nor in my days of happiness had I been troubled by the recollection of André's blasphemous oath. The words which with his last breath he had whispered in my ear were vain and meaningless to me. He had vented his rage in those idle threats, as he might have vented it in idle execrations. That he will haunt the footsteps of his enemy after death is the one revenge which a dying man can promise himself; and if men had power thus to avenge themselves the earth would be peopled with phantoms.

I had lived for three years at Puy Verdun; sitting alone in the solemn midnight by the hearth where he had sat, pacing the corridors that had echoed his footfall; and in all that time my fancy had never so played me false as to shape the shadow of the dead. Is it strange, then, if I had forgotten André's horrible promise?

There was no portrait of my cousin at Puy Verdun. It was the age of boudoir art, and a miniature set in the lid of a gold bonbonnière, or hidden artfully in a massive bracelet, was more fashionable than a clumsy life-size image, fit only to hang on the gloomy walls of a provincial château rarely visited by its owner. My cousin's fair face had adorned more than one bonbonniére, and had been concealed in more than one bracelet; but it was not among the faces that looked down from the pannelled walls of Puy Verdun.

In the library I found a picture which awoke painful associations. It was the portrait of a de Brissac, who had flourished in the time of Francis the First; and it was from this picture that my cousin André had copied the quaint hunting dress he wore at the Regent's ball. The library was a room in which I spent a good deal of my life; and I ordered a curtain to be hung before this picture.

We had been married three months, when Eveline one day asked: "Who is the lord of the château nearest to this?"

I looked at her in astonishment.

"My dearest," I answered, "do you not know that there is no other château within forty miles of Puy Verdun?"

"Indeed!" she said. "That is strange."

I asked her why the fact seemed strange to her; and

after much entreaty I obtained from her the reason of her surprise.

In her walks about the park and woods during the last month she had met a man who, by his dress and bearing, was obviously of noble rank. She had imagined that he occupied some château near at hand, and that his estate adjoined ours. I was at a loss to imagine who this stranger could be; for my estate at Puy Verdun lay in the heart of a desolate region, and unless when some traveller's coach went lumbering and jingling through the village, one had little more chance of encountering a gentlemen than of meeting a demigod.

"Have you seen this man often, Eveline?" I asked.

She answered, in a tone which had a touch of sadness: "I see him every day."

"Where, dearest?"

"Sometimes in the park, sometimes in the wood. You know the little cascade, Hector, where there is some old neglected rock-work that forms a kind of cavern. I have taken a fancy to that spot, and have spent many mornings there reading. Of late I have seen the stranger there every morning."

"He has never dared to address you?"

"Never. I have looked up from my book, and have seen him standing at a little distance, watching me silently. I have continued reading; and when I have raised my eyes again I have found him gone. He must approach and depart with a

291

stealthy tread, for I never hear his footfall. Sometimes I have almost wished that he would speak to me. It is so terrible to see him standing silently there."

"He is some insolent peasant who seeks to frighten you."

My wife shook her head.

"He is no peasant," she answered. "It is not by his dress alone I judge, for that is strange to me. He has an air of nobility which it is impossible to mistake."

"Is he young or old?"

"He is young and handsome."

I was much disturbed by the idea of this stranger's intrusion on my wife's solitude; and I went straight to the village to enquire if any stranger had been seen there. I could hear of no one. I questioned the servants closely, but without result. Then I determined to accompany my wife in her walks, and to judge for myself of the rank of the stranger.

For a week I devoted all my mornings to rustic rambles with Eveline in the park and woods; and in all that week we saw no one but the occasional peasant in *sabos*, or one of our own household returning from a neighbouring farm.

I was a man of studious habits, and those summer rambles disturbed the even current of my life. My wife perceived this, and entreated me to trouble myself no further.

"I will spend my mornings in the pleasaunce, Hector," she said; "the stranger cannot intrude upon me there."

"I began to think the stranger is only a phantasm of your own romantic brain," I replied, smiling at the earnest face lifted to mine. "A châtelaine who is always reading romances may well meet handsome cavaliers in the woodlands. I dare say I have Mademoiselle Scuderi to thank for this noble stranger, and that he is only the great Cyrus in modern costume."

"Ah, that is the point which mystifies me, Hector," she said. "The stranger's costume is not modern. He looks as an old picture might look if it could descend from its frame."

Her words pained me, for they reminded me of that hidden picture in the library, and the quaint hunting costume of orange and purple, which André de Brissac wore at the Regent's ball.

After this my wife confined her walks to the pleasaunce; and for many weeks I heard no more of the nameless stranger. I dismissed all thought of him from my mind, for a graver and heavier care had come upon me. My wife's health began to droop. The change in her was so gradual as to be almost imperceptible to those who watched her day by day. It was only when she put on a rich gala dress which she had not worn for months that I saw how wasted the form must be on which the embroidered bodice hung so loosely, and how wan and dim were the eyes which had once been brilliant as the jewels she wore in her hair.

I sent a messenger to Paris to summon one of the court physicians; but I knew that many days must needs elapse before he could arrive at Puy Verdun.

In the interval I watched my wife with unutterable fear.

It was not her health only that had declined. The change was more painful to behold than any physical alteration. The bright and sunny spirit had vanished, and in the place of my joyous young bride I beheld a woman weighed down by rooted melancholy. In vain I sought to fathom the cause of my darling's sadness. She assured me that she had no reason for sorrow or discontent, and that if she seemed sad without a motive, I must forgive her sadness, and consider it as a misfortune rather than a fault.

I told her that the court physician would speedily find some cure for her despondency, which needs must arise from physical causes, since she had no real ground for sorrow. But although she said nothing, I could see she had no hope or belief in the healing powers of medicine.

One day, when I wished to beguile her from that pensive silence in which she was wont to sit an hour at a time, I told her, laughing, that she appeared to have forgotten her mysterious cavalier in the wood, and it seemed also as if he had forgotten her.

To my wonderment, her pale face became a sudden crimson; and from crimson changed to pale again in a breath.

"You have never seen him since you deserted your woodland grotto?" I said.

She turned to me with a heart-rending look.

"Hector," she cried, "I see him every day; and it is that which is killing me."

She burst into a passion of tears when she had said this. I took her in my arms as if she had been a frightened child, and tried to comfort her.

"My darling, this is madness," I said. "You know that no stranger can come to you in the pleasaunce. The moat is ten feet wide and always full of water, and the gates are kept locked day and night by old Massou. The châtelaine of a medieval fortress need fear no intruder in her antique garden."

My wife shook her head sadly.

"I see him every day," she said.

On this I believed that my wife was mad. I shrank from questioning her more closely concerning her myserious visitant. It would be ill, I thought, to give form and substance to the shadow that tormented her, by too close inquiry about its looks and manner, its coming and going.

I took care to assure myself that no stranger to the household could by any possibility penetrate to the pleasaunce. Having done this, I was fain to await the coming of the physician.

He came at last. I revealed to him the conviction which

was my misery. I told him that I believed my wife to be mad. He saw her—spent an hour alone with her, and then came to me. To my unspeakable relief he assured me of her sanity.

"It is just possible that she may be affected by one delusion," he said; "but she is so reasonable upon all other points that I can scarcely bring myself to believe her the subject of a monomania. I am rather inclined to think that she really sees the person of whom she speaks. She described him to me with a perfect minuteness. The descriptions of scenes or individuals given by patients afflicted with monomainia are always more or less disjointed; but your wife spoke to me as clearly and calmly as I am now speaking to you. Are you sure there is no one who can approach her in that garden where she walks?"

"I am quite sure."

"Is there any kinsman of your steward, or hanger-on of your household—a young man with a fair, womanish face, very pale and rendered remarkable by a crimson scar, which looks like the mark of a blow?"

"My God!" I cried, as the light broke in upon me all at once. "And the dress—the strange, old-fashioned dress?"

"The man wears a hunting costume of purple and orange," answered the doctor.

I knew then that André de Brissac had kept his word, and that in the hour when my life was brightest his shadow had come between me and happiness.

I showed my wife the picture in the library, for I would fain assure myself that there was some error in my fancy about my cousin. She shook like a leaf when she beheld it, and clung to me convulsively.

"This is witchcraft Hector," she said. "The dress in that picture is the dress of the man I see in the pleasaunce; but the face is not his."

Then she described to me the face of the stranger; and it was my cousin's face line for line—André de Brissac, whom she had never seen in the flesh. Most vividly of all did she describe the cruel mark upon his face, the trace of a fierce blow from an open hand.

After this I carried my wife away from Puy Verdun. We wandered far—through the southern provinces, and into the very heart of Switzerland. I thought to distance the ghastly phantom, and I fondly hoped that change of scene would bring peace to my wife.

It was not so. Go where we would, the ghost of André de Brissac followed us. To my eyes that fatal shadow never revealed itself. *That* would have been too poor a vengeance. It was my wife's innocent heart which André made the instrument of his revenge. The unholy presence destroyed her life. My constant companionship could not shield her from the horrible intruder. In vain did I watch her; in vain did I strive to comfort her.

"He will not let me be at peace," she said. "He comes between us, Hector. He is standing between us now. I can see his face with the red mark upon it plainer than I see yours."

One fair moonlight night, when we were together in a mountain village in the Tyrol, my wife cast herself at my feet, and told me she was the worst and vilest of women. "I have confessed all to my Director," she said; "from the first I have not hidden my sin from heaven. But I feel that death is near me; and before I die I would fain reveal my sin to you."

"What sin, my sweet one?"

"When first the stranger came to me in the forest, his presence bewildered and distressed me, and I shrank from him as from something strange and terrible. He came again and again; by and by I found myself thinking of him, and watching for his coming. His image haunted me perpetually; I strove in vain to shut his face out of my mind. Then followed an interval in which I did not see him; and, to my shame and anguish, I found that life seemed dreary and desolate without him. After that came the time in which he haunted the pleasaunce; and—oh, Hector, kill me if you will, for I deserve no mercy at your hands!—I grew in those days to count the hours that must elapse before his coming, to take no pleasure save in the sight of that pale face with the red brand upon it. He plucked all old familiar joys out of my heart, and left in it but one weird, unholy pleasure—the delight of his presence. For a year I lived but to see him. And now curse me, Hector; for this is my sin. Whether it comes of the baseness of my own heart, or is the work of witchcraft, I know not; but I know that I have striven against this wickedness in vain."

I took my wife to my breast, and forgave her. In sooth, what had I to forgive? Was the fatality that overshadowed us any work of hers? On the next night she died, with her hand in mine; and at the very last she told me, sobbing and affrighted, that *he* was by her side.

SANDY THE TINKER

Mrs. Riddell

"Before commencing my story, I wish to state it is perfectly true in every particular."

"We quite understand that," said the sceptic of our party, who was wont, in the security of friendly intercourse, to characterise all such prefaces as mere introductions to some tremendously exaggerated tale.

On the occasion in question, however, we had donned our best behaviour, a garment which did not sit ungracefully on some of us; and our host, who was about to draw out from the stores of memory one narrative for our entertainment, was scarcely the person before whom even Jack Hill, the sceptic, would have cared to express his cynical and unbelieving views.

We were seated, an incongruous company of ten persons, in the best room of an old manse among the Scottish hills. Accident had thrown us together, and accident had driven us under the minister's hospitable roof. Cold, wet and hungry, drenched with rain, sorely beaten by the wind, we had crowded through the door opened by a friendly hand, and now, wet no longer, the pangs of hunger assuaged with smoking rashers of ham, poached eggs, and steaming potatoes, we sat around a blazing fire, drinking toddy out of tumblers, whilst the two ladies who graced the assemblage partook of a modicum of the same beverage from wine glasses.

Everything was eminently comfortable, but conducted upon the most correct principles. Jack could no more have taken it upon himself to shock the minister's ear with some of the opinions he aired in Fleet Street, than he could have asked for more whisky with his water.

"Yes, it is perfectly true," continued the minister, looking thoughtfully at the fire. "I can't explain it, I cannot even try to explain it. I will tell you the story exactly as it occurred, however, and leave you to draw your own deductions from it."

None of us answered. We fell into listening attitudes instantly, and eighteen eyes fixed themselves by one accord upon our host.

He was an old man, but hale. The weight of eighty winters had whitened his head, but not bowed it. He seemed young as any of us—younger than Jack Hill, who was a reviewer and a newspaper hack, and whose way through life had not been altogether on easy lines.

"Thirty years ago, upon a certain Friday morning in August," began the minister, "I was sitting at breakfast in the room on the other side of the passage, where you ate your supper, when the servant girl came in with a letter. She said a laddie, all out of breath, had brought it over from Dendeldy Manse. "He was bidden to rin a' the way," she went on, "and he's fairly beaten."

'I told her to make the messenger sit down, and put food before him; and then, when she went to do my bidding, proceeded, I must confess with some curiosity, to break the seal of a missive forwarded in such hot haste.

"It was from the minister at Dendeldy, who had been newly chosen to occupy the pulpit his deceased father occupied for a quarter of a century and more.

"The call from the congregation originated rather out of respect to the father's memory than any extraordinary liking for the son. He had been reared for the most part in England, and was somewhat distant and formal in his manners; and, though full of Greek and Latin and Hebrew, wanted the true Scotch accent, that goes straight to the heart of those accustomed to the broad, honest, tender Scottish tongue.

"His people were proud of him, but they did not like some of his ways. They could remember him a lad running about the whole country-side, and they could not understand,

and did not approve of his holding them at arm's length, and shutting himself up among his books and refusing their hospitality, and sending out word he was busy when maybe some very decent man wanted speech with him. I had taken it upon myself to point out that I thought he was wrong, and that he would alienate his flock from him. Perhaps it was for this very reason, because I was blunt and plain, he took to me kindly, and never got on his high horse, no matter what I said to him.

"Well, to return to the letter. It was written in the wildest haste, and entreated me not to lose a moment in coming to him, as he was in the very *greatest distress* and *anxiety*. 'Let *nothing* delay you,' he proceeded. 'If I cannot speak to you soon I believe I shall go out of my senses.'

"What could be the matter? I thought. What in all the wide earth could have happened?

"I had seen him but a few days before and he was in good health and spirits, getting on better with his people, feeling hopeful of so altering his style of preaching as to touch their hearts more sensibly.

"What could have happened, however, puzzled me sorely. As I made my hurried preparations for setting out I fairly perplexed myself with speculation. I went into the kitchen, where his messenger was eating some breakfast, and asked if Mr. Crawley was ill.

" 'I dinna ken,' he answered. 'He mad' no complaint, but he luiked awful bad, just awful.'

" 'In what way?'I inquired.

" 'As if he had seen a ghaist,' was the reply.

"This made me very uneasy, and I jumped to the conclusion the trouble was connected with money matters. Young men will be young men." Here the minister looked significantly at the callow bird of our company, a youth who had never owed a sixpence in his life or given away a cent; while Jack Hill—no chicken, by the way—was over head and ears in debt, and could not keep a sovereign in his pocket, though spending or bestowing it involved going dinner-less the next day.

"Young men will be young men," repeated the minister, in his best pulpit manner ("Just as though any one expected them to be young women!" grumbled Jack to me afterwards), "and I feared that now he was settled and comfortably off, some old creditor he had been paying as best he could, might have become pressing. I knew nothing of his liabilities, or, beyond the amount of the stipend paid him, the state of his pecuniary affairs; but, having once in my own life made myself responsible for a debt, I was aware of all the trouble putting your arm out further than you can draw it back involves. And I considered that most probably money, which is the root of all evil" ("and all good" Jack's eyes suggested to me), "was the cause of my young friend's agony of mind. Blessed with a large family—every one of whom is now alive and doing well, I thank God, out in the world—you may imagine I had not much opportunity for laying by. Still, I had put aside a little for a rainy day, and that little I placed in my pocket-book, hoping even a small sum might prove of use in case of emergency.'

"By the road," proceeded our host, "Dendeldy is distant from here ten long miles, but by a short cut across the hills it can be reached in something under six. For me it was nothing of a walk, and accordingly I arrived at the manse ere noon."

He paused, and, though thirty years had elapsed, drew a handkerchief across his forehead before he continued his narrative.

"I had to climb a steep brae to reach the front door, but before I could breast it my friend met me.

" 'Thank God you are come,' he said, pressing my hand in his. 'Oh, I am grateful.'

"He was trembling with excitement. His face was a ghastly pallor. His voice was that of a person suffering from some terrible shock, labouring under some awful fear.

" 'What *has* happened, Edward?' I asked. I had known him since he was a little boy. 'I am distressed to see you in such a state. Rouse yourself; be a man; whatever may have gone wrong can possibly be righted. I have come over to do all that lies in my power for you. If it is a matter of money——'

" 'No, no; it is not money,' he interrupted; 'would that it were!' and he began to tremble again so violently that really he communicated some part of his nervousness to me, and put me into a state of perfect terror.

" 'Whatever it is, Crawley, out with it,' I said; 'have you murdered anybody?'

" 'No, it is worse than that,' he answered.

" 'But that's just nonsense,' I declared. 'Are you in your right mind, do you think?'

" 'I wish I were not,' he returned. 'I'd like to know I was stark staring mad; it would be happier for me—far, far happier.'

" 'If you don't tell me this minute what is the matter, I shall turn on my heel and tramp my way home again,' I said, half in anger at what I thought was his folly.

" 'Come into the house,' he entreated, 'and try to have patience with me; for indeed, Mr. Morison, I am sorely troubled. I have been through my deep waters, and they have gone clean over my head.'

"We went into his little study and sat down. For a while he remained silent, his head resting upon his hand, struggling with some strong emotion; but after about five minutes he asked in a low subdued voice:

" 'Do you believe in dreams?'

" 'What has my belief to do with the matter in hand?' I inquired.

" 'It is a dream, an awful dream, that is troubling me.'

"I rose from my chair.

" 'Do you mean to say,' I asked, 'you have brought me from my business and my parish to tell me you have had a bad dream?'

" 'That is just what I do mean to say,' he answered. 'At least it was not a dream—it was a vision; no, I don't mean a vision—I can't tell you what it was; but nothing I ever went through in actual life was half so real, and I have bound myself to go through it all again. There is no hope for me, Mr. Morison. I sit before you a lost creature, the most miserable man on the face of the whole earth.'

" 'What did you dream?' I inquired.

"A dreadful fit of trembling again seized him; but at last he managed to say: 'I have been like this ever since, and I shall be like this for evermore, till—till—the end comes.'

" 'When did you have your bad dream?' I asked.

" 'Last night, or rather this morning,' he answered. 'I'll tell you all about it. I was as well when I went to bed about eleven o'clock as ever I was in my life. I had been considering my sermon and felt satisfied I should be able to deliver a good one next Sunday morning. I had taken nothing after my tea and I lay down in my bed feeling at peace with all mankind, and satisfied with my lot. How long I slept, or what I dreamt about at first, if I dreamt at all, I don't know; but after a time the mists seemed to clear from before my eyes, to roll away like clouds from a mountain summit, and I found myself walking on a beautiful summer's evening beside the River Deldy.'

"He paused for a moment, and an irrepressible shudder shook his frame.

" 'Go on,' I said, for I felt afraid of his breaking down again.

"He looked at me pitifully, with a hungry entreaty in his weary eyes, and continued.

" 'It was a lovely evening and I never thought the earth had looked so beautiful before. I walked on and on, till I came to that point where, as you may perhaps remember, the path, growing very narrow, winds round the base of a great crag, and leads the wayfarer suddenly into a little green amphitheatre, bounded on one side by the river, and on the other by rocks, that rise in places sheer to a height of a hundred feet or more.'

" 'I remember it,' I said; 'a little farther on three streams meet and fall with a tremendous roar into the Witches' Cauldron. A fine sight in the winter time, only there is scarce any reaching it from below, as the path you mention and the little green oasis are mostly covered with water.'

" 'I had not been there before since I was a child,' he went on mournfully, 'but I recollected it as one of the most solitary spots possible; and my astonishment was great, to see a man standing in the pathway, with a drawn sword in his hand. He did not stir as I drew near, so I stepped aside on the grass. Instantly he barred my way.

" '"You can't pass here," he said.

" '"Why not?" I asked.

" '"Because I say so," he answered.

" '"And who are you that say so?" I inquired, looking full at him.

" 'He was like a god. Majesty and power were written on every feature, were expressed in every gesture. But, oh, the awful scorn of his smile, the contempt with which he regarded me! The beams of the setting sun fell full upon him, and seemed to bring out, as in letters of fire, the wickedness and terrible beauty of his face.

" 'I felt afraid; but I managed to say:

" '"Stand out of my way, the river bank is as free to me as to you."

" '"Not this part of it," he answered; "this place belongs to me."

" '"Very well," I agreed, for I did not want to stand there

bandying words with him, and a sudden darkness seemed to be falling around. "It is getting late, and so I'll turn round."

" 'He gave a laugh, the like of which never fell on human ear before, and made reply: "You can't turn back—of your own free will you have come on my ground and from it there is no return."

" 'I did not speak; I only just turned round and made as fast as I could for the path at the foot of the crag. He did not pass me, yet before I could reach the point I desired he stood barring my progress, with the scornful smile still on his lips, and his gigantic form assuming tremendous proportions in the narrow way.

" '"Let me pass," I entreated, "and I will never come here again, never trespass more on your ground."

" '"No, you shall not pass."

" '"Who are you that takes such power on yourself?" I asked.

" '"Come closer, and I will tell you," he said.

" 'I drew a step nearer, and he spoke one word. I never heard it before, but, by some extraordinary intuition, I knew what it meant. He was the Evil One. The name seemed to be taken up by the echoes, and repeated from rock to rock and crag to crag. The whole air seemed full of that one word— and then a great horror of darkness came about us, only the place where we stood remained light. We occupied a small circle walled round with the thick blackness of night.

" "'You must come with me," he said.

" 'I refused and then he threatened me. I implored and entreated and wept, but at last I agreed to do what he wanted if he would promise to let me return. Again he laughed, and said, Yes, I should return—and the rocks and trees and mountains, ay, and the very rivers, seemed to take up the answer and bear it in sobbing whispers away into the darkness.'

"He stopped, and lay back in his chair, shivering like one in an ague fit.

" 'Go on,' I repeated again, 'it was only a dream, you know.'

" 'Was it?' he murmured, mournfully. 'Ah, you have not heard the end of it yet.'

" 'Let me hear it then,' I said. 'What happened afterwards?'

" 'The darkness seemed in part to clear away and we walked side by side across the grass in the twilight, straight up to the bare, black wall of rock. With the hilt of his sword he struck a heavy blow, and the solid rock opened as though it were a door. We passed through and it closed behind us with a tremendous clang—yes, it closed behind us'; and at that point he fairly broke down, crying and sobbing as I had never seen a man even in the most frightful grief cry and sob before."

The minister paused in his narrative. At that moment there came a tremendous blast of wind which shook the windows of the manse, and burst open the hall door, and caused the candles to flicker and the fire to go roaring up the chimney. It is not too much to say that, what with the uncanny story, and the howling storm, we all felt that creeping sort of uneasiness which so often seems like the touch of something from another world—a hand stretched across the boundary-line of time and eternity, the coldness and mystery of which make the stoutest heart tremble.

"I am telling you this tale," said Mr. Morison, resuming his seat after a brief absence to see that the fastenings of the house were properly attended to, "exactly as I heard it. You must draw your own deductions from the facts I put before you. Part of that great and terrible region in which he found himself, my friend went on to tell me, he penetrated, compelled by a power he could not resist, to see the most awful sights and the most frightful sufferings. There was no form of vice that had not there its representative. As they moved along, his companion told him the special sin for which such horrible punishment was being inflicted. Shuddering, and in mortal agony, he was unable to withdraw his eyes from the dreadful spectacle. The atmosphere grew more unendurable, the sights more and more terrible, the cries, groans, blasphemies more awful and heartrending.

" 'I can bear no more,' he gasped at last; 'let me go!'

"With a mocking laugh, the Presence beside him answered the appeal; a laugh which was taken up, even by the lost and anguished spirits around.

" 'There is no return' said the pitiless voice.

" 'But you promised,' he cried, 'you promised me faithfully.'

" 'What are promises here?' and the words were the sound of doom.

"Still he prayed and entreated; he fell on his knees and in his agony spoke words that seemed to cause the purpose of the Evil One to falter.

" 'You shall go,' he said, 'on one condition: that you agree to return to me on Wednesday next—or send a substitute.'

" 'I could not do that,' said my friend. 'I could not send any fellow-creature here. Better stop myself than do that.'

" 'Then stop,' said Satan, with the bitterest contempt; and he was turning away when the poor distracted soul asked for a minute more before he made his choice.

"He was in an awful strait: on the one hand, how could he remain himself? on the other, how could he doom another to such fearful torments? Who could he send? Who would come? And then suddenly there flashed into his mind the thought of an old man to whom it could not signify much whether he took up his place in this abode a few days sooner or a few days later. He was travelling to it as fast as he knew how. He was the reprobate of the parish; the sinner without hope that successive ministers had striven in vain to reclaim from the error of his ways; a man marked and doomed— Sandy the Tinker. Sandy, who was mostly drunk and always godless. Sandy, who, it was said, believed in nothing, and gloried in his infidelity. Sandy, whose soul really did not signify much. He would send him. Lifting his eyes, he saw those of his tormentor surveying him scornfully.

" 'Well, have you made your choice?' he asked.

" 'Yes, I think I can send a substitute,' was the hesitating answer.

" 'See you do then,' was the reply; 'for if you do not, and fail to return yourself, *I shall come for you.* Wednesday, remember, before midnight.' And with these words ringing in his ears he was flung violently through the rock, and found himself in the middle of his bedroom floor, as if he had just been kicked there.

"This is not the end of the story, is it?" asked one of our party, as the minister came to a full stop, and looked earnestly at the fire.

"No," he answered, "it is not the end; but before proceeding I must ask you to bear carefully in mind the circumstances already recounted. Especially remember the date mentioned—*Wednesday next, before midnight.*

"Whatever I thought, and you may think, about my friend's dream, it made the most remarkable impression upon *his* mind. He could not shake off its influence; he passed from one state of nervousness to another. It was in vain I entreated him to exert his common sense, and call all his strength of mind to his assistance. I might as well have spoken to the wind. He implored me not to leave him, and I agreed to remain. Indeed, to leave him in his then frame of mind would have been an act of the greatest cruelty. He wanted me also to preach in his place on the Sunday following; but this I flatly refused.

" 'If you do not make an effort now,' I said, 'you will never make it. Rouse yourself, get on with your sermon, and if you buckle down to work you will soon forget all about that foolish dream.'

"Well, to cut a long story short, the sermon was somehow composed and Sunday came, and my friend, a little better and getting over his fret, walked up into the pulpit to preach. He looked dreadfully ill; but I thought the worst was over now and that he would go on mending.

"Vain hope! He gave out the text and then looked over the congregation—and the first person on whom his eyes lighted was Sandy the Tinker. Sandy, who had never before been known to enter a place of worship of any sort; Sandy, whom he had mentally chosen as his substitute, and who was *due on the following Wednesday*—sitting just below him, quite sober, and comparatively clean, waiting with a great show of attention for the opening words of the sermon.

"With a terrible cry my friend caught the front of the pulpit, then swayed back and fell down in a fainting fit. He was carried home and a doctor sent for. I said a few words, addressed apparently to the congregation, but really to Sandy, for my heart somehow came into my mouth at the sight of him. And then, after I had dismissed the people, I paced slowly back to the manse, almost afraid of what might meet me.

"Mr. Crawley was not dead; but he was in the most dreadful state of physical exhaustion and mental agitation. It was dreadful to hear him. How could he go himself? How could he send Sandy?—poor old Sandy whose soul, in the sight of God, was just as precious as his own.

"His whole cry was for us to deliver him from the Evil One; to save him from committing a sin which would render him a wretched man for life. He counted the hours and the minutes before he must return to that horrible place.

" 'I can't send Sandy,' he would moan. 'I cannot. Oh, I cannot save myself at such a price!'

"And then he would cover his face with the bedclothes, only to start up and wildly entreat me not to leave him; to stand between the enemy and himself, to save him, or, if that were impossible, to give him the courage to do what was right.

" 'If this continues,' said the doctor, 'Wednesday will find him either dead or a raving lunatic.'

"We talked the matter over, the doctor and I, as we walked to and fro in the meadow behind the manse; and we decided, having to make our choice of two evils, to risk giving him such an opiate as should carry him over the dreaded interval. We knew it was a perilous thing to do even with one in his condition, but, as I said before; we could only take the lesser of two evils.

"What we dreaded most was his awaking before the time expired, so I kept watch beside him. He lay like one dead through the whole of Tuesday night and Wednesday and Wednesday evening. Eight, nine, ten, eleven o'clock came and passed—then twelve. 'God be thanked!' I said, as I stooped over him and heard he was breathing quietly.

" 'He will do now, I hope,' said the doctor, who had come in just before midnight, 'You will stay with him till he wakes?'

"I promised that I would and in the beautiful dawn of a summer's morning he opened his eyes and smiled. He had no recollection then of what had occurred; he was as weak as an infant and when I bade him try to go to sleep again turned on his pillow and sank to rest once more.

"Worn out with watching, I stepped softly from the room and passed into the fresh, sweet air. I strolled down to the garden-gate, and stood looking at the great mountains and the fair country, and the Deldy wandering like a silver thread through the green fields below.

"All at once my attention was attracted by a group of people coming slowly along the road leading from the hills. I could not at first see that in their midst something was being borne on men's shoulders; but when at last I made this out, I hurried to meet them and learn what was the matter.

" 'Has there been an accident?' I asked, as I drew near.

"They stopped and one man came towards me.

" 'Ay,' he said, 'the warst accident that could befa' him, puir fella. He's deid.'

" 'Who is it?' I asked, pressing forward; and lifting the cloth they had flung over his face, I saw *Sandy the Tinker*!

" 'He had been coming home, I tak' it,' remarked one who stood by, 'puir Sandy, and gaed over the cliff afore he could save himself. We found him just on this side of the Witches's Caldron, where there's a bonny strip of green turf, and his cuddy was feeding on the hill-top with the bit cart behind her.' "

There was silence for a minute—then one of the ladies said softly, "Poor Sandy."

"And what became of Mr. Crawley?" asked the other.

"He gave up his parish and went abroad as a missionary. He is still living."

"What a most extraordinary story!" I remarked.

"Yes, I think so," said the minister. "If you like to go round by Deldy tomorrow, my son, who now occupies the manse, would show you the scene of the occurrence."

The next day we all stood looking at the frowning cliff and at the Deldy, swollen by recent rains, rushing on its way.

The youngest of the party went up to the rock and knocked upon it loudly with his cane.

"Oh, don't do that, pray!" cried both the ladies nervously—the spirit of the weird story still brooded over us.

"What do you think of the coincidence, Jack?" I inquired of my friend, as we talked apart from the others.

"Ask me when we get back to Fleet Street," he answered.

A TALE OF A GAS-LIGHT GHOST

Anonymous

'Tis an easy thing for me to tell you a story of ghosts, for from my childhood I have been accustomed to hear of them; from my infancy I was taught to believe in them. Not the old nurses' tales of white-draped spectres, of grinning skulls and ghastly goblins; but the well-authenticated appearances after death of those known upon earth, in the dress they wore when toiling in the world.

Ghosts ran in the Dale family, people said jeeringly— insanity too, they added; and from time to time we have been made the butts for jokes of those would-be wags, who refuse to believe anything which does not happen to have come under their own narrow experience. I could tell you a story of my great-grandfather, who was haunted by the spirit of a man he slew in a duel, who followed him in the spirit form wherever he went, beckoning to him from the midst of a crowd at times; at others visiting him in the solitude of his chamber, till my great-grandfather, driven to frenzy, one day drew his sword and nearly ran his butler through the body for denying the ghost of the murdered man stood by him. The constant terror of this continual appearance drove my ancestor out of his mind though, of course, there were people who declared he was out of his mind in the first instance.

So of Roderick Dale, his son, who was haunted by an unknown figure, and finished his days in a lunatic asylum; so of Charles Mervyn, his nephew, who was again and again surprised by the apparition of his father, starting as it were from out the wall upon him. I could tell you all these stories, but you would not even pretend to listen to them.

The story I am about to tell you is quite different from these. It happened less than two years ago. There are a dozen men alive at the present day to vouch for its truth; and it does not depend on any of the usual ghost properties for its effect. In it there is no dismal ruined mansion, no desolate churchyard, no bell tolling the hour of midnight, no rattling of chains or hollow groanings; in short, it is a matter-of-fact ghost story, with none of the ordinary paraphernalia generally supposed to appertain to the spirit world. In order, however, that you may understand it properly, I must give you a short description of the parish of Mapleton, and a few of its inhabitants some twenty months since.

Mapleton is an essentially agricultural parish; its acreage is large, and so are its tillers; its population is small, and so are its wants; its politics are conservative, its society is exclusive, and its ignorance of the other parts of the world is great. Furthermore, its landowners are few and wealthy, and its tenant-farmers well-to-do and contented. It was on record that only one farmer had ever been dissatisfied with the state of things at Mapleton—a young man who had considered the old house in which generations of his ancestors had been born and died too gloomy for him, and had built himself a brand new house, of a mixture of the cottage and villa style, on the outskirts of the village, and had immediately afterwards gone to the dogs, and had been forced to seek a living away from his native place.

Thus it came about that there was a house to let in Mapleton; but how Gregory Barnstake came to know of it, and how, knowing it, he came to take it, after it had remained empty several years, was never understood. Where he came from nobody knew—who he was no one could find out. He was a severely handsome man, by which I mean that his face in marble would have been called superb, but in flesh and blood it was too hard and too expressionless; he was neither young nor old; he had no friends who came to see him, and he appeared to be well off. Society at Mapleton settled that from such a man it would be well to keep aloof until something was known of his antecedents, but Gregory

Barnstake never gave society an opportunity of showing its feelings, for he avoided as much as possible even necessary intercourse with his neighbours, and, as the villagers put it, "kept himself to himself".

The doctor was the only man in the parish who had ever entered his house. Gregory Barnstake one afternoon fell down in a fit, and his servant ran to Dr. Sweetman and brought him in all haste to where the new inhabitant of Mapleton lay stretched on a couch, with his limbs cold and stiff and his eyes fixed and glassy, looking more like a corpse than a man.

In an hour's time the rigidity left his limbs, and his eyes assumed their ordinary expression. Sitting up, his glance rested somewhat angrily on the doctor.

"Who are you?" he asked abruptly.

"Doctor Sweetman. I heard from your servant that you were ill, and came to see if I could be of any service."

"Thank you. When I want physic I will send for you."

The doctor, who was as merry and good-natured a little round man as you could wish to meet with, took this, of course, as a dismissal, and not a very polite one. He was not prone to take offence, but he could not feel pleased with such a reception.

"Good day, sir," he said, opening the door.

"Stay a moment, doctor, I beg," said Mr. Barnstake; "I fear

I have offended you. Let me explain to you that these fits of mine come upon me at intervals. I can never tell when to expect them. They seize me and leave me in a state of torpor for one, two, or sometimes three hours, during which time no doctor's skill could benefit me. When they have passed I recover at once, as you see I have done now."

"Is your mind unconscious at the time?' asked Dr. Sweetman.

"Unconscious of the present, but living in the past," was the answer with a weary sigh.

"Have you any pain when you are attacked in the first instance?"

"Yes. I feel as if a hand of ice were laid over my heart; then that its hold tightens, causing me exquisite pain, till at last I fall senseless."

"Hum!" said the doctor; "a curious but not an unprecedented case. If you would allow me to send you something I fancy I could alleviate your sufferings."

"Quite a mistake. You doctors go on prescribing medicine till you believe in their efficacy."

"You have a bad opinion of the profession," responded the doctor.

"Not of the profession so much, perhaps, as of those who practise it. The world is composed of knaves and fools; the fools take the medicines, the knaves prescribe."

Retorted the doctor hotly:

"Then, sir, I am to conclude that you alone are superior to the world at large, as you are neither knave enough to prescribe, nor fool enough to take, prescriptions."

"You are to conclude nothing of the sort, but to see in me an unfortunate man whose love of playing the knave led him on to play the fool, and reduced him to what he now is. If you knew the story of my life you——"

"Well, sir?"

"You would know the story of a miserable man."

The doctor had to be content with that ending to the sentence, and took his leave, puzzling his head to make out whether he had been talking to a man whose brains were a little touched, or whether his conversation had been with one of those dark and mysterious heroes so often met with in books and melodramas, but so seldom in real life.

The months went by at Mapleton, the crops were gathered in and sown again, and Gregory Barnstake remained as great a mystery as ever. With the doctor he had had on one or two occasions short conversations, but with no one else had he interchanged more than a few words of abrupt courtesy.

A time came, however, when he was driven to consort with his neighbours. An enterprising railway company, having discovered there was no iron road near Mapleton, sent out its staff of surveyors to walk over the farms and inspect the country, with a view to making a branch line from Overbury through Mapleton to Harstone Heath, and the landowners rose in a body to repel the intrusive steam engines.

Gregory Barnstake received a letter to inform him of these facts, and that a meeting, commencing with a dinner, was to be held at the "Seven Stars" on a certain day for the purpose of remonstrating, petitioning, and doing anything that might be necessary to stop the proposed railway. To this letter he returned no answer.

A second was sent, repeating the substance of the first and adding the information that his house was the proposed site of the station. To this he rejoined that he was sorry to hear it, as he should certainly leave the place in the event of a railroad coming there, but that at the same time he must decline to attend the dinner.

However, still further pressure was put upon him, till at last, in an interview with Dr. Sweetman, he said angrily:

"Well, well, to save further words I will attend, but bear in mind whatever may happen I am not responsible."

There were many reasons why his presence was so much desired at the meeting, the principal being that he was a person much interested, as the whole of the land he held on lease would be required by the railway company. Another, that it was whispered that he was very clever; that he read Latin and Greek books for amusement; and that mysterious volumes of matter incomprehensible, save to the learned, lay generally on the table by his side. Now the Mapletonians, as a rule, knew more of farming than of literature, and it was deemed that to have a man amongst them who would polish up any petition they might send forward, and to see to the correctness of expression in such letters as they might consider it incumbent on them to write, would be of the greatest advantage; and so it was that Gregory Barnstake was worried into a reluctant assent to attend the meeting.

The day, big with fate for the Mapletonians, arrived. The landowners and the majority of tenant-farmers met in the largest room of the "Seven Stars", and, punctual to the minute, Gregory Barn-stake entered. As the door opened to give him admission, he happened to be the subject of the conversation, and an awkward silence ensued as he came forward; but one or two speedily advanced towards him and gave him a hearty welcome, thanking him for breaking through his rule of never mixing with his neighbours, and hoping that, now he had commenced, they might often have the pleasure of seeing him, to all of which he answered, gravely and seriously, that it was no pleasure to him to mix in what was called society; but, as they had pressed him so much to be present on this occasion, he had felt he must do as they desired, "but," he added, speaking loudly enough for the whole room to hear, "in accepting your invitation, I omitted to state that it would be impossible for me to come alone, and, therefore, I must beg that a chair may be set apart for another guest."

Everyone was astonished, for never had Gregory Barnstake been seen talking familiarly with anyone, never had he been supposed to have any intimate; and yet there was some one from whom he could not be separated himself even for a few hours.

"Is your friend in any way interested in this proposed railway encroachment?" asked the squire.

"Not in the least."

"Has he any property about here?"

"None whatever."

"We have not expected anyone here today," stammered the squire, getting very red in the face, "who was not in some way connected or, at all events, interested in the subject we have met to discuss, but, of course——"

"If you have any objection I will at once withdraw."

"No, no; on no account. I was about to add that any friend of yours we would accept."

There was a silence, then a short desultory conversation, and in the middle of it dinner was announced.

"Has your friend arrived?" asked the squire of his strange acquaintance. "I see no unfamiliar face amongst us."

"He is not here, yet, but he is sure to come. If I may keep

this seat next to me vacant for him, it is all I require."

No objection was made, the party took their seats, leaving that one chair unoccupied; the covers were removed, and the dinner commenced.

There was not much conversation then, for the Mapletonians held that to dine was one of the chief duties of man; but ere the first course was at an end the entire party, with one accord, raised their eyes from their plates and fixed them on a figure sitting in the chair that had been left vacant. Gregory Barnstake alone seemed quiet and unsurprised. In the chair by his side sat a man, remarkable more for his aristocratic appearance than for any beauty of feature. His age, apparently, was between forty and fifty; his hair and whiskers were iron grey, and arranged with scrupulous neatness and precision; but the most extraordinary thing about him was his complexion, which was of a pale ash hue, such as to cause more than one to shudder and wonder. Another peculiarity about him was his attire. He was in full evening dress. His black coat and spotless shirt front, his sparkling studs and snowy cravat, contrasted strangely with the farmers' shooting jackets and the squire's bird's-eye neckerchief.

Quietly he sat at table, eating nothing, but trifling with the fork laid beside his plate. No one had seen him enter, no one had observed him take his seat, but there he sat as calmly and unconcernedly as if he were a bidden guest, known to the whole company.

As he played with the fork with his left hand another fact was apparent, which was that the second and third fingers on that hand were wanting.

It was strange that, while the whole table paused to regard the stranger the only person who seemed unconscious of his presence was he who sat by his side, and through whose agency he was in the room. There was a great awkwardness about it, the squire thought, for Gregory Barnstake had apparently no intention of introducing him, and not one of the company seated in that warm gas-lighted room, with a good dinner on the table before them, but felt a sensation of uneasiness, for which they were totally unable to account.

"Come, gentlemen," said the squire, feeling it incumbent upon some one to break the silence, "there's no occasion for so much solemnity, I hope. Mr. Parkhurst, pleasure of a glass of wine with you."

Mr. Parkhurst filled his glass.

"Ah," continued the squire, "I remember old Tony buying this wine—very good it is, too—let me see when was it; '44, I think."

"No," said the stranger, " '48."

"I beg your pardon sir. Did you know Tony Bean?"

The stranger shook his head.

"Anyhow it was in the year Jem Hales was transported for poaching. His time's up now; he'll be coming home soon, I suppose."

"Jem Hales will never come home," said the stranger.

"Do you know him then?"

"I saw him a short time since."

"Indeed. In England?"

"No."

"Where is he now?"

"In his grave."

The squire gazed, not without a certain amount of fear, on the uninvited guest, and pursued the matter no further.

The conversation at the dinner-table languished, and, in spite of one or two attempts to revive it, finally died into confidential whisperings between those sitting next each other.

With the removal of the cloth the spirits of the company revived, and the squire, getting on his legs, inveighed with all the eloquence of which he was master against all the railway companies, and that one in particular which threatened to destroy the primitive innocence of Mapleton. Everybody spoke at once, and the meeting had like to have proved a failure, but Gregory Barnstake, rousing himself, made a speech such as had never been heard in Mapleton, putting all the facts before them clearly and concisely, and urging the immediate drawing up and signing of the proposed petition.

All this time the stranger sat calm and immovable, but when preparations were being made for framing the petition he spoke.

"You may spare yourself trouble," he said; "your petition will be of no avail."

"How do you know that?" asked the squire sharply.

"I state a fact."

"Perhaps you are a shareholder in the company," said a farmer, in a tone meant to be sarcastic.

"This day nineteen months," said the stranger, "a train will pass through Mapleton."

"I hope you are a false prophet, sir," said the squire.

"I am not," rejoined the other.

In spite of his prediction, the petition was drawn up and signed, and the meeting broke up.

"You see we persevere in our plan, although you predict failure," said the squire, putting on his hat.

The stranger bowed.

"Good evening, sir."

"We shall meet again. In eight weeks."

"You are certainly a very circumstantial prophet," answered the squire, and with a slight bow he left the room.

Said Dr. Sweetman, taking Gregory Barnstake by the

button, "an extraordinary-looking man, your friend."

"Very."

"Excuse me, I don't wish to be impertinent, but, in the interest of my profession, do you know if he is suffering from any internal disease?"

"He is not. I can answer for it," said Gregory with a slight shudder.

"It is strange. I never saw a living man with such a complexion."

"He is not a living man," was the reply, and the speaker walked away, leaving the little doctor gazing after him in frightened astonishment.

Eight weeks after this dinner the squire was out with the hounds, and his horse, in taking a hedge, stumbled, and pitched his rider over his head. The squire was not hurt, neither was the horse, for he trotted away, leaving his owner to follow as best he might, and over fields and hedges he went, till, on emerging from a small copse, he saw his steed standing by a pond, and near to him the figure of a man. The man was dressed in spotless evening attire, and was without a hat and the squire in a moment identified him as the stranger at the dinner two months before.

His appearance had been singular enough within the walls of the "Seven Stars", but now to meet him in a precisely similar dress in the open country was much more startling, and the squire, though a brave man, would have avoided him if possible; he would have given a well-filled purse to have been able to reach his horse without passing by the motionless figure, but it was an impossibility, so, raising his hat and putting as bold a face on it as he could, he thanked the stranger for catching his beast, but received not a syllable in response. Only, at last, when he had remounted his horse did the figure move, then it turned towards him, and, stretching out the hand on which the two fingers were missing, pointed to the water.

The squire set spurs to his horse and rode away.

The days became weeks, and the weeks months, the railway company got permission to make their line through Mapleton, and some hundred nawys were busily employed in making an embankment. In draining the pond which was memorable to the squire they found something which induced them to leave off work for the time, and send for the authorities to the spot, and that something was the skeleton of a man half-buried in the mud.

Dr. Sweetman was, of course, amongst those summoned. The bones were left untouched for his inspection.

"It's strange," he said, when he had finished his inspection, "but there are two fingers wanting."

There was nothing to be done after the inquiry but to place the bones in a coffin and inter them in the churchyard;

but an idea had come into the doctor's head—a fancy—that Gregory Barnstake might know something of the skeleton. Had not that mysterious friend of his lacked two fingers of his left hand? So the doctor, on his way home, called at the house at the end of the village.

He rapped at the door with his knuckles, but received no answer. The door was on the latch and he pushed it open. He entered the sitting-room where he had had his first interview with its strange occupant, and the first thing that met his eyes was Gregory Barnstake stretched on the floor, his handsome face terribly distorted with pain—dead!

Was he really dead, or was it only one of those strange fits to which he was subject? The little doctor tried every test, and decided it was really death that had come upon him; that the agony of one of those fits had killed him. For the rest, I hardly dare tell you; but nevertheless it is true that, when the body came to be examined, over the heart were distinctly discernable the livid marks as of a hand pressed tightly there, but of a hand of which the second and third fingers were wanting.

That is the story I had to tell you. You are welcome to put what interpretation on it you please. It was a mystery, and a mystery it will always remain. I cannot attempt to give you a clue to one of the strangest stories it has ever been my lot to hear and know to be true.

In conclusion, I can only add that there are now at least a dozen men alive who can vouch for the accuracy of the facts I have stated, but who, like myself, whatever may be their opinions, forbear to attempt an explanation of this strange occurrence to which I, perhaps without sufficient reason, have given the name of "The Tale of a Gas-light Ghost."

EYES OF TERROR

Mrs. L. T. Meade

The strange story which I am about to tell happened just when the late war in South Africa was at its height. I was in a very nervous condition at the time, having lost my dear father, who was killed in action shortly before the taking of Pretoria. The news of my father's death reached us on a certain evening in May, just when the days were approaching their longest, and summer, with all its beauties, was about to visit the land. It was immediately afterwards that the visitations which I am about to describe took place. They were of a very alarming character, and so much did they upset my mental equilibrium that I determined to put my case into the hands of a certain Professor Ellicott, who was not only a physician and surgeon in the ordinary sense, but was also a man of great learning and keen original research.

I had met the Professor once at the house of a neighbour, and on that occasion had admired him, not only for his intellectual appearance, but also for the massive strength of his face and the calmness of his bearing. I knew that a strong man, who was also sympathetic and tactful, would not laugh at a girl's fears, however unreasonable he might consider them, and had not the least doubt that I should receive a patient hearing when I told him my story.

My name is Nora Dallas. I am twenty-one years of age. I have lived all my life in a beautiful old place about a mile and a half from the town of Ashingford. Professor Ellicott lived in the High Street, and I was fortunate enough to find him at home.

I sent in my card and was immediately admitted into his presence. He was a man of about thirty, with resolute grey eyes and a determined chin. He gave me a quick glance when I entered the room; then, without uttering a word, pointed to a chair.

"I am called Nora Dallas," I said.

"I know," he replied, in a gentle voice. "You are the daughter of that Colonel Dallas whose gallant action, when he sacrificed his life for his country on the march to Pretoria, is the talk and admiration of the country."

My eyes filled with tears.

"It is only three weeks since I heard of my father's death," I said. "You will forgive me sir, but I cannot bear any sympathetic reference to the subject, at least for the present."

"I understand," he replied, his hard face softening. "And now, what can I do for you?"

"I want to consult you as a doctor."

"But I am not a consultant—I mean that I do not practise medicine in the ordinary sense."

"I am aware of that fact," I answered. "And just for that very reason, Professor Ellicott, I have been compelled to come to you."

"I do not quite understand."

He looked at me with the dawn of a smile on his lips.

"I think you will give me a frank opinion, and be unbiased by the red-tapism which causes many medical men to hide the truth from their patients."

"Ah, you think well of me," he said, with a smile, "and I perceive that you are a brave woman. Nevertheless, I must inform you that I am scarcely qualified to enter into your case. My work lies altogether in the regions of original research."

"May I at least tell you my story?" I insisted. "You can make up your mind afterwards whether you will help me or not."

His reply to this was to get up and pace the room, stopping once or twice to look at me, then continuing his slow, measured tread up and down. I did not interrupt him. I sat as still as though carved in marble.

"You must forgive my apparent rudeness, Miss Dallas," he said, "but I was endeavouring to recall what I had already heard about you. I remember everything now. I met you a month ago at Sir John Newcome's. You live at Courtlands, one of the finest places in the neighbourhood. You are an only child. Doubtless, now that your father is dead, you are wealthy. You have lived at Courtlands almost all your life. Of course, Miss Dallas, you have your own family physician?"

"Yes," I answered.

"Will you not consult him?"

"No; for he is not the man for my purpose."

He smiled.

"You think that I am?"

"If anyone can help me, you can."

"How like a woman!" he said, somewhat impatiently. "And yet you know nothing about me. As I said just now, I am not a consultant. I have come to Ashingford for quiet, and for the opportunity to examine into the length and breadth of a problem which, if I can bring it to a successful issue, will mean health and happiness to millions. And yet a girl, little more than a child, wants to interrupt my train of thought. Do you think you are fair to me?"

"I don't know anything about that," I replied, with vehemence. "I only know that I want help. Will you give it to me?"

My voice broke.

"Of course I will," he said, cordially, and his whole manner completely altered. "I only said what I did to test you. Now we will preamble no more. Tell me your story."

"I was twenty-one last March," I began, immediately, "and now that my dear father is dead I am absolutely my own mistress. With the exception of my Aunt Sophia, my father's sister, who lives with me, and my two cousins, I am without relations. It is about these cousins that I wish specially to speak. They are the sons of my father's younger brother, who has long been dead. My father adopted them in their infancy, brought them up, sent them to school, and gave them all they required. They are twins and are now five-and twenty years of age. Rudolf has been called to the Bar and Lionel is a solicitor. Professor Ellicott, I must be truthful—I must be truthful even at the risk of failing in charity. My cousins are not good men. I have nothing to say against them—I have no means at present of proving my words—nevertheless, instinct tells me that I am right. Rudolf is the sort of man who imposes on people. I have seen him rhapsodize over poetry or a sunset, and his friends then imagine that he has a great love for the beautiful. But I know better. The only love in his wicked heart is the love of money. Lionel is his weak shadow—his dupe and tool."

"Surely you are hard on your cousins?"

"You would naturally think so; and yet I hope to convince you that I have read their characters aright.

"My father, before he went to South Africa, made a will, the contents of which he fully explained to me. In the event of his death I was to inherit the house and estate and also the bulk of his money, with the exception of a sum of sixty thousand pounds, which was to be divided between my two cousins. He fully explained all that he wanted to tell me with regard to his last will, and gave me directions as to certain affairs which he wished to be specially attended to. My dear father then continued to say some words which astonished and distressed me very much. He declared that it was the darling wish of his heart that Rudolf and I should marry. My father said that he had the highest opinion of my cousin and assured me that nothing would make him happier than such a marriage. Rudolf had told him of his attachment to me—an attachment which I knew well did not exist.

"I heard my father in silence. Then I gave an emphatic negative to the whole proposal. My father listened in amazement. I said that I neither liked nor trusted my cousin, and that nothing—no words, no conditions—would make me accept him. After a pause my father said that my feelings must be my guide, but he continued:

" 'I cannot agree with your opinion, and I sincerely hope that time may alter it.'

"From the hour of his depature there began for me a detestable period, during which I was persecuted by Rudolf's odious attentions. As he and Lionel practically lived in our house, you can imagine that it was impossible for me to escape altogether from his presence. But at last it became so intolerable that I wrote to my father on the subject. I told Rudolf quite frankly that I was doing so, and even made him acquainted with the greater part of my letter. In that letter I told my father that he did not rightly gauge his nephew's character, that he was not what he believed him to be, and, in order to prove my words, I mentioned a few instances which, unconvincing to a stranger like yourself, might have the effect of opening his eyes.

"That letter was posted two months ago. Up to the present I have had no reply to it, but am even now waiting and hoping to hear my father's views on the subject. Important letters must be on the road from South Africa for me. I have only received the news of my dear father's death by cablegram."

My voice broke. I paused, struggling with emotion; then I continued:

"I am sorry to trouble you, Professor Ellicott, with this long preamble. I am now approaching that strange thing about which I wish to consult you.

"We received the cablegram acquainting us with the news

of my father's death on a certain morning towards the end of last month. On the evening of that same day another long cablegram from South Africa was put into Rudolf's hands. He was sitting with my aunt and me in the drawing-room when he received it. He opened it, was evidently very much upset, but refused to divulge its contents. He called Lionel to his side, and they left the room together. I saw them pacing up and down in the shrubbery, evidently consulting with regard to the contents of the cablegram, but never from that hour till now have I heard the slightest inkling of what it was about.

"Three days later my father's will was read and my cousins heard of the large sums of money which would fall to their share. They fully expected to be remembered in my father's will, but not to such a generous extent, and their satisfaction was very great. As to Rudolf, his face quite beamed with delight, and they were both in feverish haste to possess themselves of the money. Mr. Brewster, our family lawyer, however, said that it would be impossible for them to receive their legacies for several weeks, as probate would have to be taken and other preliminaries attended to. Finally he made the remark:

"Nothing can really be done until Colonel Dallas's letters and papers arrive from South Africa. This can scarcely be expected until a month from the present date.'

"On that very evening my elder cousin came to me again and once more implored me to become his wife. He spoke of my father and his well-known wishes on the subject, and pleaded with such power that had I not known him well I might have been touched into a semblance of kindness by his manner. I did know my cousin, however, and told him so in unmistakable terms. He seemed to struggle with emotion for a minute; then he said, rising as he spoke:

" 'All right, Nora, I see I must accept your verdict. You may be sure that I will not trouble you on this subject again. It would be brutal to do so," he added, "for you are looking very ill. I see it in your eyes.'

" 'I am not exactly ill,' I answered. 'I am naturally in very great trouble, but I am no more really ill than you are.'

" 'I am all right,' he said, with a shrug of his shoulders. 'But your nerves, poor Nora, are in a sad condition. You have received a most serious shock, and it is telling on you. You ought to be exceedingly careful. I mean it is your duty to be much more careful than most women.'

" 'I don't understand you,' I answered. 'And I wish,' I added, 'that you would leave me now.'

" 'I will in a minute,' he said, and then he approached quite close to my side.

" 'One word before I go,' he went on, and he fixed his great, strong, dark eyes on mine. 'Whether you like me or whether you hate me we are cousins, Nora. Our family history is well known to each of us. I in particular, however, have studied medicine, and am therefore in a position to speak. I only gave up medicine for the Bar because I thought I saw a more speedy way of earning money in that profession. Now, Nora, listen. Raise your eyes to mine. Don't shrink, child. If you encourage the morbid fancies which are now filling your brain you will share the fate of poor Aunt Ethel. I know what I am talking about. The pupils of your eyes point to a disordered brain.'

"He left me. I sat still for a minute, feeling more nervous and disturbed than I cared to own. Then I went to Aunt Sophia.

" 'What is the matter, Nora?' she said, when I found her. 'You are trembling all over and looking so ill. What is wrong child?'

" 'I want to ask you a straight question,' I replied. 'Who was, or who is, Aunt Ethel? I have never heard of her.'

"Aunt Sophia looked startled. She did not speak for a minute; then she said, with considerable reluctance:

" 'It doesn't matter about your Aunt Ethel. She has been long in her grave. Let her memory rest in peace.'

" 'But what about her?' I said. 'I *will* know,' I continued, and then I repeated what Rudolf had told me.

"Aunt Sophia looked very queer. After a futher pause

she said:

" 'Rudolf has done wrong, but as you know so much you may as well know all. Your Aunt Ethel was your father's eldest sister. She went mad when about your age, and eventually ended her days by suicide.'

" 'And I was never told,' I said, turning white.

" 'Why should you be told?'

" 'But there must be insanity in our family.'

" 'Hers was the only case. Don't think about it again, child. Busy yourself with those active employments which a woman in your position has naturally so much to do with.'

"I left Aunt Sophia and returned to my room. There was a moon in the sky. My bedroom windows were open. I lit a pair of candles at each side of the long mirror at one end of the room, and deliberately studied my face. I had always known that my eyes were somewhat peculiar, my pupils being more dilated than those of most women."

"That fact merely betokens a high degree of nervous sensibility," said the Professor.

"I examined my eyes that night," I continued, "and it did seem to me that they had a wild and startled glance. I called my courage to my aid, however, and determined not to be fanciful, and to try to forget my cousin's words. That was easily said, but very difficult to act upon. My courage certainly did ebb as night went on. I found that my thoughts dwelt on Aunt Ethel and her horrible fate, and also found that I could turn them in no other direction. Presently I went to the window and looked out into the beautiful night. The moonlight was falling across the grass and causing black shadows under the trees.

"Suddenly I uttered a scream and fell back, too startled to keep my self-control. For gazing at me fixedly out of the deep mass of foliage were two very bright, luminous eyes, eyes full of a strange and terrifying gleam. I saw them as distinctly as I now see you. I watched them move, and saw them glitter as they disappeared into the darkness. When they had quite vanished I knew that I was cold all over. I shivered with a most awful sense of dread. My first desire was to run straight to Aunt Sophia, tell her the whole truth, and beg of her to share my room for the night. But on reflection I resolved not to do this. I did not want Aunt Sophia to know. She would certainly not have believed my tale, and she would put down the vision which I had seen to the same cause of which Rudolf would doubtless attribute it.

"There was no repose for me that night. The thought of those eyes kept me company—the eyes themselves and Rudolf's significant words: 'If you encourage those morbid fancies you will share the fate of poor Aunt Ethel. The pupils of your eyes point to a disordered brain.'

"In the afternoon of the next day I went for a solitary walk by myself. We have pine woods at the back of our house. From there I could see at intervals the tower which is the oldest part of the mansion. It is situated at the end of a long, rambling building, and was in existence at least four centuries ago. It is a curious Old Norman tower, with arches over the windows and a castellated roof. The tower contains only two rooms, the lower one being the library of our house and the upper my father's study. Since his death no one has been near that part of the building. I felt a sense of reproach as I remembered his room now. Was his study neglected and covered with dust? Were the flowers in the vases dried up and dead? I would go to the study tomorrow and see that it was made fresh and clean. I would open the windows and let in the sweet air. Nay, more, when the long-looked-for and eagerly expected letters arrived from South Africa I would read them in my father's study.

"That evening I paced up and down for a long time in the pine woods, then I returned to the house. I took up a novel and tried to read, but the book did not suit my mood. I remembered another which had begun to interest me, and which I had left in one of the drawing-rooms. I went downstairs to fetch it. There was no one in the room. I found the book in a distant corner and returned slowly to my bedroom. To do this I had to go down a long corridor into which many opened. For some extraordinary reason the electric light in this corridor was not turned on. I noticed how dark it was, and just as I reached my own door I looked back, impelled, I suppose, by instinct. In the darkness at the father end of the corridor I again saw the gleaming eyes. They stared fixedly at me without blinking, and with a horrible leering expression in their gaze. Again I screamed, rushed into my room, and locked the door. I could scarcely endure my misery.

" 'Am I going mad or am I the victim of an apparition?' I said to myself. 'Is my brain giving way? What am I to do? How am I to endure this? How am I to live?'

"The next week or ten days passed without any futher disturbance, and I was beginning to recover my mental balance. Rudolf was away from home during the greater part of that time, engaged on some very special business in the North of England. I was undoubtedly happier and less nervous when he was absent, but when he returned his affectionate and concerned manner about me made me self-reproachful, and I almost wondered at myself for the intolerable feeling of repugnance which I always felt towards him.

"Two or three nights after his return I saw the eyes again. On this occasion they stared at me from the centre of the rose-lawn. The night was black as pitch, and there were the eyes raised between five and six feet above the ground, and staring full at me with unblinking directness. After this visitation I determined to see you at once. Now, can you help me? Have I been visited by an apparition or am I mad? Tell me what you really think."

For reply the Professor said, quietly:

"I will examine your own eyes before I pronounce an opinion."

I rose at once. He placed me in a chair in front of a large window and, taking up some powerful lenses, carefully looked into both my eyes. When the examination was over he said:—

"You are very nervous. Some of the higher nerve centres are in a state of irritation. Your Father's death, joined to the shock of this apparition, trick, or what you like to call it, has been too much for you. You ought really to leave home."

"But am I going mad?"

"There is no trace of a disordered brain. Nevertheless you are nervous, and nerves are kittle cattle, and ought to be attended to."

"But, Dr. Ellicott, why should I be nervous? Why should I see those ghastly eyes? What is the mystery?"

"I should like much to unravel it," he said, with a shrug of his shoulders.

"How I wish you would!"

He looked thoughtful for a minute or two; then he said:

"Would it be possible for you to invite me to stay at Courtlands?"

"Would you come?"

"Could you give me a room where I could continue my business without interruption?"

"I could hand you over the library in the old tower. There you need never hear a footfall, for the tower is at the end of an unused wing at a remote part of the building."

"In that case I will bring my things and spend a few days at Courtlands. I do not believe in your apparition as an apparition, nor do I think that you are becoming insane. Your case interests me. May I arrive in time for dinner this evening?"

"I don't know how to thank you," was my answer.

"Expect me at Courtlands about seven o'clock. And now leave me, like a good girl, for I have many things to attend to."

I returned home with a great sense of relief, just in time for lunch. The only people at table were Aunt Sophia and my Cousin Lionel.

"Why, Nora," cried my aunt, "how much better you look! Have you had good news?"

"Yes and no," I replied. "By the way, Aunt Sophy, can we entertain a visitor for the next few days?'

"A visitor now?" she said, raising her brows in

astonishment.

Lionel laid down his knife and fork and looked hard at me.

"To receive a visitor in the house now would be unusual, would it not, Nora?" he said, gently. "My uncle has not been dead a month yet."

I took no notice of him, but turned again to Aunt Sophia.

"Dr. Ellicott, the well-known Professor, is staying at Ashingford," I said. "I met him some time ago at the Newcomes'. He is a remarkably clever man, and I may as well confess that I consulted him medically this morning. No more Dr. Jessops for me. I preferred to consult one who was well up-to-date on medical matters. The Professor interests me and I interest him. He wishes to come here for a few days in order to watch my symptoms. He will arrive in time for dinner. Please, Aunt Sophy, will you order the green room to be got ready for him, and also the library in the old tower?"

I spoke in a decided manner, and neither my aunt nor Lionel ventured to remonstrate, for, after all, I was really mistress.

Suddenly I turned to my cousin.

"Is Rudolf away again?" I asked.

"No," he replied; "Rudolf is unwell. His eyes are hurting

him. He is obliged to stay in a darkened room."

"I did not know that Rudolf suffered from his eyes."

"He never did until lately. We neither of us can imagine what is the matter with them," was Lionel's response.

I said a word or two of commonplace condolence, and then left the room.

That evening the Professor arrived, and when I entered the drawing-room before dinner I noticed that my aunt and both my cousins were waiting to receive him. During dinner he made himself generally agreeable, and Rudolf in especial seemed to be attracted by his manner and powers of conversation. I noticed, however, rather to my amazement, that my elder cousin wore a shade over his eyes, and in the course of dinner I inquired what really ailed them.

"I don't know," he said. "I am in considerable pain. My eyes are very much inflamed."

"Will you permit me to do something to relieve your symptoms?" said Professor Ellicott, suddenly, turning as he spoke, raising his pince-nez, and fixing his gaze on Rudolf's face.

"I wish you would," was the reply.

"I will look at your eyes after dinner. And now, Miss Dallas," he continued, turning with courtesy to my aunt, "let me explain that knotty point to you."

He was discussing a little matter with regard to the growth

of ferns, and Aunt Sophia, a keen botanist, was listening to him with rapt attention.

By-and-by I made the signal to leave the room, and the gentlemen were left to themselves. In the course of that same evening the Professor came to sit near me.

"I have examined your cousin's eyes. There is considerable inflammation both in the eyelids and the eyes themselves. Their condition points to a strange diagnosis, but as it seems impossible that it can be the right one I am not prepared to say anything further on the subject—at least now. Tell me are you going to have a good sleep tonight?"

"I hope so."

"I think you will, for I have prepared a small, but effectual, draught, which I want you to take just as you are lying down. Get your maid to sleep in your room, and believe me that, eyes or no eyes, you will be in a state of oblivion five minutes after you take my draught."

I smiled, with a sense of relief.

"I believe," I said, "that in any case I should sleep well with you in the house."

The next few days passed without anything fresh occurring. We saw but little of the Professor. He was absorbed with his own work in the old library in the tower.

At last the day arrived when we expected letters and news from the beloved dead. Even Aunt Sophia was agitated, and

Lionel and Rudolf were like restless ghosts, hovering here, there and everywhere. Rudolf's eyes looked worse than ever, and he also complained of a strange sore at his side. At dinner that evening the Professor said, abruptly:

"By the way, Dallas, do you happen to know anything about that new substance—radium?"

"I have heard of it," was the reply.

Lionel's face became suddenly rigid and very pale. Rudolf, on the contrary, looked with the utmost composure at Professor Ellicott.

"You, of course, have studied its properties," he said. "Tell me about them. I dabble in many things, and, above all enjoyments, to peer into the mysteries of science delights me most. But give me an account of the properties of radium."

"They are too varied to mention here. I will but allude to one or two. In close contact with the skin, radium has the effect of absolutely destroying the epidermis and the true skin beneath, thus in time producing an open sore. Moreover," said the Professor, "were you really dabbling with this strange substance the state of your eyes would be accounted for."

"I have never even seen the thing," was the abrupt answer.

The conversation turned to other matters. After dinner we all went to the drawing-room. Professor Ellicott came and seated himself near me.

"You will receive a letter from your father by the next post?" he asked.

"Yes."

"Where will you read it?"

"In his study. I have always read his letters there. I made him a promise that I would do so. He said he would like to think of me sitting under my mother's portrait, reading his letters and thinking of him."

A few minutes afterwards the postman's ring was heard, and a servant entered with several letters on a salver. The one I had expected was handed to me, and there was also a foreign letter for Aunt Sophia. Rudolf, who had come into the room just before the servant brought the letters, came up to me.

"You will go away by yourself and read your letter," he said, kindly. "You will read it in your father's study, won't you?"

I nodded. He smiled.

"I felt sure you would go there, Nora. He will be with you in spirit."

As Rudolf uttered the last words he glanced towards Lionel, and the two left the room a minute or two before I did.

To reach the tower I had to go down a long corridor which was seldom used. At the farther end of the corridor was a baize door which opened on to some narrow stone stairs. They were worn with age. Mounting them, I soon reached my father's study on the top floor of the tower. It was octagonal in shape, with many windows. These windows were closely barred and the panes of glass were small. When I entered the room I gave a start of surprise. I expected to see it in darkness, but instead of that a small table had been drawn up within a foot or two of the high, old-fashioned grate, and on it were placed a pair of brass candlesticks with candles in them already lighted. But why were the blinds not drawn down at the windows? I felt a momentary inclination to repair this omission myself, but my father's letter occupied all my thoughts and I soon forgot everything but the fact that I was about to read the beloved words—in short, to receive a message from the dead.

The contents of my father's letter absorbed my complete attention, and I-soon perceived that only the very early portion was written by himself; most of it had evidently been dictated to a certain Edward Vincent, whose name, as one of the young lieutenants in my father's regiment, was already familiar to me. The letter told me that my father was mortally wounded, and that he was now partly writing, partly dictating his last good-bye to me in the tent where they had removed him after the skirmish with the enemy. In the letter he told me that he had received my last communication, and, in consequence, had made inquiries, which took some little time to come to fruition. On that very morning, however, he had received a long letter from London, which contained a complete confirmation of what I had told him, and also many other revelations had been forthcoming, which filled him with the utmost displeasure and horror. He therefore resolved immediately to change his will, leaving none of his property to my cousins, but all to me. The last words of his letter desired me to turn to the opposite page, on which a formally-worded will was written. This will left everything to me. I turned to it and read it. It was very short, and was signed by my father, and had also the signatures of two witnesses.

Tears flowed from my eyes. In one sense I was relieved, and yet my heart was torn. I covered my face. Just then a slight noise, which might have been attributed to the tapping of a bough against the window-pane, caused me to turn my head. I did so tremblingly. I felt convinced that I was not alone. Something, or someone, was looking at me. Fascinated, I gazed straight before me. Again came that ghastly tap, which I felt sure, proceeded from no human hand. I looked towards the upper panes of one of the windows, and there were the eyes. Never had they seemed more malicious or horrible. I lost my nerve, gave one shrill and terrified scream, and rushed towards the door, altogether forgetting my letter, which lay upon the table.

I had just reached the door when a fresh thing happened. The room became full of a sudden and terrible wind. It caught at the table-cloth, flapping it violently. The letter, written on thin foreign paper and consequently light as air, floated off the table with one or two other loose letters, was carried straight to the fireplace, and then up the chimney. The next instant I felt my dress dragged as by an unseen power. Something seemed to draw me back into the room, and the candles on the table flickered and went out: I was in the dark and alone, yet not alone. What awful thing had happened? My brain swam for a minute. I felt sick and cold; then I lost consciousness.

When I returned to my senses I was lying on the sofa and Professor Ellicott was bending over me.

"Now, control yourself, Miss Dallas," he said. "We have not a moment to lose. Tell me exactly what occurred."

I pressed my hand to my face. There was a light again in the room.

"Be quick," said the Professor. "What did you see? Why did you cry out? I was coming into the house in a hurry—in fact, I was on my way to this room—when I heard your shriek. I had been smoking and walking up and down in the grounds. Something induced me to look towards the tower. All of a sudden I saw—but tell me first what did you see?"

"The eyes," I answered. "They looked at me through one of the windows—that one exactly facing the table."

"Through what part of the window did they look?"

"Through one of the topmost panes."

"Good! I thought so. Now go on. Tell me the rest."

"I lost my nerve. I rushed towards the door, and just as I got there I turned, for the room was full of wind."

"Wind!" said the Professor. "Why, the night is as calm as death."

"Nevertheless, the room was full of a sort of gale, and the letter—my father's letter—was lifted and carried towards the chimney, up which it disappeared, and I myself was dragged back into the room. Then the candles were put out. Oh, I do believe at last in the ghost. Professor Ellicott, I wish I were dead."

"Don't be so silly, child. I assure you there is no ghost. Now, listen. I also saw something."

"The eyes?"

He nodded.

"They flashed at me for an instant. I fancy, Miss Dallas, this is a very tangible ghost. I saw a figure crouching on the roof, bending down over the turret towards that very window. I was just under the tower, hastening in, when you screamed, and I looked up and saw it disappear behind the parapet. The eyes were visible for about half a second.

We shall catch your ghost, don't be afraid, and solve your mystery. I shall remain here for the present, but we must have the roof examined, and at once. Do you know of any other way to get to it except by a ladder from the ground? There surely must be a trap-door somewhere."

"There is," I answered, "There's a trap-door at the end of this very wing."

"Good!" said the Professor. "Go downstairs at once and get several men, your cousins amongst them, to examine the roof from end to end, and in especial to look on the roof of this tower. I will stay here. Don't be long."

I ran away. The Professor's words had excited me, and my courage had returned. I gave the alarm. I could not find my cousins, but soon the rest of the house was in a state of ferment. Some of the men-servants and two of the gardeners immediately ascended to the roof. They carefully examined not only the roof of the house, but that of the tower. But look as they would they could not see a single trace of any individual hiding there. It is true that a rope, fastened to one of the chimneys, was hanging close to one of the parapets of the tower. This alone pointed conclusively to the fact that someone had been there. Nothing else, however, was to be discovered.

Accompanied by Aunt Sophia I returned to the Professor.

"Four of our men have been on the roof," I said, "and they brought away this rope. You can see it, There was no one there."

"Ah!" He shrugged his shoulders. "I thought there must have been a rope. He could not have bent over so far without being secured against the possibility of falling."

"The rope was fastened round one of the chimneys," I continued.

"Profesor, what does this mean?" said poor Aunt Sophia.

"Where are your nephews, madam?" was his answer. "Why are they not helping in this search?"

"We cannot find my cousins anywhere," I answered. "The last I saw of them was when I was going upstairs to read my father's letter. They then left the drawing-room and went out of the house arm-in-arm."

"I will go and have a further search made for them," said my aunt. "They certainly ought to be acquainted with this most remarkable occurrence."

She gave me a suspicious and, I fancied, unbelieving glance. Did she really think that I was imagining the whole thing? The Professor's attitude, however, comforted me.

"Don't be alarmed, child," he said. "The clue which we seek is close at hand. I am convinced of it. Now we must do something. I shall remain in this room for the night, and one or two of the servants must watch on the roof of the tower. But you must go to bed and rest, otherwise you will be down with nervous fever. Now, tell me, please, Miss Dallas, who are the most trustworthy and absolutely reliable servants in your house?"

"Harris, the old gardener, for one," I answered. "He has been with us since before I was born."

"Who else?"

"Franks, the butler."

"Then Harris and Franks shall watch on the roof of the tower tonight. Now go to bed."

Against my will I was forced to go to my room. Another sleeping-draught, administered by the Professor, ensured my repose, and in the morning I was sufficiently calm even to defy Aunt Sophia's looks of suspicion, for suspect me now of incipient insanity she evidently did.

The mysterious disappearance of both my cousins caused a great deal of talk and speculation on the following morning, and I went to the tower to visit the Professor in a state of great excitement on the subject. His manners were absolutely non-committal. He refused to say anything about my cousins, and he also refused to leave the study.

"When I go someone else must take my place," he said. "This room must not be left unguarded for a single moment, nor must the roof above."

Towards the latter part of the day he suggested that I

should take his place in the study while he himself examined the roof. In about half an hour he returned to me. I saw that he held a tiny glass tube in his hand.

"Can you make anything of this?" he said, laying it on the table before me.

"Nothing," I answered. "What is it?"

"A very valuable piece of evidence, I take it."

"What do you mean?"

"I will try to tell you. I found this tube in the gutter just above the window. It is, as you see, sealed up at each end. It looks innocent enough; nevertheless, it contains a very minute portion of that new substance—radium. You heard what I said to your Cousin Rudolf with regard to the effect of radium on the human skin, but I did not tell him that it does something else. When held for a short time in front of the eyes, the eyes take to themselves a certain amount of its properties, and they glow in the dark with a great luminosity which gives them a most terrifying appearance. It strikes me, Miss Dallas, that in this little bottle I hold the solution of your ghost. The eyes of a man who held radium a short distance from his pupils would also become very much inflamed. Consider the condition of your Cousin Rudolf's eyes. I found this tube in the gutter. We are getting near the clue; eh, don't you think so?"

I felt myself turning pale. I know that I trembled.

"Could any man living be so wicked?" was my next remark.

"Men will do strange things for money," was his answer. "But how your cousin would know that your father intended to change his will is a mystery which I cannot fathom."

"What do you mean to do next?" I asked.

"Watch for the scoundrels. They are hiding somewhere, and all in good time they will reappear. By the way, you say that your father's letter, containing the will, was blown up the chimney. James," he continued, turning to the servant who had just entered the room, "you and Andrews must come up here within an hour and take my place while I visit the roof. I may have to remain there for some hours this evening. Meanwhile, Miss Dallas," he continued, giving me a quick smile, "you shall go and take a constitutional."

I did not want to go out, but the Professor's word just then was my law. The evening was a lovely one, and I walked for some little time. As I returned I looked towards the tower. Suddenly I perceived the tall figure of the Professor. He was standing absolutely motionless near one of the chimneys. He evidently saw me, but did not make the slightest movement. A wild desire to be with him and to share his watch came over me. Quick as thought I entered the house, reached the trap-door, which was open, and soon was standing on the low roof of Courtlands. I walked warily and presently reached the edge of the parapet. There were two steps here leading from the roof of the house to the roof of the tower. I mounted them and stood by the Professor's side.

"Child," he said, in a whisper, "what are you doing?"

"I must share your watch," I said.

"I would rather be alone."

I shook my head.

"Something forces me to remain with you. Don't deny me my wish."

He held up his hand with a warning gesture to me.

"Then you must crouch by this parapet," he said, "and remain motionless. I shall hide behind the chimney. My suspicions are confirmed. There are men not far from here. I heard a movement not along ago. Absolute quiet will force the scoundrels from their lair."

I now perceived that he carried a revolver. Moving away from him a few paces I crouched down behind the parapet. He did likewise a little way off. We were the only watchers on the silent tower, but I knew that there were servants also on guard in the room below.

By-and-by the sun sank towards the west and twilight reigned over the scene. Twilight deepened into night.

The Professor and I had remained motionless, as though we were dead, for from two to three hours.

All of a sudden I saw Professor Ellicot raise himself and

glance towards me. I could but dimly see his face, but I knew that something was about to happen. The next minute, peering hard towards the stack of chimneys, I noticed, to my unbounded horror, the head of my Cousin Rudolf show itself. He did not see us, and cautiously began to descend from the chimney on to the roof. Just as he was about to place his feet on the roof, Professor Ellicott, strong as steel, sprang upon him and dragged him by the shoulders and arms down upon his knees.

"I have been waiting for you," he said. As he spoke he held his revolver to my cousin's ear. "If you stir you are a dead man. Confess your crime at once. Your game is up! Now, then, what does this mean?"

Rudolf groaned.

"The agony in my eyes is past bearing," he said.

"Call to your brother to come out of his hiding-place. I will take you both to the Colonel's study. There you shall explain your villainies."

"Let me rise, and I promise you I will not try to escape," answered Rudolf. "I am in such pain that I am past caring for anything but the chance of relief. I will shout to Lionel. We have been starving and have been in the dark. Oh, the agony in my eyes!"

The Professor allowed Rudolf to rise. He went to the chimney and called down. In a moment Lionel made his appearance. Professor Ellicott then escorted the two men across the roof, down through the trap-door, and back again to my father's study.

"I cannot face the light," said Rudolf at once, covering his eyes with his hands. "I have endured more than I bargained for. If I am happy enough to escape without the punishment of the law, I will confess everything."

"That remains with Miss Dallas, for she is the person you have injured," said the Professor.

"Tell the truth, Rudolf. I won't be too hard on you," I answered, my voice trembling. I saw him shiver slightly. His tall, athletic figure was bowed. He still kept his face covered with his hand. As to Lionel, he was crouching in the attitude of an unmistakable cur in a distant corner.

"This is the story," said Rudolf. "There is no use any longer hiding things. I was in serious money trouble—Stock Exchange debts, the usual thing. The money left to me in my uncle's will would, however, have put me again on my feet. Were it for any reason withdrawn, nothing remained for me but open disgrace and ruin.

"For years it has been my one effort to keep my transgressions from my uncle's ears, and only for the extraordinary instinct which you, Nora, possessed, and which caused you to watch me as a cat watches a mouse, I should have succeeded in securing the fortune which he meant to leave me. Lionel was much in the same boat. We decided, therefore, to act together. For a long time we have been in league with a certain Lieutenant Vincent, a young officer in the same regiment as my uncle. My uncle was much attached to Vincent. In the hour of his death Vincent happened to be near, and it was to him my uncle dictated his letter, the letter which you received last night. On the afternoon of the day when the news of my uncle's death was received here I had a long cablegram from Vincent, in which he gave me briefly the contents of the new will, which was already on its way to England, and also said that both the witnesses, privates in my uncle's regiment, had been shot dead shortly after he breathed his last. Thus there were no witnesses to prove this will. He said we must make the best of his information, and we had a month to mature our plans in. We put our heads together and resolved on a course of action. We knew the history of Aunt Ethel. Nora has always had very highly strung nerves, and we perceived to our satisfaction that they were terribly upset by her father's death. I had been reading a good deal about the newly discovered substance—radium, and thought it possible that it might serve my purpose. I purchased a minute portion and began at once to work on my cousin's fears. Radium, as you know, when held near the eyes, can give them a luminous and very ghastly appearance. I got Nora to believe that she was the victim of a terrifying disorder, and you are aware how successfully my purpose worked. I further arranged, with Lionel's help, to deprive Nora of the fresh will as soon as she had read it; our belief being that her story would not be credited, and that when she spoke of a new will having been sent to her the whole thing, in combination with her story of the ghostly eyes, would be put down to insanity.

"Now, this was our plan: We knew that her habit was to read all letters received from her father in his study. We investigated this room thoroughly and made an important discovery. A few feet up the wide chimney was a secret chamber. The entrance to this chamber was approached by climbing down the inside of the chimney from the roof. This mode of entrance was facilitated by projecting bricks left for the purpose. We resolved to utilise the chamber for our requirements.

"As soon, therefore, as the post arrived from South Africa, Lionel and I left the drawing-room. We immediately went by the trap-door on to the roof. Lionel disappeared down the chimney into the secret chamber, where we had previously taken an immensely powerful exhaust-pump. In the bottom of the chimney there was placed a short time ago a large register, thus closing up the space except for a small hole in the centre, in order to let the smoke pass up. Leading from the exhaust-pump we had arranged a large tube, the mouth of which fitted exactly into the hole in the register. We had also put in order a small electric bell which communicated from the roof to the chamber. After Lionel had disappeared down the chimney I prepared my eyes, and at the right moment bent over the parapet.

"All the time Nora was reading her letter I was looking at her, and when I perceived that she had quite taken in its contents I attracted her attention by gently tapping on the window with a spray of ivy. She turned instinctively. Again I tapped, and she looked up and saw me. As my brother and I guessed she would, she uttered a scream and immediately tried to leave the room, forgetting the letter, which still lay on the table. I immediately rang the bell. Nora was too terrified to hear it. At the signal Lionel began to work the exhaust-pump by means of a hand wheel. It sucked the air out of the study, and drew the letter and other small papers up the chimney right into the tube. Thus we secured the letter and the new will.

"I then joined Lionel in the secret room, not forgetting to take with me the wires from the electric bell. We both immediately set to work to draw back the tube into the secret chamber, and by the time Nora had recovered consciousness all trace of our plot had virtually disappeared."

"What about the will? Have you destroyed it?" said the Professor.

"Strange to say, we have not," replied Lionel. "The fact is, we were in the dark and starving. We had hoped, but for your interference to get away in a few minutes. We have been incarcerated for twenty-four hours. Rudolf was in agony with his eyes. We wanted to read the will before tearing it up."

"Then you can give it to me?"

"Yes. We have it here intact, and, if our cousin will permit us, we will leave the country tomorrow and never trouble her again."

They did so. I did not wish to pursue them, as I doubtless could, with the punishment of the law. My terrors were over. Never more would the ghastly eyes alarm me.

AT THE DIP OF THE ROAD

Mrs. Molesworth

Have I ever seen a ghost? I do not know.

That is the only reply I can truthfully make to the question nowadays so often asked. And sometimes, if inquirers care to hear more, I go on to tell them the one experience which makes it impossible for me to reply positively either in the affirmative or negative, and restricts me to "I do not know."

This was the story.

I was staying with relations in the country. Not a very isolated or out-of-the-way part of the world, and yet rather inconvenient of access by the railway, for the nearest station was six miles off. Though the family I was visiting were nearly connected with me I did not know much of their home or its neighbourhood, as the head of the house, an uncle of mine by marriage, had only come into the property a year or two previously to the date of which I am writing, through the death of an elder brother.

It was a nice place. A good comfortable old house, a

prosperous, satisfactory estate. Everything about it was in good order from the farmers—who always paid their rents—to the shooting—which was always good—and from the vineries—which were noted—to the woods, where the earliest primroses in all the countryside were to be found each year.

And my uncle and aunt and their family deserved these pleasant things and made a good use of them.

But there was a touch of the commonplace about it all. There was nothing picturesque or romantic. The country was flat though fertile, and the house, though old, was conveniently modern in its arrangements, airy, cheery and bright.

"Not even a ghost, or the shadow of one," I remember saying one day with a faint grumble.

"Ah, well—as to that," said my uncle, "perhaps we—" but just then something interrupted him, and I forgot his unfinished speech.

Into the happy party of which for the time being I was one, there fell one morning a sudden thunderbolt of calamity. The post brought news of the alarming illness of the eldest daughter, Frances, married a year or two ago and living—as the crow flies—at no very great distance. But as the crow flies is not always as the railroad runs, and to reach the Aldoyn's home from Fawne Court, my uncle's place, was a complicated business. In fact it was scarcely possible to go and return in a day.

"Can one of you come over?" wrote the young husband. "She is already out of danger, but longing to see her mother or one of you. She is worrying about the baby"—a child of a few months old—"and wishing for a nurse."

We looked at each other.

"Nurse must go at once," said my uncle to me, as the eledest of the party. Perhaps I should here say that I am a widow, though not old, and with no close ties or responsibilities. "But for your aunt it is impossible."

"Quite so," I agreed. For she was at the moment painfully lamed by rheumatism.

"And the other girls are almost too young at such a crisis," my uncle continued. "Would you, Charlotte—" and he hesitated. "It would be such a comfort to have personal news of her."

"Of course I will go," I said. "Nurse and I can start at once. I will leave her there, and return alone to give you, I have no doubt, better news of poor Frances."

He was full of gratitude. So were they all.

"Don't hurry back tonight," said my uncle. "Stay till—till Monday if you like." But I could not promise. I knew they would be glad of news at once, and in a small house like my cousin's, at such a time, an inmate the more might be inconvenient.

"I will try to return tonight," I said. And as I sprang into the carriage I added: "Send someone to meet the last train, unless I telegraph to the contrary."

My uncle nodded; the boys called after me, "All right"; the old butler bowed assent, and I was satisfied.

Nurse and I reached our journey's end promptly, considering the four or five junctions at which we had to change carriages. But on the whole, the trains fitted astonishingly.

We found Frances better, delighted to see us, eager for news of her mother, and, finally, disposed to sleep peacefully now that she knew that there was an experienced person in charge. And both she and her husband thanked me so much that I felt ashamed of the little I had done. Mr. Aldoyn begged me to stay till Monday—but the house was upset and I was eager to carry back my good tidings.

"They are meeting me from the last train," I said. "No thank you, I think it is best I go."

"You will have an uncomfortable journey," he replied. "It is Saturday, and the trains will be late, and the stations crowded with the market people. It will be horrid for you, Charlotte."

But I persisted.

It *was* rather horrid. And it was queer. There was a sort of uncanny eeriness about that Saturday evening's journey that I have never forgotten. The season was very early spring. It was not very cold, but chilly and ungenial. And there were such odd sorts of people about. I travelled second-class; for I am not rich and I am very independent. I did not want my uncle to pay my fare, for I liked the feeling of rendering some small service in return for his steady kindness to me. The first stage of my journey was performed in the company of two old naturalists travelling to Scotland to look for some small plant which was to be found only in one spot in the Highlands. This I gathered from their talk to each other. You never saw two such extraordinary creatures as they were. They both wore black kid gloves much too large for them, and the ends of the fingers waved about like feathers.

Then followed two or three short transits, interspersed with weary waitings at stations. The last of these was the worst, and tantalising too, for by this time I was within a few miles of Moore. The station was crowded with rough folk, all, it seemed to me, more or less tipsy. So I took refuge in a dark waiting-room on the small side of the line by which I was to proceed, where I felt I might have been robbed and murdered and no one the wiser.

But at last came my slow train and I jumped in—to jump out again more joyfully some fifteen minutes later when we drew up.

I peered about for the carriage. It was not to be seen; only two or three tax-carts or dog-carts, farmers' vehicles, standing about, while their owners, it was easy to hear, were drinking far more than was good for them in the taproom of the Unicorn. Thence, nevertheless—not to the taproom, but to the front of the inn—I made my way, though not undismayed by the shouts and roars breaking the stillness of the quiet night. "Was the Fawne Court carriage not here?" I asked.

The landlady was a good-natured woman, especially civil to any member of the "Court" family. But she shook her head.

"No, no carriage has been down today. There must have been some mistake."

There was nothing for it but to wait till she could somehow or other disinter a fly and horse, and, worst of all a driver. For the men she had to call were all rather . . . "well, ma'am, you see it's Saturday night. We weren't expecting any one."

And when, after waiting half an hour, the fly at last emerged, my heart almost failed me. Even before he drove out of the yard, it was very plain that if we ever reached Fawne Court alive, it would certainly be more thanks to good luck than to the driver's management.

But the horse was old and the man had a sort of instinct about him. We got on all right till we were more than half way to our journey's end. The road was straight and the moonlight bright, especially after we had passed a certain corner, and got well out of the shade of the trees which skirted the first part of the way.

Just past this turn there came a dip in the road. It went down, down gradually, for a quarter of a mile or more, and I looked up anxiously, fearful of the horse taking advantage of the slope. But no, he jogged on, if possible more slowly than before, though new terrors assailed me when I saw that the driver was now fast asleep, his head swaying from side to side with extraordinary regularity. After a bit I grew easier again; he seemed to keep his equilibrium, and I looked out at the side window on the moon-flooded landscape, with some interest. I had never seen brighter moonlight.

Suddenly from out of the intense stillness and loneliness a figure, a human figure, became visible. It was that of a man, a young and active man, running along the footpath a few feet to our left, apparently from some whim, keeping pace with the fly. My first feeling was of satisfaction that I was no longer alone, at the tender mercies of my stupified charioteer. But, as I gazed, a slight misgiving came over me. Who could be running along this lonely road so late, and what was his motive in keeping up with us so steadily. It almost seemed as if he had been waiting for us, yet that, of course, was impossible. He was not very highwayman-like certainly; he was well dressed—neatly dressed that is to say, like a superior gamekeeper—his figure was remarkably good, tall and slight, and he ran gracefully. But there was something queer about him, and suddenly the curiosity that had mingled in my observation of him was entirely submerged in alarm, when I saw that, as he ran, he was slowly but steadily drawing nearer and nearer the fly.

"In another moment he will be opening the door and jumping in," I thought, and I glanced before me only to see that the driver was more hopelessly asleep than before; there was no chance of his hearing if I called out. And get out I could not without attracting the strange runner's attention, for as ill-luck would have it, the window was drawn up on the right side and I could not open the door without rattling the glass. While, worse and worse, the left-hand window was down! Even that slight protection wanting!

I looked out once more. By this time the figure was close—very close to the fly. Then an arm was stretched out and laid along the edge of the door, as if preparatory to opening it, and then, for the first time, I saw his face.

It was a young face, but terribly, horribly pale and ghastly, and the eyes—all was so visible in the moonlight—had an expression such as I had never seen before or since. It terrified me, though afterwards on recalling it, it seemed to me that it might have been more a look of agonised appeal than of menace of any kind.

I cowered back into my corner and shut my eyes, feigning sleep. It was the only idea that occurred to me. My heart was beating like a sledge hammer. All sorts of thoughts rushed through me; amongst them I remember saying to myself: "He must be an escaped lunatic—his eyes are so awfully wild."

How long I sat thus I don't know—whenever I dared to glance out furtively he was still there. But all at once a strange feeling of relief came over me. I sat up—yes, he was gone! And though, as I took courage, I leant out and looked round in every direction, not a trace of him was to be seen, though the road and the fields were bare and clear for a long distance around.

When I got to Fawne Court I had to wake the lodge-keeper—everyone was asleep. But my uncle was still up, though not expecting me, and very distressed he was at the mistake about the carriage.

"However," he concluded, "all's well that ends well. It's delightful to have your good news. But you look sadly pale and tired, Charlotte."

Then I told him of my fright—it seemed now so foolish of me, I said. But my uncle did not smile—on the contrary.

"My dear," he said, "it sounds very like our ghost, though, of course, it may have been only one of the keepers."

He told me the story. Many years ago in his grandfather's time, a young and favourite gamekeeper had been found dead in a field skirting the road down there. There was no sign of violence upon the body; it was never explained what had killed him. But he had had in his charge a watch—a very valuable one—which his master for some reason or other had handed him to take home to the house, not wishing to keep it on him. And when the body was found late that night, the watch was not on it. Since then, so the story goes, on a moonlight night the spirit of the poor fellow haunts the spot. It is supposed that he wants to tell what had become of his master's watch, which was never found. But no one has ever had the courage to address him.

"He never comes farther than the dip in the road," said my uncle. "If you had spoken to him, Charlotte, I wonder if he would have told you his secret?"

He spoke half laughingly, but I have never quite forgiven myself for my cowardice. It was the look in those terrible eyes!

THE GORGON'S HEAD

Miss Gertrude Bacon

"They that go down to the sea in ships" see strange things, but what they tell is oft-times stranger still. A faculty for romancing is imparted by a seafaring life as readily and surely as a rolling gait and a weather-beaten countenance. A fine imagination is one of the gifts of the ocean—witness the surprising and unlimited power of expression and epithet possessed by the sailor. And a fine imagination will frequently manifest itself in other ways besides swear words.

Captain Brander is one of the most gifted men in this way in the whole merchant service. His officers say of him with pride that he possesses the largest vocabulary in the great steamship company of which he is one of the oldest and most respected skippers, and his yarns are only equalled in their utter impossibility by the genius he displays in furnishing them with minute detail and all the outward circumstance of truth.

I first learned this fact from the second engineer the

evening of the sixth day of our voyage, as we leant across the bulwarks and watched the sunset. The second engineer was a bit of a liar—or I should say romancer—himself. The day he took me down into the engine-room he told me, as personal experiences, tales of mutinous Lascar firemen, unpopular officers who disappeared suddenly into the fiery maw of blazing furnaces, and so forth, which, whatever foundation of fact they may have possessed, certainly did not lose in the telling. As a humble aspirant in the same branch of art he naturally was quick to recognise the genius of that past master, the captain, and his admiration for his chief was as boundless as it was sincere.

"I say, Miss Baker," he said, *à propos* of nothing, "have you had the skipper 'on' yet?"

"Not that I am aware of," I said. "What do you mean?"

"Why, has he been spinning you any yarns yet? There isn't a man in the service can touch him for stories. I don't deny that he has seen some service, and been in some tight places, but for a real out-and-out lie, commend me to old Monkey Brand!" (It was by this sobriquet, I regret to say, suggested partly by his name, and mostly by his undoubted resemblance to a well-known advertisement, that the worthy captain was known in the unregenerate engine-room.)

"Oh, I should just love to hear him," I cried. "There is nothing I should like better. Do tell me how I can manage to draw him."

"Well, he doesn't want much drawing as a rule," said the engineer. "He likes to give vent to his imagination. Let me see," he continued; "tomorrow afternoon we shall be about passing the Grecian Islands. Ask him about them, and try and get him on the subject of Gorgons."

"Gorgons!" I said. "What a strange topic! Why, since I've left school I have almost forgotten what they were. Weren't they mythological creatures who turned people into stone when they looked at them?"

"That's about it, I believe," said the engineer, "and a fellow called Perseus cut off their heads, or something of that kind. It's a lie anyhow, but you ask the skipper."

It was the custom of Captain Brander every afternoon to make a kind of royal progress among his passengers. Going the entire circuit of the ship; passing slowly from group to group, with a joke here and a chat there, and bestowing his favours in lordly and impartial fashion—especially among the ladies. I have watched him often coming the whole length of the promenade deck, making some outrageous compliment to one girl, patting another on the shoulder, even chucking a third under the chin; a sense of supreme self-satisfaction animating his red cheeks, curling his grey hair, and suffusing his whole short, portly person. Eccentric he was; indifferent to his personal appearance—his battered old cap had seen almost as much service as he had—but a more popular man or an abler officer never walked the bridge. On this particular occasion I was at the end of the deck, and had so arranged that an inviting deck chair stood vacant beside me. Wearied by his progress by the time he reached me, he fell at once into my little trap, and sat down on the empty chair, leant back, and spread his legs. He and I were fast friends, and had been since the day when I tried to photograph him, and he had frustrated my design by unscrewing the front lens of my camera and keeping it in his pocket for the rest of the morning.

"Captain," I said, pointing to a cloudy grey outline faintly visible against the eastern horizon, "what land is that?"

"My dear young lady," said he, "I am quite sick of answering that question! If I have been asked it once I have been asked it twenty times in the last half-hour. That old Mrs. Matherson in the red shawl buttonholed me on the subject to such an extent that I thought I should never get away again. Wonderful thirst for information that old party has! And she appears to think that because I'm captain I must have a complete knowledge of geography, geology, history, etymology, mythology, *and* navigation. Well, for the twenty-first time, then, we are passing the isles off the coast of Greece, and that one straight ahead is Zante."

"So that is Greece, is it?" I mused aloud. "Well, from here

at least it looks old enough and romantic enough to be the home of all those ancient heroes we read about—Alexander and Hercules and—and—Gorgons and those sort of things." I felt I had introduced the subject somewhat lamely, after all, and the captain looked me full in the face as if suspecting a plot. But if I am not very adroit in conversation, I can at least look innocent upon occasions, and he merely said, "And what do you know about Gorgons, pray?"

"Oh, as much as most people, I expect!" I answered. "They are only a sort of fairly tale, you know."

"I am not so sure of that," said Captain Brander. "Those fairy tales, as you call them, have often truth at the bottom of them. And as to Gorgons, why, I could tell you a little incident that happened to me once—but it's rather a long story."

Then I urged my best persuasions—not that he needed much pressing—and pushing his old cap off his bald forehead, and speaking slowly and with that almost American accent peculiar to him, he unfolded his tale of wonder as follows:

"It's nearly thirty years ago, Miss Baker—that's long before *you* were ever born or thought of—that I was fourth officer of the *Haslar*, 2,000-ton vessel of this same company I serve to this day. How times have altered, to be sure! The *Haslar* was reckoned a fine ship in those days, and if you had told me that I should presently command an 8,000-tonner, such as I do this day, with 11,000 horsepower engines, and more men for the crew alone than the *Haslar* could hold when she was packed her tightest, I very probably wouldn't have believed you. However, that is neither here nor there. But thirty years ago in the spring time—now I come to think of it, it was in the month of April—we were cruising in this very neighbourhood, and one thick foggy night our skipper lost his bearings a bit, got too near the coast, and ran us ashore off the south point of Zante.

"Of course there was a great fuss, and everybody came up on deck with lifebelts, and all the girls screamed, and all the young fellows swore to save them or die in the attempt; and the skipper turned as white as paper—not that he was afraid, for he was no coward—none of our officers are that—but because he knew his prospects were ruined, and he would be turned out of the company and perhaps lose his certificate, and he'd got a wife and a big family, poor chap! Of course that consideration didn't affect *me*, for I was in my bunk and asleep at the time, but it was certainly unfortunate for him.

"Well, it was very soon discovered that the ship wasn't going down in a hurry, and nobody got into the boats, though they were lowered ready. And when daylight came we saw we were fast on the rocks, with half the stern under water, and the saloon and a lot of the cabins flooded. But more than that the *Haslar* couldn't sink, and at low water you might almost walk dryshod on to the shore. There was no getting her off, however, and so all the passengers were landed and sent home as best they could across country, and a rough time they had of it, for Zante is not an over-hospitable sort of a place; while we officers had to stick to the ship till we could get help, and then till she was repaired sufficiently to work her into dock somewhere.

"It was a tedious job, for help was slow in coming; and then all her boilers had to be taken out before she would float, and we fellows got jolly sick of it, I can tell you, for we were hard worked, and Zante is a wretched hole to spend more than half an hour in. Our one amusement, when we were off duty, was to go ashore on foot or row round the island in a boat, shooting wild fowl and exploring the country. There was precious little to see and not much to shoot, and it was slow fun altogether till, one day, the second officer came back from a tramp ashore and told us he had found his way to some very remote village on the eastern coast, where there was a cave among the hills which the villagers warned him not to enter. He could not gather for what reason, because he didn't understand enough of their outlandish tongue, but as it was then growing late he was obliged to return to the ship without further investigation.

"I was always one for adventure when I was a lad, and directly the second officer told his tale I made up my mind to go and explore that cave before any of the rest had a chance. It so happened that next day was my turn for going ashore, and I went and looked up one of the assistant engineers and persuaded him to come with me. I wanted him because he was a chum of mine, and also he was the only one of us who could talk the language a bit. He had been in those parts before, and generally acted as interpreter in our dealings with the natives. His name was Travers, a queer little dark chap, with black eyes and a hot temper, but a pleasant fellow enough if you did not rub him up the wrong way, and game for anything under the sun. He readily agreed to come with me, and we started as soon as we could get away, telling no one of our destination, for we had no wish to be forestalled.

"It was a long tramp, right across the island, to the village which Jenkins, the second officer, had indicated. But at last after climbing a weary hill, we looked down on some clustering huts standing amid vineyards in the valley beneath, while another and much sheerer cliff rose on the opposite side, whose rugged scarp was all rent and riven as by an earthquake, and intersected by a deep ravine. Here and there among the rocks were dark shadows and black patches which might be the entrances to caverns in the crag. 'This must be the place,' I said, 'and one of those is the forbidden cave. How are we to find out which?'

"As if in answer to my question, at this moment there came along the hill-top towards us a burly countryman with a sunburned face and tattered garments. He regarded us with astonishment, as well he might, for they get few strangers in those parts, and he made some remark to us in his queer language, which, of course, I didn't understand, but Travers did and replied to it. Finding he was understood, the countryman stopped and talked.

" 'Ah!' he said, or so Travers interpreted. 'So you have reached the valley of the Haunted Cavern! It is far to seek and hard to find, but it lies spread beneath you.'

" 'But which is the Haunted Cavern, and why is it so called?' asked Travers.

" 'It lies in yonder cleft of the hills,' answered the man, pointing to the opposite ravine, 'and it is called the Haunted Cavern because none who venture there return alive. Nay, they return not either alive or dead. They are seen no more!'

" 'Tell that to the Marines!' said Travers, only he translated it into Greek, of course, or what the Zante people think is Greek. 'You don't expect me to believe such a yarn as that! Why, what is there up in that place?'

" 'That is what none can tell,' replied the peasant; 'for none come back to say. And, indeed, it is the truth I speak. Many men have attempted to find the secret. In bygone days, I have heard, a whole party of soldiers were sent there to search for brigands supposed to be in hiding, but not one was seen again. The cavern has an evil name, and now is shunned by one and all, but every now and again there arises a youth venturesome beyond the rest; and he heeds not the warnings of the old, but hopes to break the spell and find the treasure that some say is hidden there, and he starts in high hope and courage, but never again do we behold his face!'

" 'But what is the reason?' persisted Travers, the incredulous.

" 'Nay, that we cannot say,' reiterated the man. 'A short distance can one go up the ravine that leads to the cavern. I have been there myself, and truly there is nothing that can be seen except a barren valley, scattered all over with big black stones. Nothing more, and farther than the entrance none must venture.'

" 'Oh, I say!' exclaimed Travers, in delight, 'did you ever hear such an old liar? This beats anything I could have believed possible in the nineteenth century. Come on, Brander! We are in luck this time!' and the impetuous fellow dashed off down the hill, I at his heels, leaving the countryman dumb with amazement behind us.

"At the foot of the hill we entered the little village. An old, white-haired man of rather superior appearance was crossing the road before us. Travers accosted him and asked him the way to the Haunted Cavern. The old man turned quite pale with astonishment and apprehension.

" 'The Haunted Cavern, my son!' he said, in quavering tones; 'surely you are not going thither?'

" 'Yes, we are, though,' said Travers, his eyes dancing with excitement. It is wonderful what enterprise that boy—he was little more—had in him. 'And if you won't tell us, we'll find the way out for ourselves!' and he pushed past the old man, who held out his skinny hands as if to detain him.

"Before we had got clear of the hamlet the news had somehow got circulated that we were about to explore the ravine, and the whole of the inhabitants turned out in the wildest excitement. Some were for staying us forcibly, till Travers began to get quite nasty, drew his revolver, and talked of firing. Many reiterated and emphasised alarming warnings and assurances that we should never return. All watched us with the most intense interest, and followed close on our footsteps until we began to near the fatal spot, when they fell off singly or in parties, till finally at the very entrance of the ravine we had left even the boldest spirits behind us.

"In truth, it was a strange spot to which we had penetrated. The narrow path had led us suddenly round the spur of the mountain, and now, look which way we might, the giant rocks towered up sheer above us, hundreds of feet high, in inaccessible grey walls. The sinking sun was now too low to shine within this well-like space, which his rays could only reach at midday, and the very air struck damp and chill. We were in an open valley, thus shut in by the cliffs, of considerable extent, but not to be reached by any path except that we had traversed. The ground was firm and smooth, but littered all over with the strangest black stones of all sorts of shapes, and in all positions, though of a fairly uniform size, and alike in material. There was something uncanny and weird about these queer black boulders, which strewed the valley the thicker the farther we advanced, till at the far end of the space, where a huge black hole yawned ominous in the cliff, they almost entirely blocked the way.

"The dark cavern looked terribly grim and forbidding in the fading light. A little stream issued from its mouth and trickled among the stones. It did not gurgle and glisten as most mountain streams, but flowed noiselessly, sluggish, and dull, and gathered in stagnant pools on its rocky bed. No birds sang in that dismal nook; no sound from without penetrated to its recesses. All was silent, dim, and chill as the tomb itself.

"Despite my utmost efforts, I felt the spell of the weird, wild spot stealing over me, and a cold shudder crept down my backbone. There was but room for one at a time in the ever-narrowing track, and I was at first leading. My steps became slower and slower, and finally I paused altogether and turned to look back on Travers to see if he too was feeling the oppressive sense of evil that seemed to hang heavy in the very air. But in his face was only visible an ecstasy almost of eagerness and delight. His dark eyes sparkled again, his cheeks were flushed, his breath came quick, and his whole body was quivering with excitement.

" 'Go on, Branded' he cried. 'What are you stopping for, man? This is grand! This is luck, indeed! Did you ever see such a place? Come on, I want to get to that cave!'

"I felt utterly ashamed to confess my weakness, but it was that cave that I had begun to dread more and more. Whatever else I may be, Miss Baker, it is not boasting to say I am no coward. I have seen danger, aye, and courted it all my life, and until that moment I doubt if I had known what fear was. But I knew then: the blind, unreasoning fear that saps the strength of mind and limb and melts the heart and paralyses all thought save that one overpowering instinct to fly—somewhere. Yet, in face of Travers's eagerness, I could not bear to show the white feather. I turned my back therefore on the dark cavern, now just ahead of us, and endeavoured to temporise.

" 'Travers,' I said, 'did you ever see such queer stones? How do you suppose they have got here? They are quite a different nature from these cliffs, so they could not have fallen from the sides.'

" 'Oh, bother the stones!' said Travers. 'I can't look at them now, I want to get into the cave. Quick, before it gets dark!' and as I still hesitated, he pushed past me into a more open space beyond, almost at the cavern's mouth. I did not dare to leave him, and was scrambling after him as best I might, when I suddenly heard him cry out in a voice such as I had never heard before, and hope never to again. A shrill, high-pitched cry in which there were surprise, wonder, disgust, alarm, and awful horror all combined in one: a cry of astonishment, a shriek of agony, a shout of dismay. 'Look, Brander! look! look!'

"I could have sworn that when he spoke my companion was in full view, close beside me, touching me almost, though at the exact moment my eyes were looking from him; but when I turned my head in answer to his cry he was gone.

"For one second only had my gaze been averted, but in that time he had utterly vanished from sight, disappeared in a flash, gone—whither? A large black stone stood close beside me, similar to the rest in that ghostly valley; yet it struck me somehow that I had not noticed it there before. I placed my hand upon it as I peered round behind to see if Travers were there and a shudder I could not explain ran up my arm, for the stone felt warm to the touch. I had not time then to analyse my unreasonable horror at this trivial circumstance; I was too eager to find my friend. I rushed madly among the stones, I yelled his name again and again, but the weird echoes of my cry, returned in countless reflections from cliff and cavern, alone answered me.

"In a frenzy of despair I continued my search, for certain was I that by no natural means could Travers have disappeared so utterly in so brief a space. Blind panic seized me, and I knew not what I did, till my eye suddenly fell on a shallow pool of water collected in a rocky hollow at my very feet. It was not more than a couple of inches deep, and scarce a yard across, but on its placid face were reflected the overhanging rock and opening of the cavern just behind it, and also something else that glued my eyes to it in horror and rooted my flying feet to the ground.

"Just above the cavern's mouth was a narrow ledge of rock, running horizontally, and of a few inches in width. On this natural shelf, reflected in the water, I saw, hanging downwards, a decayed fragment of goat-skin, rotten with age, but which might have been bound round something, long years before. Upon this, as if escaped from its folds, rested a Head.

"It was a human head, severed at the neck, but fresh and unfaded as if but newly dead. It bore the features of a woman—of a woman of more perfect loveliness than was ever told of in tale, or sculptured in marble, or painted on canvas. Every feature, every line was of the truest beauty, cast in the noblest mould—the face of a goddess. But upon that perfect countenance was the mark of eternal pain, of deathless agony and suffering past words. The forehead was lined and knit, the death-white lips were tightly pressed in speechless torment; in the wide eyes seemed yet to lurk the flame of an unquenchable fire; while around the fair brows, in place of hair, curled and coiled the stark bodies of venomous serpents, stiff in death, but their loathsome forms still erect, their evil heads yet thrust forward as if to strike.

"My heart ceased beating, and the chill of death crept over my limbs, as with eyes starting from their sockets I stared at that awful head, reflected in the pool. For hours it seemed to me I gazed fascinated, as the bird by the eye of the snake that has charmed it. I was as incapable of thought as movement, till suddenly forgotten school-room learning began to cross my brain, and I knew that I looked at the reflection of Medusa, the Gorgon, fairest and foulest of living things, the unclean creature, half woman, half eagle, slain by the hero Perseus, and one glimpse of whose tortured face turned the luckless beholder into stone with the horror of it.

"If I once raised my eyes from the reflection to the actual head above I knew that I too should freeze in a moment into another black block, even as poor Travers, and every other who had entered the accursed valley had done before. And as this thought occurred to me, the longing to lift my eyes and look upon the real object become so overpowering that, in sheer self-preservation, I inclined my face closer and closer to the water till I seemed almost to touch it, when my senses fled and I knew no more.

"When I woke at last it was far on in the night, and a bright moon, riding high, shone full down upon the valley, revealing the ragged rocks and scattered stones with a cold brilliance that almost equalled the day. I was lying chilled and stiff beside the pool, and I started up in amazement, unable to recall to my mind, for a moment, where I was or what I was doing there. I had my back to the cavern, fortunately, and as I gazed over the ghostly and deserted scene the events of the day suddenly returned to my mind in a single flash of terror.

"To escape from this ghastly place was now my only thought, and in order to do this I resolved to look no more at the pool at my feet in case the terrible fascination should again take possession of me. What it cost me to adhere to this resolution I cannot tell you, but with the courage of despair I pressed blindly forward to the mouth of the ravine, only pausing a second to lay my hand upon the now ice-cold stone that once was Travers.

"Poor Travers! gay, light-hearted fellow! Ever in the forefront of mischief, of danger, of adventure. How eager he had been to solve the secret of the haunted valley, which now must be his tomb for ever. How full of health and spirits he had scrambled a few hours before among those very boulders, one of which now, standing stiffly erect among its forest of brethren, was at once the monument and sole relic of a fearless lad, a cheery friend, and a gallant seaman. Dear old Travers! Brave, foolish boy! My heart was heavy, indeed, for his awful fate, as I reverently touched the stone and murmured to the night breeze, stealing around the rocks, 'Good-bye, old fellow; sleep sound!'

"It seemed to me, in my loneliness and terror, that my fearsome journey would never be ended: that, lost in a labyrinth, I should tread that valley for ever. But at last, after endless ages, I reached the mouth of the ravine, and once on open ground I stretched my cramped limbs and ran, without ceasing, till I once more reached the ship."

Here the captain paused, more from want of breath than anything else, I think.

"Go on, Captain Brander," I cried. "You haven't half finished yet. What did they say when you returned, and how did you explain about poor Travers?"

"Young lady," said Captain Brander, "don't ask any more questions. I think I have told you enough for one afternoon," and here, an officer coming up and summoning him, he left me.

MARY SHELLEY

Mary Shelley (née Mary Wollstonecraft Godwin) was born in Somers Town, London, in 1797. She came from rich literary heritage; her father was the political philosopher William Godwin, and her mother was the philosopher and feminist Mary Wollstonecraft. In 1812, when she was just fifteen, Mary met the poet Percy Bysshe Shelley. Shelley was married at the time, but the two spent the summer of 1814 travelling around Europe together. In 1815, Mary gave birth prematurely to a girl, and the infant died twelve days later. In her journal of March 19, 1815, Mary recorded a nightmare she'd had, now cited as a possible inspiration for her future masterwork, *Frankenstein*: "Dream that my little baby came to life again - that it had only been cold & that we rubbed it before the fire & it lived."

In the summer of 1816, the couple famously visited the poet Lord Byron at his villa beside Lake Geneva, in Switzerland. Storms and tumultuous weather (common in Shelley's future novel) confined them to the indoors, where they and Byron's assorted other guests took to reading to each other from a book of ghost stories. One evening, Byron challenged all his guests to write one themselves. The guests obliged, and Mary's story went on to become *Frankenstein*. Mary and Percy married later that year, and eighteen months later, in 1818 *Frankenstein* was published. Mary was only 21, and the novel was a huge success. The first edition of the book included a preface from Percy, and many, disbelieving that a young woman could have penned such a horror story, thought that the novel was his.

In 1819, following the death of another child, Mary suffered a nervous breakdown. This was compounded three years later when her husband drowned. Widowed at just 25, Mary returned to England, determined to continue profiting from her writing in order to support her one surviving son. Between 1827 and 1840, she was busy as an author and editor, penning three more novels and a number of short stories. However, she never experienced further success of the sort that *Frankenstein* had brought. Her final decade was blighted by illness, and throughout the 1840s she suffered from terrible headaches and bouts of paralysis in parts of her body. In 1851, at Chester Square, she died at the age of fifty-three from what her physician suspected was a brain tumour.

Shelley underwent a period of critical neglect after her death, due in part to the onset of the realist movement. For a long time she was chiefly remembered as the wife of Percy Bysshe Shelley, and it was not until 1989 that a full-length scholarly biography was published. In recent decades, the republication of almost all her writing, including her short fiction, has stimulated a new recognition of its value, and scholars now consider Mary Shelley to be a major figure in Romanticism.

MARGARET OLIPHANT

Margaret Oliphant was born in Wallyford, Scotland in 1828. When she was ten years old, her family moved to Liverpool, where she began to experiment with writing. She had her first novel, *Passages in the Life of Mrs. Margaret Maitlan* (1849), published when she was just 21. It was a moderate commercial success, and following her second novel (*Caleb Field*, published in 1851) Oliphant became a regular contributor to the famous *Blackwood's Magazine*.

By the 1860s, Oliphant was a popular and recognized author, and in order to support her family (she had become a widow in 1959) she became an incredibly prolific author. Oliphant eventually went on to write more than 120 words, including novels travelogues, histories and volumes of literary criticism. Two of her better-known fictional works are *Miss Marjoribanks* (1866) and *Phoebe Junior* (1876). Towards the end of her life, she wrote a well-received series of supernatural short stories called *Tales of the Seen and Unseen* (1885), which remains popular to this day. Oliphant died in 1897, aged 69.

MRS. CROWE

Catherine Ann Crowe was born Catherine Stevens in Borough Green, England in 1790. She was educated at home, and married an army officer, Major John Crowe, in her early twenties. However, by 1838, the two of them had separated, and Mrs. Crowe was living in Edinburgh, where she was acquainted with a number of well known writers, including Thomas de Quincey and William Makepeace Thackeray.

She produced two historical plays, *Aristodemus* (1838) and *The Cruel Kindness* (1853), both of which had short runs, before establishing her reputation in 1841 with *The Adventures of Susan Hopley*. An intricately plotted crime procedural that was some way ahead of its time, the novel was well-received and sold well, and Crowe followed it with *Men and Women* (1844), *The Story of Lily Dawson* (1847), *The Adventures of a Beauty* (1852), and *Linny Lockwood* (1854). During this period, her short stories were in demand from periodicals such as *Chambers' Edinburgh Journal* and Charles Dickens' *Household Words*.

Crowe turned increasingly to supernatural subjects, and in 1848 she published the work she is best-known for: *The Night-side of Nature*. A two volume exploration of "ghosts and ghost seers," interspersed with observations on phrenology,

Mesmerism and poltergeists, the collection of tales was a publishing sensation, running through sixteen editions in just six years. It remains popular to this day.

Crowe's success waned somewhat in the late 1850s, and in 1861 she sold her copyrights. After 1852, she left Edinburgh, and in 1871 she moved to Folkestone, where – following rumours that she had gone mad - she died the following year, aged 81.

MRS. HENRY WOOD

Mrs. Henry Wood was born in Worcester, England in 1814. In 1836, she married and moved to France, where she began to write short fiction. Her early work was published in *New Monthly Magazine* and *Bentley's Miscellany*, and proved very popular. Wood published her first novel, *Danesbury House*, in 1860, and followed it a year later with her most famous work, *East Lynne* (1861). The latter novel was an overnight success, and turned her into a household name. With her newfound financial security, Wood had a prolific seven-year period in which she produced fifteen novels; none of them, however, proved as popular as *East Lynne*. In later life, she co-edited the periodical *The Argosy*, before dying in 1887, aged 73.

MRS. ELIZABETH GASKELL

Elizabeth Cleghorn Gaskell was born Elizabeth Stevenson in London, England in 1810. In her youth she attended various boarding schools, where she was a voracious reader, before living with various family members and friends following her father's death. One of these was the Reverend William Turner in Newcastle-upon-Tyne, a staunch reformist and opponent of oppressive practices such as slavery, whose attitude profoundly affected Elizabeth's values and outlook on life.

In 1832, Elizabeth married lecturer and Unitarian minister William Gaskell, and they settled in the industrial city of Manchester. Despite having a busy life and four children, Gaskell found time in the evenings to write stories and sketches, and in 1837 her first story, 'Sketches Among the Poor', was published in *Blackwood's Magazine*. Over the next decade, Gaskell had numerous short pieces published in various periodicals, including *Harper's* and Charles Dickens' *All the Year Round*, and in 1848 she produced her first novel, *Mary Barton: A Tale of Manchester Life*. A scathing critique of inegalitarian British society, the novel was an immediate success. Gaskell followed it with the novels *Cranford* (1851–3), *Ruth* (1853) and *North and South* (1854–5).

From 1850 onwards, Gaskell and her husband rented a

villa in Plymouth Grove, and she became something of a celebrity, mingling with many literary luminaries of the day. Amongst her closest friends was fellow author Charlotte Bronte, whom Gaskell penned the first biography of. She continued to produce fiction, including the novels *Sylvia's Lovers* (1863) and *Wives and Daughters: An Everyday Story* (1865), before dying in 1865, aged 55.

AMELIA EDWARDS

Amelia Ann Blanford Edwards was born in London, England in 1831. Educated at home by her mother, she began writing at a young age, publishing her first poem at the age of seven. Edwards produced her first novel in 1844, but it was her Egyptian travelogue, *A Thousand Miles* (1876) and her final novel, *Lord Brackenbury* (1880), which made her name. Both books were runaway successes, and cemented her reputation as a popular writer of her day. Over the course of her life, Edwards contributed poetry, stories and articles to a range of magazines, including *Chamber's Journal, Household Words* and *All the Year Round*, and also wrote for various newspapers. Late in her career, she abandoned her literary work to concentrate solely on Egyptology. Edwards died in 1892, aged sixty.

MARY ANN EVANS (GEORGE ELIOT)

Mary Ann Evans was born in Nuneaton, England in 1819. A highly intelligent child, she was a voracious reader, and started at a young age to question the orthodoxy of the Anglican Church in which she was raised. When she was 21, Evans moved to Coventry, and in 1846 published her first major work – an English translation of the German author Ludwig Feuerbach's *The Essence of Christianity*. Her father became increasingly inpatient with Evans' questioning of the Christian faith, and to avoid being thrown out she attended church and kept house for him. However, a matter of weeks after his death, at the age of 30, she moved to London, with the intention of becoming a full-time writer.

In 1851, Evans became assistant editor of the campaigning, left-wing journal *The Westminster Review*, contributing many of her own essays. At this time, a female author heading a literary enterprise was virtually unheard of; to many, the mere sight of an unmarried young woman mixing with the predominantly male society of London was scandalous. Additionally, she conducted what was effectively an open affair with the philosopher and critic, George Henry Lewes. In the mid 1850s, Evans resolved to become a novelist, and adopted the pseudonym for which she would become best-known: George Elliot.

In 1858 (when Evans was 39) *Amos Barton*, the first of the *Scenes of Clerical Life*, was published in *Blackwood's Magazine*. Her first complete novel, *Adam Bede* was published a year later. Both of these were instant successes, and afforded Evans some degree of fame. After the popularity of *Adam Bede*, she continued to write for the next fifteen years. She produced six more novels, including her *magnum opus, Middlemarch* (1875), as well as a good body of poetry and a somewhat out-of-character novella *The Lifted Veil* (now seen as a significant milestone in the Victorian tradition of horror fiction).

Evans died in 1880, aged 61. She was not buried in Westminster Abbey because of her denial of the Christian faith; instead, she was interred in Highgate Cemetery, London, in the area reserved for religious dissenters or agnostics. Some years after her death, American author Henry James credited her with producing "deep, masterly pictures of the multifold life of man."

MISS BRADDON

Mary Elizabeth Braddon was born in Soho, London, England in 1835. She was educated privately in England and France, and at the age of just nineteen was offered a commission by a local printer to produce a serial novel "combining the humour of Dickens with the plot and construction of G. P. R. Reynolds" What emerged was *Three Times dead, or The Secret of the Heath*, which was published five years later under the title *The Trail of the Serpent* (1861).

For the rest of her life, Braddon was an extremely prolific writer, producing more than eighty novels, while also finding time to write and act in a number of stage plays. Her most famous novel, *Lady Audley's Secret*, began serialisation in 1862, and was an overnight success, propelling her into fame and fortune. A quintessential 'sensation novel', centring on an incident of "accidental bigamy," *Lady Audley's Secret* has never been out of print, and was adapted as recently as 2000. Braddon also founded *Belgravia Magazine*, and edited *Temple Bar Magazine*. She died in 1915 in Richmond, England, aged 79.

CHARLOTTE RIDDELL

Charlotte Riddell was born in Carrickfergus, County Antrim, Ireland in 1832. In her late teens, in the space of just five years, both her parents died, and at the age of 25 she married Joseph Hadley Riddell, a civil engineer. Very little is known beyond this about Riddell's life, other than that she lived in London and was one of the most popular authors of the Victorian era, writing more than thirty novels and a good amount of short stories. She was also part-owner and editor of *St. James's Magazine*, one of the most prestigious literary magazines of the 1860s. Nowadays, her best-known work is probably her collection of ghost stories, *Weird Stories*, first published in 1882. She died of breast cancer in 1906 in Ashford, Kent, aged 75. Her obituary in *The Times* read "Mrs. Riddell always wrote carefully, displayed much insight into character, and skill in manipulating her materials. The tone of her novels was invariably wholesome."

MRS. L. T. MEADE

Elizabeth Thomasina Meade was born in County Cork, Ireland in 1844. She started writing speculative fiction at a very young age, which horrified her father, a Protestant clergyman. Upon the death of her mother, Meade moved to London, where she spent much time in the Reading Room of the British Museum. In 1879, she married Alfred Toulim Smith. Over the course of her life, Meade was a prolific author, producing more than 280 books and numerous short stories and articles for magazines such as *The Strand Magazine* and *Lady's Pictorial*. At her peak, she was publishing more than ten novels a year. She was best known for her female adventure novels, of which she penned more than thirty, but wrote in a number of genres, from romantic to detective fiction. Meade also co-edited *Atalanta*, a girl's magazine, and was an active feminist. She died in 1914.

www.ingramcontent.com/pod-product-compliance
Lightning Source LLC
Chambersburg PA
CBHW030931020726
47498CB00001B/197